T0144303

The Judgment House

The Judgment House

Gilbert Parker

MINT EDITIONS

The Judgment House was first published in 1913.

This edition published by Mint Editions 2020.

ISBN 9781513271088 | E-ISBN 9781513276083

Published by Mint Editions®

 MINT
EDITIONS

minteditionbooks.com

Publishing Director: Jennifer Newens
Design & Production: Rachel Lopez Metzger
Project Manager: Micaela Clark
Typesetting: Westchester Publishing Services

Contents

BOOK I

I

THE JASMINE FLOWER

The music throbbed in a voice of singular and delicate power; the air was resonant with melody, love and pain. The meanest Italian in the gallery far up beneath the ceiling, the most exalted of the land in the boxes and the stalls, leaned indulgently forward, to be swept by this sweet storm of song. They yielded themselves utterly to the power of the triumphant debutante who was making "Manassa" the musical feast of the year, renewing to Covent Garden a reputation which recent lack of enterprise had somewhat forfeited.

Yet, apparently, not all the vast audience were hypnotized by the unknown and unheralded singer, whose stage name was Al'mah. At the moment of the opera's supreme appeal the eyes of three people at least were not in the thraldom of the singer. Seated at the end of the first row of the stalls was a fair, slim, graciously attired man of about thirty, who, turning in his seat so that nearly the whole house was in his circle of vision, stroked his golden moustache, and ran his eyes over the thousands of faces with a smile of pride and satisfaction which in a less handsome man would have been almost a leer. His name was Adrian Fellowes.

Either the opera and the singer had no charms for Adrian Fellowes, or else he had heard both so often that, without doing violence to his musical sense, he could afford to study the effect of this wonderful effort upon the mob of London, mastered by the radiant being on the stage. Very sleek, handsome, and material he looked; of happy colour, and, apparently, with a mind and soul in which no conflicts ever raged—to the advantage of his attractive exterior. Only at the summit of the applause did he turn to the stage again. Then it was with the gloating look of the gambler who swings from the roulette-table with the winnings of a great coup, cynical joy in his eyes that he has beaten the Bank, conquered the dark spirit which has tricked him so often. Now the cold-blue eyes caught, for a second, the dark-brown eyes of the Celtic singer, which laughed at him gaily, victoriously, eagerly, and then again drank in the light and the joy of the myriad faces before her.

In a box opposite the royal box were two people, a man and a very young woman, who also in the crise of the opera were not looking at the stage. The eyes of the man, sitting well back—purposely, so that he might see her without marked observation—were fixed upon the rose-tinted, delicate features of the girl in a joyous blue silk gown, which was so perfect a contrast to the golden hair and wonderful colour of her face. Her eyes were fixed upon her lap, the lids half closed, as though in reverie, yet with that perspicuous and reflective look which showed her conscious of all that was passing round her—even the effect of her own pose. Her name was Jasmine Grenfel.

She was not oblivious of the music. Her heart beat faster because of it; and a temperament adjustable to every mood and turn of human feeling was answering to the poignancy of the opera; yet her youth, child-likeness, and natural spontaneity were controlled by an elate consciousness. She was responsive to the passionate harmony; but she was also acutely sensitive to the bold yet deferential appeal to her emotions of the dark, distinguished, bearded man at her side, with the brown eyes and the Grecian profile, whose years spent in the Foreign Office and at embassies on the Continent had given him a tact and an insinuating address peculiarly alluring to her sex. She was well aware of Ian Stafford's ambitions, and had come to the point where she delighted in them, and had thought of sharing in them, "for weal or for woe"; but she would probably have resented the suggestion that his comparative poverty was weighed against her natural inclinations and his real and honest passion. For she had her ambitions, too; and when she had scanned the royal box that night, she had felt that something only little less than a diadem would really satisfy her.

Then it was that she had turned meditatively towards another occupant of her box, who sat beside her pretty stepmother—a big, bronzed, clean-shaven, strong-faced man of about the same age as Ian Stafford of the Foreign Office, who had brought him that night at her request. Ian had called him, "my South African nabob," in tribute to the millions he had made with Cecil Rhodes and others at Kimberley and on the Rand. At first sight of the forceful and rather ungainly form she had inwardly contrasted it with the figure of Ian Stafford and that other spring-time figure of a man at the end of the first row in the stalls, towards which the prima donna had flashed one trusting, happy glance, and with which she herself had been familiar since her childhood. The contrast had not been wholly to the advantage of the nabob; though, to be sure, he was simply arrayed—as if, indeed, he were not worth a thousand a year. Certainly he had about him a sense of power, but his occasional laugh was too vigorous for one whose own great sense of humour was conveyed by an infectious, rippling murmur delightful to hear.

Rudyard Byng was worth three millions of pounds, and that she interested him was evident by the sudden arrest of his look and his movements when introduced to her. Ian Stafford had noted this look; but he had seen many another man look at Jasmine Grenfel with just as much natural and unbidden interest, and he shrugged the shoulders of his mind; for the millions alone would not influence her, that was sure. Had she not a comfortable fortune of her own? Besides, Byng was not the kind of man to capture Jasmine's fastidious sense and nature. So much had happened between Jasmine and himself, so deep an understanding had grown up between them, that it only remained to bring her to the last court of inquiry and get reply to a vital question—already put in a thousand ways and answered to his perfect satisfaction. Indeed, there was between Jasmine and himself the equivalent of a betrothal. He had asked her to marry him, and she had not said no; but she had bargained for time to "prepare"; that she should have another year in which to be gay in a gay world and, in her own words, "walk the primrose path of pleasure untrammelled and alone, save for my dear friend Mrs. Grundy."

Since that moment he had been quite sure that all was well. And now the year was nearly up, and she had not changed; had, indeed, grown more confiding and delicately dependent in manner towards him, though seeing him but seldom alone.

As Ian Stafford looked at her now, he kept saying to himself, "So exquisite and so clever, what will she not be at thirty! So well poised, and yet so sweetly child-like dear dresden-china Jasmine."

That was what she looked like—a lovely thing of the time of Boucher in dresden china.

At last, as though conscious of what was going on in his mind, she slowly turned her drooping eyes towards him, and, over her shoulder, as he quickly leaned forward, she said in a low voice which the others could not hear:

"I am too young, and not clever enough to understand all the music means—is that what you are thinking?"

He shook his head in negation, and his dark-brown eyes commanded hers, but still deferentially, as he said: "You know of what I was thinking. You will be forever young, but yours was always—will always be—the wisdom of the wise. I'd like to have been as clever at twenty-two."

"How trying that you should know my age so exactly—it darkens the future," she rejoined with a soft little laugh; then, suddenly, a cloud passed over her face. It weighed down her eyelids, and she gazed before her into space with a strange, perplexed, and timorous anxiety. What did she see? Nothing that was light and joyous, for her small sensuous lips drew closer, and the fan she held in her lap slipped from her fingers to the floor.

This aroused her, and Stafford, as he returned the fan to her, said into a face again alive to the present: "You look as though you were trying to summon the sable spirits of a sombre future."

Her fine pink-white shoulders lifted a little and, once more quite self-possessed, she rejoined, lightly, "I have a chameleon mind; it chimes with every mood and circumstance."

Suddenly her eyes rested on Rudyard Byng, and something in the rough power of the head arrested her attention, and the thought flashed through her mind: "How wonderful to have got so much at thirty-three! Three millions at thirty-three—and millions beget millions!"

. . . Power—millions meant power; millions made ready the stage for the display and use of every gift, gave the opportunity for the full occupation of all personal qualities, made a setting for the jewel of life and beauty, which reflected, intensified every ray of merit. Power—that was it. Her own grandfather had had power. He had made his fortune, a great one too, by patents which exploited the vanity of mankind, and, as though to prove his cynical contempt for his fellow-creatures, had then invented a quick-firing gun which nearly every nation in the world adopted. First, he had got power by a fortune which represented the shallowness and gullibility of human nature, then had exploited the serious gift which had always been his, the native genius which had devised the gun when he was yet a boy. He had died at last with the smile on his lips which had followed his remark, quoted in every great newspaper of two continents, that: "The world wants to be fooled, so I fooled it; it wants to be stunned, so I stunned it. My fooling will last as long as my gun; and both have paid me well. But they all love being fooled best."

Old Draygon Grenfel's fortune had been divided among his three sons and herself, for she had been her grandfather's favourite, and she was the only grandchild to whom he had left more than a small reminder of his existence. As a child her intelligence was so keen, her perception so acute, she realized him so well, that he had said she was the only one of his blood who had anything of himself in character or personality, and he predicted—too often in her presence—that she "would give the world a start or two when she had the chance." His intellectual contempt for his eldest son, her father, was reproduced in her with no prompting on his part; and, without her own mother from the age of three, Jasmine had grown up self-willed and imperious, yet with too much intelligence to carry her will and power too far. Infinite adaptability had been the result of a desire to please and charm; behind which lay an unlimited determination to get her own way and bend other wills to hers.

The two wills she had not yet bent as she pleased were those of her stepmother and of Ian Stafford—one, because she was jealous and obstinate, and the other because he had an adequate self-respect and an ambition of his own to have his way in a world which would not give save at the point of the sword. Come of as good family as there was in England, and the grandson of a duke, he still was eager for power, determined to get on, ingenious in searching for that opportunity which even the most distinguished talent must have, if it is to soar high above the capable average. That chance, the predestined alluring opening had not yet come; but his eyes were wide open, and he was ready for the spring—nerved the more to do so by the thought that Jasmine would appreciate his success above all others, even from the standpoint of intellectual appreciation, all emotions excluded. How did it come that Jasmine was so worldly wise, and yet so marvellously the insouciant child?

He followed her slow, reflective glance at Byng, and the impression of force and natural power of the millionaire struck him now, as it had often done. As though summoned by them both, Byng turned his face and, catching Jasmine's eyes, smiled and leaned forward.

"I haven't got over that great outburst of singing yet," he said, with a little jerk of the head towards the stage, where, for the moment, minor characters were in possession, preparing the path for the last rush of song by which Al'mah, the new prima donna, would bring her first night to a complete triumph.

With face turned full towards her, something of the power of his head seemed to evaporate swiftly. It was honest, alert, and almost brutally simple—the face of a pioneer. The forehead was broad and strong, and the chin was square and determined; but the full, dark-blue eyes had in them shadows of rashness and recklessness, the mouth was somewhat self-indulgent and indolent; though the hands clasping both knees were combined of strength, activity, and also a little of grace.

"I never had much chance to hear great singers before I went to South Africa," he added, reflectively, "and this swallows me like a storm on the high veld—all lightning and thunder and flood. I've missed a lot in my time."

With a look which made his pulses gallop, Jasmine leaned over and whispered—for the prima donna was beginning to sing again:

"There's nothing you have missed in your race that you cannot ride back and collect. It is those who haven't run a race who cannot ride back. You have won; and it is all waiting for you."

Again her eyes beamed upon him, and a new sensation came to him—the kind of thing he felt once when he was sixteen, and the vicar's daughter had suddenly held him up for quite a week, while all his natural occupations were neglected, and the spirit of sport was humiliated and abashed. Also he had caroused in his time—who was there in those first days at Kimberley and on the Rand who did not carouse, when life was so hard, luck so uncertain, and food so bad; when men got so dead beat, with no homes anywhere—only shake-downs and the Tents of Shem? Once he had had a native woman summoned to be his slave, to keep his home; but that was a business which had revolted him, and he had never repeated the experiment. Then, there had been an adventuress, a wandering, foreign princess who had fooled him and half a dozen of his friends to the top of their bent; but a thousand times he had preferred other sorts of pleasures—cards, horses, and the bright outlook which came with the clinking glass after the strenuous day.

Jasmine seemed to divine it all as she looked at him—his primitive, almost Edenic sincerity; his natural indolence and native force: a nature that would not stir until greatly roused, but then, with an unyielding persistence and concentrated force, would range on to its goal, making up for a slow-moving intellect by sheer will, vision and a gallant heart.

Al'mah was singing again, and Byng leaned forward eagerly. There was a rustle in the audience, a movement to a listening position, then a tense waiting and attention.

As Jasmine composed herself she said in a low voice to Ian Stafford, whose well-proportioned character, personality, and refinement of culture were in such marked contrast to the personality of the other: "They live hard lives in those new lands. He has wasted much of himself."

"Three millions at thirty-three means spending a deal of one thing to get another," Ian answered a little grimly.

"Hush! Oh, Ian, listen!" she added in a whisper.

Once more Al'mah rose to mastery over the audience. The bold and generous orchestration, the exceptional chorus, the fine and brilliant tenor, had made a broad path for her last and supreme effort. The audience had long since given up their critical sense, they were ready to be carried into captivity again, and the surrender was instant and complete. Now, not an eye was turned away from the singer. Even the Corinthian gallant at the end of the first row of stalls gave himself up to feasting on her and her success, and the characters in the opera were as electrified as the audience.

For a whole seven minutes this voice seemed to be the only thing in the world, transposing all thoughts, emotions, all elements of life into terms of melody. Then, at last, with a crash of sweetness, the voice broke over them all in crystals of sound and floated away into a world of bright dreams.

An instant's silence which followed was broken by a tempest of applause. Again, again, and again it was renewed. The subordinate singers were quickly disposed of before the curtain, then Al'mah received her memorable tribute. How many times she came and went she never knew; but at last the curtain, rising, showed her well up the stage beside a table where two huge candles flared. The storm of applause breaking forth once more, the grateful singer raised her arms and spread them out impulsively in gratitude and dramatic abandon.

As she did so, the loose, flowing sleeve of her robe caught the flame of a candle, and in an instant she was in a cloud of fire. The wild applause turned suddenly to notes of terror as, with a sharp cry, she stumbled forward to the middle of the stage.

For one stark moment no one stirred, then suddenly a man with an opera-cloak on his arm was seen to spring across a space of many feet between a box on the level of the stage and the stage itself. He crashed into the footlights, but recovered himself and ran forward. In an instant he had enveloped the agonized figure of the singer and had crushed out the flames with swift, strong movements.

Then lifting the now unconscious artist in his great arms, he strode off with her behind the scenes.

"Well done, Byng! Well done, Ruddy Byng!" cried a strong voice from the audience; and a cheer went up.

In a moment Byng returned and came down the stage. "She is not seriously hurt," he said simply to the audience. "We were just in time."

Presently, as he entered the Grenfel box again, deafening applause broke forth.

"We were just in time," said Ian Stafford, with an admiring, teasing laugh, as he gripped Byng's arm.

"'We'—well, it was a royal business," said Jasmine, standing close to him and looking up into his eyes with that ingratiating softness which had deluded many another man; "but do you realize that it was my cloak you took?" she added, whimsically.

"Well, I'm glad it was," Byng answered, boyishly. "You'll have to wear my overcoat home."

"I certainly will," she answered. "Come—the giant's robe."

People were crowding upon their box.

"Let's get out of this," Byng said, as he took his coat from the hook on the wall.

As they left the box the girl's white-haired, prematurely aged father whispered in the pretty stepmother's ear: "Jasmine'll marry that nabob—you'll see."

The stepmother shrugged a shoulder. "Jasmine is in love with Ian Stafford," she said, decisively.

"But she'll marry Rudyard Byng," was the stubborn reply.

II

The Underground World

W hat's that you say—Jameson—what?"
Rudyard Byng paused with the lighted match at the end of
his cigar, and stared at a man who was reading from a tape-machine,
which gave the club the world's news from minute to minute.

"Dr. Jameson's riding on Johannesburg with eight hundred men. He
started from Pitsani two days ago. And Cronje with his burghers are
out after him."

The flaming match burned Byng's fingers. He threw it into the
fireplace, and stood transfixed for a moment, his face hot with feeling,
then he burst out:

"But—God! they're not ready at Johannesburg. The burghers'll catch
him at Doornkop or somewhere, and—" He paused, overcome. His
eyes suffused. His hands went out in a gesture of despair.

"Jameson's jumped too soon," he muttered. "He's lost the game for
them."

The other eyed him quizzically. "Perhaps he'll get in yet. He surely
planned the thing with due regard for every chance. Johannesburg—"

"Johannesburg isn't ready, Stafford. I know. That Jameson and the
Rand should coincide was the only chance. And they'll not coincide now.
It might have been—it was to have been—a revolution at Johannesburg,
with Dr. Jim to step in at the right minute. It's only a filibustering
business now, and Oom Paul will catch the filibuster, as sure as guns.
'Gad, it makes me sick!"

"Europe will like it—much," remarked Ian Stafford, cynically,
offering Byng a lighted match.

Byng grumbled out an oath, then fixed his clear, strong look on
Stafford. "It's almost enough to make Germany and France forget 1870
and fall into each other's arms," he answered. "But that's your business,
you Foreign Office people's business. It's the fellows out there, friends
of mine, so many of them, I'm thinking of. It's the British kids that can't
be taught in their mother-tongue, and the men who pay all the taxes
and can't become citizens. It's the justice you can only buy; it's the foot
of Kruger on the necks of the subjects of his suzerain; it's eating dirt as

Englishmen have never had to eat it anywhere in the range of the Seven Seas. And when they catch Dr. Jim, it'll be ten times worse. Yes, it'll be at Doornkop, unless—But, no, they'll track him, trap him, get him now. Johannesburg wasn't ready. Only yesterday I had a cable that—" he stopped short. . . "but they weren't ready. They hadn't guns enough, or something; and Englishmen aren't good conspirators, not by a damned sight! Now it'll be the old Majuba game all over again. You'll see."

"It certainly will set things back. Your last state will be worse than your first," remarked Stafford.

Rudyard Byng drained off a glass of brandy and water at a gulp almost, as Stafford watched him with inward adverse comment, for he never touched wine or spirits save at meal-time, and the between-meal swizzle revolted his aesthetic sense. Byng put down the glass very slowly, gazing straight before him for a moment without speaking. Then he looked round. There was no one very near, though curious faces were turned in his direction, as the grim news of the Raid was passed from mouth to mouth. He came up close to Stafford and touched his chest with a firm forefinger.

"Every egg in the basket is broken, Stafford. I'm sure of that. Dr. Jim'll never get in now; and there'll be no oeufs a la coque for breakfast. But there's an omelette to be got out of the mess, if the chef doesn't turn up his nose too high. After all, what has brought things to this pass? Why, mean, low tyranny and injustice. Why, just a narrow, jealous race-hatred which makes helots of British men. Simple farmers, the sentimental newspapers call them—simple Machiavellis in veldschoen!"*

Stafford nodded assent. "But England is a very conventional chef," he replied. "She likes the eggs for her omelette broken in the orthodox way."

"She's not so particular where the eggs come from, is she?"

Stafford smiled as he answered: "There'll be a good many people in England who won't sleep to-night some because they want Jameson to get in; some because they don't; but most because they're thinking of the millions of British money locked up in the Rand, with Kruger standing over it with a sjambak, which he'll use. Last night at the opera we had a fine example of presence of mind, when a lady burst into flames on the stage. That spirited South African prima donna, the Transvaal, is in flames. I wonder if she really will be saved, and who will save her, and—"

---

* A glossary of South African words will be found at the end of the book.

A light, like the sun, broke over the gloomy and rather haggard face of Rudyard Byng, and humour shot up into his eyes. He gave a low, generous laugh, as he said with a twinkle: "And whether he does it at some expense to himself—with his own overcoat, or with some one else's cloak. Is that what you want to say?"

All at once the personal element, so powerful in most of us—even in moments when interests are in existence so great that they should obliterate all others—came to the surface. For a moment it almost made Byng forget the crisis which had come to a land where he had done all that was worth doing, so far in his life; which had burned itself into his very soul; which drew him, sleeping or waking, into its arms of memory and longing.

He had read only one paper that morning, and it—the latest attempt at sensational journalism—had so made him blush at the flattering references to himself in relation to the incident at the opera, that he had opened no other. He had left his chambers to avoid the telegrams and notes of congratulation which were arriving in great numbers. He had gone for his morning ride in Battersea Park instead of the Row to escape observation; had afterwards spent two hours at the house he was building in Park Lane; had then come to the club, where he had encountered Ian Stafford and had heard the news which overwhelmed him.

"Well, an opera cloak did the work better than an overcoat would have done," Stafford answered, laughing. "It was a flash of real genius to think of it. You did think it all out in the second, didn't you?"

Stafford looked at him curiously, for he wondered if the choice of a soft cloak which could more easily be wrapped round the burning woman than an overcoat was accidental, or whether it was the product of a mind of unusual decision.

Byng puffed out a great cloud of smoke and laughed again quietly as he replied:

"Well, I've had a good deal of lion and rhinoceros shooting in my time, and I've had to make up my mind pretty quick now and then; so I suppose it gets to be a habit. You don't stop to think when the trouble's on you; you think as you go. If I'd stopped to think, I'd have funked the whole thing, I suppose—jumping from that box onto the stage, and grabbing a lady in my arms, all in the open, as it were. But that wouldn't have been the natural man. The natural man that's in most of us, even when we're not very clever, does things right. It's when the conventional man comes in and says, Let us consider, that we go wrong. By Jingo, Al'mah was as near having her beauty spoiled as any woman ever was; but she's only got a few nasty burns on the arm and has singed her hair a little."

"You've seen her to-day, then?"

Stafford looked at him with some curiosity, for the event was one likely to rouse a man's interest in a woman. Al'mah was unmarried, so far as the world knew, and a man of Byng's kind, if not generally inflammable, was very likely to be swept off his feet by some unusual woman in some unusual circumstance. Stafford had never seen Rudyard Byng talk to any woman but Jasmine for more than five minutes at a time, though hundreds of eager and avaricious eyes had singled him out for attention; and, as it seemed absurd that any one should build a palace in Park Lane to live in by himself, the glances sent in his direction from many quarters had not been without hopefulness. And there need not have been, and there was not, any loss of dignity on the part of match-making mothers in angling for him, for his family was quite good enough; his origin was not obscure, and his upbringing was adequate. His external ruggedness was partly natural; but it was also got from the bitter rough life he had lived for so many years in South Africa before he had fallen on his feet at Kimberley and Johannesburg.

As for "strange women," during the time that had passed since his return to England there had never been any sign of loose living. So, to Stafford's mind, Byng was the more likely to be swept away on a sudden flood that would bear him out to the sea of matrimony. He had put his question out of curiosity, and he had not to wait for a reply. It came frankly and instantly:

"Why, I was at Al'mah's house in Bruton Street at eight o'clock this morning—with the milkman and the newsboy; and you wouldn't believe it, but I saw her, too. She'd been up since six o'clock, she said. Couldn't sleep for excitement and pain, but looking like a pansy blossom all the same, rigged out as pretty as could be in her boudoir, and a nurse doing the needful. It's an odd dark kind of beauty she has, with those full lips and the heavy eyebrows. Well, it was a bull in a china-shop, as you might judge—and thank you kindly, Mr. Byng, with such a jolly laugh, and ever and ever and ever so grateful and so wonderfully—thoughtful, I think, was the word, as though one had planned it all. And wouldn't I stay to breakfast? And not a bit stagey or actressy, and rather what you call an uncut diamond—a gem in her way, but not fine beur, not exactly.

A touch of the karoo, or the prairie, or the salt-bush plains in her, but a good chap altogether; and I'm glad I was in it last night with her. I laughed a lot at breakfast—why yes, I stayed to breakfast. Laugh before breakfast and cry before supper, that's the proverb, isn't it? And I'm crying, all right, and there's weeping down on the Rand too."

As he spoke Stafford made inward comment on the story being told to him, so patently true and honest in every particular. It was rather contradictory and unreasonable, however, to hear this big, shy, rugged fellow taking exception, however delicately and by inference only, to the lack of high refinement, to the want of fine fleur, in Al'mah's personality. It did not occur to him that Byng was the kind of man who would be comparing Jasmine's quite wonderful delicacy, perfumed grace, and exquisite adaptability with the somewhat coarser beauty and genius of the singer. It seemed natural that Byng should turn to a personality more in keeping with his own, more likely to make him perfectly at ease mentally and physically.

Stafford judged Jasmine by his own conversations with her, when he was so acutely alive to the fact that she was the most naturally brilliant woman he had ever known or met; and had capacities for culture and attainment, as she had gifts of discernment and skill in thought, in marked contrast to the best of the ladies of their world. To him she had naturally shown only the one side of her nature—she adapted herself to him as she did to every one else; she had put him always at an advantage, and, in doing so, herself as well.

Full of dangerous coquetry he knew her to be—she had been so from a child; and though this was culpable in a way, he and most others had made more than due allowance, because mother-care and loving surveillance had been withdrawn so soon. For years she had been the spoiled darling of her father and brothers until her father married again; and then it had been too late to control her. The wonder was that she had turned out so well, that she had been so studious, so determined, so capable. Was it because she had unusual brain and insight into human nature, and had been wise and practical enough to see that there was a point where restraint must be applied, and so had kept herself free from blame or deserved opprobrium, if not entirely from criticism? In the day when girls were not in the present sense emancipated, she had the savoir faire and the poise of a married woman of thirty. Yet she was delicate, fresh, and flower-like, and very amusing, in a way which delighted men; and she did not antagonize women.

Stafford had ruled Byng out of consideration where she was concerned. He had not heard her father's remark of the night before, "Jasmine will marry that nabob—you'll see."

He was, however, recalled to the strange possibilities of life by a note which was handed to Byng as they stood before the club-room fire. He could not help but see—he knew the envelope, and no other handwriting was like Jasmine's, that long, graceful, sliding hand. Byng turned it over before opening it.

"Hello," he said, "I'm caught. It's a woman's hand. I wonder how she knew I was here."

Mentally Stafford shrugged his shoulders as he said to himself: "If Jasmine wanted to know where he was, she'd find out. I wonder—I wonder."

He watched Byng, over whose face passed a pleased smile.

"Why," Byng said, almost eagerly, "it's from Miss Grenfel—wants me to go and tell her about Jameson and the Raid."

He paused for an instant, and his face clouded again. "The first thing I must do is to send cables to Johannesburg. Perhaps there are some waiting for me at my rooms. I'll go and see. I don't know why I didn't get news sooner. I generally get word before the Government. There's something wrong somewhere. Somebody has had me."

"If I were you I'd go to our friend first. When I'm told to go at once, I go. She wouldn't like cablegrams and other things coming between you and her command—even when Dr. Jim's riding out of Matabeleland on the Rand for to free the slaves."

Stafford's words were playful, but there was, almost unknown to himself, a strange little note of discontent and irony behind.

Byng laughed. "But I'll be able to tell her more, perhaps, if I go to my rooms first."

"You are going to see her, then?"

"Certainly. There's nothing to do till we get news of Jameson at bay in a conga or balled up at a kopje." Thrusting the delicately perfumed letter in his pocket, he nodded, and was gone.

"I was going to see her myself," thought Stafford, "but that settles it. It will be easier to go where duty calls instead, since Byng takes my place. Why, she told me to come to-day at this very hour," he added, suddenly, and paused in his walk towards the door.

"But I want no triangular tea-parties," he continued to reflect. . . "Well, there'll be work to do at the Foreign Office, that's sure. France,

Austria, Russia can spit out their venom now and look to their mobilization. And won't Kaiser William throw up his cap if Dr. Jim gets caught! What a mess it will be! Well—well—well!"

He sighed, and went on his way brooding darkly; for he knew that this was the beginning of a great trial for England and all British people.

III

A Daughter of Tyre

M onsieur voleur!"

Jasmine looked at him again, as she had done the night before at the opera, standing quite confidentially close to him, her hand resting in his big palm like a pad of rose-leaves; while a delicate perfume greeted his senses. Byng beamed down on her, mystified and eager, yet by no means impatient, since the situation was one wholly agreeable to him, and he had been called robber in his time with greater violence and with a different voice. Now he merely shook his head in humorous protest, and gave her an indulgent look of inquiry. Somehow he felt quite at home with her; while yet he was abashed by so much delicacy and beauty and bloom.

"Why, what else are you but a robber?" she added, withdrawing her hand rather quickly from the too frank friendliness of his grasp. "You ran off with my opera-cloak last night, and a very pretty and expensive one it was."

"Expensive isn't the word," he rejoined; "it was unpurchasable."

She preened herself a little at the phrase. "I returned your overcoat this morning—before breakfast; and I didn't even receive a note of thanks for it. I might properly have kept it till my opera cloak came back."

"It's never coming back," he answered; "and as for my overcoat, I didn't know it had been returned. I was out all the morning."

"In the Row?" she asked, with an undertone of meaning.

"Well, not exactly. I was out looking for your cloak."

"Without breakfast?" she urged with a whimsical glance.

"Well, I got breakfast while I was looking."

"And while you were indulging material tastes, the cloak hid itself—or went out and hanged itself?"

He settled himself comfortably in the huge chair which seemed made especially for him. With a rare sense for details she had had this very chair brought from the library beyond, where her stepmother, in full view, was writing letters. He laughed at her words—a deep, round chuckle it was.

"It didn't exactly hang itself; it lay over the back of a Chesterfield where I could see it and breakfast too."

"A Chesterfield in a breakfast-room! That's more like the furniture of a boudoir."

"Well, it was a boudoir." He blushed a little in spite of himself.

"Ah! . . . Al'mah's? Well, she owed you a breakfast, at least, didn't she?"

"Not so good a breakfast as I got."

"That is putting rather a low price on her life," she rejoined; and a little smile of triumph gathered at her pink lips; lips a little like those Nelson loved not wisely yet not too well, if love is worth while at all.

"I didn't see where you were leading me," he gasped, helplessly. "I give up. I can't talk in your way."

"What is my way?" she pleaded with a little wave of laughter in her eyes.

"Why, no frontal attacks—only flank movements, and getting round the kopjes, with an ambush in a drift here and there."

"That sounds like Paul Kruger or General Joubert," she cried in mock dismay. "Isn't that what they are doing with Dr. Jameson, perhaps?"

His face clouded. Storm gathered slowly in his eyes, a grimness suddenly settled in his strong jaw. "Yes," he answered, presently, "that's what they will be doing; and if I'm not mistaken they'll catch Jameson just as you caught me just now. They'll catch him at Doornkop or thereabouts, if I know myself—and Oom Paul."

Her face flushed prettily with excitement. "I want to hear all about this empire-making, or losing, affair; but there are other things to be settled first. There's my opera-cloak and the breakfast in the prima donna's boudoir, and—"

"But, how did you know it was Al'mah?" he asked blankly.

"Why, where else would my cloak be?" she inquired with a little laugh. "Not at the costumier's or the cleaner's so soon. But, all this horrid flippancy aside, do you really think I should have talked like this, or been so exigent about the cloak, if I hadn't known everything; if I hadn't been to see Al'mah, and spent an hour with her and knew that she was recovering from that dreadful shock very quickly? But could you think me so inhuman and unwomanly as not to have asked about her?"

"I wouldn't be in a position to investigate much when you were talking—not critically," he replied, boldly. "I would only be thinking that everything you said was all right. It wouldn't occur to me to—"

She half closed her eyes, looking at him with languishing humour. "Now you must please remember that I am quite young, and may have my head turned, and—"

"It wouldn't alter my mind about you if you turned your head," he broke in, gallantly, with a desperate attempt to take advantage of an opportunity, and try his hand at a game entirely new to him.

There was an instant's pause, in which she looked at him with what was half-assumed, half-natural shyness. His attempt to play with words was so full of nature, and had behind it such apparent admiration, that the unspoiled part of her was suddenly made self-conscious, however agreeably so. Then she said to him: "I won't say you were brave last night— that doesn't touch the situation. It wasn't bravery, of course; it was splendid presence of mind which could only come to a man with great decision of character. I don't think the newspapers put it at all in the right way. It wasn't like saving a child from the top of a burning building, was it?"

"There was nothing in it at all where I was concerned," he replied. "I've been living a life for fifteen years where you had to move quick—by instinct, as it were. There's no virtue in it. I was just a little quicker than a thousand other men present, and I was nearer to the stage."

"Not nearer than my father or Mr. Stafford."

"They had a bigger shock than I had, I suppose. They got struck numb for a second. I'm a coarser kind. I have seen lots of sickening things; and I suppose they don't stun me. We get callous, I fancy, we veld-rangers and adventurers."

"You seem sensitive enough to fine emotions," she said, almost shyly. "You were completely absorbed, carried away, by Al'mah's singing last night. There wasn't a throb of music that escaped you, I should think."

"Well, that's primary instinct. Music is for the most savage natures. The boor that couldn't appreciate the Taj Mahal, or the sculpture of Michael Angelo, might be swept off his feet by the music of a master, though he couldn't understand its story. Besides, I've carried a banjo and a cornet to the ends of the earth with me. I saved my life with the cornet once. A lion got inside my zareba in Rhodesia. I hadn't my gun within reach, but I'd been playing the cornet, and just as he was crouching I blew a blast from it—one of those jarring discords of Wagner in the "Gotterdammerung"—and he turned tail and got away into the bush with a howl. Hearing gets to be the most acute of all the senses with the pioneer. If you've ever been really dying of thirst, and have reached water again, its sounds become wonderful to you ever after that—the trickle of a creek, the wash of a wave on the shore, the drip on a tin roof, the drop over a fall, the swish of a rainstorm. It's the same with birds and trees. And trees all make different sounds—that's the shape of the leaves. It's all music, too."

Her breath came quickly with pleasure at the imagination and observation of his words. "So it wasn't strange that you should be ravished by Al'mah's singing last night was it?" She looked at him keenly. "Isn't it curious that such a marvellous gift should be given to a woman who in other respects—" she paused.

"Yes, I know what you mean. She's so untrained in lots of ways. That's what I was saying to Stafford a little while ago. They live in a world of their own, the stage people. There's always a kind of irresponsibility. The habit of letting themselves go in their art, I suppose, makes them, in real life, throw things down so hard when they don't like them. Living at high pressure is an art like music. It alters the whole equilibrium, I suppose. A woman like Al'mah would commit suicide, or kill a man, without realizing the true significance of it all."

"Were you thinking that when you breakfasted with her?"

"Yes, when she was laughing and jesting—and when she kissed me good-bye."

"When—she—kissed you—good-bye?"

Jasmine drew back, then half-glanced towards her stepmother in the other room. She was only twenty-two, and though her emancipation had been accomplished in its way somewhat in advance of her generation, it had its origin in a very early period of her life, when she had been allowed to read books of verse—Shelley, Byron, Shakespeare, Verlaine, Rossetti, Swinburne, and many others—unchallenged and unguided. The understanding of things, reserved for "the wise and prudent," had been at first vaguely and then definitely conveyed to her by slow but subtle means—an apprehension from instinct, not from knowledge. There had never been a shock to her mind.

The knowledge of things had grown imperceptibly, and most of life's ugly meanings were known—at a great distance, to be sure, but still known. Yet there came a sudden half-angry feeling when she heard Rudyard Byng say, so loosely, that Al'mah had kissed him. Was it possible, then, that a man, that any man, thought she might hear such things without resentment; that any man thought her to know so much of life that it did not matter what was said? Did her outward appearance, then, bear such false evidence?

He did not understand quite, yet he saw that she misunderstood, and he handled the situation with a tact which seemed hardly to belong to a man of his training and calibre.

"She thought no more of kissing me," he continued, presently, in a calm voice—"a man she had seen only once before, and was not likely to see again, than would a child of five. It meant nothing more to her than kissing Fanato on the stage. It was pure impulse. She forgot it as soon as it was done. It was her way of showing gratitude. Somewhat unconventional, wasn't it? But then, she is a little Irish, a little Spanish, and the rest Saxon; and she is all artist and bohemian."

Jasmine's face cleared, and her equilibrium was instantly restored. She was glad she had misunderstood. Yet Al'mah had not kissed her when she left, while expressing gratitude, too. There was a difference. She turned the subject, saying: "Of course, she insists on sending me a new cloak, and keeping the other as a memento. It was rather badly singed, wasn't it?"

"It did its work well, and it deserves an honoured home. Do you know that even as I flung the cloak round her, in the excitement of the moment I 'sensed,' as my young nephew says, the perfume you use."

He lifted his hand, conscious that his fingers still carried some of that delicate perfume which her fingers left there as they lay in his palm when she greeted him on his entrance. "It was like an incense from the cloak, as it blanketed the flames. Strange, wasn't it, that the undersense should be conscious of that little thing, while the over-sense was adding a sensational postscript to the opera?"

She smiled in a pleased way. "Do you like the perfume? I really use very little of it."

"It's like no other. It starts a kind of cloud of ideas floating. I don't know how to describe it. I imagine myself—"

She interrupted, laughing merrily. "My brother says it always makes him angry, and Ian Stafford calls it 'The Wild Tincture of Time'— frivolously and sillily says that it comes from a bank whereon the 'wild thyme' grows! But now, I want to ask you many questions. We have been mentally dancing, while down beyond the Limpopo—"

His demeanour instantly changed, and she noted the look of power and purpose coming into the rather boyish and good-natured, the rash and yet determined, face. It was not quite handsome. The features were not regular, the forehead was perhaps a little too low, and the hair grew very thick, and would have been a vast mane if it had not been kept fairly close by his valet. This valet was Krool, a half-caste—Hottentot and Boer—whom he had rescued from Lobengula in the Matabele war, and who had in his day been ship-steward, barber, cook, guide, and native recruiter. Krool had attached himself to Byng, and he would not be shaken off even when his master came home to England.

Looking at her visitor with a new sense of observation alive in her, Jasmine saw the inherent native drowsiness of the nature, the love of sleep and good living, the healthy primary desires, the striving, adventurous, yet, in one sense, unambitious soul. The very cleft in the chin, like the alluring dimple of a child's cheek, enlarged and hardened, was suggestive of animal beauty, with its parallel suggestion of indolence. Yet, somehow, too ample as he was both in fact and by suggestion to the imagination there was an apparent underlying force, a capacity to do huge things when once roused. He had been roused in his short day. The life into which he had been thrown with men of vaster ambition and much more selfish ends than his own, had stirred him to prodigies of activity in those strenuous, wonderful, electric days when gold and diamonds changed the hard-bitten, wearied prospector, who had doggedly delved till he had forced open the hand of the Spirit of the Earth and caught the treasure that flowed forth, into a millionaire, into a conqueror, with the world at his feet. He had been of those who, for many a night and many a year, eating food scarce fit for Kaffirs, had, in poverty and grim endeavour, seen the sun rise and fall over the Magaliesberg range, hope alive in the morning and dead at night. He had faced the devilish storms which swept the high veld with lightning and the thunderstone, striking men dead as they fled for shelter to the boulders of some barren, mocking kopje; and he had had the occasional wild nights of carousal, when the miseries and robberies of life and time and the ceaseless weariness and hope deferred, were forgotten.

It was all there in his face—the pioneer endeavour, the reckless effort, the gambler's anxiety, the self-indulgence, the crude passions, with a far-off, vague idealism, the selfish outlook, and yet great breadth of feeling, with narrowness of individual purpose. The rough life, the sordid struggle, had left their mark, and this easy, coaxing, comfortable life of London had not covered it up—not yet. He still belonged to other—and higher—spheres.

There was a great contrast between him and Ian Stafford. Ian was handsome, exquisitely refined, lean and graceful of figure, with a mind which saw the end of your sentences from the first word, with a skill of speech like a Damascus blade, with knowledge of a half-dozen languages. Ian had an allusiveness of conversation which made human intercourse a perpetual entertainment, and Jasmine's intercourse with him a delight which lingered after his going until his coming again. The contrast was prodigious—and perplexing, for Rudyard Byng had qualities which compelled her interest. She sighed as she reflected.

"I suppose you can't get three millions all to yourself with your own hands without missing a good deal and getting a good deal you could do without," she said to herself, as he wonderingly interjected the exclamation:

"Now, what do you know of the Limpopo? I'll venture there isn't another woman in England who even knows the name."

"I always had a thirst for travel, and I've read endless books of travel and adventure," she replied. "I'd have been an explorer, or a Cecil Rhodes, if I had been a man."

"Can you ride?" he asked, looking wonderingly at her tiny hand, her slight figure, her delicate face with its almost impossible pink and white.

"Oh, man of little faith!" she rejoined. "I can't remember when I didn't ride. First a Shetland pony, and now at last I've reached Zambesi—such a wicked dear."

"Zambesi—why Zambesi? One would think you were South African."

She enjoyed his mystification. Then she grew serious and her eyes softened. "I had a friend—a girl, older than I. She married. Well, he's an earl now, the Earl of Tynemouth, but he was the elder son then, and wild for sport. They went on their honeymoon to shoot in Africa, and they visited the falls of the Zambesi. She, my friend, was standing on the edge of the chasm—perhaps you know it—not far from Livingstone's tree, between the streams. It was October, and the river was low. She put up her big parasol. A gust of wind suddenly caught it, and instead of letting the thing fly, she hung on, and was nearly swept into the chasm. A man with them pulled her back in time—but she hung on to that red parasol. Only when it was all over did she realize what had really happened. Well, when she came back to England, as a kind of thank-offering she gave me her father's best hunter. That was like her, too; she could always make other people generous. He is a beautiful Satan, and I rechristened him Zambesi. I wanted the red parasol, too, but Alice Tynemouth wouldn't give it to me."

"So she gave it to the man who pulled her back. Why not?"

"How do you know she did that?"

"Well, it hangs in an honoured place in Stafford's chambers. I conjecture right, do I?"

Her eyes darkened slowly, and a swift-passing shadow covered her faintly smiling lips; but she only said, "You see he was entitled to it, wasn't he?" To herself, however, she whispered, "Neither of them—neither ever told me that."

At that moment the door opened, and a footman came forward to Rudyard Byng. "If you please, sir, your servant says, will you see him. There is news from South Africa."

Byng rose, but Jasmine intervened. "No, tell him to come here," she said to the footman. "Mayn't he?" she asked.

Byng nodded, and remained standing. He seemed suddenly lost to her presence, and with head dropped forward looked into space, engrossed, intense.

Jasmine studied him as an artist would study a picture, and decided that he had elements of the unusual, and was a distinct personality. Though rugged, he was not uncouth, and there was nothing of the nouveau riche about him. He did not wear a ring or scarf-pin, his watch-chain was simple and inconspicuous enough for a school-boy—and he was worth three million pounds, with a palace building in Park Lane and a feudal castle in Wales leased for a period of years. There was nothing greatly striking in his carriage; indeed, he did not make enough of his height and bulk; but his eye was strong and clear, his head was powerful, and his quick smile was very winning. Yet—yet, he was not the type of man who, to her mind should have made three millions at thirty-three. It did not seem to her that he was really representative of the great fortune-builders—she had her grandfather and others closely in mind. She had seen many captains of industry and finance in her grandfather's house, men mostly silent, deliberate and taciturn, and showing in their manner and persons the accumulated habits of patience, force, ceaseless aggression and domination.

Was it only luck which had given Rudyard Byng those three millions? It could not be just that alone. She remembered her grandfather used to say that luck was a powerful ingredient in the successful career of every man, but that the man was on the spot to take the luck, knew when to take it, and how to use it. "The lucky man is the man that sits up watching for the windfall while other men are sleeping"—that was the way he had put it. So Rudyard Byng, if lucky, had also been of those who had grown haggard with watching, working and waiting;

but not a hair of his head had whitened, and if he looked older than he was, still he was young enough to marry the youngest debutante in England and the prettiest and best-born. He certainly had inherent breeding. His family had a long pedigree, and every man could not be as distinguished-looking as Ian Stafford—as Ian Stafford, who, however, had not three millions of pounds; who had not yet made his name and might never do so.

She flushed with anger at herself that she should be so disloyal to Ian, for whom she had pictured a brilliant future—ambassador at Paris or Berlin, or, if he chose, Foreign Minister in Whitehall—Ian, gracious, diligent, wonderfully trained, waiting, watching for his luck and ready to take it; and to carry success, when it came, like a prince of princelier days. Ian gratified every sense in her, met every demand of an exacting nature, satisfied her unusually critical instinct, and was, in effect, her affianced husband. Yet it was so hard to wait for luck, for place, for power, for the environment where she could do great things, could fill that radiant place which her cynical and melodramatic but powerful and sympathetic grandfather had prefigured for her. She had been the apple of that old man's eye, and he had filled her brain— purposely—with ambitious ideas. He had done it when she was very young, because he had not long to stay; and he had overcoloured the pictures in order that the impression should be vivid and indelible when he was gone. He had meant to bless, for, to his mind, to shine, to do big things, to achieve notoriety, to attain power, "to make the band play when you come," was the true philosophy of life. And as this philosophy, successful in his case, was accompanied by habits of life which would bear the closest inspection by the dean and chapter, it was a difficult one to meet by argument or admonition. He had taught his grandchild as successfully as he had built the structure of his success. He had made material things the basis of life's philosophy and purpose; and if she was not wholly materialistic, it was because she had drunk deep, for one so young, at the fountains of art, poetry, sculpture and history. For the last she had a passion which was represented by books of biography without number, and all the standard historians were to be found in her bedroom and her boudoir. Yet, too, when she had opportunity—when Lady Tynemouth brought them to her—she read the newest and most daring productions of a school of French novelists and dramatists who saw the world with eyes morally astigmatic and out of focus. Once she had remarked to Alice Tynemouth:

"You say I dress well, yet it isn't I. It's my dressmaker. I choose the over-coloured thing three times out of five—it used to be more than that. Instinctively I want to blaze. It is the same in everything. I need to be kept down, but, alas! I have my own way in everything. I wish I hadn't, for my own good. Yet I can't brook being ruled."

To this Alice had replied: "A really selfish husband—not a difficult thing to find—would soon keep you down sufficiently. Then you'd choose the over-coloured thing not more than two times, perhaps one time, out of five. Your orientalism is only undisciplined self-will. A little cruelty would give you a better sense of proportion in colour—and everything else. You have orientalism, but little or no orientation."

Here, now, standing before the fire, was that possible husband who, no doubt, was selfish, and had capacities for cruelty which would give her greater proportion—and sense of colour. In Byng's palace, with three millions behind her—she herself had only the tenth of one million—she could settle down into an exquisitely ordered, beautiful, perfect life where the world would come as to a court, and—

Suddenly she shuddered, for these thoughts were sordid, humiliating, and degrading. They were unbidden, but still they came. They came from some dark fountain within herself. She really wanted—her idealistic self wanted—to be all that she knew she looked, a flower in life and thought. But, oh, it was hard, hard for her to be what she wished! Why should it be so hard for her?

She was roused by a voice. "Cronje!" it said in a deep, slow, ragged note.

Byng's half-caste valet, Krool, sombre of face, small, lean, ominous, was standing in the doorway.

"Cronje! . . . Well?" rejoined Byng, quietly, yet with a kind of smother in the tone.

Krool stretched out a long, skinny, open hand, and slowly closed the fingers up tight with a gesture suggestive of a trap closing upon a crushed captive.

"Where?" Byng asked, huskily.

"Doornkop," was the reply; and Jasmine, watching closely, fascinated by Krool's taciturnity, revolted by his immobile face, thought she saw in his eyes a glint of malicious and furtive joy. A dark premonition suddenly flashed into her mind that this creature would one day, somehow, do her harm; that he was her foe, her primal foe, without present or past cause for which she was responsible; but still a foe—one of those antipathies foreordained, one of those evil influences which exist somewhere in the universe against every individual life.

"Doornkop—what did I say!" Byng exclaimed to Jasmine. "I knew they'd put the double-and-twist on him at Doornkop, or some such place; and they've done it—Kruger and Joubert. Englishmen aren't slim enough to be conspirators. Dr. Jim was going it blind, trusting to good luck, gambling with the Almighty. It's bury me deep now. It's Paul Kruger licking his chops over the savoury mess. 'Oh, isn't it a pretty dish to set before the king!' What else, Krool?"

"Nothing, Baas."

"Nothing more in the cables?"

"No, Baas."

"That will do, Krool. Wait. Go to Mr. Whalen. Say I want him to bring a stenographer and all the Partners—he'll understand—to me at ten to-night."

"Yes, Baas."

Krool bowed slowly. As he raised his head his eyes caught those of Jasmine. For an instant they regarded each other steadily, then the man's eyes dropped, and a faint flush passed over his face. The look had its revelation which neither ever forgot. A quiver of fear passed through Jasmine, and was followed by a sense of self-protection and a hardening of her will, as against some possible danger.

As Krool left the room he said to himself: "The Baas speaks her for his vrouw. But the Baas will go back quick to the Vaal—p'r'aps."

Then an evil smile passed over his face, as he thought of the fall of the Rooinek—of Dr. Jim in Oom Paul's clutches. He opened and shut his fingers again with a malignant cruelty.

Standing before the fire, Byng said to Jasmine meditatively, with that old ironic humour which was always part of him: "'Fee, fo, fi, fum, I smell the blood of an Englishman.'"

Her face contracted with pain. "They will take Dr. Jim's life?" she asked, solemnly.

"It's hard to tell. It isn't him alone. There's lots of others that we both know."

"Yes, yes, of course. It's terrible, terrible," she whispered.

"It's more terrible than it looks, even now. It's a black day for England. She doesn't know yet how black it is. I see it, though; I see it. It's as plain as an open book. Well, there's work to do, and I must be about it. I'm off to the Colonial Office. No time to lose. It's a job that has no eight-hours shift."

Now the real man was alive. He was transformed. The face was set and quiet. He looked concentrated will and power as he stood with his hands clasped behind him, his shoulders thrown back, his eyes alight with fire and determination. To herself Jasmine seemed to be moving in the centre of great events, having her fingers upon the levers which work behind the scenes of the world's vast schemes, standing by the secret machinery of government.

"How I wish I could help you," she said, softly, coming nearer to him, a warm light in her liquid blue eyes, her exquisite face flushing with excitement, her hands clasped in front of her.

As Byng looked at her, it seemed to him that sweet honesty and high-heartedness had never had so fine a setting; that never had there been in the world such an epitome of talent, beauty and sincerity. He had suddenly capitulated, he who had ridden unscathed so long. If he had dared he would have taken her in his arms there and then; but he had known her only for a day. He had been always told that a woman must be wooed and won, and to woo took time. It was not a task he understood, but suddenly it came to him that he was prepared to do it; that he must be patient and watch and serve, and, as he used to do, perhaps, be elate in the morning and depressed at night, till the day of triumph came and his luck was made manifest.

"But you can help me, yes, you can help me as no one else can," he said almost hoarsely, and his hands moved a little towards her.

"You must show me how," she said, scarce above a whisper, and she drew back slightly, for this look in his eyes told its own story.

"When may I come again?" he asked.

"I want so much to hear everything about South Africa. Won't you come to-morrow at six?" she asked.

"Certainly, to-morrow at six," he answered, eagerly, "and thank you."

His honest look of admiration enveloped her as her hand was again lost in his strong, generous palm, and lay there for a moment thrilling him. . . He turned at the door and looked back, and the smile she gave seemed the most delightful thing he had ever seen.

"She is a flower, a jasmine-flower," he said, happily, as he made his way into the street.

When he had gone she fled to her bedroom. Standing before the mirror, she looked at herself long, laughing feverishly. Then suddenly she turned and threw herself upon the bed, bursting into a passion of tears. Sobs shook her.

"Oh, Ian," she said, raising her head at last, "oh, Ian, Ian, I hate myself!"

Down in the library her stepmother was saying to her father, "You are right, Jasmine will marry the nabob."

"I am sorry for Ian Stafford," was the response.

"Men get over such things," came the quietly cynical reply.

"Jasmine takes a lot of getting over," answered Jasmine's father. "She has got the brains of all the family, the beauty her family never had—the genius of my father, and the wilfulness, and—"

He paused, for, after all, he was not talking to the mother of his child.

"Yes, all of it, dear child," was the enigmatical reply.

"I wish—Nelly, I do wish that—"

"Yes, I know what you wish, Cuthbert, but it's no good. I'm not of any use to her. She will work out her own destiny alone—as her grandfather did."

"God knows I hope not! A man can carry it off, but a woman—"

Slow and almost stupid as he was, he knew that her inheritance from her grandfather's nature was a perilous gift.

IV

The Partners Meet

E ngland was more stunned than shocked. The dark significance, the evil consequences destined to flow from the Jameson Raid had not yet reached the general mind. There was something gallant and romantic in this wild invasion: a few hundred men, with no commissariat and insufficient clothing, with enough ammunition and guns for only the merest flurry of battle, doing this unbelievable gamble with Fate— challenging a republic of fighting men with well-stocked arsenals and capable artillery, with ample sources of supply, with command of railways and communications. It was certainly magnificent; but it was magnificent folly.

It did not take England long to decide that point; and not even the Laureate's paean in the organ of the aristocracy and upper middle class could evoke any outburst of feeling. There was plenty of admiration for the pluck and boldness, for the careless indifference with which the raiders risked their lives; for the romantic side of the dash from Pitsani to the Rand; but the thing was so palpably impossible, as it was carried out, that there was not a knowing mind in the Islands which would not have echoed Rhodes' words, "Jameson has upset the apple-cart."

Rudyard Byng did not visit Jasmine the next evening at six o'clock. His world was all in chaos, and he had not closed his eyes to sleep since he had left her. At ten o'clock at night, as he had arranged, "The Partners" and himself met at his chambers, around which had gathered a crowd of reporters and curious idlers; and from that time till the grey dawn he and they had sat in conference. He had spent two hours at the Colonial Office after he left Jasmine, and now all night he kneaded the dough of a new policy with his companions in finance and misfortune.

There was Wallstein, the fairest, ablest, and richest financier of them all, with a marvellous head for figures and invaluable and commanding at the council-board, by virtue of his clear brain and his power to co-ordinate all the elements of the most confusing financial problems. Others had by luck and persistence made money—the basis of their fortunes; but Wallstein had showed them how to save those fortunes and make them grow; had enabled them to compete successfully with the games of other great financiers in the world's stock-markets. Wallstein was short and stout, with a big blue eye and an unwrinkled forehead; prematurely aged from lack of exercise and the exciting air of the high veld; from planning and scheming while others slept; from an inherent physical weakness due to the fact that he was one of twin sons, to his brother being given great physical strength, to himself a powerful brain for finance and a frail if ample body. Wallstein knew little and cared less about politics; yet he saw the use of politics in finance, and he did not stick his head into the sand as some of his colleagues did when political activities hampered their operations. In Johannesburg he had kept aloof from the struggle with Oom Paul, not from lack of will, but because he had no stomach for daily intrigue and guerrilla warfare and subterranean workings; and he was convinced that only a great and bloody struggle would end the contest for progress and equal rights for all white men on the Rand. His inquiries had been bent towards so disposing the financial operations, so bulwarking the mining industry by sagacious designs, that, when the worst came, they all would be able to weather the storm. He had done his work better than his colleagues knew, or indeed even himself knew.

Probably only Fleming the Scotsman—another of the Partners— with a somewhat dour exterior, an indomitable will, and a caution which compelled him to make good every step of the way before him, and so cultivate a long sight financially and politically, understood how extraordinary Wallstein's work had been—only Fleming, and Rudyard Byng, who knew better than any and all.

There was also De Lancy Scovel, who had become a biggish figure in the Rand world because he had been a kind of financial valet to Wallstein and Byng, and, it was said, had been a real unofficial valet to Rhodes, being an authority on cooking, and on brewing a punch, and a master of commissariat in the long marches which Rhodes made in the days when he trekked into Rhodesia. It was indeed said that he had made his first ten thousand pounds out of two trips which Rhodes made en route to Lobengula, and had added to this amount on the principle of compound multiplication when the Matabele war came; for here again he had a collateral interest in the commissariat.

Rhodes, with a supreme carelessness in regard to money, with an indifference to details which left his mind free for the working of a few main ideas, had no idea how many cheques he gave on the spur of the moment to De Lancy Scovel in this month or in that, in this year or in that, for this thing or for that—cheques written very often on the backs of envelopes, on the white margin of a newspaper, on the fly-leaf of a book or a blank telegraph form. The Master Man was so stirred by half-contemptuous humour at the sycophancy and snobbery of his vain slave, who could make a salad out of anything edible, that, caring little what men were, so long as they did his work for him, he once wrote a cheque for two thousand pounds on the starched cuff of his henchman's "biled shirt" at a dinner prepared for his birthday.

So it was that, with the marrow-bones thrown to him, De Lancy Scovel came to a point where he could follow Wallstein's and Rhodes' lead financially, being privy to their plans, through eavesdropping on the conferences of his chiefs. It came as a surprise to his superiors that one day's chance discovery showed De Lancy Scovel to be worth fifty thousand pounds; and from that time on they used him for many a purpose in which it was expedient their own hands should not appear. They felt confident that a man who could so carefully and secretly build up his own fortune had a gift which could be used to advantage. A man who could be so subterranean in his own affairs would no doubt be equally secluded in their business. Selfishness would make him silent. And so it was that "the dude" of the camp and the kraal, the factotum, who in his time had brushed Rhodes' clothes when he brushed his own, after the Kaffir servant had messed them about, came to be a millionaire and one of the Partners. For him South Africa had no charms. He was happy in London, or at his country-seat in Leicestershire, where he followed the hounds with a temerity which was at base vanity; where he gave the county the best food to be got outside St. Petersburg or Paris; where his so-called bachelor establishment was cared for by a coarse, gray-haired housekeeper who, the initiated said, was De Lancy's South African wife, with a rooted objection to being a lady or "moving in social circles"; whose pleasure lay in managing this big household under De Lancy's guidance. There were those who said they had seen her brush a speck of dust from De Lancy's coat-collar, as she emerged from her morning interview with him; and others who said they had seen her hidden in the shrubbery listening to the rather flaccid conversation of her splendid poodle of a master.

There were others who had climbed to success in their own way, some by happy accident, some by a force which disregarded anything in their way, and some by sheer honest rough merit, through which the soul of the true pioneer shone.

There was also Barry Whalen, who had been educated as a doctor, and, with a rare Irish sense of adaptability and amazing Celtic cleverness, had also become a mining engineer, in the days when the Transvaal was emerging from its pioneer obscurity into the golden light of mining prosperity. Abrupt, obstinately honest, and sincere; always protesting against this and against that, always the critic of authority, whether the authority was friend or foe; always smothering his own views in the moment when the test of loyalty came; always with a voice like a young bull and a heart which would have suited a Goliath, there was no one but trusted Barry, none that had not hurried to him in a difficulty; not because he was so wise, but because he was so true. He would never have made money, in spite of the fact that his prescience, his mining sense, his diagnosis of the case of a mine, as Byng called it, had been a great source of wealth to others, had it not been for Wallstein and Byng.

Wallstein had in him a curious gentleness and human sympathy, little in keeping with the view held of him by that section of the British press which would willingly have seen England at the mercy of Paul Kruger—for England's good, for her soul's welfare as it were, for her needed chastisement. He was spoken of as a cruel, tyrannical, greedy German Jew, whose soul was in his own pocket and his hand in the pockets of the world. In truth he was none of these things, save that he was of German birth, and of as good and honest German origin as George of Hanover and his descendants, if not so distinguished. Wallstein's eye was an eye of kindness, save in the vision of business; then it saw without emotion to the advantage of the country where he had made his money, and to the perpetual advantage of England, to whom he gave an honourable and philanthropic citizenship. His charities were not of the spectacular kind; but many a poor and worthy, and often unworthy, unfortunate was sheltered through bad days and heavy weather of life by the immediate personal care of "the Jew Mining Magnate, who didn't care a damn what happened to England so long as his own nest was well lined!"

It was Wallstein who took heed of the fact that, as he became rich, Barry Whalen remained poor; and it was he who took note that Barry had a daughter who might any day be left penniless with frail health and no protector; and taking heed and note, it was he made all the Partners unite in taking some financial risks and responsibilities for Barry, when two new mines were opened—to Barry's large profit. It was characteristic of Barry, however, that, if they had not disguised their action by financial devices, and by making him a Partner, because he was needed professionally and intellectually and for other business reasons, nicely phrased to please his Celtic vanity, he would have rejected the means to the fortune which came to him. It was a far smaller fortune than any of the others had; but it was sufficient for him and for his child. So it was that Barry became one of the Partners, and said things that every one else would hesitate to say, but were glad to hear said.

Others of the group were of varying degrees of ability and interest and importance. One or two were poltroons in body and mind, with only a real instinct for money-making and a capacity for constructive individualism. Of them the most conspicuous was Clifford Melville, whose name was originally Joseph Sobieski, with habitat Poland, whose small part in this veracious tale belongs elsewhere.

Each had his place, and all were influenced by the great schemes of Rhodes and their reflection in the purposes and actions of Wallstein. Wallstein was inspired by the dreams and daring purposes of Empire which had driven Rhodes from Table Mountain to the kraal of Lobengula and far beyond; until, at last, the flag he had learned to love had been triumphantly trailed from the Cape to Cairo.

Now in the great crisis, Wallstein, of them all, was the most self-possessed, save Rudyard Byng. Some of the others were paralyzed. They could only whine out execrations on the man who had dared something; who, if he had succeeded, would have been hailed as the great leader of a Revolution, not the scorned and humiliated captain of a filibustering expedition. A triumphant rebellion or raid is always a revolution in the archives of a nation. These men were of a class who run for cover before a battle begins, and can never be kept in the fighting-line except with the bayonet in the small of their backs. Others were irritable and strenuous, bitter in their denunciations of the Johannesburg conspirators, who had bungled their side of the business and who had certainly shown no rashness. At any rate, whatever the merits of their case, no one in England accused the Johannesburgers of foolhardy courage or impassioned daring. They were so busy in trying to induce Jameson to go back that they had no time to go forward themselves. It was not that they lost their heads, their hearts were the disappearing factors.

At this gloomy meeting in his house, Byng did not join either of the two sections who represented the more extreme views and the unpolitical minds. There was a small section, of which he was one, who were not cleverer financially than their friends, but who had political sense and intuition; and these, to their credit, were more concerned, at this dark moment, for the political and national consequences of the Raid, than for the certain set-back to the mining and financial enterprises of the Rand. A few of the richest of them were the most hopeless politically— ever ready to sacrifice principle for an extra dividend of a quarter per cent.; and, in their inmost souls, ready to bow the knee to Oom Paul and his unwholesome, undemocratic, and corrupt government, if only the dividends moved on and up.

Byng was not a great genius, and he had never given his natural political talent its full chance; but his soul was bigger than his pocket. He had a passionate love for the land—for England—which had given him birth; and he had a decent pride in her honour and good name. So it was that he had almost savagely challenged some of the sordid deliberations of this stern conference. In a full-blooded and manly appeal he begged them "to get on higher ground." If he could but have heard it, it would have cheered the heart of the broken and discredited pioneer of Empire at Capetown, who had received his death-warrant, to take effect within five years, in the little cottage at Muizenberg by the sea; as great a soul in posse as ever came from the womb of the English mother; who said as he sat and watched the tide flow in and out, and his own tide of life ebbed, "Life is a three days' trip to the sea-shore: one day in going, one day in settling down, and one day in packing up again."

Byng had one or two colleagues who, under his inspiration, also took the larger view, and who looked ahead to the consequences yet to flow from the fiasco at Doornkop, which became a tragedy. What would happen to the conspirators of Johannesburg? What would happen to Jameson and Willoughby and Bobby White and Raleigh Grey? Who was to go to South Africa to help in holding things together, and to prevent the worst happening, if possible? At this point they had arrived when they saw—

> . . . *The dull dank morn stare in,*
> *Like a dim drowned face with oozy eyes.*

A more miserable morning seldom had broken, even in England.

"I will go. I must go," remarked Byng at last, though there was a strange sinking of the heart as he said it. Even yet the perfume of

Jasmine's cloak stole to his senses to intoxicate them. But it was his duty to offer to go; and he felt that he could do good by going, and that he was needed at Johannesburg. He, more than all of them, had been in open conflict with Oom Paul in the the past, had fought him the most vigorously, and yet for him the old veldschoen Boer had some regard and much respect, in so far as he could respect a Rooinek at all.

"I will go," Byng repeated, and looked round the table at haggard faces, at ashen faces, at the faces of men who had smoked to quiet their nerves, or drunk hard all night to keep up their courage. How many times they had done the same in olden days, when the millions were not yet arrived, and their only luxury was companionship and champagne— or something less expensive.

As Byng spoke, Krool entered the room with a great coffee-pot and a dozen small white bowls. He heard Byng's words, and for a moment his dark eyes glowed with a look of evil satisfaction. But his immobile face showed nothing, and he moved like a spirit among them his lean hand putting a bowl before each person, like a servitor of Death passing the hemlock-brew.

At his entrance there was instant silence, for, secret as their conference must be, this half-caste, this Hottentot-Boer, must hear nothing and know nothing. Not one of them but resented his being Byng's servant. Not one but felt him a danger at any time, and particularly now. Once Barry Whalen, the most outwardly brusque and apparently frank of them all, had urged Byng to give Krool up, but without avail; and now Barry eyed the half-caste with a resentful determination. He knew that Krool had heard Byng's words, for he was sitting opposite the double doors, and had seen the malicious eyes light up. Instantly, however, that light vanished. They all might have been wooden men, and Krool but a wooden servitor, so mechanical and concentrated were his actions. He seemed to look at nobody; but some of them shrank a little as he leaned over and poured the brown, steaming liquid and the hot milk into the bowls. Only once did the factotum look at anybody directly, and that was at Byng just as he was about to leave the room. Then Barry Whalen saw him glance searchingly at his master's face in a mirror, and again that baleful light leaped up in his eyes.

When he had left the room, Barry Whalen said, impulsively: "Byng, it's all damn foolery your keeping that fellow about you. It's dangerous, 'specially now."

"Coffee's good, isn't it? Think there's poison in it?" Byng asked with a contemptuous little laugh. "Sugar—what?" He pushed the great bowl of sugar over the polished table towards Barry.

"Oh, he makes you comfortable enough, but—"

"But he makes you uncomfortable, Barry? Well, we're bound to get on one another's nerves one way or another in this world when the east wind blows; and if it isn't the east wind, it's some other wind. We're living on a planet which has to take the swipes of the universe, because it has permitted that corrupt, quarrelsome, and pernicious beast, man, to populate the hemispheres. Krool is staying on with me, Barry."

"We're in heavy seas, and we don't want any wreckers on the shore," was the moody and nervously indignant reply.

"Well, Krool's in the heavy seas, all right, too—with me."

Barry Whalen persisted. "We're in for complications, Byng. England has to take a hand in the game now with a vengeance. We don't want any spies. He's more Boer than native."

"There'll be nothing Krool can get worth spying for. If we keep our mouths shut to the outside world, we'll not need fear any spies. I'm not afraid of Krool. We'll not be sold by him. Though some one inside will sell us perhaps—as the Johannesburg game was sold by some one inside."

There was a painful silence, and more than one man looked at his fellows furtively.

"We will do nothing that will not bear the light of day, and then we need not fear any spying," continued Byng.

"If we have secret meetings and intentions which we don't make public, it is only what governments themselves have; and we keep them quiet to prevent any one taking advantage of us; but our actions are justifiable. I'm going to do nothing I'm ashamed of; and when it's necessary, or when and if it seems right to do so, I'll put all my cards on the table. But when I do, I'll see that it's a full hand—if I can."

There was a silence for a moment after he had ended, then some one said:

"You think it's best that you should go? You want to go to Johannesburg?"

"I didn't say anything about wanting to go. I said I'd go because one of us—or two of us—ought to go. There's plenty to do here; but if I can be any more use out there, why, Wallstein can stay here, and—"

He got no further, for Wallstein, to whom he had just referred, and who had been sitting strangely impassive, with his eyes approvingly fixed on Byng, half rose from his chair and fell forward, his thick, white hands sprawling on the mahogany table, his fat, pale face striking the polished wood with a thud. In an instant they were all on their feet and at his side.

Barry Whalen lifted up his head and drew him back into the chair, then three of them lifted him upon a sofa. Barry's hand felt the breast of the prostrate figure, and Byng's fingers sought his wrist. For a moment there was a dreadful silence, and then Byng and Whalen looked at each other and nodded.

"Brandy!" said Byng, peremptorily.

"He's not dead?" whispered some one.

"Brandy—quick," urged Byng, and, lifting up the head a little, he presently caught the glass from Whalen's hand and poured some brandy slowly between the bluish lips. "Some one ring for Krool," he added.

A moment later Krool entered. "The doctor—my doctor and his own—and a couple of nurses," Byng said, sharply, and Krool nodded and vanished. "Perhaps it's only a slight heart-attack, but it's best to be on the safe side."

"Anyhow, it shows that Wallstein needs to let up for a while," whispered Fleming.

"It means that some one must do Wallstein's work here," said Barry Whalen. "It means that Byng stays in London," he added, as Krool entered the room again with a rug to cover Wallstein.

Barry saw Krool's eyes droop before his words, and he was sure that the servant had reasons for wishing his master to go to South Africa. The others present, however, only saw a silent, magically adept figure stooping over the sick man, adjusting the body to greater ease, arranging skilfully the cushion under the head, loosening and removing the collar and the boots, and taking possession of the room, as though he himself were the doctor; while Byng looked on with satisfaction.

"Useful person, eh?" he said, meaningly, in an undertone to Barry Whalen.

"I don't think he's at home in England," rejoined Barry, as meaningly and very stubbornly: "He won't like your not going to South Africa."

"Am I not going to South Africa?" Byng asked, mechanically, and looking reflectively at Krool.

"Wallstein's a sick man, Byng. You can't leave London. You're the only real politician among us. Some one else must go to Johannesburg."

"You—Barry?"

"You know I can't, Byng—there's my girl. Besides, I don't carry enough weight, anyhow, and you know that too."

Byng remembered Whalen's girl—stricken down with consumption a few months before. He caught Whalen's arm in a grip of friendship. "All right, dear old man," he said, kindly. "Fleming shall go, and I'll stay. Yes, I'll stay here, and do Wallstein's work."

He was still mechanically watching Krool attend to the sick man, and he was suddenly conscious of an arrest of all motion in the half-caste's lithe frame. Then Krool turned, and their eyes met. Had he drawn Krool's eyes to his—the master-mind influencing the subservient intelligence?

"Krool wants to go to South Africa," he said to himself with a strange, new sensation which he did not understand, though it was not quite a doubt. He reassured himself. "Well, it's natural he should. It's his home. . . But Fleming must go to Johannesburg. I'm needed most here."

There was gratitude in his heart that Fate had decreed it so. He was conscious of the perfume from Jasmine's cloak searching his senses, even in this hour when these things that mattered—the things of Fate—were so enormously awry.

V

A Woman Tells Her Story

"S oon he will speak you. Wait here, madame."

Krool passed almost stealthily out.

Al'mah looked round the rather formal sitting-room, with its somewhat incongruous furnishing—leopard-skins from Bechuanaland; lion-skins from Matabeleland; silver-mounted tusks of elephants from Eastern Cape Colony and Portuguese East Africa; statues and statuettes of classical subjects; two or three Holbeins, a Rembrandt, and an El Greco on the walls; a piano, a banjo, and a cornet; and, in the corner, a little roulette-table. It was a strange medley, in keeping, perhaps, with the incongruously furnished mind of the master of it all; it was expressive of tastes and habits not yet settled and consistent.

Al'mah's eyes had taken it all in rather wistfully, while she had waited for Krool's return from his master; but the wistfulness was due to personal trouble, for her eyes were clouded and her motions languid. But when she saw the banjo, the cornet, and the roulette-table, a deep little laugh rose to her full red lips.

"How like a subaltern, or a colonial civil servant!" she said to herself.

She reflected a moment, then pursued the thought further: "But there must be bigness in him, as well as presence of mind and depth of heart—yes, I'm sure his nature is deep."

She remembered the quick, protecting hands which had wrapped her round with Jasmine Grenfel's cloak, and the great arms in which she had rested, the danger over.

"There can't be much wrong with a nature like his, though Adrian hates him so. But, of course, Adrian would. Besides, Adrian will never get over the drop in the mining-stock which ruined him—Rudyard Byng's mine. . . It's natural for Adrian to hate him, I suppose," she added with a heavy sigh.

Mentally she took to comparing this room with Adrian Fellowes' sitting-room overlooking the Thames Embankment, where everything was in perfect taste and order, where all was modulated, harmonious, soigne and artistic. Yet, somehow, the handsome chambers which hung over the muddy river with its wonderful lights and shades, its mists and radiance, its ghostly softness and greyness, lacked in something that roused imagination, that stirred her senses here—the vital being in her.

It was power, force, experience, adventure. They were all here. She knew the signs: the varied interests, the primary emotions, music, art, hunting, prospecting, fighting, gambling. They were mixed with the solid achievement of talent and force in the business of life. Here was a model of a new mining-drill, with a picture of the stamps working in the Work-and-Wonder mine, together with a model of the Kaffir compound at Kimberley, with the busy, teeming life behind the wire boundaries.

Thus near was Byng to the ways of a child, she thought, thus near to the everlasting intelligence and the busy soul of a constructive and creative Deity—if there was a Deity. Despite the frequent laughter on her tongue and in her eyes, she doubted bitterly at times that there was a Deity. For how should happen the awful tragedies which encompassed men and peoples, if there was a Deity. No benign Deity could allow His own created humanity to be crushed in bleeding masses, like the grapes trampled in the vats of a vineyard. Whole cities swallowed up by earthquake; islands swept of their people by a tidal wave; a vast ship pierced by an iceberg and going down with its thousand souls; provinces spread with the vile elements of a plague which carpeted the land with dead; mines flooded by water or devastated by fire; the little new-born babe left without the rightful breast to feed it; the mother and her large family suddenly deprived of the breadwinner; old men who had lived like saints, giving their all to their own and to the world, driven to the degradation of the poorhouse in the end—ah, if one did not smile, one would die of weeping, she thought.

Al'mah had smiled her way through the world; with a quick word of sympathy for any who were hurt by the blows of life or time; with an open hand for the poor and miserable,—now that she could afford it—and hiding her own troubles behind mirth and bonhommie; for her humour, as her voice, was deep and strong like that of a man. It was sometimes too pronounced, however, Adrian Fellowes had said; and Adrian was an acute observer, who took great pride in her. Was it not to Adrian she had looked first for approval the night of her triumph at Covent Garden—why, that was only a few days ago, and it seemed a hundred days, so much had happened since. It was Adrian's handsome face which had told her then of the completeness of her triumph.

The half-caste valet entered again. "Here come, madame," he said with something very near a smile; for he liked this woman, and his dark, sensual soul would have approved of his master liking her.

"Soon the Baas, madame," he said as he placed a chair for her, and with the gliding footstep of a native left the room.

"Sunny creature!" she remarked aloud, with a little laugh, and looked round. Instantly her face lighted with interest. Here was nothing of that admired disorder, that medley of incongruous things which marked the room she had just left; but perfect order, precision, and balance of arrangement, the most peaceful equipoise. There was a great carved oak-table near to sun-lit windows, and on it were little regiments of things, carefully arranged—baskets with papers in elastic bands; classified and inscribed reference-books, scales, clips, pencils; and in one clear space, with a bunch of violets before it, the photograph of a woman in a splendid silver frame—a woman of seventy or so, obviously Rudyard Byng's mother.

Al'mah's eyes softened. Here was insight into a nature of which the world knew so little. She looked further. Everywhere were signs of disciplined hours and careful hands—cabinets with initialed drawers, shelves filled with books. There is no more impressive and revealing moment with man or woman than when you stand in a room empty of their actual presence, but having, in every inch of it, the pervasive influences of the absent personality. A strange, almost solemn quietness stole over Al'mah's senses. She had been admitted to the inner court, not of the man's house, but of his life. Her eyes travelled on with the gratified reflection that she had been admitted here. Above the books were rows of sketches—rows of sketches!

Suddenly, as her eyes rested on them, she turned pale and got to her feet. They were all sketches of the veld, high and low; of natives; of bits of Dutch architecture; of the stoep with its Boer farmer and his vrouw; of a kopje with a dozen horses or a herd of cattle grazing; of a spruit, or a Kaffir's kraal; of oxen leaning against the disselboom of a cape-wagon; of a herd of steinboks, or a little colony of meerkats in the karoo.

Her hand went to her heart with a gesture of pain, and a little cry of misery escaped her lips.

Now there was a quick footstep, and Byng entered with a cordial smile and an outstretched hand.

"Well, this is a friendly way to begin the New Year," he said, cheerily, taking her hand. "You certainly are none the worse for our little unrehearsed drama the other night. I see by the papers that you have been repeating your triumph. Please sit down. Do you mind my having a little toast while we talk? I always have my petit dejeuner here; and I'm late this morning."

"You look very tired," she said as she sat down.

Krool here entered with a tray, placing it on a small table by the big desk. He was about to pour out the tea, but Byng waved him away.

"Send this note at once by hand," he said, handing him an envelope. It was addressed to Jasmine Grenfel.

"Yes, I'm tired—rather," he added to his guest with a sudden weariness of manner. "I've had no sleep for three nights—working all the time, every hour; and in this air of London, which doesn't feed you, one needs plenty of sleep. You can't play with yourself here as you can on the high veld, where an hour or two of sleep a day will do. On-saddle and off-saddle, in-span and outspan, plenty to eat and a little sleep; and the air does the rest. It has been a worrying time."

"The Jameson Raid—and all the rest?"

"Particularly all the rest. I feel easier in my mind about Dr. Jim and the others. England will demand—so I understand," he added with a careful look at her, as though he had said too much—"the right to try Jameson and his filibusters from Matabeleland here in England; but it's different with the Jo'burgers. They will be arrested—"

"They have been arrested," she intervened.

"Oh, is it announced?" he asked without surprise.

"It was placarded an hour ago," she replied, heavily.

"Well, I fancied it would be," he remarked. "They'll have a close squeak. The sympathy of the world is with Kruger—so far."

"That is what I have come about," she said, with an involuntary and shrinking glance at the sketches on the walls.

"What you have come about?" he said, putting down his cup of tea and looking at her intently. "How are you concerned? Where do you come in?"

"There is a man—he has been arrested with the others; with Farrar, Phillips, Hammond, and the rest—"

"Oh, that's bad! A relative, or—"

"Not a relative, exactly," she replied in a tone of irony. Rising, she went over to the wall and touched one of the water-colour sketches.

"How did you come by these?" she asked.

"Blantyre's sketches? Well, it's all I ever got for all Blantyre owed me, and they're not bad. They're lifted out of the life. That's why I bought them. Also because I liked to think I got something out of Blantyre; and that he would wish I hadn't. He could paint a bit—don't you think so?"

"He could paint a bit—always," she replied.

A silence followed. Her back was turned to him, her face was towards the pictures.

Presently he spoke, with a little deferential anxiety in the tone. "Are you interested in Blantyre?" he asked, cautiously. Getting up, he came over to her.

"He has been arrested—as I said—with the others."

"No, you did not say so. So they let Blantyre into the game, did they?" he asked almost musingly; then, as if recalling what she had said, he added: "Do you mind telling me exactly what is your interest in Blantyre?"

She looked at him straight in the eyes. For a face naturally so full of humour, hers was strangely dark with stormy feeling now.

"Yes, I will tell you as much as I can—enough for you to understand," she answered.

He drew up a chair to the fire, and she sat down. He nodded at her encouragingly. Presently she spoke.

"Well, at twenty-one I was studying hard, and he was painting—"

"Blantyre?"

She inclined her head. "He was full of dreams—beautiful, I thought them; and he was ambitious. Also he could talk quite marvellously."

"Yes, Blantyre could talk—once," Byng intervened, gently.

"We were married secretly."

Byng made a gesture of amazement, and his face became shocked and grave. "Married! Married! You were married to Blantyre?"

"At a registry office in Chelsea. One month, only one month it was, and then he went away to Madeira to paint—'a big commission,' he said; and he would send for me as soon as he could get money in hand— certainly in a couple of months. He had taken most of my half-year's income—I had been left four hundred a year by my mother."

Byng muttered a malediction under his breath and leaned towards her sympathetically.

With an effort she continued. "From Madeira he wrote to tell me he was going on to South Africa, and would not be home for a year. From South Africa he wrote saying he was not coming back; that I could divorce him if I liked. The proof, he said, would be easy; or I needn't divorce him unless I liked, since no one knew we were married."

For an instant there was absolute silence, and she sat with her fingers pressed tight to her eyes. At last she went on, her face turned away from the great kindly blue eyes bent upon her, from the face flushed with honourable human sympathy.

"I went into the country, where I stayed for nearly three years, till—till I could bear it no longer; and then I began to study and sing again."

"What were you doing in the country?" he asked in a low voice.

"There was my baby," she replied, her hands clasping and unclasping in pain. "There was my little Nydia."

"A child—she is living?" he asked gently.

"No, she died two years ago," was the answer in a voice which tried to be firm.

"Does Blantyre know?"

"He knew she was born, nothing more."

"We were married secretly."

"And after all he has done, and left undone, you want to try and save him now?"

He was thinking that she still loved the man. "That offscouring!" he said to himself. "Well, women beat all! He treats her like a Patagonian; leaves her to drift with his child not yet born; rakes the hutches of the towns and the kraals of the veld for women—always women, black or white, it didn't matter; and yet, by gad, she wants him back!"

She seemed to understand what was passing in his mind. Rising, with a bitter laugh which he long remembered, she looked at him for a moment in silence, then she spoke, her voice shaking with scorn:

"You think it is love for him that prompts me now?" Her eyes blazed, but there was a contemptuous laugh at her lips, and she nervously pulled at the tails of her sable muff. "You are wrong—absolutely. I would rather bury myself in the mud of the Thames than let him touch me. Oh, I know what his life must have been—the life of him that you know! With him it would either be the sewer or the sycamore-tree of Zaccheus; either the little upper chamber among the saints or eating husks with the swine. I realize him now. He was easily susceptible to good and evil, to the clean and the unclean; and he might have been kept in order by some one who would give a life to building up his character; but his nature was rickety, and he has gone down and not up."

"Then why try to save him? Let Oom Paul have him. He'll do no more harm, if—"

"Wait a minute," she urged. "You are a great man"—she came close to him—"and you ought to understand what I mean, without my saying it. I want to save him for his own sake, not for mine—to give him a chance. While there's life there's hope. To go as he is, with the mud up to his lips—ah, can't you see! He is the father of my dead child. I like to feel that he may make some thing of his life and of himself yet. That's why I haven't tried to divorce him, and—"

"If you ever want to do so—" he interrupted, meaningly.

"Yes, I know. I have always been sure that nothing could be quite so easy; but I waited, on the chance of something getting hold of him which would lift him out of himself, give him something to think of so much greater than himself, some cause, perhaps—"

"He had you and your unborn child," he intervened.

"Me—!" She laughed bitterly. "I don't think men would ever be better because of me. I've never seen that. I've seen them show the worst of human nature because of me—and it wasn't inspiring. I've not met many men who weren't on the low levels."

"He hasn't stood his trial for the Johannesburg conspiracy yet. How do you propose to help him? He is in real danger of his life."

She laughed coldly, and looked at him with keen, searching eyes. "You ask that, you who know that in the armory of life there's one all-powerful weapon?"

He nodded his head whimsically. "Money? Well, whatever other weapons you have, you must have that, I admit. And in the Transvaal—"

"Then here," she said, handing him an envelope—"here is what may help."

He took it hesitatingly. "I warn you," he remarked, "that if money is to be used at all, it must be a great deal. Kruger will put up the price to the full capacity of the victim."

"I suppose this victim has nothing," she ventured, quietly.

"Nothing but what the others give him, I should think. It may be a very costly business, even if it is possible, and you—"

"I have twenty thousand pounds," she said.

"Earned by your voice?" he asked, kindly.

"Every penny of it."

"Well, I wouldn't waste it on Blantyre, if I were you. No, by Heaven, you shall not do it, even if it can be done! It is too horrible."

"I owe it to myself to do it. After all, he is still my husband. I have let it be so; and while it is so, and while"—her eyes looked away, her face suffused slightly, her lips tightened—"while things are as they are, I am bound—bound by something, I don't know what, but it is not love, and it is not friendship—to come to his rescue. There will be legal expenses—"

Byng frowned. "Yes, but the others wouldn't see him in a hole—yet I'm not sure, either, Blantyre being Blantyre. In any case, I'm ready to do anything you wish."

She smiled gratefully. "Did you ever know any one to do a favor who wasn't asked to repeat it—paying one debt by contracting another, finding a creditor who will trust, and trading on his trust? Yet I'd rather owe you two debts than most men one." She held out her hand to him. "Well, it doesn't do to mope—'The merry heart goes all the day, the sad one tires in a mile-a.' And I am out for all day. Please wish me a happy new year."

He took her hand in both of his. "I wish you to go through this year as you ended the last—in a blaze of glory."

"Yes, really a blaze if not of glory," she said, with bright tears, yet laughing, too, a big warm humour shining in her strong face with the dark brown eyes and the thick, heavy eyebrows under a low, broad forehead like his own. They were indeed strangely alike in many ways both of mind and body.

"They say we end the year as we begin it," he said, cheerily. "You proved to Destiny that you were entitled to all she could give in the old year, and you shall have the best that's to be had in 1897. You are a woman in a million, and—"

"May I come and breakfast with you some morning?" she asked, gaily.

"Well, if ever I'm thought worthy of that honour, don't hesitate. As the Spanish say, It is all yours." He waved a hand to the surroundings.

"No, it is all yours," she said, reflectively, her eyes slowly roaming about her. "It is all you. I'm glad to have been here, to be as near as this to your real life. Real life is so comforting after the mock kind so many of us live; which singers and actors live anyhow."

She looked round the room again. "I feel—I don't know why it is, but I feel that when I'm in trouble I shall always want to come to this room. Yes, and I will surely come; for I know there's much trouble in store for me. You must let me come. You are the only man I would go to like this, and you can't think what it means to me—to feel that I'm not misunderstood, and that it seems absolutely right to come. That's because any woman could trust you—as I do. Good-bye."

In another moment she had gone, and he stood beside the table with the envelope she had left with him. Presently he opened it, and unfolded the cheque which was in it. Then he gave an exclamation of astonishment.

"Seven thousand pounds!" he exclaimed. "That's a better estimate of Krugerism than I thought she had. It'll take much more than that, though, if it's done at all; but she certainly has sense. It's seven thousand times too much for Blantyre," he added, with an exclamation of disgust. "Blantyre—that outsider!" Then he fell to thinking of all she had told him. "Poor girl—poor girl!" he said aloud. "But she must not come here, just the same. She doesn't see that it's not the thing, just because she thinks I'm a Sir Galahad—me!" He glanced at the picture of his mother, and nodded toward it tenderly. "So did she always. I might have turned Kurd and robbed caravans, or become a Turk and kept concubines, and she'd never have seen that it was so. But Al'mah mustn't come here any more, for her own sake. . . I'd find it hard to explain if ever, by any chance—"

He fell to thinking of Jasmine, and looked at the clock. It was only ten, and he would not see Jasmine till six; but if he had gone to South Africa he would not have seen her at all! Fate and Wallstein had been kind.

Presently, as he went to the hall to put on his coat and hat to go out, he met Barry Whalen. Barry looked at him curiously; then, as though satisfied, he said: "Early morning visitor, eh? I just met her coming away. Card of thanks for kind services au theatre, eh?"

"Well, it isn't any business of yours what it is, Barry," came the reply in tones which congealed.

"No, perhaps not," answered his visitor, testily, for he had had a night of much excitement, and, after all, this was no way to speak to a friend, to a partner who had followed his lead always. Friendship should be allowed some latitude, and he had said hundreds of things less carefully to Byng in the past. The past—he was suddenly conscious that Byng had changed within the past few days, and that he seemed to have put restraint on himself. Well, he would get back at him just the same for the snub.

"It's none of my business," he retorted, "but it's a good deal of Adrian Fellowes' business—"

"What is a good deal of Adrian Fellowes' business?"

"Al'mah coming to your rooms. Fellowes is her man. Going to marry her, I suppose," he added, cynically.

Byng's jaw set and his eyes became cold. "Still, I'd suggest your minding your own business, Barry. Your tongue will get you into trouble some day. . . You've seen Wallstein this morning—and Fleming?"

Barry replied sullenly, and the day's pressing work began, with the wires busy under the seas.

VI

Within the Power-House

At a few moments before six o'clock Byng was shown into Jasmine's sitting-room. As he entered, the man who sat at the end of the front row of stalls the first night of "Manassa" rose to his feet. It was Adrian Fellowes, slim, well groomed, with the colour of an apple in his cheeks, and his gold-brown hair waving harmoniously over his unintellectual head.

"But, Adrian, you are the most selfish man I've ever known," Jasmine was saying as Byng entered.

Either Jasmine did not hear the servant announce Byng, or she pretended not to do so, and the words were said so distinctly that Byng heard them as he came forward.

"Well, he is selfish," she added to Byng, as she shook hands. "I've known him since I was a child, and he has always had the best of everything and given nothing for it." Turning again to Fellowes, she continued: "Yes, it's true. The golden apples just fall into your hands."

"Well, I wish I had the apples, since you give me the reputation," Fellowes replied, and, shaking hands with Byng, who gave him an enveloping look and a friendly greeting, he left the room.

"Such a boy—Adrian," Jasmine said, as they sat down.

"Boy—he looks thirty or more!" remarked Byng in a dry tone.

"He is just thirty. I call him a boy because he is so young in most things that matter to people. He is the most sumptuous person—entirely a luxury. Did you ever see such colouring—like a woman's! But selfish, as I said, and useful, too, is Adrian. Yes, he really is very useful. He would be a private secretary beyond price to any one who needed such an article. He has tact—as you saw—and would make a wonderful master of ceremonies, a splendid comptroller of the household and equerry and lord-chamberlain in one. There, if ever you want such a person, or if—"

She paused. As she did so she was sharply conscious of the contrast between her visitor and Ian Stafford in outward appearance. Byng's clothes were made by good hands, but they were made by tailors who knew their man was not particular, and that he would not "try on." The result was a looseness and carelessness of good things—giving him, in a way, the look of shambling power. Yet in spite of the tie a little crooked, and the trousers a little too large and too short, he had touches of that distinction which power gives. His large hands with the square-pointed fingers had obtrusive veins, but they were not common.

"Certainly," he intervened, smiling indulgently; "if ever I want a comptroller, or an equerry, or a lord-chamberlain, I'll remember 'Adrian.' In these days one can never tell. There's the Sahara. It hasn't been exploited yet. It has no emperor."

"I like you in this mood," she said, eagerly. "You seem on the surface so tremendously practical and sensible. You frighten me a little, and I like to hear you touch things off with raillery. But, seriously, if you can ever put anything in that boy's way, please do so. He has had bad luck—in your own Rand mine. He lost nearly everything in that, speculating, and—"

Byng's face grew serious again. "But he shouldn't have speculated; he should have invested. It wants brains, good fortune, daring and wealth to speculate. But I will remember him, if you say so. I don't like to think that he has been hurt in any enterprise of mine. I'll keep him in mind. Make him one of my secretaries perhaps."

Then Barry Whalen's gossip suddenly came to his mind, and he added: "Fellowes will want to get married some day. That face and manner will lead him into ways from which there's only one outlet."

"Matrimony?" She laughed. "Oh dear, no, Adrian is much too selfish to marry."

"I thought that selfishness was one of the elements of successful marriages. I've been told so."

A curious look stole into her eyes. All at once she wondered if his words had any hidden meaning, and she felt angrily self-conscious; but she instantly put the reflection away, for if ever any man travelled by the straight Roman road of speech and thought, it was he. He had only been dealing in somewhat obvious worldly wisdom.

"You ought not to give encouragement to such ideas by repeating them," she rejoined with raillery. "This is an age of telepathy and suggestion, and the more silent we are the safer we are. Now, please, tell me everything—of the inside, I mean—about Cecil Rhodes and the Raiders. Is Rhodes overwhelmed? And Mr. Chamberlain—you have seen him? The papers say you have spent many hours at the Colonial Office. I suppose you were with him at six o'clock last evening, instead of being here with me, as you promised."

He shook his head. "Rhodes? The bigger a man is the greater the crash when he falls; and no big man falls alone."

She nodded. "There's the sense of power, too, which made everything vibrate with energy, which gave a sense of great empty places filled—of that power withdrawn and collapsed. Even the bad great man gone leaves a sense of desolation behind. Power—power, that is the thing of all," she said, her eyes shining and her small fingers interlacing with eager vitality: "power to set waves of influence in motion which stir the waters on distant shores. That seems to me the most wonderful thing."

Her vitality, her own sense of power, seemed almost incongruous. She was so delicately made, so much the dresden-china shepherdess, that intensity seemed out of relation to her nature. Yet the tiny hands playing before her with natural gestures like those of a child had, too, a decision and a firmness in keeping with the perfectly modelled head and the courageous poise of the body. There was something regnant in her, while, too, there was something sumptuous and sensuous and physically thrilling to the senses. To-day she was dressed in an exquisite blue gown, devoid of all decoration save a little chinchilla fur, which only added to its softness and richness. She wore no jewelry whatever except a sapphire brooch, and her hair shone and waved like gossamer in the sun.

"Well, I don't know," he rejoined, admiration unbounded in his eyes for the picture she was of maidenly charm and womanly beauty, "I should say that goodness was a more wonderful thing. But power is the most common ambition, and only a handful of the hundreds of millions get it in any large way. I used to feel it tremendously when I first heard the stamps pounding the quartz in the mills on the Rand. You never heard that sound? In the clear height of that plateau the air reverberates greatly; and there's nothing on earth which so much gives a sense of power—power that crushes—as the stamps of a great mine pounding away night and day. There they go, thundering on, till it seems to you that some unearthly power is hammering the world into shape. You get up and go to the window and look out into the night. There's the deep blue sky—blue like nothing you ever saw in any other sky, and the stars so bright and big, and so near, that you feel you could reach up and pluck one with your hand; and just over the little hill are the lights of the stamp-mills, the smoke and the mad red flare, the roar of great hammers as they crush, crush, crush; while the vibration of the earth makes you feel that you are living in a world of Titans."

"And when it all stops?" she asked, almost breathlessly. "When the stamps pound no more, and the power is withdrawn? It is empty and desolate—and frightening?"

"It is anything you like. If all the mills all at once, with the thousands of stamps on the Rand reef, were to stop suddenly, and the smoke and the red flare were to die, it would be frightening in more ways than one. But I see what you mean. There might be a sense of peace, but the minds and bodies which had been vibrating with the stir of power would feel that the soul had gone out of things, and they would dwindle too."

"If Rhodes should fall, if the stamps on the Rand should cease—?"

He got to his feet. "Either is possible, maybe probable; and I don't want to think of it. As you say, there'd be a ghastly sense of emptiness and a deadly kind of peace." He smiled bitterly.

She rose now also, and fingering some flowers in a vase, arranging them afresh, said: "Well, this Jameson Raid, if it is proved that Cecil Rhodes is mixed up in it, will it injure you greatly—I mean your practical interests?"

He stood musing for a moment. "It's difficult to say at this distance. One must be on the spot to make a proper estimate. Anything may happen."

She was evidently anxious to ask him a question, but hesitated. At last she ventured, and her breath came a little shorter as she spoke.

"I suppose you wish you were in South Africa now. You could do so much to straighten things out, to prevent the worst. The papers say you have a political mind—the statesman's intelligence, the Times said. That letter you wrote, that speech you made at the Chamber of Commerce dinner—"

She watched him, dreading what his answer might be. There was silence for a moment, then he answered: "Fleming is going to South Africa, not myself. I stay here to do Wallstein's work. I was going, but Wallstein was taken ill suddenly. So I stay—I stay."

She sank down in her chair, going a little pale from excitement. The whiteness of her skin gave a delicate beauty to the faint rose of her cheeks—that rose-pink which never was to fade entirely from her face while life was left to her.

"If it had been necessary, when would you have gone?" she asked.

"At once. Fleming goes to-morrow," he added.

She looked slowly up at him. "Wallstein is a new name for a special

Providence," she murmured, and the colour came back to her face. "We need you here. We—"

Suddenly a thought flashed into his mind and suffused his face. He was conscious of that perfume which clung to whatever she touched. It stole to his senses and intoxicated them. He looked at her with enamoured eyes. He had the heart of a boy, the impulsiveness of a nature which had been unschooled in women's ways. Weaknesses in other directions had taught him much, but experiences with her sex had been few. The designs of other women had been patent to him, and he had been invincible to all attack; but here was a girl who, with her friendly little fortune and her beauty, could marry with no difficulty; who, he had heard, could pick and choose, and had so far rejected all comers; and who, if she had shown preference at all, had shown it for a poor man like Ian Stafford. She had courage and simplicity and a downright mind; that was clear. And she was capable. She had a love for big things, for the things that mattered. Every word she had ever said to him had understanding, not of the world alone, and of life, but of himself, Rudyard Byng. She grasped exactly what he would say, and made him say things he would never have thought of saying to any one else. She drew him out, made the most of him, made him think. Other women only tried to make him feel. If he had had a girl like this beside him during the last ten years, how many wasted hours would have been saved, how many bottles of champagne would not have been opened, how many wild nights would have been spent differently!

Too good, too fine for him—yes, a hundred times, but he would try to make it up to her, if such a girl as this could endure him. He was not handsome, he was not clever, so he said to himself, but he had a little power. That he had to some degree rough power, of course, but power; and she loved power, force. Had she not said so, shown it, but a moment before? Was it possible that she was really interested in him, perhaps because he was different from the average Englishman and not of a general pattern? She was a woman of brains, of great individuality, and his own individuality might influence her. It was too good to be true; but there had ever been something of the gambler in him, and he had always plunged. If he ever had a conviction he acted on it instantly, staked everything, when that conviction got into his inner being. It was not, perhaps, a good way, and it had failed often enough; but it was his way, and he had done according to the light and the impulse that were in him. He had no diplomacy, he had only purpose.

He came over to her. "If I had gone to South Africa would you have remembered my name for a month?" he asked with determination and meaning.

"My friends never suffer lunar eclipse," she answered, gaily. "Dear sir, I am called Hold-Fast. My friends are century-flowers and are always blooming."

"You count me among your friends?"

"I hope so. You will let me make all England envious of me, won't you? I never did you any harm, and I do want to have a hero in my tiny circle."

"A hero—you mean me? Well, I begin to think I have some courage when I ask you to let me inside your 'tiny' circle. I suppose most people would think it audacity, not courage."

"You seem not to be aware what an important person you are—how almost sensationally important. Why, I am only a pebble on a shore like yours, a little unknown slip of a girl who babbles, and babbles in vain."

She got to her feet now. "Oh, but believe me, believe me," she said, with sweet and sudden earnestness, "I am prouder than I can say that you will let me be a friend of yours! I like men who have done things, who do things. My grandfather did big, world-wide things, and—"

"Yes, I know; I met your grandfather once. He was a big man, big as can be. He had the world by the ear always."

"He spoiled me for the commonplace," she replied. "If I had lived in Pizarro's time, I'd have gone to Peru with him, the splendid robber."

He answered with the eager frankness and humour of a boy. "If you mean to be a friend of mine, there are those who will think that in one way you have fulfilled your ambition, for they say I've spoiled the Peruvians, too."

"I like you when you say things like that," she murmured. "If you said them often—"

She looked at him archly, and her eyes brimmed with amusement and excitement.

Suddenly he caught both her hands in his and his eyes burned. "Will you—"

He paused. His courage forsook him. Boldness had its limit. He feared a repulse which could never be overcome. "Will you, and all of you here, come down to my place in Wales next week?" he blundered out.

She was glad he had faltered. It was too bewildering. She dared not yet face the question she had seen he was about to ask. Power—yes, he could give her that; but power was the craving of an ambitious soul. There were other things. There was the desire of the heart, the longing which came with music and the whispering trees and the bright stars, the girlish dreams of ardent love and the garlands of youth and joy—and Ian Stafford.

Suddenly she drew herself together. She was conscious that the servant was entering the room with a letter.

"The messenger is waiting," the servant said.

With an apology she opened the note slowly as Byng turned to the fire. She read the page with a strange, tense look, closing her eyes at last with a slight sense of dizziness. Then she said to the servant:

"Tell the messenger to wait. I will write an answer."

"I am sure we shall be glad to go to you in Wales next week," she added, turning to Byng again. "But won't you be far away from the centre of things in Wales?"

"I've had the telegraph and a private telephone wire to London put in. I shall be as near the centre as though I lived in Grosvenor Square; and there are always special trains."

"Special trains—oh, but it's wonderful to have power to do things like that! When do you go down?" she asked.

"To-morrow morning."

She smiled radiantly. She saw that he was angry with himself for his cowardice just now, and she tried to restore him. "Please, will you telephone me when you arrive at your castle? I should like the experience of telephoning by private wire to Wales."

He brightened. "Certainly, if you really wish it. I shall arrive at ten to-morrow night, and I'll telephone you at eleven."

"Splendid—splendid! I'll be alone in my room then. I've got a telephone instrument there, and so we could say good-night."

"So we can say good-night," he repeated in a low voice, and he held out his hand in good-bye. When he had gone, with a new, great hope in his heart, she sat down and tremblingly re-opened the note she had received a moment before.

"I am going abroad" it read—"to Paris, Berlin, Vienna, and St. Petersburg. I think I've got my chance at last. I want to see you before I go—this evening, Jasmine. May I?"

It was signed "Ian."

"Fate is stronger than we are," she murmured; "and Fate is not kind to you, Ian," she added, wearily, a wan look coming into her face.

"Mio destino," she said at last—"mio destino!" But who was her destiny—which of the two who loved her?

BOOK II

VII

Three Years Later

E xtra speshul—extra speshul—all about Kruger an' his guns!"
The shrill, acrid cry rang down St. James's Street, and a newsboy
with a bunch of pink papers under his arm shot hither and thither on
the pavement, offering his sensational wares to all he met.

"Extra speshul—extra speshul—all about the war wot's comin'—all
about Kruger's guns!"

From an open window on the second floor of a building in the street
a man's head was thrust out, listening.

"The war wot's comin'!" he repeated, with a bitter sort of smile. "And
all about Kruger's guns. So it is coming, is it, Johnny Bull; and you
do know all about his guns, do you? If it is, and you do know, then a
shattering big thing is coming, and you know quite a lot, Johnny Bull."

He hummed to himself an impromptu refrain to an impromptu
tune:

> *"Then you know quite a lot, Johnny Bull, Johnny Bull,*
> *Then you know quite a lot, Johnny Bull!"*

Stepping out of the French window upon a balcony now, he looked
down the street. The newsboy was almost below. He whistled, and
the lad looked up. In response to a beckoning finger the gutter-snipe
took the doorway and the staircase at a bound. Like all his kind, he
was a good judge of character, and one glance had assured him that
he was speeding upon a visit of profit. Half a postman's knock—a
sharp, insistent stroke—and he entered, his thin weasel-like face thrust
forward, his eyes glittering. The fire in such eyes is always cold, for
hunger is poor fuel to the native flame of life.

"Extra speshul, m'lord—all about Kruger's guns."

He held out the paper to the figure that darkened the window, and
he pronounced the g in Kruger soft, as in Scrooge.

The hand that took the paper deftly slipped a shilling into the cold,
skinny palm. At its first touch the face of the paper-vender fell, for it was
the same size as a halfpenny; but even before the swift fingers had had

a chance to feel the coin, or the glance went down, the face regained its confidence, for the eyes looking at him were generous. He had looked at so many faces in his brief day that he was an expert observer.

"Thank y' kindly," he said; then, as the fingers made assurance of the fortune which had come to him, "Ow, thank ye werry much, y'r gryce," he added.

Something alert and determined in the face of the boy struck the giver of the coin as he opened the paper to glance at its contents, and he paused to scan him more closely. He saw the hunger in the lad's eyes as they swept over the breakfast-table, still heavy with uneaten breakfast—bacon, nearly the whole of an omelette, and rolls, toast, marmalade and honey.

"Wait a second," he said, as the boy turned toward the door.

"Yes, y'r gryce."

"Had your breakfast?"

"I has me brekfist w'en I sells me pypers." The lad hugged the remaining papers closer under his arms, and kept his face turned resolutely away from the inviting table. His host correctly interpreted the action.

"Poor little devil—grit, pure grit!" he said under his breath. "How many papers have you got left?" he asked.

The lad counted like lightning. "Ten," he answered. "I'll soon get 'em off now. Luck's wiv me dis mornin'." The ghost of a smile lighted his face.

"I'll take them all," the other said, handing over a second shilling.

The lad fumbled for change and the fumbling was due to honest agitation. He was not used to this kind of treatment.

"No, that's all right," the other interposed.

"But they're only a h'ypenny," urged the lad, for his natural cupidity had given way to a certain fine faculty not too common in any grade of human society.

"Well, I'm buying them at a penny this morning. I've got some friends who'll be glad to give a penny to know all about Kruger's guns." He too softened the g in Kruger in consideration of his visitor's idiosyncrasies.

"You won't be mykin' anythink on them, y'r gryce," said the lad with a humour which opened the doors of Ian Stafford's heart wide; for to him heaven itself would be insupportable if it had no humorists.

"I'll get at them in other ways," Stafford rejoined. "I'll get my profit, never fear. Now what about breakfast? You've sold all your papers, you know."

"I'm fair ready for it, y'r gryce," was the reply, and now the lad's glance went eagerly towards the door, for the tension of labour was relaxed, and hunger was scraping hard at his vitals.

"Well, sit down—this breakfast isn't cold yet. . . But, no, you'd better have a wash-up first, if you can wait," Stafford added, and rang a bell.

"Wot, 'ere—brekfist wiv y'r gryce 'ere?"

"Well, I've had mine"—Stafford made a slight grimace—"and there's plenty left for you, if you don't mind eating after me."

"I dusted me clothes dis mornin'," said the boy, with an attempt to justify his decision to eat this noble breakfast. "An' I washed me 'ends—but pypers is muck," he added.

A moment later he was in the fingers of Gleg the valet in the bathroom, and Stafford set to work to make the breakfast piping hot again. It was an easy task, as heaters were inseparable from his bachelor meals, and, though this was only the second breakfast he had eaten since his return to England after three years' absence, everything was in order.

For Gleg was still more the child of habit—and decorous habit—than himself. It was not the first time that Gleg had had to deal with his master's philanthropic activities. Much as he disapproved of them, he could discriminate; and there was that about the newsboy which somehow disarmed him. He went so far as to heap the plate of the lad, and would have poured the coffee too, but that his master took the pot from his hand and with a nod and a smile dismissed him; and his master's smile was worth a good deal to Gleg. It was an exacting if well-paid service, for Ian Stafford was the most particular man in Europe, and he had grown excessively so during the past three years, which, as Gleg observed, had brought great, if quiet, changes in him. He had grown more studious, more watchful, more exclusive in his daily life, and ladies of all kinds he had banished from direct personal share in his life. There were no more little tea-parties and dejeuners chez lui, duly chaperoned by some gracious cousin or aunt—for there was no embassy in Europe where he had not relatives.

"'Ipped—a bit 'ipped. 'E 'as found 'em out, the 'uzzies," Gleg had observed; for he had decided that the general cause of the change in his master was Woman, though he did not know the particular woman who had 'ipped him.

As the lad ate his wonderful breakfast, in which nearly half a pot of marmalade and enough butter for three ordinary people figured, Stafford read the papers attentively, to give his guest a fair chance at the food and to overcome his self-consciousness. He got an occasional glance at the trencherman, however, as he changed the sheets, stepped across the room to get a cigarette, or poked the small fire—for, late September as it was, a sudden cold week of rain had come and gone, leaving the air raw; and a fire was welcome.

At last, when he realized that the activities of the table were decreasing, he put down his paper. "Is it all right?" he asked. "Is the coffee hot?"

"I ain't never 'ad a meal like that, y'r gryce, not never any time," the boy answered, with a new sort of fire in his eyes.

"Was there enough?"

"I've left some," answered his guest, looking at the jar of marmalade and half a slice of toast. "I likes the coffee hot—tykes y'r longer to drink it," he added.

Ian Stafford chuckled. He was getting more than the worth of his money. He had nibbled at his own breakfast, with the perturbations of a crossing from Flushing still in his system, and its equilibrium not fully restored; and yet, with the waste of his own meal and the neglect of his own appetite, he had given a great and happy half-hour to a waif of humanity.

As he looked at the boy he wondered how many thousands there were like him within rifle-shot from where he sat, and he thought each of them would thank whatever gods they knew for such a neglected meal. The words from the scare-column of the paper he held smote his sight:

"War Inevitable—Transvaal Bristling with Guns and Loaded to the Nozzle with War Stores—Milner and Kruger No Nearer a Settlement—Sullen and Contemptuous Treatment of British Outlander." . . . And so on.

And if war came, if England must do this ugly thing, fulfil her bitter and terrible task, then what about such as this young outlander here, this outcast from home and goodly toil and civilized conditions, this sickly froth of the muddy and dolorous stream of lower England? So much withdrawn from the sources of the possible relief, so much less with which to deal with their miseries—perhaps hundreds of millions, mopped up by the parched and unproductive soil of battle and disease and loss.

He glanced at the paper again. "Britons Hold Your Own," was the heading of the chief article. "Yes, we must hold our own," he said, aloud, with a sigh. "If it comes, we must see it through; but the breakfasts will be fewer. It works down one way or another—it all works down to this poor little devil and his kind."

"Now, what's your name?" he asked.

"Jigger," was the reply.

"What else?"

"Nothin', y'r gryce."

"Jigger—what?"

"It's the only nyme I got," was the reply.

"What's your father's or your mother's name?"

"I ain't got none. I only got a sister."

"What's her name?"

"Lou," he answered. "That's her real name. But she got a fancy name yistiddy. She was took on at the opera yistiddy, to sing with a hunderd uvver girls on the styge. She's Lulu Luckingham now."

"Oh—Luckingham!" said Stafford, with a smile, for this was a name of his own family, and of much account in circles he frequented. "And who gave her that name? Who were her godfathers and godmothers?"

"I dunno, y'r gryce. There wasn't no religion in it. They said she'd have to be called somefink, and so they called her that. Lou was always plenty for 'er till she went there yistiddy."

"What did she do before yesterday?"

"Sold flowers w'en she could get 'em to sell. 'Twas when she couldn't sell her flowers that she piped up sort of dead wild—for she 'adn't 'ad nothin' to eat, an' she was fair crusty. It was then a gentleman, 'e 'eard 'er singin' hot, an' he says, 'That's good enough for a start,' 'e says, 'an' you come wiv me,' he says. 'Not much,' Lou says, 'not if I knows it. I seed your kind frequent.' But 'e stuck to it, an' says, 'It's stryght, an' a lydy will come for you to-morrer, if you'll be 'ere on this spot, or tell me w'ere you can be found.' An' Lou says, says she, 'You buy my flowers, so's I kin git me bread-baskit full, an' then I'll think it over.' An' he bought 'er flowers, an' give 'er five bob. An' Lou paid rent for both of us wiv that, an' 'ad brekfist; an' sure enough the lydy come next dy an' took her off. She's in the opery now, an' she'll 'ave 'er brekfist reg'lar. I seed the lydy meself. Her picture's on the 'oardings—"

Suddenly he stopped. "W'y, that's 'er—that's 'er!" he said, pointing to the mantel-piece.

Stafford followed the finger and the glance. It was Al'mah's portrait in the costume she had worn over three years ago, the night when Rudyard Byng had rescued her from the flames. He had bought it then. It had been unpacked again by Gleg, and put in the place it had occupied for a day or two before he had gone out of England to do his country's work—and to face the bitterest disillusion of his life; to meet the heaviest blow his pride and his heart had ever known.

"So that's the lady, is it?" he said, musingly, to the boy, who nodded assent.

"Go and have a good look at it," urged Stafford.

The boy did so. "It's 'er—done up for the opery," he declared.

"Well, Lulu Luckingham is all right, then. That lady will be good to her."

"Right. As soon as I seed her, I whispers to Lou 'You keep close to that there wall,' I sez. 'There's a chimbey in it, an' you'll never be cold,' I says to Lou."

Stafford laughed softly at the illustration. Many a time the lad snuggled up to a wall which had a warm chimney, and he had got his figure of speech from real life.

"Well, what's to become of you?" Stafford asked.

"Me—I'll be level wiv me rent to-day," he answered, turning over the two shillings and some coppers in his pocket; "an' Lou and me's got a fair start."

Stafford got up, came over, and laid a hand on the boy's shoulder. "I'm going to give you a sovereign," he said—"twenty shillings, for your fair start; and I want you to come to me here next Sunday-week to breakfast, and tell me what you've done with it."

"Me—y'r gryce!" A look of fright almost came into the lad's face. "Twenty bob—me!"

The sovereign was already in his hand, and now his face suffused. He seemed anxious to get away, and looked round for his cap. He couldn't do here what he wanted to do. He felt that he must burst.

"Now, off you go. And you be here at nine o'clock on Sunday-week with the papers, and tell me what you've done."

"Gawd—my Gawd!" said the lad, huskily. The next minute he was out in the hall, and the door was shut behind him. A moment later, hearing a whoop, Stafford went to the window and, looking down, he saw his late visitor turning a cart-wheel under the nose of a policeman, and then, with another whoop, shooting down into the Mall, making Lambeth way.

　　　　　　　　　　　　　　　　　　　GILBERT PARKER

With a smile he turned from the window. "Well, we shall see," he said. "Perhaps it will be my one lucky speculation. Who knows—who knows!"

His eye caught the portrait of Al'mah on the mantelpiece. He went over and stood looking at it musingly.

"You were a good girl," he said, aloud. "At any rate, you wouldn't pretend. You'd gamble with your immortal soul, but you wouldn't sell it—not for three millions, not for a hundred times three millions. Or is it that you are all alike, you women? Isn't there one of you that can be absolutely true? Isn't there one that won't smirch her soul and kill the faith of those that love her for some moment's excitement, for gold to gratify a vanity, or to have a wider sweep to her skirts? Vain, vain, vain—and dishonourable, essentially dishonourable. There might be tragedies, but there wouldn't be many intrigues if women weren't so dishonourable—the secret orchard rather than the open highway and robbery under arms. . . Whew, what a world!"

He walked up and down the room for a moment, his eyes looking straight before him; then he stopped short. "I suppose it's natural that, coming back to England, I should begin to unpack a lot of old memories, empty out the box-room, and come across some useless and discarded things. I'll settle down presently; but it's a thoroughly useless business turning over old stock. The wise man pitches it all into the junk-shop, and cuts his losses."

He picked up the Morning Post and glanced down the middle page—the social column first—with the half-amused reflection that he hadn't done it for years, and that here were the same old names reappearing, with the same brief chronicles. Here, too, were new names, some of them, if not most of them, of a foreign turn to their syllables—New York, Melbourne, Buenos Ayres, Johannesburg. His lip curled a little with almost playful scorn. At St. Petersburg, Vienna, and elsewhere he had been vaguely conscious of these social changes; but they did not come within the ambit of his daily life, and so it had not mattered. And there was no reason why it should matter now. His England was a land the original elements of which would not change, had not changed; for the old small inner circle had not been invaded, was still impervious to the wash of wealth and snobbery and push. That refuge had its sequestered glades, if perchance it was unilluminating and rather heavily decorous; so that he could let the climbers, the toadies, the gold-spillers, and the bribers have the middle of the road.

It did not matter so much that London was changing fast. The old clock on the tower of St. James's would still give the time to his step as he went to and from the Foreign Office, and there were quiet places like Kensington Gardens where the bounding person would never think to stray. Indeed, they never strayed; they only rushed and pushed where their spreading tails could be seen by the multitude. They never got farther west than Rotten Row, which was in possession of three classes of people—those who sat in Parliament, those who had seats on the Stock Exchange, and those who could not sit their horses. Three years had not done it all, but it had done a good deal; and he was more keenly alive to the changes and developments which had begun long before he left and had increased vastly since. Wealth was more and more the master of England—new-made wealth; and some of it was too ostentatious and too pretentious to condone, much less indulge.

All at once his eye, roaming down the columns, came upon the following announcement:

"Mr. and Mrs. Rudyard Byng have returned to town from Scotland for a few days, before proceeding to Wales, where they are presently to receive at Glencader Castle the Duke and Duchess of Sheffield, the Prince and Princess of Cleaves, M. Santon, the French Foreign Minister, the Slavonian Ambassador, the Earl and Countess of Tynemouth, and Mr. Tudor Tempest."

"'And Mr. Tudor Tempest,'" Ian repeated to himself. "Well, she would. She would pay that much tribute to her own genius. Four-fifths to the claims of the body and the social nervous system, and one-fifth to the desire of the soul. Tempest is a literary genius by what he has done, and she is a genius by nature, and with so much left undone. The Slavonian Ambassador—him, and the French Foreign Minister! That looks like a useful combination at this moment—at this moment. She has a gift for combinations, a wonderful skill, a still more wonderful perception—and a remarkable unscrupulousness. She's the naturally ablest woman I have ever known; but she wants to take short-cuts to a worldly Elysium, and it can't be done, not even with three times three millions—and three millions was her price."

Suddenly he got up and went over to a table where were several dispatch-boxes. Opening one, he drew forth from the bottom, where he had placed it nearly three years ago, a letter. He looked at the long, sliding handwriting, so graceful and fine, he caught the perfume which had intoxicated Rudyard Byng, and, stooping down, he sniffed the dispatch-box. He nodded.

"She's pervasive in everything," he murmured. He turned over several other packets of letters in the box. "I apologize," he said, ironically, to these letters. "I ought to have banished her long ago, but, to tell you the truth, I didn't realize how much she'd influence everything—even in a box." He laughed cynically, and slowly opened the one letter which had meant so much to him.

There was no show of agitation. His eye was calm; only his mouth showed any feeling or made any comment. It was a little supercilious and scornful. Sitting down by the table, he spread the letter out, and read it with great deliberation. It was the first time he had looked at it since he received it in Vienna and had placed it in the dispatch-box.

"Dear Ian," it ran, "our year of probation—that is the word isn't it?—is up; and I have decided that our ways must lie apart. I am going to marry Rudyard Byng next month. He is very kind and very strong, and not too ragingly clever. You know I should chafe at being reminded daily of my own stupidity by a very clever man. You and I have had so many good hours together, there has been such confidence between us, that no other friendship can ever be the same; and I shall always want to go to you, and ask your advice, and learn to be wise. You will not turn a cold shoulder on me, will you? I think you yourself realized that my wish to wait a year before giving a final answer was proof that I really had not that in my heart which would justify me in saying what you wished me to say. Oh yes, you knew; and the last day when you bade me good-bye you almost said as much! I was so young, so unschooled, when you first asked me, and I did not know my own mind; but I know it now, and so I go to Rudyard Byng for better or for worse—"

He suddenly stopped reading, sat back in his chair, and laughed sardonically.

"For richer, for poorer'—now to have launched out on the first phrase, and to have jibbed at the second was distinctly stupid. The quotation could only have been carried off with audacity of the ripest kind. 'For better, for worse, for richer, for poorer, in sickness and in health, till death us do part, amen—' That was the way to have done it, if it was to be done at all. Her cleverness forsook her when she wrote that letter. 'Our year of probation'—she called it that. Dear, dear, what a poor prevaricator the best prevaricator is! She was sworn to me, bound to me, wanted a year in which to have her fling before she settled down, and she threw me over—like that."

He did not read the rest of the letter, but got up, went over to the fire, threw it in, and watched it burn.

"I ought to have done so when I received it," he said, almost kindly now. "A thing like that ought never to be kept a minute. It's a terrible confession, damning evidence, a self-made exposure, and to keep it is too brutal, too hard on the woman. If anything had happened to me and it had been read, 'Not all the King's horses nor all the King's men could put Humpty Dumpty together again.'"

Then he recalled the brief letter he had written her in reply. Unlike him, she had not kept his answer, when it came into her hands, but, tearing it up into fifty fragments, had thrown it into the waste-basket, and paced her room in shame, anger and humiliation. Finally, she had taken the waste-basket and emptied it into the flames. She had watched the tiny fragments burn in a fire not hotter than that in her own eyes, which presently were washed by a flood of bitter tears and passionate and unavailing protest. For hours she had sobbed, and when she went out into the world the next day, it was with his every word ringing in her ears, as they had rung ever since: the sceptic comment at every feast, the ironical laughter behind every door, the whispered detraction in every loud accent of praise.

"Dear Jasmine," his letter had run, "it is kind of you to tell me of your intended marriage before it occurs, for in these distant lands news either travels slowly or does not reach one at all. I am fortunate in having my information from the very fountain of first knowledge. You have seen and done much in the past year; and the end of it all is more fitting than the most meticulous artist could desire or conceive. You will adorn the new sphere into which you enter. You are of those who do not need training or experience: you are a genius, whose chief characteristic is adaptability. Some people, to whom nature and Providence have not been generous live up to things; to you it is given to live down to them; and no one can do it so well. We have had good times together—happy conversations and some cheerful and entertaining dreams and purposes. We have made the most of opportunity, each in his and her own way. But, my dear Jasmine, don't ever think that you will need to come to me for advice and to learn to be wise. I know of no one from whom I could learn, from whom I have learned, so much. I am deeply your debtor for revelations which never could have come to me without your help. There is a wonderful future before you, whose variety let Time, not me, attempt to reveal. I shall watch your going on"—(he did not say goings on)—"your Alpine course, with clear memories of things and hours dearer to me than all the world, and with which I would not have parted for the mines of the Rand. I lose them now for nothing—and less than nothing. I shall be abroad for some years, and, meanwhile, a new planet will swim into the universe of matrimony. I shall see the light shining, but its heavenly orbit will not be within my calculations. Other astronomers will watch, and some no doubt will pray, and I shall read in the annals the bright story of the flower that was turned into a star!

> Always yours sincerely,
> IAN STAFFORD

From the filmy ashes of her letter to him Stafford now turned away to his writing-table. There he sat for a while and answered several notes, among them one to Alice Mayhew, now the Countess of Tynemouth, whose red parasol still hung above the mantel-piece, a relic of the Zambesi—and of other things.

Periodically Lady Tynemouth's letters had come to him while he was abroad, and from her, in much detail, he had been informed of the rise of Mrs. Byng, of her great future, her "delicious" toilettes, her great entertainments for charity, her successful attempts to gather round her the great figures in the political and diplomatic world; and her partial rejection of Byng's old mining and financial confreres and their belongings. It had all culminated in a visit of royalty to their place in Suffolk, from which she had emerged radiantly and delicately aggressive, and sweeping a wider circle with her social scythe.

Ian had read it all unperturbed. It was just what he knew she could and would do; and he foresaw for Byng, if he wanted it, a peerage in the not distant future. Alice Tynemouth was no gossip, and she was not malicious. She had a good, if wayward, heart, was full of sentiment, and was a constant and helpful friend. He, therefore, accepted her invitation now to spend the next week-end with her and her husband; and then, with letters to two young nephews in his pocket, he prepared to sally forth to buy them presents, and to get some sweets for the children of a poor invalid cousin to whom for years he had been a generous friend. For children he had a profound love, and if he had married, he would not have been content with a childless home—with a childless home like that of Rudyard Byng. That news also had come to him from Alice Tynemouth, who honestly lamented that Jasmine Byng had no "balance-wheel," which was the safety and the anchor of women "like her and me," Lady Tynemouth's letter had said.

Three millions then—and how much more now?—and big houses, and no children. It was an empty business, or so it seemed to him, who had come of a large and agreeably quarrelsome and clever family, with whom life had been checkered but never dull.

He took up his hat and stick, and went towards the door. His eyes caught Al'mah's photograph as he passed.

"It was all done that night at the opera," he said. "Jasmine made up her mind then to marry him, . . . I wonder what the end will be. . . Sad little, bad little girl. . . The mess of pottage at the last? Quien sabe!"

VIII

"He Shall Not Treat Me So"

The air of the late September morning smote Stafford's cheeks pleasantly, and his spirits rose as he walked up St. James's Street. His step quickened imperceptibly to himself, and he nodded to or shook hands with half a dozen people before he reached Piccadilly. Here he completed the purchases for his school-boy nephews, and then he went to a sweet-shop in Regent Street to get chocolates for his young relatives. As he entered the place he was suddenly brought to a standstill, for not two dozen yards away at a counter was Jasmine Byng.

She did not see him enter, and he had time to note what matrimony, and the three years and the three million pounds, had done to her. She was radiant and exquisite, a little paler, a little more complete, but increasingly graceful and perfectly appointed. Her dress was of dark green, of a most delicate shade, and with the clinging softness and texture of velvet. She wore a jacket of the same material, and a single brilliant ornament at her throat relieved the simplicity. In the hat, too, one big solitary emerald shone against the lighter green.

She was talking now with animation and amusement to the shop-girl who was supplying her with sweets, and every attendant was watching her with interest and pleasure. Stafford reflected that this was always her way: wherever she went she attracted attention, drew interest, magnetized the onlooker. Nothing had changed in her, nothing of charm and beauty and eloquence,—how eloquent she had always been!—of esprit, had gone from her; nothing. Presently she turned her face full toward him, still not seeing him, half hidden as he was behind some piled-up tables in the centre of the shop.

Nothing changed? Yes, instantly he was aware of a change, in the eyes, at the mouth. An elusive, vague, distant kind of disturbance—he could not say trouble—had stolen into her eyes, had taken possession of the corners of the mouth; and he was conscious of something exotic, self-indulgent, and "emancipated." She had always been self-indulgent and selfish, and, in a wilful, innocent way, emancipated, in the old days; but here was a different, a fuller, a more daring expression of these qualities. . . Ah, he had it now! That elusive something was a lurking recklessness, which, perhaps, was not bold enough yet to leap into full exercise, or even to recognize itself.

So this was she to whom he had given the best of which he had been capable—not a very noble or priceless best, he was willing to acknowledge, but a kind of guarantee of the future, the nucleus of fuller things. As he looked at her now his heart did not beat faster, his pulses did not quicken, his eye did not soften, he did not even wish himself away. Love was as dead as last year's leaves—so dead that no spirit of resentment, or humiliation, or pain of heart was in his breast at this sight of her again. On the contrary, he was conscious of a perfect mastery of himself, of being easily superior to the situation.

Love was dead; youth was dead; the desire that beats in the veins of the young was dead; his disillusion and disappointment and contempt for one woman had not driven him, as it so often does, to other women— to that wild waste which leaves behind it a barren and ill-natured soil exhausted of its power, of its generous and native health. There was a strange apathy in his senses, an emotional stillness, as it were, the atrophy of all the passionate elements of his nature. But because of this he was the better poised, the more evenly balanced, the more perceptive. His eyes were not blurred or dimmed by any stress of emotion, his mind worked in a cool quiet, and his forward tread had leisurely decision and grace. He had sunk one part of himself far below the level of activity or sensation, while new resolves, new powers of mind, new designs were set in motion to make his career a real and striking success. He had the most friendly ear and the full confidence of the Prime Minister, who was also Foreign Secretary—he had got that far; and now, if one of his great international schemes could but be completed, an ambassadorship would be his reward, and one of first-class importance. The three years had done much for him in a worldly way, wonderfully much.

As he looked at the woman who had shaken his life to the centre— not by her rejection of him, but by the fashion of it, the utter selfishness and cold-blooded calculation of it, he knew that love's fires were out, and that he could meet her without the agitation of a single nerve. He despised her, but he could make allowance for her. He knew the strain that was in her, got from her brilliant and rather plangent grandfather. He knew the temptation of a vast fortune, the power that it would bring—and the notoriety, too, again an inheritance from her grandfather. He was not without magnanimity, and he could the more easily exercise it because his pulses of emotion were still.

She was by nature the most brilliantly endowed woman he had ever met, the most naturally perceptive and artistic, albeit there was a touch of gorgeousness to the inherent artistry which time, training and experience would have chastened. Would have chastened? Was it not, then, chastened? Looking at her now, he knew that it was not. It was still there, he felt; but how much else was also there—of charm, of elusiveness, of wit, of mental adroitness, of joyous eagerness to discover a new thought or a new thing! She was a creature of rare splendour, variety and vanity.

Why should he deny himself the pleasure of her society? His intellectual side would always be stimulated by her, she would always "incite him to mental riot," as she had often said. Time had flown, love had flown, and passion was dead; but friendship stayed. Yes, friendship stayed—in spite of all. Her conduct had made him blush for her, had covered him with shame, but she was a woman, and therefore weak— he had come to that now. She was on a lower plateau of honour, and therefore she must be—not forgiven—that was too banal; but she must be accepted as she was. And, after all, there could be no more deception; for opportunity and occasion no longer existed. He would go and speak to her now.

At that moment he was aware that she had caught sight of him, and that she was startled. She had not known of his return to England, and she was suddenly overwhelmed by confusion. The words of the letter he had written her when she had thrown him over rushed through her brain now, and hurt her as much as they did the first day they had been received. She became a little pale, and turned as though to find some other egress from the shop. There being none, there was but one course, and that was to go out as though she had not seen him. He had not even been moved at all at seeing her; but with her it was different. She was disturbed—in her vanity? In her peace? In her pride? In her senses? In her heart? In any, or each, or all? But she was disturbed: her equilibrium was shaken. He had scorched her soul by that letter to her, so gently cold, so incisive, so subtly cruel, so deadly in its irony, so final—so final.

She was ashamed, and no one else in the world but Ian Stafford could so have shamed her. Power had been given to her, the power of great riches—the three millions had been really four—and everything and everybody, almost, was deferential towards her. Had it brought her happiness, or content, or joy? It had brought her excitement—much of that—and elation, and opportunity to do a thousand things, and to fatigue herself in a thousand ways; but had it brought happiness?

If it had, the face of this man who was once so much to her, and whom she had flung into outer darkness, was sufficient to cast a cloud over it. She felt herself grow suddenly weak, but she determined to go out of the place without appearing to see him.

He was conscious of it all, saw it out of a corner of his eye, and as she started forward, he turned, deliberately walked towards her, and, with a cheerful smile, held out his hand.

"Now, what good fortune!" he said, spiritedly. "Life plays no tricks, practices no deception this time. In a book she'd have made us meet on a grand staircase or at a court ball."

As he said this, he shook her hand warmly, and again and again, as would be fitting with old friends. He had determined to be master of the situation, and to turn the moment to the credit of his account—not hers; and it was easy to do it, for love was dead, and the memory of love atrophied.

Colour came back to her face. Confusion was dispelled, a quick and grateful animation took possession of her, to be replaced an instant after by the disconcerting reflection that there was in his face or manner not the faintest sign of emotion or embarrassment. From his attitude they might have been good friends who had not met for some time; nothing more.

"Yes, what a place to meet!" she said. "It really ought to have been at a green-grocer's, and the apotheosis of the commonplace would have been celebrated. But when did you return? How long do you remain in England?"

Ah, the sense of relief to feel that he was not reproaching her for anything, not impeaching her by an injured tone and manner, which so many other men had assumed with infinitely less right or cause than he!

"I came back thirty-six hours ago, and I stay at the will of the master-mind," he answered.

The old whimsical look came into her face, the old sudden flash which always lighted her eyes when a daring phrase was born in her mind, and she instantly retorted:

"The master-mind—how self-centred you are!"

Whatever had happened, certainly the old touch of intellectual diablerie was still hers, and he laughed good-humoredly. Yes, she might be this or that, she might be false or true, she might be one who had sold herself for mammon, and had not paid tribute to the one great natural principle of being, to give life to the world, man and woman perpetuating man and woman; but she was stimulating and delightful without effort.

"And what are you doing these days?" he asked. "One never hears of you now."

This was cruel, but she knew that he was "inciting her to riot," and she replied: "That's because you are so secluded—in your kindergarten for misfit statesmen. Abandon knowledge, all ye who enter there!"

It was the old flint and steel, but the sparks were not bright enough to light the tinder of emotion. She knew it, for he was cool and buoyant and really unconcerned, and she was feverish—and determined.

"You still make life worth living," he answered, gaily.

"It is not an occupation I would choose," she replied. "It is sure to make one a host of enemies."

"So many of us make our careers by accident," he rejoined.

"Certainly I made mine not by design," she replied instantly; and there was an undercurrent of meaning in it which he was not slow to notice; but he disregarded her first attempt to justify, however vaguely, her murderous treatment of him.

"But your career is not yet begun," he remarked.

Her eyes flashed—was it anger, or pique, or hurt, or merely the fire of intellectual combat?

"I am married," she said, defiantly, in direct retort.

"That is not a career—it is casual exploration in a dark continent," he rejoined.

"Come and say that to my husband," she replied, boldly. Suddenly a thought lighted her eyes. "Are you by any chance free to-morrow night to dine with us—quite, quite en famille' Rudyard will be glad to see you—and hear you," she added, teasingly.

He was amused. He felt how much he had really piqued her and provoked her by showing her so plainly that she had lost every vestige of the ancient power over him; and he saw no reason why he should not spend an evening where she sparkled.

"I am free, and will come with pleasure," he replied.

"That is delightful," she rejoined, "and please bring a box of bons mots with you. But you will come, then—?" She was going to add, "Ian," but she paused.

"Yes, I'll come—Jasmine," he answered, coolly, having read her hesitation aright.

She flushed, was embarrassed and piqued, but with a smile and a nod she left him.

In her carriage, however, her breath came quick and fast, her tiny hand clenched, her face flushed, and there was a devastating fire in her eyes.

"He shall not treat me so. He shall show some feeling. He shall—he shall—he shall!" she gasped, angrily.

IX

The Appian Way

C ape to Cairo be damned!"

The words were almost spat out. The man to whom they were addressed slowly drew himself up from a half-recumbent position in his desk-chair, from which he had been dreamily talking into the ceiling, as it were, while his visitor leaned against a row of bookshelves and beat the floor impatiently with his foot.

At the rude exclamation, Byng straightened himself, and looked fixedly at his visitor. He had been dreaming out loud again the dream which Rhodes had chanted in the ears of all those who shared with him the pioneer enterprises of South Africa. The outburst which had broken in on his monologue was so unexpected that for a moment he could scarcely realize the situation. It was not often, in these strenuous and perilous days—and for himself less often than ever before, so had London and London life worked upon him—that he, or those who shared with him the vast financial responsibilities of the Rand, indulged in dreams or prophecies; and he resented the contemptuous phrase just uttered, and the tone of the speaker even more.

Byng's blank amazement served only to incense his visitor further. "Yes, be damned to it, Byng!" he continued. "I'm sick of the British Empire and the All Red, and the 'immense future.' What I want is the present. It's about big enough for you and me and the rest of us. I want to hold our own in Johannesburg. I want to pull thirty-five millions a year out of the eighty miles of reef, and get enough native labour to do it. I want to run the Rand like a business concern, with Kruger gone to Holland; and Leyds gone to blazes. That's what I want to see, Mr. Invincible Rudyard Byng."

The reply to this tirade was deliberate and murderously bitter. "That's what you want to see, is it, Mr. Blasphemous Barry Whalen? Well, you can want it with a little less blither and a little more manners."

A hard and ugly look was now come into the big clean-shaven face which had become sleeker with good living, and yet had indefinably coarsened in the three years gone since the Jameson raid; and a gloomy anger looked out of the deep-blue eyes as he slowly went on:

"It doesn't matter what you want—not a great deal, if the others agree generally on what ought to be done; and I don't know that it matters much in any case. What have you come to see me about?"

"I know I'm not welcome here, Byng. It isn't the same as it used to be. It isn't—"

Byng jerked quickly to his feet and lunged forward as though he would do his visitor violence; but he got hold of himself in time, and, with a sudden and whimsical toss of the head, characteristic of him, he burst into a laugh.

"Well, I've been stung by a good many kinds of flies in my time, and I oughtn't to mind, I suppose," he growled. . . "Oh, well, there," he broke off; "you say you're not welcome here? If you really feel that, you'd better try to see me at my chambers—or at the office in London Wall. It can't be pleasant inhaling air that chills or stifles you. You take my advice, Barry, and save yourself annoyance. But let me say in passing that you are as welcome here as anywhere, neither more nor less. You are as welcome as you were in the days when we trekked from the Veal to Pietersburg and on into Bechuanaland, and both slept in the cape-wagon under one blanket. I don't think any more of you than I did then, and I don't think any less, and I don't want to see you any more or any fewer. But, Barry"—his voice changed, grew warmer, kinder—"circumstances are circumstances. The daily lives of all of us are shaped differently—yours as well as mine—here in this pudding-faced civilization and in the iron conventions of London town; and we must adapt ourselves accordingly. We used to flop down on our Louis Quinze furniture on the Vaal with our muddy boots on—in our front drawing-room. We don't do it in Thamesfontein, my noble buccaneer—not even in Barry Whalen's mansion in Ladbroke Square, where Barry Whalen, Esq., puts his silk hat on the hall table, and—and, 'If you please, sir, your bath is ready'! . . . Don't be an idiot-child, Barry, and don't spoil my best sentences when I let myself go. I don't do it often these days—not since Jameson spilt the milk and the can went trundling down the area. It's little time we get for dreaming, these sodden days, but it's only dreams that do the world's work and our own work in the end. It's dreams that do it, Barry; it's dreams that drive us on, that make us see beyond the present and the stupefying, deadening grind of the day. So it'll be Cape to Cairo in good time, dear lad, and no damnation, if you please. . . Why, what's got into you? And again, what have you come to see me about, anyhow? You knew we were to meet at dinner at Wallstein's to-night. Is there anything that's skulking at our heels to hurt us?"

The scowl on Barry Whalen's dissipated face cleared a little. He came over, rested both hands on the table and leaned forward as he spoke, Byng resuming his seat meanwhile.

Barry's voice was a little thick with excitement, but he weighed his words too. "Byng, I wanted you to know beforehand what Fleming intends to bring up to-night—a nice kind of reunion, isn't it, with war ahead as sure as guns, and the danger of everything going to smash, in spite of Milner and Jo?"

A set look came into Byng's face. He caught the lapels of his big, loose, double-breasted jacket, and spread his feet a little, till he looked as though squaring himself to resist attack.

"Go on with your story," he interposed. "What is Fleming going to say—or bring up, you call it?"

"He's going to say that some one is betraying us—all we do that's of any importance and most we say that counts—to Kruger and Leyds. He's going to say that the traitor is some one inside our circle."

Byng started, and his hands clutched at the chairback, then he became quiet and watchful. "And whom does Fleming—or you—suspect?" he asked, with lowering eyelids and a slumbering malice in his eyes.

Barry straightened himself and looked Byng rather hesitatingly in the face; then he said, slowly:

"I don't know much about Fleming's suspicions. Mine, though, are at least three years old, and you know them.

"Krool?"

"Krool—for sure."

"What would be Krool's object in betraying us, even if he knew all we say and do?"

"Blood is thicker than water, Byng, and double pay to a poor man is a consideration."

"Krool would do nothing that injured me, Barry. I know men. What sort of thing has been given away to Brother Boer?"

Barry took from his pocket a paper and passed it over. Byng scanned it very carefully and slowly, and his face darkened as he read; for there were certain things set down of which only he and Wallstein and one or two others knew; which only he and one high in authority in England knew, besides Wallstein. His face slowly reddened with anger.

London life, and its excitements multiplied by his wife and not avoided by himself, had worn on him, had affected his once sunny and even temper, had given him greater bulk, with a touch of flabbiness under the chin and at the neck, and had slackened the firmness of the muscles. Presently he got up, went over to a table, and helped himself to brandy and soda, motioning to Barry to do the same. There were two or three minutes' silence, and then he said:

"There's something wrong, certainly, but it isn't Krool. No, it isn't Krool."

"Nevertheless, if you're wise you'll ship him back beyond the Vaal, my friend."

"It isn't Krool. I'll stake my life on that. He's as true to me as I am to myself; and, anyhow, there are things in this Krool couldn't know." He tossed the paper into the fire and watched it burn.

He had talked over many, if not all, of these things with Jasmine, and with no one else; but Jasmine would not gossip. He had never known her to do so. Indeed, she had counselled extreme caution so often to himself that she would, in any case, be innocent of having babbled. But certainly there had been leakage—there had been leakage regarding most critical affairs. They were momentous enough to cause him to say reflectively now, as he watched the paper burn:

"You might as well carry dynamite in your pocket as that."

"You don't mind my coming to see you?" Barry asked, in an anxious tone.

He could not afford to antagonize Byng; in any case, his heart was against doing so; though, like an Irishman, he had risked everything by his maladroit and ill-mannered attack a little while ago.

"I wanted to warn you, so's you could be ready when Fleming jumped in," Barry continued.

"No; I'm much obliged, Barry," was Byng's reply, in a voice where trouble was well marked, however. "Wait a minute," he continued, as his visitor prepared to leave. "Go into the other room"—he pointed. "Glue your ear to the door first, then to the wall, and tell me if you can hear anything—any word I say."

Barry did as he was bidden. Presently Byng spoke in a tone rather louder than in ordinary conversation to an imaginary interlocutor for some minutes. Then Barry Whalen came back into the room.

"Well?" Byng asked. "Heard anything?"

"Not a word—scarcely a murmur."

"Quite so. The walls are thick, and those big mahogany doors fit like a glove. Nothing could leak through. Let's try the other door, leading into the hall." They went over to it. "You see, here's an inside baize-door as well. There's not room for a person to stand between the two. I'll go out now, and you stay. Talk fairly loud."

The test produced the same result.

"Maybe I talk in my sleep," remarked Byng, with a troubled, ironical laugh.

Suddenly there shot into Barry Whalen's mind a thought which startled him, which brought the colour to his face with a rush. For years he had suspected Krool, had considered him a danger. For years he had regarded Byng as culpable, for keeping as his servant one whom the Partners all believed to be a spy; but now another, a terrible thought came to him, too terrible to put into words—even in his own mind.

There were two other people besides Krool who were very close to Byng. There was Mrs. Byng for one; there was also Adrian Fellowes, who had been for a long time a kind of handy-man of the great house, doing the hundred things which only a private secretary, who was also a kind of master-of-ceremonies and lord-in-waiting, as it were, could do. Yes, there was Adrian Fellowes, the private secretary; and there was Mrs. Byng, who knew so much of what her husband knew! And the private secretary and the wife necessarily saw much of each other. What came to Barry's mind now stunned him, and he mumbled out some words of good-bye with an almost hang-dog look to his face; for he had a chivalrous heart and mind, and he was not prone to be malicious.

"We'll meet at eight, then?" said Byng, taking out his watch. "It's a quarter past seven now. Don't fuss, Barry. We'll nose out the spy, whoever he is, or wherever to be found. But we won't find him here, I think—not here, my friend."

Suddenly Barry Whalen turned at the door. "Oh, let's go back to the veld and the Rand!" he burst out, passionately. "This is no place for us, Byng—not for either of us. You are getting flabby, and I'm spoiling my temper and my manners. Let's get out of this infernal jack-pot. Let's go where we'll be in the thick of the broiling when it comes. You've got a political head, and you've done more than any one else could do to put things right and keep them right; but it's no good. Nothing'll be got except where the red runs. And the red will run, in spite of all Jo or Milner or you can do. And when it comes, you and I will be sick if we're not there—yes, even you with your millions, Byng."

With moist eyes Byng grasped the hand of the rough-hewn comrade of the veld, and shook it warmly.

"England has got on your nerves, Barry," he said, gently. "But we're all right in London. The key-board of the big instrument is here."

"But the organ is out there, Byng, and it's the organ that makes the music, not the keys. We're all going to pieces here, every one of us. I see it. Herr Gott, I see it plain enough! We're in the wrong shop. We're not buying or selling; we're being sold. Baas—big Baas, let's go where there's room to sling a stone; where we can see what's going on round us; where there's the long sight and the strong sight; where you can sell or get sold in the open, not in the alleyways; where you can have a run for your money."

Byng smiled benevolently. Yet something was stirring his senses strangely. The smell of the karoo was in his nostrils. "You're not ending up as you began, Barry," he replied. "You started off like an Israelite on the make, and you're winding up like Moody and Sankey."

"Well, I'm right now in the wind-up. I'm no better, I'm no worse, than the rest of our fellows, but I'm Irish—I can see. The Celt can always see, even if he can't act. And I see dark days coming for this old land. England is wallowing. It's all guzzle and feed and finery, and nobody cares a copper about anything that matters—"

"About Cape to Cairo, eh?"

"Byng, that was one of my idiocies. But you think over what I say, just the same. I'm right. We're rotten cotton stuff now in these isles. We've got fatty degeneration of the heart, and in all the rest of the organs too."

Again Byng shook him by the hand warmly. "Well, Wallstein will give us a fat dinner to-night, and you can moralize with lime-light effects after the foie gras, Barry."

Closing the door slowly behind his friend, whom he had passed into the hands of the dark-browed Krool, Byng turned again to his desk. As he did so he caught sight of his face in the mirror over the mantel-piece. A shadow swept over it; his lips tightened.

"Barry was right," he murmured, scrutinizing himself. "I've degenerated. We've all degenerated. What's the matter, anyhow? What is the matter? I've got everything—everything—everything."

Hearing the door open behind him, he turned to see Jasmine in evening dress smiling at him. She held up a pink finger in reproof.

"Naughty boy," she said. "What's this I hear—that you have thrown me over—me—to go and dine with the Wallstein! It's nonsense! You can't go. Ian Stafford is coming to dine, as I told you."

His eyes beamed protectingly, affectionately, and yet, somehow, a little anxiously, on her "But I must go, Jasmine. It's the first time we've all been together since the Raid, and it's good we should be in the full circle once again. There's work to do—more than ever there was. There's a storm coming up on the veld, a real jagged lightning business, and men will get hurt, hosts beyond recovery. We must commune together, all of us. If there's the communion of saints, there's also the communion of sinners. Fleming is back, and Wolff is back, and Melville and Reuter and Hungerford are back, but only for a few days, and we all must meet and map things out. I forgot about the dinner. As soon as I remembered it I left a note on your dressing-table."

With sudden emotion he drew her to him, and buried his face in her soft golden hair. "My darling, my little jasmine-flower," he whispered, softly, "I hate leaving you, but—"

"But it's impossible, Ruddy, my man. How can I send Ian Stafford away? It's too late to put him off."

"There's no need to put him off or to send him away—such old friends as you are. Why shouldn't he dine with you a deux? I'm the only person that's got anything to say about that."

She expressed no surprise, she really felt none. He had forgotten that, coming up from Scotland, he had told her of this dinner with his friends, and at the moment she asked Ian Stafford to dine she had forgotten it also; but she remembered it immediately afterwards, and she had said nothing, done nothing.

As Byng spoke, however, a curious expression emerged from the far depths of her eyes—emerged, and was instantly gone again to the obscurity whence it came. She had foreseen that he would insist on Stafford dining with her; but, while showing no surprise—and no perplexity—there was a touch of demureness in her expression as she answered:

"I don't want to seem too conventional, but—"

"There should be a little latitude in all social rules," he rejoined. "What nonsense! You are prudish, Jasmine. Allow yourself some latitude."

"Latitude, not license," she returned. Having deftly laid on him the responsibility for this evening's episode, this excursion into the dangerous fields of past memory and sentiment and perjured faith, she closed the book of her own debit and credit with a smile of satisfaction.

"Let me look at you," he said, standing her off from him.

Holding her hand, he turned her round like a child to be inspected. "Well, you're a dream," he added, as she released herself and swept into a curtsey, coquetting with her eyes as she did so. "You're wonderful in blue—a flower in the azure," he added. "I seem to remember that gown before—years ago—"

She uttered an exclamation of horror. "Good gracious, you wild and ruthless ruffian! A gown—this gown—years ago! My bonny boy, do you think I wear my gowns for years?"

"I wear my suits for years. Some I've had seven years. I've got a frock-coat I bought for my brother Jim's wedding, ten years ago, and it looks all right—a little small now, but otherwise 'most as good as new."

"What a lamb, what a babe, you are, Ruddy! Like none that ever lived. Why, no woman wears her gowns two seasons, and some of them rather hate wearing them two times."

"Then what do they do with them—after the two times?"

"Well, for a while, perhaps, they keep them to look at and gloat over, if they like them; then, perhaps, they give them away to their poor cousins or their particular friends—"

"Their particular friends—?"

"Why, every woman has some friends poorer than herself who love her very much, and she is good to them. Or there's the Mart—"

"Wait. What's 'the Mart'?"

"The place where ladies can get rid of fine clothes at a wicked discount."

"And what becomes of them then?"

"They are bought by ladies less fortunate."

"Ladies who wear them?"

"Why, what else would they do? Wear them—of course, dear child."

Byng made a gesture of disgust. "Well, I call it sickening. To me there's something so personal and intimate about clothes. I think I could kill any woman that I saw wearing clothes of yours—of yours."

She laughed mockingly. "My beloved, you've seen them often enough, but you haven't known they were mine; that's all."

"I didn't recognize them, because no one could wear your clothes like you. It would be a caricature. That's a fact, Jasmine."

She reached up and swept his cheek with a kiss. "What a darling you are, little big man! Yet you never make very definite remarks about my clothes."

He put his hands on his hips and looked her up and down approvingly. "Because I only see a general effect, but I always remember colour. Tell me, have you ever sold your clothes to the Mart, or whatever the miserable coffin-shop is called?"

"Well, not directly."

"What do you mean by 'not directly'?"

"Well, I didn't sell them, but they were sold for me." She hesitated, then went on hurriedly. "Adrian Fellowes knew of a very sad case—a girl in the opera who had had misfortune, illness, and bad luck; and he suggested it. He said he didn't like to ask for a cheque, because we were always giving, but selling my old wardrobe would be a sort of lucky find—that's what he called it."

Byng nodded, with a half-frown, however. "That was ingenious of Fellowes, and thoughtful, too. Now, what does a gown cost, one like that you have on?"

"This—let me see. Why, fifty pounds, perhaps. It's not a ball gown, of course."

He laughed mockingly. "Why, 'of course,' And what does a ball gown cost—perhaps?" There was a cynical kind of humour in his eye.

"Anything from fifty to a hundred and fifty—maybe," she replied, with a little burst of merriment.

"And how much did you get for the garments you had worn twice, and then seen them suddenly grow aged in their extreme youth?"

"Ruddy, do not be nasty—or scornful. I've always worn my gowns more than twice—some of them a great many times, except when I detested them. And anyhow, the premature death of a gown is very, very good for trade. That influences many ladies, of course."

He burst out laughing, but there was a satirical note in the gaiety, or something still harsher.

"'We deceive ourselves and the truth is not in us,'" he answered. "It's all such a hollow make-believe."

"What is?"

She gazed at him inquiringly, for this mood was new to her. She was vaguely conscious of some sort of change in him—not exactly toward her, but a change, nevertheless.

"The life we rich people lead is a hollow make-believe, Jasmine," he said, with sudden earnestness. "I don't know what's the matter, but we're not getting out of life all we ought to get; and we're not putting into it all we ought to put in. There's a sense of emptiness—of famine somewhere."

He caught the reflection of his face in the glass again, and his brow contracted. "We get sordid and sodden, and we lose the proportions of life. I wanted Dick Wilberforce to do something with me the other day, and he declined. 'Why, my dear fellow,' I said, 'you know you want to do it?' 'Of course I do,' he answered, 'but I can't afford that kind of thing, and you know it.' Well, I did know it, but I had forgotten. I was only thinking of what I myself could afford to do. I was setting up my own financial standard, and was forgetting the other fellows who hadn't my standard. What's the result? We drift apart, Wilberforce and I—well, I mean Wilberforce as a type. We drift into sets of people who can afford to do certain things, and we leave such a lot of people behind that we ought to have clung to, and that we would have clung to, if we hadn't been so much thinking of ourselves, or been so soddenly selfish."

A rippling laugh rang through the room. "Boanerges—oh, Boanerges Byng! 'Owever can you be so heloquent!"

Jasmine put both hands on his shoulders and looked up at him with that look which had fascinated him—and so many others—in their day. The perfume which had intoxicated him in the first days of his love of her, and steeped his senses in the sap of youth and Eden, smote them again, here on the verge of the desert before him. He suddenly caught her in his arms and pressed her to him almost roughly.

"You exquisite siren—you siren of all time," he said, with a note of joy in which there was, too, a stark cry of the soul. He held her face back from him. . . "If you had lived a thousand years ago you would have had a thousand lovers, Jasmine. Perhaps you did—who knows! And now you come down through the centuries purified by Time, to be my jasmine-flower."

His lip trembled a little. There was a strange melancholy in his eyes, belying the passion and rapture of his words.

In all their days together she had never seen him in this mood. She had heard him storm about things at times, had watched his big impulses working; had drawn the thunder from his clouds; but there was something moving in him now which she had never seen before. Perhaps it was only a passing phase, even a moment's mood, but it made a strange impression on her. It was remembered by them both long after, when life had scattered its vicissitudes before their stumbling feet and they had passed through flood and fire.

She drew back and looked at him steadily, reflectively, and with an element of surprise in her searching look. She had never thought him gifted with perception or insight, though he had eloquence and an eye for broad effects. She had thought him curiously ignorant of human nature, born to be deceived, full of child-like illusions, never understanding the real facts of life, save in the way of business—and politics. Women he never seemed by a single phrase or word to understand, and yet now he startled her with a sudden revelation and insight of which she had not thought him capable.

"If you had lived a thousand years ago you would have had a thousand lovers. Perhaps you did—who knows! . . . And now you come down through the centuries purified by Time—"

The words slowly repeated themselves in her brain. Many and many a time she had imagined herself as having lived centuries ago, and again and again in her sleep these imaginings had reflected themselves in wild dreams of her far past—once as a priestess of Isis, once as a Slavonian queen, once as a peasant in Syria, and many times as a courtezan of Alexandria or Athens—many times as that: one of the gifted, beautiful, wonderful women whose houses were the centres of culture, influence, and power. She had imagined herself, against her will, as one of these women, such as Cleopatra, for whom the world were well lost; and who, at last, having squeezed the orange dry, but while yet the sun was coming towards noon, in scorn of Life and Time had left the precincts of the cheerful day without a lingering look. . . Often and often such dreams, to her anger and confusion, had haunted her, even before she was married; and she had been alternately humiliated and fascinated by them. Years ago she had told Ian Stafford of one of the dreams of a past life—that she was a slave in Athens who saved her people by singing to the Tyrant; and Ian had made her sing to him, in a voice quite in keeping with her personality, delicate and fine and wonderfully high in its range, bird-like in its quality, with trills like a lark—a little meretricious but captivating. He had also written for her two verses which were as sharp and clear in her mind as the letter he wrote when she had thrown him over so dishonourably:

> *"Your voice I knew, its cadences and trill;*
> *It stilled the tumult and the overthrow*
> *When Athens trembled to the people's will;*
> *I knew it—'twas a thousand years ago.*

> *"I see the fountains, and the gardens where*
> *You sang the fury from the Satrap's brow;*
> *I feel the quiver of the raptured air*
> *I heard you in the Athenian grove—I hear you now."*

As the words flashed into her mind now she looked at her husband steadfastly. Were there, then, some unexplored regions in his nature, where things dwelt, of which she had no glimmering of knowledge? Did he understand more of women than she thought? Could she then really talk to him of a thousand things of the mind which she had ever ruled out of any commerce between them, one half of her being never opened up to his sight? Not that he was deficient in intellect, but, to her thought, his was a purely objective mind; or was it objective because it had not been trained or developed subjectively? Had she ever really tried to find a region in his big nature where the fine allusiveness and subjectivity of the human mind could have free life and untrammelled exercise, could gambol in green fields of imagination and adventure upon strange seas of discovery? A shiver of pain, of remorse, went through her frame now, as he held her at arm's length and looked at her. . . Had she started right? Had she ever given their natures a chance to discover each other? Warmth and passion and youth and excitement and variety—oh, infinite variety there had been!—but had the start been a fair one, had she, with a whole mind and a full soul of desire, gone to him first and last? What had been the governing influence in their marriage where she was concerned?

Three years of constant motion, and never an hour's peace; three years of agitated waters, and never in all that time three days alone together. What was there to show for the three years? That for which he had longed with a great longing had been denied him; for he had come of a large family, and had the simple primitive mind and heart. Even in his faults he had ever been primitively simple and obvious. She had been energetic, helping great charities, aiding in philanthropic enterprises, with more than a little shrewdness preventing him from being robbed right and left by adventurers of all descriptions; and yet—and yet it was all so general, so soulless, her activity in good causes. Was there a single afflicted person, one forlorn soul whom she had directly and personally helped, or sheltered from the storm for a moment, one bereaved being whose eyes she had dried by her own direct personal sympathy?

Was it this which had been more or less vaguely working in his mind a little while before when she had noticed a change in him; or was it that he was disappointed that they were two and no more—always two, and no more? Was it that which was working in his mind, and making him say hard things about their own two commendable selves?

"If you had lived a thousand years ago you would have had a thousand lovers. . . And now you come down through the centuries purified by Time, to be my jasmine-flower"—

She did not break the silence for some time, but at last she said: "And what were you a thousand years ago, my man?"

He drew a hot hand across a troubled brow. "I? I was the Satrap whose fury you soothed away, or I was the Antony you lured from fighting Caesar."

It was as though he had read those lines written by Ian Stafford long ago.

Again that perfume of hers caught his senses, and his look softened wonderfully. A certain unconscious but underlying discontent appeared to vanish from his eyes, and he said, abruptly: "I have it—I have it. This dress is like the one you wore the first night that we met. It's the same kind of stuff, it's just the same colour and the same style. Why, I see it all as plain as can be—there at the opera. And you wore blue the day I tried to propose to you and couldn't, and asked you down to Wales instead. Lord, how I funked it!" He laughed, happily almost. "Yes, you wore blue the first time we met—like this."

"It was the same skirt, and a different bodice, of course both those first times," she answered. Then she stepped back and daintily smoothed out the gown she was wearing, smiling at him as she did that day three years ago. She had put on this particular gown, remembering that Ian Stafford had said charming things about that other blue gown just before he bade her good-bye three years ago. That was why she wore blue this night—to recall to Ian what it appeared he had forgotten. And presently she would dine alone with Ian in her husband's house—and with her husband's blessing. Pique and pride were in her heart, and she meant Ian Stafford to remember. No man was adamantine; at least she had never met one—not one, neither bishop nor octogenarian.

"Come, Ruddy, you must dress, or you'll be late," she continued, lightly, touching his cheek with her fingers; "and you'll come down and apologize, and put me right with Ian Stafford, won't you?"

"Certainly. I won't be five minutes. I'll—"

There was a tap at the door and a footman, entering, announced that Mr. Stafford was in the drawing-room.

"Show him into my sitting-room," she said. "The drawing-room, indeed," she added to her husband—"it is so big, and I am so small. I feel sometimes as though I wanted to live in a tiny, tiny house."

Her words brought a strange light to his eyes. Suddenly he caught her arm.

"Jasmine," he said, hurriedly, "let us have a good talk over things—over everything. I want to see if we can't get more out of life than we do. There's something wrong. What is it? I don't know; but perhaps we could find out if we put our heads together—eh?" There was a strange, troubled longing in his look.

She nodded and smiled. "Certainly—to-night when you get back," she said. "We'll open the machine and find what's wrong with it." She laughed, and so did he.

As she went down the staircase she mused to herself and there was a shadow in her eyes and over her face.

"Poor Ruddy! Poor Ruddy!" she said.

Once again before she entered the sitting-room, as she turned and looked back, she said:

"Poor boy. . . Yet he knew about a thousand years ago!" she added with a nervous little laugh, and with an air of sprightly eagerness she entered to Ian Stafford.

X

An Arrow Finds a Breast

As he entered the new sphere of Jasmine's influence, charm, and existence, Ian Stafford's mind became flooded by new impressions. He was not easily moved by vastness or splendour. His ducal grandfather's houses were palaces, the estates were a fair slice of two counties, and many of his relatives had sumptuous homes stored with priceless legacies of art. He had approached the great house which Byng had built for himself with some trepidation; for though Byng came of people whose names counted for a good deal in the north of England, still, in newly acquired fortunes made suddenly in new lands there was something that coarsened taste—an unmodulated, if not a garish, elegance which "hit you in the eye," as he had put it to himself. He asked himself why Byng had not been content to buy one of the great mansions which could always be had in London for a price, where time had softened all the outlines, had given that subdued harmony in architecture which only belongs to age. Byng could not buy with any money those wonderful Adam's mantels, over-mantels and ceilings which had a glory quite their own. There must, therefore, be an air of newness in the new mansion, which was too much in keeping with the new money, the gold as yet not worn smooth by handling, the staring, brand-new sovereigns looking like impostors.

As he came upon the great house, however, in the soft light of evening, he was conscious of no violence done to his artistic sense. It was a big building, severely simple in design, yet with the rich grace, spacious solidity, and decorative relief of an Italian palace: compact, generous, traditionally genuine and wonderfully proportionate.

"Egad, Byng, you had a good architect—and good sense!" he said to himself. "It's the real thing; and he did it before Jasmine came on the scene too."

The outside of the house was Byng's, but the inside would, in the essentials, of course, be hers; and he would see what he would see.

When the door opened, it came to him instantly that the inside and outside were in harmony. How complete was that harmony remained to be seen, but an apparently unstudied and delightful reticence was noticeable at once. The newness had been rubbed off the gold somehow, and the old furniture—Italian, Spanish—which relieved the spaciousness of the entrance gave an air of Time and Time's eloquence to this three-year-old product of modern architectural skill.

As he passed on, he had more than a glimpse of the ball-room, which maintained the dignity and the refined beauty of the staircase and the hallways; and only in the insistent audacity and intemperate colouring of some Rubens pictures did he find anything of that inherent tendency to exaggeration and Oriental magnificence behind the really delicate artistic faculties possessed by Jasmine.

The drawing-room was charming. It was not quite perfect, however. It was too manifestly and studiously arranged, and it had the finnicking exactness of the favourite gallery of some connoisseur. For its nobility of form, its deft and wise softness of colouring, its half-smothered Italian joyousness of design in ceiling and cornice, the arrangement of choice and exquisite furniture was too careful, too much like the stage. He smiled at the sight of it, for he saw and knew that Jasmine had had his playful criticism of her occasionally flamboyant taste in mind, and that she had over-revised, as it were. She had, like a literary artist, polished and refined and stippled the effect, till something of personal touch had gone, and there remained classic elegance without the sting of life and the idiosyncrasy of its creator's imperfections. No, the drawing-room would not quite do, though it was near the perfect thing. His judgment was not yet complete, however. When he was shown into Jasmine's sitting-room his breath came a little quicker, for here would be the real test; and curiosity was stirring greatly in him.

Yes, here was the woman herself, wilful, original, delightful, with a flower-like delicacy joined to a determined and gorgeous audacity. Luxury was heaped on luxury, in soft lights from Indian lamps and lanterns, in the great divan, the deep lounge, the piled-up cushions, the piano littered with incongruous if artistic bijouterie; but everywhere, everywhere, books in those appealing bindings and with that paper so dear to every lover of literature. Instinctively he picked them up one by one, and most of them were affectionately marked by marginal notes of criticism, approval, or reference; and all showing the eager, ardent mind of one who loved books. He noticed, however, that most of the books he had seen before, and some of them he had read with her in the days which were gone forever. Indeed, in one of them he found some of his own pencilled marginal notes, beneath which she had written her insistent opinions, sometimes with amazing point. There were few new books, and they were mostly novels; and it was borne in on him that not many of these annotated books belonged to the past three years. The millions had come, the power and the place; but something had gone with their coming.

He was turning over the pages of a volume of Browning when she entered; and she had an instant to note the grace and manly dignity of his figure, the poise of the intellectual head—the type of a perfect, well-bred animal, with the accomplishment of a man of purpose and executive design. A little frown of trouble came to her forehead, but she drove it away with a merry laugh, as he turned at the rustle of her skirts and came forward.

He noted her blue dress, he guessed the reason she had put it on; and he made an inward comment of scorn. It was the same blue, and it was near the same style of the dress she wore the last time he saw her. She watched to see whether it made any impression on him, and was piqued to observe that he who had in that far past always swept her with an admiring, discriminating, and deferential glance, now only gave her deference of a courteous but perfunctory kind. It made the note to all she said and did that evening—the daring, the brilliance, the light allusion to past scenes and happenings, the skilful comment on the present, the joyous dominance of a position made supreme by beauty and by gold; behind which were anger and bitterness, and wild and desperate revolt.

For, if love was dead in him, and respect, and all that makes man's association with woman worth while, humiliation and the sting of punishment and penalty were alive in her, flaying her spirit, rousing that mad streak which was in her grandfather, who had had many a combat, the outcome of wild elements of passion in him. She was not happy; she had never been happy since she married Rudyard Byng; yet she had said to herself so often that she might have been at peace, in a sense, had it not been for the letter which Ian Stafford had written her, when she turned from him to the man she married.

The passionate resolve to compel him to reproach himself in soul for his merciless, if subtle, indictment of her to bring him to the old place where he had knelt in spirit so long ago—ah, it was so long!—came to her. Self-indulgent and pitifully mean as she had been, still this man had influenced her more than any other in the world—in that region where the best of herself lay, the place to which her eyes had turned always when she wanted a consoling hour. He belonged to her realm of the imagination, of thought, of insight, of intellectual passions and the desires of the soul. Far above any physical attraction Ian had ever possessed for her was the deep conviction that he gave her mind what no one else gave it, that he was the being who knew the song her spirit sang. . . He should not go forever from her and with so cynical a completeness. He should return; he should not triumph in his self-righteousness, be a living reproach to her always by his careless indifference to everything that had ever been between them. If he treated her so because of what she had done to him, with what savagery might not she be treated, if all that had happened in the last three years were open as a book before him!

Her husband—she had not thought of that. So much had happened in the past three years; there had been so much adulation and worship and daring assault upon her heart—or emotions—from quarters of unusual distinction, that the finest sense of her was blunted, and true proportions were lost. Rudyard ought never to have made that five months' visit to South Africa a year before, leaving her alone to make the fight against the forces round her. Those five months had brought a change in her, had made her indignant at times against Rudyard.

"Why did he go to South Africa? Why did he not take me with him? Why did he leave me here alone?" she had asked herself. She did not realize that there would have been no fighting at all, that all the forces contending against her purity and devotion would never have gathered at her feet and washed against the shores of her resolution, if she had loved Rudyard Byng when she married him as she might have loved him, ought to have loved him.

The faithful love unconsciously announces its fidelity, and men instinctively are aware of it, and leave it unassailed. It is the imperfect love which subtly invites the siege, which makes the call upon human interest, selfishness, or sympathy, so often without intended unscrupulousness at first. She had escaped the suspicion, if not the censure, of the world—or so she thought; and in the main she was right. But she was now embarked on an enterprise which never would have been begun, if she had not gambled with her heart and soul three years ago; if she had not dragged away the veil from her inner self, putting her at the mercy of one who could say, "I know you—what you are."

Just before they went to the dining-room Byng came in and cheerily greeted Stafford, apologizing for having forgotten his engagement to dine with Wallstein.

"But you and Jasmine will have much to talk about," he said—"such old friends as you are; and fond of books and art and music and all that kind of thing... Glad to see you looking so well, Stafford," he continued. "They say you are the coming man. Well, au revoir. I hope Jasmine will give you a good dinner." Presently he was gone—in a heavy movement of good-nature and magnanimity.

"Changed—greatly changed, and not for the better," said Ian Stafford to himself. "This life has told on him. The bronze of the veld has vanished, and other things are disappearing."

At the table with the lights and the flowers and the exquisite appointments, with appetite flattered and tempted by a dinner of rare simplicity and perfect cooking, Jasmine was radiant, amusing, and stimulating in her old way. She had never seemed to him so much a mistress of delicate satire and allusiveness. He rose to the combat with an alacrity made more agile by considerable abstinence, for clever women were few, and real talk was the rarest occurrence in his life, save with men in his own profession chiefly.

But later, in her sitting-room, after the coffee had come, there was a change, and the transition was made with much skill and sensitiveness. Into Jasmine's voice there came another and more reflective note, and the drift of the conversation changed. Books brought the new current; and soon she had him moving almost unconsciously among old scenes, recalling old contests of ideas, and venturing on bold reproductions of past intellectual ideals. But though they were in this dangerous field of the past, he did not once betray a sign of feeling, not even when, poring over Coventry Patmore's poems, her hand touched his, and she read the lines which they had read together so long ago, with no thought of any significance to themselves:

> *"With all my will, but much against my heart,*
> *We two now part.*
> *My very Dear,*
> *Our solace is the sad road lies so clear...*
> *Go thou to East, I West.*
> *We will not say*
> *There's any hope, it is so far away..."*

He read the verses with a smile of quiet enjoyment, saying, when he had finished:

"A really moving and intimate piece of work. I wonder what their story was—a hopeless love, of course. An affaire—an 'episode'—London ladies now call such things."

"You find London has changed much since you went away—in three years only?" she asked.

"Three years—why, it's an eternity, or a minute, as you are obliged to live it. In penal servitude it is centuries, in the Appian Way of pleasure it is a sunrise moment. Actual time has nothing to do with the clock."

She looked up to the little gold-lacquered clock on the mantel-piece. "See, it is going to strike," she said. As she spoke, the little silver hammer softly struck. "That is the clock-time, but what time is it really—for you, for instance?"

"In Elysium there is no time," he murmured with a gallantry so intentionally obvious and artificial that her pulses beat with anger.

"It is wonderful, then, how you managed the dinner-hour so exactly. You did not miss it by a fraction."

"It is only when you enter Elysium that there is no time. It was eight o'clock when I arrived—by the world's time. Since then I have been dead to time—and the world."

"You do not suggest that you are in heaven?" she asked, ironically.

"Nothing so extreme as that. All extremes are violent."

"Ah, the middle place—then you are in purgatory?"

"But what should you be doing in purgatory? Or have you only come with a drop of water to cool the tongue of Dives?" His voice trailed along so coolly that it incensed her further.

"Certainly Dives' tongue is blistering," she said with great effort to still the raging tumult within her. "Yet I would not cool it if I could."

Suddenly the anger seemed to die out of her, and she looked at him as she did in the days before Rudyard Byng came across her path—eagerly, childishly, eloquently, inquiringly. He was the one man who satisfied the intellectual and temperamental side of her; and he had taught her more than any one else in the world. She realized that she had "Tossed him violently like a ball into a far country," and that she had not now a vestige of power over him—either of his senses or his mind; that he was master of the situation. But was it so that there was a man whose senses could not be touched when all else failed? She was very woman, eager for the power which she had lost, and power was hard to get—by what devious ways had she travelled to find it!

As they leaned over a book of coloured prints of Gainsborough, Romney, and Vandyke, her soft, warm breast touched his arm and shoulder, a strand of her cobweb, golden hair swept his cheek, and a sigh came from her lips, so like those of that lass who caught and held her Nelson to the end, and died at last in poverty, friendless, homeless, and alone. Did he fancy that he heard a word breathing through her sigh—his name, Ian? For one instant the wild, cynical desire came over him to turn and clasp her in his arms, to press those lips which never but once he had kissed, and that was when she had plighted her secret troth to him, and had broken it for three million pounds. Why not? She was a woman, she was beautiful, she was a siren who had lured him and used him and tossed him by. Why not? All her art was now used, the art of the born coquette which had been exquisitely cultivated since she was a child, to bring him back to her feet—to the feet of the wife of Rudyard Byng. Why not? For an instant he had the dark impulse to treat her as she deserved, and take a kiss "as long as my exile, as sweet as my revenge"; but then the bitter memory came that this was the woman to whom he had given the best of which he was capable and the promise of that other best which time and love and life truly lived might accomplish; and the wild thing died in him.

The fever fled, and his senses became as cold as the statue of Andromeda on the pedestal at his hand. He looked at her. He did not for the moment realize that she was in reality only a girl, a child in so much; wilful, capricious, unregulated in some ways, with the hereditary taint of a distorted moral sense, and yet able, intuitive and wise, in so many aspects of life and conversation. Looking, he determined that she should never have that absolution which any outward or inward renewal of devotion would give her. Scorn was too deep—that arrogant, cruel, adventitious attribute of the sinner who has not committed the same sin as the person he despises—

"Sweet is the refuge of scorn."

His scorn was too sweet; and for the relish of it on his tongue, the price must be paid one way or another. The sin of broken faith she had sinned had been the fruit of a great temptation, meaning more to a woman, a hundred times, than to a man. For a man there is always present the chance of winning a vast fortune and the power that it brings;

but it can seldom come to a woman except through marriage. It ill became him to be self-righteous, for his life had not been impeccable—

> *"The shaft of slander shot*
> *Missed only the right blot!"*

Something of this came to him suddenly now as she drew away from him with a sense of humiliation, and a tear came unbidden to her eye.

She wiped the tear away, hastily, as there came a slight tapping at the door, and Krool entered, his glance enveloping them both in one lightning survey—like the instinct of the dweller in wild places of the earth, who feels danger where all is most quiet, and ever scans the veld or bush with the involuntary vigilance belonging to the life. His look rested on Jasmine for a moment before he spoke, and Stafford inwardly observed that here was an enemy to the young wife whose hatred was deep. He was conscious, too, that Jasmine realized the antipathy. Indeed, she had done so from the first days she had seen Krool, and had endeavoured, without success, to induce Byng to send the man back to South Africa, and to leave him there last year when he went again to Johannesburg. It was the only thing in which Byng had proved invulnerable, and Krool had remained a menace which she vaguely felt and tried to conquer, which, in vain, Adrian Fellowes had endeavoured to remove. For in the years in which Fellowes had been Byng's secretary his relations with Krool seemed amiable and he had made light of Jasmine's prejudices.

"The butler is out and they come me," Krool said. "Mr. Stafford's servant is here. There is a girl for to see him, if he will let. The boy, Jigger, his name. Something happens."

Stafford frowned, then turned to Jasmine. He told her who Jigger was, and of the incident the day before, adding that he had no idea of the reason for the visit; but it must be important, or nothing would have induced his servant to fetch the girl.

"I will come," he said to Krool, but Jasmine's curiosity was roused.

"Won't you see her here?" she asked.

Stafford nodded assent, and presently Krool showed the girl into the room.

For an instant she stood embarrassed and confused, then she addressed herself to Stafford. "I'm Lou—Jigger's sister," she said, with white lips. "I come to ask if you'd go to him. 'E's been hurt bad—

knocked down by a fire-engine, and the doctor says 'e can't live. 'E made yer a promise, and 'e wanted me to tell yer that 'e meant to keep it; but if so be as you'd come, and wouldn't mind a-comin', 'e'd tell yer himself. 'E made that free becos 'e had brekfis wiv ye. 'E's all right—the best as ever—the top best." Suddenly the tears flooded her eyes and streamed down her pale cheeks. "Oh, 'e was the best—my Gawd, 'e was the best! If it 'd make 'im die happy, you'd come, y'r gryce, wouldn't y'r?"

Child of the slums as she was, she was exceedingly comely and was simply and respectably dressed. Her eyes were big and brown like Stafford's; her face was a delicate oval, and her hair was a deep black, waving freely over a strong, broad forehead. It was her speech that betrayed her; otherwise she was little like the flower-girl that Adrian Fellowes had introduced to Al'mah, who had got her a place in the chorus of the opera and had also given her personal care and friendly help.

"Where is he? In the hospital?" Stafford asked.

"It was just beside our own 'ome it 'appened. We got two rooms now, Jigger and me. 'E was took in there. The doctor come, but 'e says it ain't no use. 'E didn't seem to care much, and 'e didn't give no 'ope, not even when I said I'd give him all me wages for a year."

Jasmine was beside her now, wiping her tears and holding her hand, her impulsive nature stirred, her heart throbbing with desire to help. Suddenly she remembered what Rudyard had said up-stairs three hours ago, that there wasn't a single person in the world to whom they had done an act which was truly and purely personal during the past three years: and she had a tremulous desire to help this crude, mothering, passionately pitiful girl.

"What will you do?" Jasmine said to Stafford.

"I will go at once. Tell my servant to have up a cab," he said to Krool, who stood outside the door.

"Truly, 'e will be glad," the girl exclaimed. "'E told me about the suvring, and Sunday-week for brekfis," she murmured. "You'll never miss the time, y'r gryce. Gawd knows you'll not miss it—an' 'e ain't got much left."

"I will go, too—if you will let me," said Jasmine to Stafford. "You must let me go. I want to help—so much."

"No, you must not come," he replied. "I will pick up a surgeon in Harley Street, and we'll see if it is as hopeless as she says. But you must not come to-night. To-morrow, certainly, to-morrow, if you will. Perhaps you can do some good then. I will let you know."

He held out his hand to say good-bye, as the girl passed out with Jasmine's kiss on her cheek and a comforting assurance of help.

Jasmine did not press her request. First there was the fact that Rudyard did not know, and might strongly disapprove; and secondly, somehow, she had got nearer to Stafford in the last few minutes than in all the previous hours since they had met again. Nowhere, by all her art, had she herself touched him, or opened up in his nature one tiny stream of feeling; but this girl's story and this piteous incident had softened him, had broken down the barriers which had checked and baffled her. There was something almost gentle in his smile as he said good-bye, and she thought she detected warmth in the clasp of his hand.

Left alone, she sat in the silence, pondering as she had not pondered in the past three years. These few days in town, out of the season, were sandwiched between social functions from which their lives were never free. They had ever passed from event to event like minor royalties with endless little ceremonies and hospitalities; and there had been so little time to meditate—had there even been the wish?

The house was very still, and the far-off, muffled rumble of omnibuses and cabs gave a background of dignity to this interior peace and luxurious quiet. For long she sat unmoving—nearly two hours—alone with her inmost thoughts. Then she went to the little piano in the corner where stood the statue of Andromeda, and began to play softly. Her fingers crept over the keys, playing snatches of things she knew years before, improvising soft, passionate little movements. She took no note of time. At last the clock struck twelve, and still she sat there playing. Then she began to sing a song which Alice Tynemouth had written and set to music two years before. It was simply yet passionately written, and the wail of anguished disappointment, of wasted chances was in it—

> "Once in the twilight of the Austrian hills,
>   A word came to me, beautiful and good;
> If I had spoken it, that message of the stars,
>   Love would have filled thy blood:
> Love would have sent thee pulsing to my arms,
>   Thy heart a nestling bird;
> A moment fled—it passed:
>   I seek in vain
> For that forgotten word."

In the last notes the voice rose in passionate pain, and died away into an aching silence.

She leaned her arms on the piano in front of her and laid her forehead on them.

"When will it all end—what will become of me!" she cried in pain that strangled her heart. "I am so bad—so bad. I was doomed from the beginning. I always felt it so—always, even when things were brightest. I am the child of black Destiny. For me—there is nothing, nothing, for me. The straight path was before me, and I would not walk in it."

With a gesture of despair, and a sudden faintness, she got up and went over to the tray of spirits and liqueurs which had been brought in with the coffee. Pouring out a liqueur-glass of brandy, she was about to drink it, when her ear became attracted by a noise without, a curious stumbling, shuffling sound. She put down the glass, went to the door that opened into the hall, and looked out and down. One light was still burning below, and she could see distinctly. A man was clumsily, heavily, ascending the staircase, holding on to the balustrade. He was singing to himself, breaking into the maudlin harmony with an occasional laugh—

"For this is the way we do it on the veld,
When the band begins to play;
With one bottle on the table and one below the belt,
When the band begins to play—"

It was Rudyard, and he was drunk—almost helplessly drunk.

A cry of pain rose to her lips, but her trembling hand stopped it. With a shudder she turned back to her sitting-room. Throwing herself on the divan where she had sat with Ian Stafford, she buried her face in her arms. The hours went by.

XI

In Wales, Where Jigger Plays His Part

Really, the unnecessary violence with which people take their own lives, or the lives of others, is amazing. They did it better in olden days in Italy and the East. No waste or anything—all scientifically measured."

With a confident and satisfied smile Mr. Mappin, the celebrated surgeon, looked round the little group of which he was the centre at Glencader, Rudyard Byng's castle in Wales.

Rudyard blinked at him for a moment with ironical amusement, then remarked: "When you want to die, does it matter much whether you kill yourself with a bludgeon or a pin, take gas from a tap or cyanide of potassium, jump in front of a railway train or use the revolting razor? You are dead neither less nor more, and the shock to the world is the same. It's only the housemaid or the undertaker that notices any difference. I knew a man at Vleifontein who killed himself by jumping into the machinery of a mill. It gave a lot of trouble to all concerned. That was what he wanted—to end his own life and exasperate the foreman."

"Rudyard, what a horrible tale!" exclaimed his wife, turning again to the surgeon, eagerly. "It is most interesting, and I see what you mean. It is, that if we only really knew, we could take our own lives or other people's with such ease and skill that it would be hard to detect it?"

The surgeon nodded. "Exactly, Mrs. Byng. I don't say that the expert couldn't find what the cause of death was, if suspicion was aroused; but it could be managed so that 'heart failure' or some such silly verdict would be given, because there was no sign of violence, or of injury artificially inflicted."

"It is fortunate the world doesn't know these ways to euthanasia," interposed Stafford. "I fancy that murders would be more numerous than suicides, however. Suicide enthusiasts would still pursue their melodramatic indulgences—disfiguring themselves unnecessarily."

Adrian Fellowes, the amiable, ever-present secretary and "chamberlain" of Rudyard's household, as Jasmine teasingly called him, whose handsome, unintellectual face had lighted with amusement at the conversation, now interposed. "Couldn't you give us some idea how it can be done, this smooth passage of the Styx?" he asked. "We'll promise not to use it."

The surgeon looked round the little group reflectively. His eyes passed from Adrian to Jasmine, who stood beside him, to Byng, and to Ian Stafford, and stimulated by their interest, he gave a pleased smile of gratified vanity. He was young, and had only within the past three years got to the top of the tree at a bound, by a certain successful operation in royal circles.

Drawing out of his pocket a small case, he took from it a needle and held it up. "Now that doesn't look very dangerous, does it?" he asked. "Yet a firm pressure of its point could take a life, and there would be little possibility of finding how the ghastly trick was done except by the aroused expert."

"If you will allow me," he said, taking Jasmine's hand and poising the needle above her palm. "Now, one tiny thrust of this steel point, which has been dipped in a certain acid, would kill Mrs. Byng as surely as though she had been shot through the heart. Yet it would leave scarcely the faintest sign. No blood, no wound, just a tiny pin-prick, as it were; and who would be the wiser? Imagine an average coroner's jury and the average examination of the village doctor, who would die rather than expose his ignorance, and therefore gives 'heart failure' as the cause of death."

Jasmine withdrew her hand with a shudder. "Please, I don't like being so near the point," she said.

"Woman-like," interjected Byng ironically.

"How does it happen you carry this murdering asp about with you, Mr. Mappin?" asked Stafford.

The surgeon smiled. "For an experiment to-morrow. Don't start. I have a favorite collie which must die. I am testing the poison with the minimum. If it kills the dog it will kill two men."

He was about to put the needle back into the case when Adrian Fellowes held out a hand for it. "Let me look at it," he said. Turning the needle over in his palm, he examined it carefully. "So near and yet so far," he remarked. "There are a good many people who would pay a high price for the little risk and the dead certainty. You wouldn't, perhaps, tell us what the poison is, Mr. Mappin? We are all very reliable people here, who have no enemies, and who want to keep their friends alive. We should then be a little syndicate of five, holding a great secret, and saving numberless lives every day by not giving the thing away. We should all be entitled to monuments in Parliament Square."

The surgeon restored the needle to the case. "I think one monument will be sufficient," he said. "Immortality by syndicate is too modern, and this is an ancient art." He tapped the case. "Turkey and the Mongol lands have kept the old cult going. In England, it's only for the dog!" He laughed freely but noiselessly at his own joke.

This talk had followed the news brought by Krool to the Baas, that the sub-manager of the great mine, whose chimneys could be seen from the hill behind the house, had thrown himself down the shaft and been smashed to a pulp. None of them except Byng had known him, and the dark news had brought no personal shock.

They had all gathered in the library, after paying an afternoon visit to Jigger, who had been brought down from London in a special carriage, and was housed near the servants' quarters with a nurse. On the night of Jigger's accident Ian Stafford on his way from Jasmine's house had caught Mr. Mappin, and the surgeon had operated at once, saving the lad's life. As it was necessary to move him in any case, it was almost as easy, and no more dangerous, to bring him to Glencader than to take him to a London hospital.

Under the surgeon's instructions Jasmine had arranged it all, and Jigger had travelled like royalty from Paddington into Wales, and there had captured the household, as he had captured Stafford at breakfast in St. James's Street.

Thinking that perhaps this was only a whim of Jasmine's, and merely done because it gave a new interest to a restless temperament, Stafford had at first rejected the proposal. When, however, the surgeon said that if the journey was successfully made, the after-results would be all to the good, Stafford had assented, and had allowed himself to be included in the house-party at Glencader.

It was a triumph for Jasmine, for otherwise Stafford would not have gone. Whether she would have insisted on Jigger going to Glencader if it had not meant that Ian would go also, it would be hard to say. Her motives were not unmixed, though there had been a real impulse to do all she could. In any case, she had lessened the distance between Ian and herself, and that gave her wilful mind a rather painful pleasure. Also, the responsibility for Jigger's well-being, together with her duties as hostess, had prevented her from dwelling on that scene in the silent house at midnight which had shocked her so—her husband reeling up the staircase, singing a ribald song.

The fullest significance of this incident had not yet come home to her. She had fought against dwelling on it, and she was glad that every moment since they had come to Glencader had been full; that Rudyard had been much away with the shooters, and occupied in trying to settle a struggle between the miners and the proprietors of the mine itself, of whom he was one. Still, things that Rudyard had said before he left the house to dine with Wallstein, leaving her with Stafford, persistently recurred to her mind.

"What's the matter?" had been Rudyard's troubled cry. "We've got everything—everything, and yet—!" Her eyes were not opened. She had had a shock, but it had not stirred the inner, smothered life; there had been no real revelation. She was agitated and disturbed—no more. She did not see that the man she had married to love and to cherish was slowly changing—was the change only a slow one now?—before her eyes; losing that brave freshness which had so appealed to London when he first came back to civilization. Something had been subtracted from his personality which left it poorer, something had been added which made it less appealing. Something had given way in him. There had been a subsidence of moral energy, and force had inwardly declined, though to all outward seeming he had played a powerful and notable part in the history of the last three years, gaining influence in many directions, without suffering excessive notoriety.

On the day Rudyard married Jasmine he would have cut off his hand rather than imagine that he would enter his wife's room helpless from drink and singing a song which belonged to loose nights on the Limpopo and the Vaal.

As the little group drew back, their curiosity satisfied, Mr. Mappin, putting the case carefully into his pocket again, said to Jasmine:

"The boy is going on so well that I am not needed longer. Mr. Wharton, my locum tenens, will give him every care."

"When did you think of going?" Jasmine asked him, as they all moved on towards the hall, where the other guests were assembled.

"To-morrow morning early, if I may. No night travel for me, if I can help it."

"I am glad you are not going to-night," she answered, graciously. "Al'mah is arriving this afternoon, and she sings for us this evening. Is it not thrilling?"

There was a general murmur of pleasure, vaguely joined by Adrian Fellowes, who glanced quickly round the little group, and met an enigmatical glance from Byng's eye. Byng was remembering what Barry Whalen had told him three years ago, and he wondered if Jasmine was cognizant of it all. He thought not; for otherwise she would scarcely bring Al'mah to Glencader and play Fellowes' game for him.

Jasmine, in fact, had not heard. Days before she had wondered that Adrian had tried to discourage her invitation to Al'mah. While it was an invitation, it was also an engagement, on terms which would have been adequate for Patti in her best days. It would, if repeated a few times, reimburse Al'mah for the sums she had placed in Byng's hands at the time of the Raid, and also, later still, to buy the life of her husband from Oom Paul. It had been insufficient, not because of the value of the article for sale, but because of the rapacity of the vender. She had paid half the cruel balance demanded; Byng and his friends had paid the rest without her knowledge; and her husband had been set free.

Byng had only seen Al'mah twice since the day when she first came to his rooms, and not at all during the past two years, save at the opera, where she tightened the cords of captivity to her gifts around her admirers. Al'mah had never met Mrs. Byng since the day after that first production of "Manassa," when Rudyard rescued her, though she had seen her at the opera again and again. She cared nothing for society or for social patronage or approval, and the life that Jasmine led had no charms for her. The only interest she had in it was that it suited Adrian from every standpoint. He loved the splendid social environment of which Jasmine was the centre, and his services were well rewarded.

When she received Jasmine's proposal to sing at Glencader she had hesitated to accept it, for society had no charms for her; but at length three considerations induced her to do so. She wanted to see Rudyard Byng, for South Africa and its shadow was ever present with her; and she dreaded she knew not what. Blantyre was still her husband, and he might return—and return still less a man than when he deserted her those sad long years ago. Also, she wanted to see Jigger, because of his sister Lou, whose friendless beauty, so primitively set, whose transparent honesty appealed to her quick, generous impulses. Last of all she wanted to see Adrian in the surroundings and influences where his days had been constantly spent during the past three years.

Never before had she had the curiosity to do so. Adrian had, however, deftly but clearly tried to dissuade her from coming to Glencader, and his reasons were so new and unconvincing that, for the first time,— she had a nature of strange trustfulness once her faith was given—a vague suspicion concerning Adrian perplexed and troubled her. His letter had arrived some hours after Jasmine's, and then her answer was immediate—she would accept. Adrian heard of the acceptance first through Jasmine, to whom he had spoken of his long "acquaintance" with the great singer.

From Byng's look, as they moved towards the hall, Adrian gathered that rumour had reached a quarter where he had much at stake; but it did not occur to him that this would be to his disadvantage. Byng was a man of the world. Besides, he had his own reasons for feeling no particular fear where Byng was concerned. His glance ran from Byng's face to that of Jasmine; but, though her eyes met his, there was nothing behind her glance which had to do with Al'mah.

In the great hall whose windows looked out on a lovely, sunny valley still as green as summer, the rest of the house-party were gathered, and Jigger's visitors were at once surrounded.

Among the visitors were Alice, Countess of Tynemouth, also the Slavonian ambassador, whose extremely pale face, stooping shoulders, and bald head with the hair carefully brushed over from each side in a vain attempt to cover the baldness, made him seem older than he really was. Count Landrassy had lived his life in many capitals up to the limit of his vitality, and was still covetous of notice from the sex who had, in a checkered career, given him much pleasure, and had provided him with far more anxiety. But he was almost uncannily able and astute, as every man found who entered the arena of diplomacy to treat with him or circumvent him. Suavity, with an attendant mordant wit, and a mastery of tactics unfamiliar to the minds and capacities of Englishmen, made him a great factor in the wide world of haute politique; but it also drew upon him a wealth of secret hatred and outward attention. His follies were lashed by the tongues of virtue and of slander; but his abilities gave him a commanding place in the arena of international politics.

As Byng and his party approached, the eyes of the ambassador and of Lady Tynemouth were directed towards Ian Stafford. The glance of the former was ironical and a little sardonic. He had lately been deeply engaged in checkmating the singularly skilful and cleverly devised negotiations by which England was to gain a powerful advantage in Europe, the full significance of which even he had not yet pierced. This he knew, but what he apprehended with the instinct of an almost scientific sense became unduly important to his mind. The author of the profoundly planned international scheme was this young man, who had already made the chancelleries of Europe sit up and look about them in dismay; for its activities were like those of underground wires; and every area of diplomacy, the nearest, the most remote, was mined and primed, so that each embassy played its part with almost startling effect. Tibet and Persia were not too far, and France was not too near to prevent the incalculably smooth working of a striking and far-reaching political move. It was the kind of thing that England's Prime Minister, with his extraordinary frankness, with his equally extraordinary secretiveness, insight and immobility, delighted in; and Slavonia and its ambassador knew, as an American high in place had colloquially said, "that they were up against a proposition which would take some moving."

The scheme had taken some moving. But it had not yet succeeded; and if M. Mennaval, the ambassador of Moravia, influenced by Count Landrassy, pursued his present tactics on behalf of his government, Ian Stafford's coup would never be made, and he would have to rise to fame in diplomacy by slower processes. It was the daily business of the Slavonian ambassador to see that M. Mennaval of Moravia was not captured either by tactics, by smooth words, or all those arts which lay beneath the outward simplicity of Ian Stafford and of those who worked with him.

With England on the verge of war, the outcome of the negotiations was a matter of vital importance. It might mean the very question of England's existence as an empire. England in a conflict with South Africa, the hour long desired by more than one country, in which she would be occupied to the limit of her capacity, with resources taxed to the utmost, army inadequate, and military affairs in confusion, would come, and with it the opportunity to bring the Titan to her knees. This diplomatic scheme of Ian Stafford, however, would prevent the worst in any case, and even in the disasters of war, would be working out advantages which, after the war was done, would give England many friends and fewer enemies, give her treaties and new territory, and set her higher than she was now by a political metre.

Count Landrassy had thought at first, when Ian Stafford came to Glencader, that this meeting had been purposely arranged; but through Byng's frankness and ingenuous explanations he saw that he was mistaken. The two subtle and combating diplomats had not yet conversed save in a general way by the smoking-room fire.

Lady Tynemouth's eyes fell on Ian with a different meaning. His coming to Glencader had been a surprise to her. He had accepted an invitation to visit her in another week, and she had only come to know later of the chance meeting of Ian and Jasmine in London, and the subsequent accident to Jigger which had brought Ian down to Wales. The man who had saved her life on her wedding journey, and whose walls were still garish with the red parasol which had nearly been her death, had a place quite his own in her consideration. She had, of course, known of his old infatuation for Jasmine, though she did not know all; and she knew also that he had put Jasmine out of his life completely when she married Byng; which was not a source of regret to her. She had written him about Jasmine, again and again,—of what she did and what the world said—and his replies had been as casual and as careless as the most jealous woman could desire; though she was not consciously jealous, and, of course, had no right to be.

She saw no harm in having a man as a friend on a basis of intimacy which drew the line at any possibility of divorce-court proceedings. Inside this line she frankly insisted on latitude, and Tynemouth gave it to her without thought or anxiety. He was too fond of outdoor life, of racing and hunting and shooting and polo and travel, to have his eye unnerved by any such foolishness as jealousy.

"Play the game—play the game, Alice, and so will I, and the rest of the world be hanged!" was what Tynemouth had said to his wife; and it would not have occurred to him to suspect Stafford, or to read one of his letters to Lady Tynemouth. He had no literary gifts; in truth, he had no "culture," and he looked upon his wife's and Stafford's interest in literature and art as a game of mystery he had never learned. Inconsequent he thought it in his secret mind, but played by nice, clever, possible, "livable" people; and, therefore, not to be pooh-poohed openly or kicked out of the way. Besides, it "gave Alice something to do, and prevented her from being lonely—and all that kind of thing."

Thus it was that Lady Tynemouth, who had played the game all round according to her lights, and thought no harm of what she did, or of her weakness for Ian Stafford—of her open and rather gushing friendship for him—had an almost honest dislike to seeing him brought into close relations again with the woman who had dishonourably treated him. Perhaps she wanted his friendship wholly for herself; but that selfish consideration did not overshadow the feeling that Jasmine had cheated at cards, as it were; and that Ian ought not to be compelled to play with her again.

"But men, even the strongest, are so weak," she had said to Tynemouth concerning it, and he had said in reply, "And the weakest are so strong—sometimes."

At which she had pulled his shoulder, and had said with a delighted laugh, "Tynie, if you say clever things like that I'll fall in love with you."

To which he had replied: "Now, don't take advantage of a moment's aberration, Alice; and for Heaven's sake don't fall in love wiv me" (he made a v of a th, like Jigger). "I couldn't go to Uganda if you did."

To which she had responded, "Dear me, are you going to Uganda?" and was told with a nod that next month he would be gone. This conversation had occurred on the day of their arrival at Glencader; and henceforth Alice had forcibly monopolized Stafford whenever and wherever possible. So far, it had not been difficult, because Jasmine had, not ostentatiously, avoided being often with Stafford. It seemed to Jasmine that she must not see much of him alone. Still there was some new cause to provoke his interest and draw him to herself. The Jigger episode had done much, had altered the latitudes of their association, but the perihelion of their natures was still far off; and she was apprehensive, watchful, and anxious.

This afternoon, however, she felt that she must talk with him. Waiting and watching were a new discipline for her, and she was not yet the child of self-denial. Fate, if there be such a thing, favoured her, however, for as they drew near to the fireplace where the ambassador and Alice Tynemouth and her husband stood, Krool entered, came forward to Byng, and spoke in a low tone to him.

A minute afterward, Byng said to them all: "Well, I'm sorry, but I'm afraid we can't carry out our plans for the afternoon. There's trouble again at the mine, and I am needed, or they think I am. So I must go there—and alone, I'm sorry to say; not with you all, as I had hoped. Jasmine, you must plan the afternoon. The carriages are ready. There's the Glen o' Smiling, well worth seeing, and the Murderer's Leap, and Lover's Land—something for all tastes," he added, with a dry note to his voice.

"Take care of yourself, Ruddy man," Jasmine said, as he left them hurriedly, with an affectionate pinch of her arm. "I don't like these mining troubles," she added to the others, and proceeded to arrange the afternoon.

She did it so deftly that she and Ian and Adrian Fellowes were the only ones left behind out of a party of twelve. She had found it impossible to go on any of the excursions, because she must stay and welcome Al'mah. She meant to drive to the station herself, she said. Adrian stayed behind because he must superintend the arrangements of the ball-room for the evening, or so he said; and Ian Stafford stayed because he had letters to write—ostensibly; for he actually meant to go and sit with Jigger, and to send a code message to the Prime Minister, from whom he had had inquiries that morning.

When the others had gone, the three stood for a moment silent in the hall, then Adrian said to Jasmine, "Will you give me a moment in the ball-room about those arrangements?"

Jasmine glanced out of the corner of her eye at Ian. He showed no sign that he wanted her to remain. A shadow crossed her face, but she laughingly asked him if he would come also.

"If you don't mind—!" he said, shaking his head in negation; but he walked with them part of the way to the ball-room, and left them at the corridor leading to his own little sitting-room.

A few minutes later, as Jasmine stood alone at a window looking down into the great stone quadrangle, she saw him crossing toward the servants' quarters.

"He is going to Jigger," she said, her heart beating faster. "Oh, but he is 'the best ever,'" she added, repeating Lou's words—"the best ever!"

Her eye brightened with intention. She ran down the corridor, and presently made her way to the housekeeper's room.

XII

The Key in the Lock

A quarter of an hour later Jasmine softly opened the door of the room where Jigger lay, and looked in. The nurse stood at the foot of the bed, listening to talk between Jigger and Ian, the like of which she had never heard. She was smiling, for Jigger was original, to say the least of it, and he had a strange, innocent, yet wise philosophy. Ian sat with his elbows on his knees, hands clasped, leaning towards the gallant little sufferer, talking like a boy to a boy, and getting revelations of life of which he had never even dreamed.

Jasmine entered with a little tray in one hand, bearing a bowl of delicate broth, while under an arm was a puzzle-box, which was one of the relics of a certain house-party in which a great many smart people played at the simple life, and sought to find a new sensation in making believe they were the village rector's brood of innocents. She was dressed in a gown almost as simple in make as that of the nurse, but of exquisite material—the soft green velvet which she had worn when she met Ian in the sweetshop in Regent Street. Her hair was a perfect gold, wavy and glistening and prettily fine, and her eyes were shining—so blue, so deep, so alluring.

The boy saw her first, and his eyes grew bigger with welcome and interest.

"It's her—me lydy," he said with a happy gasp, for she seemed to him like a being from another sphere. When she came near him the faint, delicious perfume exhaling from her garments was like those flower-gardens and scented fields to which he had once been sent for a holiday by some philanthropic society.

Ian rose as the nurse came forward quickly to relieve Jasmine of the tray and the box. His first glance was enigmatical—almost suspicious—then, as he saw the radiance in her face and the burden she carried, a new light came into his eyes. In this episode of Jigger she had shown all that gentle charm, sympathy, and human feeling which he had once believed belonged so much to her. It seemed to him in the old days that at heart she was simple, generous, and capable of the best feelings of woman, and of living up to them; and there began to grow at the back of his mind now the thought that she had been carried away by a great temptation—the glitter and show of power and all that gold can buy, and a large circle for the skirts of woman's pride and vanity. If she had married him instead of Byng, they would now be living in a small house in Curzon Street, or some such fashionable quarter, with just enough to enable them to keep their end up with people who had five thousand a year—with no box at the opera, or house in the country, or any of the great luxuries, and with a thriving nursery which would be a promise of future expense—if she had married him! . . . A kinder, gentler spirit was suddenly awake in him, and he did not despise her quite so much. On her part, she saw him coming nearer, as, standing in the door of a cottage in a valley, one sees trailing over the distant hills, with the light behind, a welcome and beloved figure with face turned towards the home in the green glade.

A smile came to his lips, as suspicion stole away ashamed, and he said: "This will not do. Jigger will be spoiled. We shall have to see Mr. Mappin about it."

As she yielded to him the puzzle-box, which she had refused to the nurse, she said: "And pray who sets the example? I am a very imitative person. Besides, I asked Mr. Mappin about the broth, so it's all right; and Jigger will want the puzzle-box when you are not here," she added, quizzically.

"Diversion or continuity?" he asked, with a laugh, as she held the bowl of soup to Jigger's lips. At this point the nurse had discreetly left the room.

"Continuity, of course," she replied. "All diplomatists are puzzles, some without solution."

"Who said I was a diplomatist?" he asked, lightly.

"Don't think that I'm guilty of the slander," she rejoined. "It was the Moravian ambassador who first suggested that what you were by profession you were by nature."

Jasmine felt Ian hold his breath for a moment, then he said in a low tone, "M. Mennaval—you know him well?"

She did not look towards him, but she was conscious that he was eying her intently. She put aside the bowl, and began to adjust Jigger's pillow with deft fingers, while the lad watched her with a worship worth any money to one attacked by ennui and stale with purchased pleasures.

"I know him well—yes, quite well," she replied. "He comes sometimes of an afternoon, and if he had more time—or if I had—he would no doubt come oftener. But time is the most valuable thing I have, and I have less of it than anything else."

"A diminishing capital, too," he returned with a laugh; while his mind was suddenly alert to an idea which had flown into his vision, though its full significance did not possess him yet.

"The Moravian ambassador is not very busy," he added with an undertone of meaning.

"Perhaps; but I am," she answered with like meaning, and looked him in the eyes, steadily, serenely, determinedly. All at once there had opened out before her a great possibility. Both from the Count Landrassy and from the Moravian ambassador she had had hints of some deep, international scheme of which Ian Stafford was the engineer-in-chief, though she did not know definitely what it was. Both ambassadors had paid their court to her, each in a different way, and M. Mennaval would have been as pertinacious as he was vain and somewhat weak (albeit secretive, too, with the feminine instinct so strong in him) if she had not checked him at all points. From what Count Landrassy had said, it would appear that Ian Stafford's future hung in the balance—dependent upon the success of his great diplomatic scheme.

Could she help Ian? Could she help him? Had the time come when she could pay her debt, the price of ransom from the captivity in which he held her true and secret character? It had been vaguely in her mind before; but now, standing beside Jigger's bed, with the lad's feverish hand in hers, there spread out before her a vision of a lien lifted, of an ugly debt redeemed, of freedom from this man's scorn. If she could do some great service for him, would not that wipe out the unsettled claim? If she could help to give him success, would not that, in the end, be more to him than herself? For she would soon fade, the dust would soon gather over her perished youth and beauty; but his success would live on, ever freshening in his sight, rising through long years to a great height, and remaining fixed and exalted. With a great belief she believed in him and what he could do. He was a Sisyphus who could and would roll the-huge stone to the top of the hill—and ever with easier power.

The old touch of romance and imagination which had been the governing forces of her grandfather's life, the passion of an idea, however essentially false and meretricious and perilous to all that was worth while keeping in life, set her pulses beating now. As a child her pulses used to beat so when she had planned with her good-for-nothing brother some small escapade looming immense in the horizon of her enjoyment. She had ever distorted or inflamed the facts of life by an overheated fancy, by the spirit of romance, by a gift—or curse—of imagination, which had given her also dark visions of a miserable end, of a clouded and piteous close to her brief journey. "I am doomed—doomed," had been her agonized cry that day before Ian Stafford went away three years ago, and the echo of that cry was often in her heart, waking and sleeping. It had come upon her the night when Rudyard reeled, intoxicated, up the staircase. She had the penalties of her temperament shadowing her footsteps always, dimming the radiance which broke forth for long periods, and made her so rare and wonderful a figure in her world. She was so young, and so exquisite, that Fate seemed harsh and cruel in darkening her vision, making pitfalls for her feet.

Could she help him? Had her moment come when she could force him to smother his scorn and wait at her door for bounty? She would make the effort to know.

"But, yes, I am very busy," she repeated. "I have little interest in Moravia—which is fortunate; for I could not find the time to study it."

"If you had interest in Moravia, you would find the time with little difficulty," he answered, lightly, yet thinking ironically that he himself had given much time and study to Moravia, and so far had not got much return out of it. Moravia was the crux of his diplomacy. Everything depended on it; but Landrassy, the Slavonian ambassador, had checkmated him at every move towards the final victory.

"It is not a study I would undertake con amore," she said, smiling down at Jigger, who watched her with sharp yet docile eyes. Then, suddenly turning towards him again, she said:

"But you are interested in Moravia—do you find it worth the time?"

"Did Count Landrassy tell you that?" he asked.

"And also the ambassador for Moravia; but only in the vaguest and least consequential way," she replied.

She regarded him steadfastly. "It is only just now—is it a kind of telepathy'—that I seem to get a message from what we used to call the power-house, that you are deeply interested in Moravia and Slavonia. Little things which have been said seem to have new meaning now, and I feel"—she smiled significantly—"that I am standing on the brink of some great happening, and only a big secret, like a cloud, prevents me from seeing it, realizing it. Is it so?" she added, in a low voice.

He regarded her intently. His look held hers. It would seem as though he tried to read the depths of her soul; as though he was asking if what had once proved so false could in the end prove true; for it came to him with sudden force, with sure conviction, that she could help him as no one else could; that at this critical moment, when he was trembling between success and failure, her secret influence might be the one reinforcement necessary to conduct him to victory. Greater and better men than himself had used women to further their vast purposes; could one despise any human agency, so long as it was not dishonourable, in the carrying out of great schemes?

It was for Britain—for her ultimate good, for the honour and glory of the Empire, for the betterment of the position of all men of his race in all the world, their prestige, their prosperity, their patriotism; and no agency should be despised. He knew so well what powers of intrigue had been used against him, by the embassy of Slavonia and those of other countries. His own methods had been simple and direct; only the scheme itself being intricate, complicated, and reaching further than any diplomatist, except his own Prime Minister, had dreamed. If carried, it would recast the international position in the Orient, necessitating new adjustments in Europe, with cession of territory and gifts for gifts in the way of commercial treaties and the settlement of outstanding difficulties.

His key, if it could be made to turn in the lock, would open the door to possibilities of prodigious consequence.

He had been three years at work, and the end must come soon. The crisis was near. A game can only be played for a given time, then it works itself out, and a new one must take its place. His top was spinning hard, but already the force of the gyration was failing, and he must presently make his exit with what the Prime Minister called his Patent, or turn the key in the lock and enter upon his kingdom. In three months—in two months—in one month—it might be too late, for war was coming; and war would destroy his plans, if they were not fulfilled now. Everything must be done before war came, or be forever abandoned.

This beautiful being before him could help him. She had brains, she was skilful, inventive, supple, ardent, yet intellectually discreet. She had as much as told him that the ambassador of Moravia had paid her the compliment of admiring her with some ardour. It would not grieve him to see her make a fool and a tool of the impressionable yet adroit diplomatist, whose vanity was matched by his unreliability, and who had a passion for philandering—unlike Count Landrassy, who had no inclination to philander, who carried his citadels by direct attack in great force. Yes, Jasmine could help him, and, as in the dead years when it seemed that she would be the courier star of his existence, they understood each other without words.

"It is so," he said at last, in a low voice, his eyes still regarding her with almost painful intensity.

"Do you trust me—now—again?" she asked, a tremor in her voice and her small hand clasping ever and ever tighter the fingers of the lad, whose eyes watched her with such dog-like adoration.

A mournful smile stole to his lips—and stayed. "Come where we can be quiet and I will tell you all," he said. "You can help me, maybe."

"I will help you," she said, firmly, as the nurse entered the room again and, approaching the bed, said, "I think he ought to sleep now"; and forthwith proceeded to make Jigger comfortable.

When Stafford bade Jigger good-bye, the lad said: "I wish I could 'ear the singing to-night, y'r gryce. I mean the primmer donner. Lou says she's a fair wonder."

"We will open your window," Jasmine said, gently. "The ball-room is just across the quadrangle, and you will be able to hear perfectly."

"Thank you, me lydy," he answered, gratefully, and his eyes closed.

"Come," said Jasmine to Stafford. "I will take you where we can talk undisturbed."

They passed out, and both were silent as they threaded the corridors and hallways; but in Jasmine's face was a light of exaltation and of secret triumph.

"We must give Jigger a good start in life," she said, softly, as they entered her sitting-room. Jigger had broken down many barriers between her and the man who, a week ago, had been eternities distant from her.

"He's worth a lot of thought," Ian answered, as the pleasant room enveloped him, and they seated themselves on a big couch before the fire.

Again there was a long silence; then, not looking at her, but gazing into the fire, Ian Stafford slowly unfolded the wide and wonderful enterprise of diplomacy in which his genius was employed. She listened with strained attention, but without moving. Her eyes were fixed on his face, and once, as the proposed meaning of the scheme was made clear by the turn of one illuminating phrase, she gave a low exclamation of wonder and delight. That was all until, at last, turning to her as though from some vision that had chained him, he saw the glow in her eyes, the profound interest, which was like the passion of a spirit moved to heroic undertaking. Once again it was as in the years gone by—he trusted her, in spite of himself; in spite of himself he had now given his very life into her hands, was making her privy to great designs which belonged to the inner chambers of the chancelleries of Europe.

Almost timorously, as it seemed, she put out her hand and touched his shoulder. "It is wonderful—wonderful," she said. "I can, I will help you. Will let you let me win back your trust—Ian?"

"I want your help, Jasmine," he replied, and stood up. "It is the last turn of the wheel. It may be life or death to me professionally."

"It shall be life," she said, softly.

He turned slowly from her and went towards the door.

"Shall we not go for a walk," she intervened—"before I drive to the station for Al'mah?"

He nodded, and a moment afterward they were passing along the corridors. Suddenly, as they passed a window, Ian stopped. "I thought Mr. Mappin went with the others to the Glen?" he said.

"He did," was the reply.

"Who is that leaving his room?" he continued, as she followed his glance across the quadrangle. "Surely, it's Fellowes," he added.

"Yes, it looked like Mr. Fellowes," she said, with a slight frown of wonder.

XIII

"I Will Not Sing"

I will not sing—it's no use, I will not." Al'mah's eyes were vivid with anger, and her lips, so much the resort of humour, were set in determination. Her words came with low vehemence.

Adrian Fellowes' hand nervously appealed to her. His voice was coaxing and gentle.

"Al'mah, must I tell Mrs. Byng that?" he asked. "There are a hundred people in the ball-room. Some of them have driven thirty miles to hear you. Besides, you are bound in honour to keep your engagement."

"I am bound to keep nothing that I don't wish to keep—you understand!" she replied, with a passionate gesture. "I am free to do what I please with my voice and with myself. I will leave here in the morning. I sang before dinner. That pays my board and a little over," she added, with bitterness. "I prefer to be a paying guest. Mrs. Byng shall not be my paying hostess."

Fellowes shrugged his shoulders, but his lips twitched with excitement. "I don't know what has come over you, Al'mah," he said helplessly and with an anxiety he could not disguise. "You can't do that kind of thing. It isn't fair, it isn't straight business; from a social standpoint, it isn't well-bred."

"Well-bred!" she retorted with a scornful laugh and a look of angry disdain. "You once said I had the manners of Madame Sans Gene, the washer-woman—a sickly joke, it was. Are you going to be my guide in manners? Does breeding only consist in having clothes made in Savile Row and eating strawberries out of season at a pound a basket?"

"I get my clothes from the Stores now, as you can see," he said, in a desperate attempt to be humorous, for she was in a dangerous mood. Only once before had he seen her so, and he could feel the air charged with catastrophe. "And I'm eating humble pie in season now at nothing a dish," he added. "I really am; and it gives me shocking indigestion."

Her face relaxed a little, for she could seldom resist any touch of humour, but the stubborn and wilful light in her eyes remained.

"That sounds like last year's pantomime," she said, sharply, and, with a jerk of her shoulders, turned away.

"For God's sake wait a minute, Al'mah!" he urged, desperately. "What has upset you? What has happened? Before dinner you were yourself; now—" he threw up his hands in despair—"Ah, my dearest, my star—"

She turned upon him savagely, and it seemed as though a storm of passion would break upon him; but all at once she changed, came up close to him, and looked him steadily in the eyes.

"I do not think I trust you," she said, quite quietly.

His eyes could not meet hers fairly. He felt them shrinking from her inquisition. "You have always trusted me till now. What has happened?" he asked, apprehensively and with husky voice.

"Nothing has happened," she replied in a low, steady voice. "Nothing. But I seem to realize you to-night. It came to me suddenly, at dinner, as I listened to you, as I saw you talk—I had never before seen you in surroundings like these. But I realized you then: I had a revelation. You need not ask me what it was. I do not know quite. I cannot tell. It is all vague, but it is startling, and it has gone through my heart like a knife. I tell you this, and I tell you quite calmly, that if you prove to be what, for the first time, I have a vision you are, I shall never look upon your face again if I can help it. If I come to know that you are false in nature and in act, that all you have said to me is not true, that you have degraded me—Oh," she fiercely added, breaking off and speaking with infinite anger and scorn—"it was only love, honest and true, however mistaken, which could make what has been between us endurable in my eyes! What I have thought was true love, and its true passion, helped me to forget the degradation and the secret shame—only the absolute honesty of that love could make me forget. But suppose I find it only imitation; suppose I see that it is only selfishness, only horrible, ugly self-indulgence; suppose you are a man who plays with a human soul! If I find that to be so, I tell you I shall hate you; and I shall hate myself; but I shall hate you more—a thousand times more."

She paused with agony and appealing, with confusion and vague horror in her face. Her look was direct and absorbing, her eyes like wells of sullen fire.

"Al'mah," he replied with fluttered eagerness, "let us talk of this later—not now—later. I will answer anything—everything. I can and I will prove to you that this is only a mad idea of yours, that—"

"No, no, no, not mad," she interrupted. "There is no madness in it. I had a premonition before I came. It was like a cloud on my soul. It left me when we met here, when I heard your voice again; and for a moment I was happy. That was why I sang before dinner that song of Lassen's, 'Thine Eyes So Blue and Tender.' But it has come back. Something deep within me says, 'He is not true.' Something whispers, 'He is false by nature; it is not in him to be true to anything or anybody.'"

He made an effort to carry off the situation lightly. With a great sense of humour, she had also an infinite capacity for taking things seriously—with an almost sensational gravity. Yet she had always responded to his cheerful raillery when he had declined to be tragical. He essayed the old way now.

"This is just absurd, old girl;"—she shrank—"you really are mad. Your home is Colney Hatch or thereabouts. Why, I'm just what I always was to you—your constant slave, your everlasting lover, and your friend. I'll talk it all over with you later. It's impossible now. They're ready for you in the ball-room. The accompanist is waiting. Do, do, do be reasonable. I will see you—afterwards—late."

A determined poignant look came into her eyes. She drew still farther away from him. "You will not, you shall not, see me 'afterwards—late.' No, no, no; I will trust my instinct now. I am natural, I am true, I hide nothing. I take my courage in both hands. I do not hide my head in the sands. I have given, because I chose to give, and I made and make no presences to myself. I answer to myself, and I do not play false with the world or with you. Whatever I am the world can know, for I deceive no one, and I have no fears. But you—oh, why, why is it I feel now, suddenly, that you have the strain of the coward in you! Why it comes to me now I do not know; but it is here"—she pressed her hand tremblingly to her heart—"and I will not act as though it wasn't here. I'm not of this world."

She waved a hand towards the ball-room. "I am not of the world that lives in terror of itself. Mine is a world apart, where one acts and lives and sings the passion and sorrows and joys of others—all unreal, unreal. The one chance of happiness we artists have is not to act in our own lives, but to be true—real and true. For one's own life as well as one's work to be all grease-paint—no, no, no. I have hid all that has been between us, because of things that have nothing to do with fear or courage, and for your sake; but I haven't acted, or pretended. I have not flaunted my private life, my wretched sin—"

"The sin of an angel—"

She shrank from the blatant insincerity of the words, and still more from the tone. Why had it not all seemed insincere before?

"But I was true in all I did, and I believed you were," she continued. "And you don't believe it now?"

"To-night I do not. What I shall feel to-morrow I cannot tell. Maybe I shall go blind again, for women are never two days alike in their minds or bodies." She threw up her hands with a despairing helplessness. "But we shall not meet till to-morrow, and then I go back to London. I am going to my room now. You may tell Mrs. Byng that I am not well enough to sing—and indeed I am not well," she added, huskily. "I am sick at heart with I don't know what; but I am wretched and angry and dangerous—and bad."

Her eyes fastened his with a fateful bitterness and gloom. "Where is Mr. Byng?" she added, sharply. "Why was he not at dinner?"

He hailed the change of idea gladly. He spoke quickly, eagerly. "He was kept at the mine. There's trouble—a strike. He was needed. He has great influence with the men, and the masters, too. You heard Mrs. Byng say why he had not returned."

"No; I was thinking of other things. But I wanted—I want to see him. When will he be back?"

"At any moment, I should think. But, Al'mah, no matter what you feel about me, you must keep your engagement to sing here. The people in there, a hundred of the best people of the county—"

"The best people of the county—such abject snobbery!" she retorted, sharply. "Do you think that would influence me? You ought to know me well enough—but that's just it, you do not know me. I realize it at last. Listen now. I will not sing to-night, and you will go and tell Mrs. Byng so."

Once again she turned away, but her exit was arrested by another voice, a pleasant voice, which said:

"But just one minute, please. Mr. Fellowes is quite right. . . Fellowes, won't you go and say that Madame Al'mah will be there in five minutes?"

It was Ian Stafford. He had come at Jasmine's request to bring Al'mah, and he had overheard her last words. He saw that there had been a scene, and conceived that it was the kind of quarrel which could be better arranged by a third disinterested person.

After a moment's hesitation, with an anxious yet hopeful look, Fellowes disappeared, Al'mah's brown eyes following him with dark inquisition. Presently she looked at Ian Stafford with a flash of malice. Did this elegant and diplomatic person think that all he had to do was to speak, and she would succumb to his blandishment? He should see.

He smiled, and courteously motioned her to a chair.

"You said to Mr. Fellowes that I should sing in five minutes," she remarked maliciously and stubbornly, but she moved forward to the chair, nevertheless.

"Yes, but there is no reason why we should not sit for three out of the five minutes. Energy should be conserved in a tiring world."

"I have some energy to spare—the overflow," she returned with a protesting flash of the eyes, as, however, she slowly seated herself.

"We call it power and magnetism in your case," he answered in that low, soothing voice which had helped to quiet storms in more than one chancellerie of Europe. . . "What are you going to sing to-night?" he added.

"I am not going to sing," she answered, nervously. "You heard what I said to Mr. Fellowes."

"I was an unwilling eavesdropper; I heard your last words. But surely you would not be so unoriginal, so cliche, as to say the same thing to me that you said to Mr. Fellowes!"

His smile was winning and his humour came from a deep well. On the instant she knew it to be real, and his easy confidence, his assumption of dominancy had its advantage.

"I'll say it in a different way to you, but it will be the same thing. I shall not sing to-night," she retorted, obstinately.

"Then a hundred people will go hungry to bed," he rejoined. "Hunger is a dreadful thing—and there are only three minutes left out of the five," he added, looking at his watch.

"I am not the baker or the butler," she replied with a smile, but her firm lips did not soften.

He changed his tactics with adroitness. If he failed now, it would be final. He thought he knew where she might be really vulnerable.

"Byng will be disappointed and surprised when he hears of the famine that the prima donna has left behind her. Byng is one of the best that ever was. He is trying to do his fellow-creatures a good turn down there at the mine. He never did any harm that I ever heard of—and this is his house, and these are his guests. He would, I'll stake my life, do Al'mah a good turn if he could, even if it cost him something quite big. He is that kind of a man. He would be hurt to know that you had let the best people of the county be parched, when you could give them drink."

"You said they were hungry a moment ago," she rejoined, her resolution slowly breaking under the one influence which could have softened her.

"They would be both hungry and thirsty," he urged. "But, between ourselves, would you like Byng to come home from a hard day's work, as it were, and feel that things had gone wrong here while he was away on humanity's business? Just try to imagine him having done you a service—"

"He has done me more than one service," she interjected. "You know it as well as I do. You were there at the opera, three years ago, when he saved me from the flames, and since then—"

Stafford looked at his watch again with a smile. "Besides, there's a far more important reason why you should sing to-night. I promised some one who's been hurt badly, and who never heard you sing, that he should hear you to-night. He is lying there now, and—"

"Jigger?" she asked, a new light in her eyes, something fleeing from her face and leaving a strange softness behind it.

"Quite so," he replied. "That's a lad really worth singing for. He's an original, if ever there was one. He worships you for what you have done for his sister, Lou. I'd undergo almost any humiliation not to disappoint Jigger. Byng would probably get over his disappointment— he'd only feel that he hadn't been used fairly, and he's used to that; but Jigger wouldn't sleep to-night, and it's essential that he should. Think of how much happiness and how much pain you can give, just by trilling a simple little song with your little voice oh, madame la cantatrice?"

Suddenly her eyes filled with tears. She brushed them away hastily. "I've been upset and angry and disturbed—and I don't know what," she said, abruptly. "One of my black moods was on me. They only come once in a blue moon; but they almost kill me when they do." . . . She stopped and looked at him steadily for a moment, the tears still in her eyes. "You are very understanding and gentle—and sensible," she added, with brusque frankness and cordiality. "Yes, I will sing for Rudyard Byng and for Jigger; and a little too for a very clever diplomatist." She gave a spasmodic laugh.

"Only half a minute left," he rejoined with gay raillery. "I said you'd sing to them in five minutes, and you must. This way."

He offered her his arm, she took it, and in cheerful silence he hurried her to the ball-room.

Before her first song he showed her the window which looked across to that out of which Jigger gazed with trembling eagerness. The blinds and curtains were up at these windows, and Jigger could see her as she sang.

Never in all her wonderful career had Al'mah sung so well—with so much feeling and an artist's genius—not even that night of all when she made her debut. The misery, the gloom, the bitterness of the past hour had stirred every fibre of her being, and her voice told with thrilling power the story of a soul.

Once after an outburst of applause from the brilliant audience, there came a tiny echo of it from across the courtyard. It was Jigger, enraptured by a vision of heaven and the sounds of it. Al'mah turned towards the window with a shining face, and waved a kiss out of the light and glory where she was, to the sufferer in the darkness. Then, after a whispered word to the accompanist she began singing Gounod's memorable song, "There is a Green Hill Far Away." It was not what the audience expected; it was in strangest contrast to all that had gone before; it brought a hush like a benediction upon the great chamber. Her voice seemed to ache with the plaintive depth of the song, and the soft night filled its soul with melody.

A wonderful and deep solemnity was suddenly diffused upon the assembly of world-worn people, to most of whom the things that mattered were those which gave them diversion. They were wont to swim with the tide of indolence, extravagance, self-seeking, and sordid pleasure now flowing through the hardy isles, from which had come much of the strength of the Old World and the vision and spirit of the New World.

Why had she chosen this song? Because, all at once, as she thought of Jigger lying there in the dark room, she had a vision of her own child lying near to death in the grasp of pneumonia five years ago; and the misery of that time swept over her—its rebellion, its hideous fear, its bitter loneliness. She recalled how a woman, once a great singer, now grown old in years as in sorrow, had sung this very song to her then, in the hour of her direst apprehension. She sang it now to her own dead child, and to Jigger. When she ceased, there was not a sound save of some woman gently sobbing. Others were vainly trying to choke back their tears.

Presently, as Al'mah stood still in the hush which was infinitely more grateful to her than any applause, she saw Krool advancing hurriedly up the centre aisle. He was drawn and haggard, and his eyes were sunken and wild. Turning at the platform, he said in a strange, hollow voice:

"At the mine—an accident. The Baas he go down to save—he not come up."

With a cry Jasmine staggered to her feet. Ian Stafford was beside her in an instant.

"The Baas—the Baas!" said Krool, insistently, painfully. "I have the horses—come."

XIV

The Baas

There had been an explosion in the Glencader Mine, and twenty men had been imprisoned in the stark solitude of the underground world. Or was it that they lay dead in that vast womb of mother-earth which takes all men of all time as they go, and absorbs them into her fruitful body, to produce other men who will in due days return to the same great mother to rest and be still? It mattered little whether malevolence had planned the outrage in the mine, or whether accident alone had been responsible; the results were the same. Wailing, woebegone women wrung their hands, and haggard, determined men stood by with bowed heads, ready to offer their lives to save those other lives far down below, if so be it were possible.

The night was serene and quiet, clear and cold, with glimmering stars and no moon, and the wide circle of the hills was drowsy with night and darkness. All was at peace in the outer circle, but at the centre was travail and storm and outrage and death. What nature had made beautiful, man had made ugly by energy and all the harsh necessities of progress. In the very heart of this exquisite and picturesque country-side the ugly, grim life of the miner had established itself, and had then turned an unlovely field of industrial activity into a cock-pit of struggle between capital and labour. First, discontent, fed by paid agitators and scarcely steadied by responsible and level-headed labour agents and leaders; then active disturbance and threatening; then partial strike, then minor outrages, then some foolishness on the part of manager or man, and now tragedy darkening the field, adding bitterness profound to the discontent and strife.

Rudyard Byng had arrived on the scene in the later stages of the struggle, when a general strike with all its attendant miseries, its dangers and provocations, was hovering. Many men in his own mine in South Africa had come from this very district, and he was known to be the most popular of all the capitalists on the Rand. His generosity to the sick and poor of the Glencader Mine had been great, and he had given them a hospital and a club with adequate endowment. Also, he had been known to take part in the rough sports of the miners, and had afterwards sat and drunk beer with them—as much as any, and carrying it better than any.

If there was any one who could stay the strike and bring about a settlement it was he; and it is probable he would have stayed it, had it not been for a collision between a government official and a miners' leader. Things had grown worse, until the day of catastrophe, when Byng had been sent for by the leaders of both parties to the quarrel. He had laboured hours after hour in the midst of grave unrest and threats of violence, for some of the men had taken to drinking heavily—but without success. Still he had stayed on, going here and there, mostly among the men themselves, talking to them in little groups, arguing simply with them, patiently dealing with facts and figures, quietly showing them the economic injustice which lay behind their full demands, and suggesting compromises.

He was received with good feeling, but in the workers' view it was "class against class—labour against capital, the man against the master." In their view Byng represented class, capital and master, not man; his interests were not identical with theirs; and though some were disposed to cheer him, the majority said he was "as good a sort as that sort can be," but shrugged their shoulders and remained obstinate. The most that he did during the long afternoon and evening was to prevent the worst; until, as he sat eating a slice of ham in a miner's kitchen, there came the explosion: the accident or crime—which, like the lances in an angry tumour, let out the fury, enmity, and rebellion, and gave human nature its chance again. The shock of the explosion had been heard at Glencader, but nothing was thought of it, as there had been much blasting in the district for days.

"There's twenty men below," said the grimy manager who had brought the news to Byng. Together they sped towards the mine, little groups running beside them, muttering those dark sayings which, either as curses or laments, are painful comments on the relations of life on the lower levels with life on the higher plateaux.

Among the volunteers to go below, Byng was of the first, and against the appeal of the mine-manager, and of others who tried to dissuade him, he took his place with two miners with the words:

"I know this pit better than most; and I'd rather be down there knowing the worst, than waiting to learn it up here. I'm going; so lower away, lads."

He had disappeared, and for a long time there was no sign; but at last there came to the surface three of the imprisoned miners and two dead bodies, and these were followed by others still alive; but Byng did not come up. He remained below, leading the search, the first in the places of danger and exploration, the last to retreat from any peril of falling timbers or from fresh explosion. Twelve of the twenty men were rescued. Six were dead, and their bodies were brought to the surface and to the arms of women whose breadwinners were gone; whose husbands or sons or brothers had been struck out into darkness without time to strip themselves of the impedimenta of the soul. Two were left below, and these were brothers who had married but three months before. They were strong, buoyant men of twenty-five, with life just begun, and home still welcome and alluring—warm-faced, bonny women to meet them at the door, and lay the cloth, and comfort their beds, and cheer them away to work in the morning. These four lovers had been the target for the good-natured and half-affectionate scoffing of the whole field; for the twins, Jabez and Jacob, were as alike as two peas, and their wives were cousins, and were of a type in mind, body, and estate. These twin toilers were left below, with Rudyard Byng forcing his way to the place where they had worked. With him was one other miner of great courage and knowledge, who had gone with other rescue parties in other catastrophes.

It was this man who was carried to the surface when another small explosion occurred. He brought the terrible news that Byng, the rescuer of so many, was himself caught by falling timbers and imprisoned near a spot where Jabez and Jacob Holyhoke were entombed.

Word had gone to Glencader, and within an hour and a half Jasmine, Al'mah, Stafford, Lord Tynemouth, the Slavonian Ambassador, Adrian Fellowes, Mr. Tudor Tempest and others were at the pit's mouth, stricken by the same tragedy which had made so many widows and orphans that night. Already two attempts had been made to descend, but they had not been successful. Now came forward a burly and dour-looking miner, called Brengyn, who had been down before, and had been in command. His look was forbidding, but his face was that of a man on whom you could rely; and his eyes had a dogged, indomitable expression. Behind him were a dozen men, sullen and haggard, their faces showing nothing of that pity in their hearts which drove them to risk all to save the lives of their fellow-workers. Was it all pity and humanity? Was there also something of that perdurable cohesion of class against class; the powerful if often unlovely unity of faction, the shoulder-to-shoulder combination of war; the tribal fanaticism which makes brave men out of unpromising material? Maybe something of this element entered into the heroism which had been displayed; but whatever the impulse or the motive, the act and the end were the same—men's lives were in peril, and they were risking their own to rescue them.

When Jasmine and her friends arrived, Ian Stafford addressed himself to the groups of men at the pit's mouth, asking for news. Seeing Brengyn approach Jasmine, he hurried over, recognizing in the stalwart miner a leader of men.

"It's a chance in a thousand," he heard Brengyn say to Jasmine, whose white face showed no trace of tears, and who held herself with courage. There was something akin in the expression of her face and that of other groups of women, silent, rigid and bitter, who stood apart, some with children's hands clasped in theirs, facing the worst with regnant resolution. All had that horrible quietness of despair so much more poignant than tears and wailing. Their faces showed the weariness of labour and an ill-nourished daily life, but there was the same look in them as in Jasmine's. There was no class in this communion of suffering and danger.

"Not one chance in a thousand," Brengyn added, heavily. "I know where they are, but—"

"You think they are—dead?" Jasmine asked in a hollow voice.

"I think, alive or dead, it's all against them as goes down to bring them out. It's more lives to be wasted."

Stafford heard, and he stepped forward. "If there's a chance in a thousand, it's good enough for a try," he said. "If you were there, Mr. Byng would take the chance in the thousand for you."

Brengyn looked Stafford up and down slowly. "What is it you've got to say?" he asked, gloomily.

"I am going down, if there's anybody will lead," Stafford replied. "I was brought up in a mining country. I know as much as most of you about mines, and I'll make one to follow you, if you'll lead—you've been down, I know."

Brengyn's face changed. "Mr. Byng isn't our class, he's with capital," he said, "but he's a man. He went down to help save men of my class, and to any of us he's worth the risk. But how many of his own class is taking it on?"

"I, for one," said Lord Tynemouth, stepping forward.

"I—I," answered three other men of the house-party.

Al'mah, who was standing just below Jasmine, had her eyes fixed on Adrian Fellowes, and when Brengyn called for volunteers, her heart almost stood still in suspense. Would Adrian volunteer?

Brengyn's look rested on Adrian for an instant, but Adrian's eyes dropped. Brengyn had said one chance in a thousand, and Adrian said to himself that he had never been lucky—never in all his life. At games of chance he had always lost. Adrian was for the sure thing always.

Al'mah's face flushed with anger and shame at the thing she saw, and a weakness came over her, as though the springs of life had been suddenly emptied.

Brengyn once again fastened the group from Glencader with his eyes. "There's a gentleman in danger," he said, grimly, again. "How many gentlemen volunteer to go down—ay, there's five!" he added, as Stafford and Tynemouth and the others once again responded.

Jasmine saw, but at first did not fully realize what was happening. But presently she understood that there was one near, owing everything to her husband, who had not volunteered to help to save him—on the thousandth chance. She was stunned and stricken.

"Oh, for God's sake, go!" she said, brokenly, but not looking at Adrian Fellowes, and with a heart torn by misery and shame.

Brengyn turned to the men behind him, the dark, determined toilers who sustained the immortal spirit of courage and humanity on thirty shillings a week and nine hours' work a day. "Who's for it, mates?" he asked, roughly. "Who's going wi' me?"

Every man answered hoarsely, "Ay," and every hand went up. Brengyn's back was on Fellowes, Al'mah, and Jasmine now. There was that which filled the cup of trembling for Al'mah in the way he nodded to the men.

"Right, lads," he said with a stern joy in his voice. "But there's only one of you can go, and I'll pick him. Here, Jim," he added to a small, wiry fellow not more than five feet four in height—"here, Jim Gawley, you're comin' wi' me, an' that's all o' you as can come. No, no," he added, as there was loud muttering and dissent. "Jim's got no missis, nor mother, and he's tough as leather and can squeeze in small places, and he's all right, too, in tight corners." Now he turned to Stafford and Tynemouth and the others. "You'll come wi' me," he said to Stafford—"if you want. It's a bad look-out, but we'll have a try. You'll do what I say?" he sharply asked Stafford, whose face was set.

"You know the place," Stafford answered. "I'll do what you say."

"My word goes?"

"Right. Your word goes. Let's get on."

Jasmine took a step forward with a smothered cry, but Alice Tynemouth laid a hand on her arm.

"He'll bring Rudyard back, if it can be done," she whispered.

Stafford did not turn round. He said something in an undertone to Tynemouth, and then, without a glance behind, strode away beside Brengyn and Jim Gawley to the pit's mouth.

Adrian Fellowes stepped up to Tynemouth. "What do you think the chances are?" he asked in a low tone.

"Go to—bed!" was the gruff reply of the irate peer, to whom cowardice was the worst crime on earth, and who was enraged at being left behind. Also he was furious because so many working-men had responded to Brengyn's call for volunteers and Adrian Fellowes had shown the white feather. In the obvious appeal to the comparative courage of class his own class had suffered.

"Or go and talk to the women," he added to Fellowes. "Make 'em comfortable. You've got a gift that way."

Turning on his heel, Lord Tynemouth hastened to the mouth of the pit and watched the preparations for the descent.

Never was night so still; never was a sky so deeply blue, nor stars so bright and serene. It was as though Peace had made its habitation on the wooded hills, and a second summer had come upon the land, though wintertime was near. Nature seemed brooding, and the generous odour of ripened harvests came over the uplands to the watchers in the valley. All was dark and quiet in the sky and on the hills; but in the valley were twinkling lights and the stir and murmur of troubled life—that sinister muttering of angry and sullen men which has struck terror to the hearts of so many helpless victims of revolution, when it has been the mutterings of thousands and not of a few rough, discontented toilers. As Al'mah sat near to the entrance of the mine, wrapped in a warm cloak, and apart from the others who watched and waited also, she seemed to realize the agony of the problem which was being worked out in these labour-centres where, between capital and the work of men's hands, there was so apparent a gulf of disproportionate return.

The stillness of the night was broken now by the hoarse calls of the men, now by the wailing of women, and Al'mah's eyes kept turning to those places where lights were shining, which, as she knew, were houses of death or pain. For hours she and Jasmine and Lady Tynemouth had gone from cottage to cottage where the dead and wounded were, and had left everywhere gifts, and the promises of gifts, in the attempt to soften the cruelty of the blow to those whose whole life depended on the weekly wage. Help and the pledge of help had lightened many a dark corner that night; and an unexplainable antipathy which had suddenly grown up in Al'mah's mind against Jasmine after her arrival at Glencader was dissipated as the hours wore on.

Pale of face, but courageous and solicitous, Jasmine, accompanied by Al'mah, moved among the dead and dying and the bitter and bereaved living, with a gentle smile and a soft word or touch of the hand. Men near to death, or suffering torture, looked gratefully at her or tried to smile; and more than once Mr. Mappin, whose hands were kept busy and whose skill saved more than a handful of lives that night, looked at her in wonder.

Jasmine already had a reputation in the great social world for being of a vain lightness, having nothing of that devotion to good works which Mr. Mappin had seen so often on those high levels where the rich and the aristocratic lived. There was, then, more than beauty and wit and great social gift, gaiety and charm, in this delicate personality? Yes, there was something good and sound in her, after all. Her husband's life was in infinite danger,—had not Brengyn said that his chances were only one in a thousand?—death stared her savagely in the face; yet she bore herself as calmly as those women who could not afford the luxury of tears or the self-indulgence of a despairing indolence; to whom tragedy was but a whip of scorpions to drive them into action. How well they all behaved, these society butterflies—Jasmine, Lady Tynemouth, and the others! But what a wonderful motherliness and impulsive sympathy steadied by common sense did Al'mah the singing-woman show!

Her instinct was infallible, her knowledge of how these poor people felt was intuitive, and her great-heartedness was to be seen in every motion, heard in every tone of her voice. If she had not had this work of charity to do, she felt she would have gone shrieking through the valley, as, this very midnight, she had seen a girl with streaming hair and bare breast go crying through the streets, and on up the hills to the deep woods, insane with grief and woe.

Her head throbbed. She felt as though she also could tear the coverings from her own bosom to let out the fever which was there; for in her life she had loved two men who had trampled on her self-respect, had shattered all her pride of life, had made her ashamed to look the world in the face. Blantyre, her husband, had been despicable and cruel, a liar and a deserter; and to-night she had seen the man to whom she had given all that was left of her heart and faith disgrace himself and his class before the world by a cowardice which no woman could forgive.

Adrian Fellowes had gone back to Glencader to do necessary things, to prepare the household for any emergency; and she was grateful for the respite. If she had been thrown with him in the desperate mood of the moment, she would have lost her self-control. Happily, fate had taken him away for a few hours; and who could tell what might not happen in a few hours? Meanwhile, there was humanity's work to be done.

About four o'clock in the morning, when she came out from a cottage where she had assisted Mr. Mappin in a painful and dangerous operation, she stood for a moment in reverie, looking up at the hills, whose peace had been shrilly broken a few hours before by that distracted waif of the world, fleeing from the pain of life.

An ample star of rare brilliancy came stealing up over the trees against the sky-line, twinkling and brimming with light.

"No," she said, as though in reply to an inner voice, "there's nothing for me—nothing. I have missed it all." Her hands clasped her breast in pain, and she threw her face upwards. But the light of the star caught her eyes, and her hands ceased to tremble. A strange quietness stole over her.

"My child, my lost beloved child," she whispered.

Her eyes swam with tears now, the lines of pain at her mouth relaxed, the dark look in her eyes stole away. She watched the star with sorrowful eyes. "How much misery does it see!" she said. Suddenly, she thought of Rudyard Byng. "He saved my life," she murmured. "I owe him—ah, Adrian might have paid the debt!" she cried, in pain. "If he had only been a man to-night—"

At that moment there came a loud noise up the valley from the pit's mouth—a great shouting. An instant later two figures ran past her. One was Jasmine, the other was a heavy-footed miner. Gathering her cloak around her Al'mah sped after them.

A huddled group at the pit's mouth, and men and women running toward it; a sharp voice of command, and the crowd falling back, making way for men who carried limp bodies past; then suddenly, out of wild murmurs and calls, a cry of victory like the call of a muezzin from the tower of a mosque—a resonant monotony, in which a dominant principle cries.

A Welsh preaching hillman, carried away by the triumph of the moment, gave the great tragedy the bugle-note of human joy and pride.

Ian Stafford and Brengyn and Jim Gawley had conquered. The limp bodies carried past Al'mah were not dead. They were living, breathing men whom fresh air and a surgeon's aid would soon restore. Two of them were the young men with the bonny wives who now with murmured endearments grasped their cold hands. Behind these two was carried Rudyard Byng, who could command the less certain concentration of a heart. The men whom Rudyard had gone to save could control a greater wealth, a more precious thing than anything he had. The boundaries of the interests of these workers were limited, but their souls were commingled with other souls bound to them by the formalities; and every minute of their days, every atom of their forces, were moving round one light, the light upon the hearthstone. These men were carried ahead of Byng now, as though by the ritual of nature taking their rightful place in life's procession before him.

Something of what the working-women felt possessed Jasmine, but it was an impulse born of the moment, a flood of feeling begotten by the tragedy. It had in it more of remorse than aught else; it was, in part, the agitation of a soul surprised into revelation. Yet there was, too, a strange, deep, undefined pity welling up in her heart,—pity for Rudyard, and because of what she did not say directly even to her own soul. But pity was there, with also a sense of inevitableness, of the continuance of things which she was too weak to alter.

Like the two women of the people ahead, she held Rudyard's hand, as she walked beside him, till he was carried into the manager's office near by. She was conscious that on the other side of Rudyard was a tall figure that staggered and swayed as it moved on, and that two dark eyes were turned towards her ever and anon.

Into those eyes she had looked but once since the rescue, but all that was necessary of gratitude was said in that one glance: "You have saved Rudyard—you, Ian," it said.

With Al'mah it was different. In the light of the open door of the manager's office, she looked into Ian Stafford's face. "He saved my life, you remember," she said; "and you have saved his. I love you."

"I love you!" Greatness of heart was speaking, not a woman's emotions. The love she meant was of the sort which brings no darkness in its train. Men and women can speak of it without casting down their eyes or feeling a flush in their cheeks.

To him came also the two women whose husbands, Jacob and Jabez, were restored to them.

"Man, we luv ye," one said, and the other laid a hand on his breast and nodded assent, adding, "Ay, we luv ye."

That was all; but greater love hath no man than this, that he lay down his life for his friend—and for his enemies, maybe. Enemies these two rescued men were in one sense—young socialists—enemies to the present social order, with faces set against the capitalist and the aristocrat and the landlord; yet in the crisis of life dipping their hands in the same dish, drinking from the same cup, moved by the same sense of elementary justice, pity, courage, and love.

"Man, we luv ye!" And the women turned away to their own—to their capital, which in the slump of Fate had suffered no loss. It was theirs, complete and paying large dividends.

To the crowd, Brengyn, with gruff sincerity, said, loudly: "Jim Gawley, he done as I knowed he'd do. He done his best, and he done it prime. We couldn't ha' got on wi'out him. But first there was Mr. Byng as had sense and knowledge more than any; an' he couldn't be denied; an' there was Mr. Stafford—him—" pointing to Ian, who, with misty eyes, was watching the women go back to their men. "He done his bit better nor any of us. And Mr. Byng and Jacob and Jabez, they can thank their stars that Mr. Stafford done his bit. Jim's all right an' I done my duty, I hope, but these two that ain't of us, they done more—Mr. Byng and Mr. Stafford. Here's three cheers, lads—no, this ain't a time for cheerin'; but ye all ha' got hands."

His hand caught Ian's with the grip of that brotherhood which is as old as Adam, and the hand of miner after miner did the same.

The strike was over—at a price too big for human calculation; but it might have been bigger still.

Outside the open door of the manager's office Stafford watched and waited till he saw Rudyard, with a little laugh, get slowly to his feet and stretch his limbs heavily. Then he turned away gloomily to the darkness of the hills. In his soul there was a depression as deep as in that of the singing-woman.

"Al'mah had her debt to pay, and I shall have mine," he said, wearily.

BOOK III

XV

The World Well Lost

People were in London in September and October who seldom arrived before November. War was coming. Hundreds of families whose men were in the army came to be within touch of the War Office and Aldershot, and the capital of the Empire was overrun by intriguers, harmless and otherwise. There were ladies who hoped to influence officers in high command in favour of their husbands, brothers, or sons; subalterns of title who wished to be upon the staff of some famous general; colonels of character and courage and scant ability, craving commands; high-placed folk connected with great industrial, shipping, or commercial firms, who were used by these firms to get "their share" of contracts and other things which might be going; and patriotic amateurs who sought to make themselves notorious through some civilian auxiliary to war organization, like a voluntary field hospital or a home of convalescence. But men, too, of the real right sort, longing for chance of work in their profession of arms; ready for anything, good for anything, brave to a miracle: and these made themselves fit by hard riding or walking or rowing, or in some school of physical culture, that they might take a war job on, if, and when, it was going.

Among all these Ian Stafford moved with an undercurrent of agitation and anxiety unseen in his face, step, motion, or gesture. For days he was never near the Foreign Office, and then for days he was there almost continuously; yet there was scarcely a day when he did not see Jasmine. Also there were few days in the week when Jasmine did not see M. Mennaval, the ambassador for Moravia—not always at her own house, but where the ambassador chanced to be of an evening, at a fashionable restaurant, or at some notable function. This situation had not been difficult to establish; and, once established, meetings between the lady and monsieur were arranged with that skill which belongs to woman and to diplomacy.

Once or twice at the beginning Jasmine's chance question concerning the ambassador's engagements made M. Mennaval keen to give information as to his goings and comings. Thus if they met naturally, it was also so constantly that people gossiped; but at first, certainly, not to

Jasmine's grave disadvantage, for M. Mennaval was thought to be less dangerous than impressionable.

In that, however, he was somewhat maligned, for his penchant for beautiful and "select" ladies had capacities of development almost unguessed. Previously Jasmine had never shown him any marked preference; and when, at first, he met her in town on her return from Wales he was no more than watchfully courteous and admiring. When, however, he found her in a receptive mood, and evidently taking pleasure in his society, his vanity expanded greatly. He at once became possessed by an absorbing interest in the woman who, of all others in London, had gifts which were not merely physical, but of a kind that stimulate the mind and rouse those sensibilities so easily dulled by dull and material people. Jasmine had her material side; but there was in her the very triumph of the imaginative also; and through it the material became alive, buoyant and magnetic.

Without that magnetic power which belonged to the sensuous part of her she would not have gained control of M. Mennaval's mind, for it was keen, suspicious, almost abnormally acute; and, while lacking real power, it protected itself against the power of others by assembled and well-disciplined adroitness and evasions.

Very soon, however, Jasmine's sensitive beauty, which in her desire to intoxicate him became voluptuousness, enveloped his brain in a mist of rainbow reflections. Under her deft questions and suggestions he allowed her to see the springs of his own diplomacy and the machinery inside the Moravian administration. She caught glimpses of its ambitions, its unscrupulous use of its position in international relations, to gain advantage for itself, even by a dexterity which might easily bear another name, and by sudden disregard of international attachments not unlike treachery.

Rudyard was too busy to notice the more than cavalier attitude of M. Mennaval; and if he had noticed it, there would have been no intervention. Of late a lesion of his higher moral sense made him strangely insensitive to obvious things. He had an inborn chivalry, but the finest, truest chivalry was not his—that which carefully protects a woman from temptation, by keeping her unostentatiously away from it; which remembers that vanity and the need for admiration drive women into pitfalls out of which they climb again maimed for life, if they climb at all.

He trusted Jasmine absolutely, while there was, at the same time, a great unrest in his heart and life—an unrest which the accident at the Glencader Mine, his own share in a great rescue, and her gratitude for his safety did little to remove. It produced no more than a passing effect upon Jasmine or upon himself. The very convention of making light of bravery and danger, which has its value, was in their case an evil, preventing them from facing the inner meaning of it all. If they had been less rich, if their house had been small, if their acquaintances had been fewer, if. . .

It was not by such incidents that they were to be awakened, and with the wild desire to make Stafford grateful to her, and owe her his success, the tragedy yonder must, in the case of Jasmine, have been obscured and robbed of its force. At Glencader Jasmine had not got beyond desire to satisfy a vanity, which was as deep in her as life itself. It was to regain her hold upon a man who had once acknowledged her power and, in a sense, had bowed to her will. But that had changed, and, down beneath all her vanity and wilfulness, there was now a dangerous regard and passion for him which, under happy circumstances, might have transformed her life—and his. Now it all served to twist her soul and darken her footsteps. On every hand she was engaged in a game of dissimulation, made the more dangerous by the thread of sincerity and desire running through it all. Sometimes she started aghast at the deepening intrigue gathering in her path; at the deterioration in her husband; and at the hollow nature of her home life; but the excitement of the game she was playing, the ardour of the chase, was in her veins, and her inherited spirit of great daring kept her gay with vitality and intellectual adventure.

Day after day she had strengthened the cords by which she was drawing Ian to her; and in the confidence begotten of her services to him, of her influence upon M. Mennaval and the progress of her efforts, a new intimacy, different from any they had ever known, grew and thrived. Ian scarcely knew how powerful had become the feeling between them. He only realized that delight which comes from working with another for a cherished cause, the goal of one's life, which has such deeper significance when the partner in the struggle is a woman. They both experienced that most seductive of all influences, a secret knowledge and a pact of mutual silence and purpose.

"You trust me now?" Jasmine asked at last one day, when she had been able to assure Ian that the end was very near, that M. Mennaval had turned his face from Slavonia, and had carried his government with him—almost. In the heir-apparent to the throne of Moravia, whose influence with the Moravian Prime Minister was considerable, there still remained one obdurate element; but Ian's triumph only lacked the removal of this one obstructive factor, and thereafter England would be secure from foreign attack, if war came in South Africa. In that case Ian's career might culminate at the head of the Foreign Office itself, or as representative of the throne in India, if he chose that splendid sphere.

"You do trust me, Ian?" Jasmine repeated, with a wistfulness as near reality as her own deceived soul could permit.

With a sincerity as deep as one can have who embarks on enterprises in which one regrets the means in contemplation of the end, Ian replied:

"Yes, yes, I trust you, Jasmine, as I used to do when I was twenty and you were five. You have brought back the boy in me. All the dreams of youth are in my heart again, all the glow of the distant sky of hope. I feel as though I lived upon a hill-top, under some greenwood tree, and—"

"And 'sported with Amaryllis in the shade,'" she broke in with a little laugh of triumph, her eyes brighter than he had ever seen them. They were glowing with a fire of excitement which was like a fever devouring the spirit, with little dark, flying banners of fate or tragedy behind.

Strange that he caught the inner meaning of it as he looked into her eyes now. In the depths of those eyes, where long ago he had drowned his spirit, it was as though he saw an army of reckless battalions marching to a great battle; but behind all were the black wings of vultures—pinions of sorrow following the gay brigades. Even as he gazed at her, something ominous and threatening caught his heart, and, with the end of his great enterprise in sight, a black premonition smothered him.

But with a smile he said: "Well, it does look as though we are near the end of the journey."

"And 'journeys end in lovers' meeting,'" she whispered softly, lowered her eyes, and then raised them again to his.

The light in them blinded him. Had he not always loved her—before any one came, before Rudyard came, before the world knew her? All that he had ever felt in the vanished days rushed upon him with intolerable force. Through his life-work, through his ambition, through helping him as no one else could have done at the time of crisis, she had reached the farthest confines of his nature. She had woven, thread by thread, the magic carpet of that secret companionship by which the best as the worst of souls are sometimes carried into a land enchanted—

for a brief moment, before Fate stoops down and hangs a veil of plague over the scene of beauty, passion, and madness.

Her eyes, full of liquid fire, met his. They half closed as her body swayed slightly towards him.

With a cry, almost rough in its intensity, he caught her in his arms and buried his face in the soft harvest of her hair. "Jasmine—Jasmine, my love!" he murmured.

Suddenly she broke from him. "Oh no—oh no, Ian! The work is not done. I can't take my pay before I have earned it—such pay—such pay."

He caught her hands and held them fast. "Nothing can alter what is. It stands. Whatever the end, whatever happens to the thing I want to do, I—"

He drew her closer.

"You say this before we know what Moravia will do; you—oh, Ian, tell me it is not simply gratitude, and because I tried to help you; not only because—"

He interrupted her with a passionate gesture. "It belonged at first to what you were doing for me. Now it is by itself, that which, for good or ill, was to be between you and me—the foreordained thing."

She drew back her head with a laugh of vanity and pride and bursting joy. "Ah, it doesn't matter now!" she said. "It doesn't matter."

He looked at her questioningly.

"Nothing matters now," she repeated, less enigmatically. She stretched her arms up joyously, radiantly.

"The world well lost!" she cried.

Her reckless mood possessed him also. They breathed that air which intoxicates, before it turns heavy with calamity and stifles the whole being; by which none ever thrived, though many have sought nourishment in daring draughts of it.

"The world well lost!" he repeated; and his lips sought hers.

Her determined patience had triumphed. Hour by hour, by being that to his plans, to his work of life, which no one else could be, she had won back what she had lost when the Rand had emptied into her lap its millions, at the bidding of her material soul. With infinite tact and skill she had accomplished her will. The man she had lost was hers again. What it must mean, what it must do, what price must be paid for this which her spirit willed had never yet been estimated. But her will had been supreme, and she took all out of the moment which was possible to mortal pleasure.

Like the Columbus, however, who plants his flag upon the cliffs of a new land, and then, leaving his vast prize unharvested, retreats upon the sea by which he came, so Ian suddenly realized that here was no abiding-place for his love. It was no home for his faith, for those joys which the sane take gladly, when it is right to take them, and the mad long for and die for when their madness becomes unbearable.

A cloud suddenly passed over him, darkened his eyes, made his bones like water. For, whatever might come, he knew in his heart of hearts that the "old paths" were the only paths which he could tread in peace—or tread at all without the ruin of all he had slowly builded.

Jasmine, however, did not see his look or realize the sudden physical change which passed over him, leaving him cold and numbed; for a servant now entered with a note.

Seeing the handwriting on the envelope, with an exclamation of excitement and surprise, Jasmine tore the letter open. One glance was sufficient.

"Moravia is ours—ours, Ian!" she cried, and thrust the letter into his hands.

> "Dearest lady," it ran, "the Crown has intervened successfully. The Heir Apparent has been set aside. The understanding may now be ratified. May I dine with you to-night?
>
> > Yours,
> >
> > M.

> "P.S.—You are the first to know, but I have also sent a note to our young friend, Ian Stafford. Mais, he cannot say, 'Alone I did it.'
>
> > M.

"Thank God—thank God, for England!" said Ian solemnly, the greater thing in him deeply stirred. "Now let war come, if it must; for we can do our work without interference."

"Thank God," he repeated, fervently, and the light in his eyes was clearer and burned brighter than the fire which had filled them during the past few moments.

Then he clasped her in his arms again.

As Ian drove swiftly in a hansom to the Foreign Office, his brain putting in array and reviewing the acts which must flow from this international agreement now made possible, the note Mennaval had written Jasmine flashed before his eyes: "Dearest lady. . . May I dine with you to-night? . . . M."

His face flushed. There was something exceedingly familiar—more in the tone of the words than the words themselves—which irritated and humiliated him. What she had done for him apparently warranted this intimate, self-assured tone on the part of Mennaval, the philanderer. His pride smarted. His rose of triumph had its thorns.

A letter from Mennaval was at the Foreign Office awaiting him. He carried it to the Prime Minister, who read it with grave satisfaction.

"It is just in time, Stafford," he remarked. "You ran it close. We will clinch it instantly. Let us have the code."

As the Prime Minister turned over the pages of the code, he said, dryly: "I hear from Pretoria, through Mr. Byng, that President Kruger may send the ultimatum tomorrow. I fear he will have the laugh on us, for ours is not ready. We have to make sure of this thing first. . . I wonder how Landrassy will take it."

He chuckled deeply. "Landrassy made a good fight, but you made a better one, Stafford. I shouldn't wonder if you got on in diplomacy," he added, with quizzical humour. . . "Ah, here is the code! Now to clinch it all before Oom Paul's challenge arrives."

XVI

The Coming of the Baas

The Baas—where the Baas?"

Barry Whalen turned with an angry snort to the figure in the doorway. "Here's the sweet Krool again," he said. "Here's the faithful, loyal offspring of the Vaal and the karoo, the bulwark of the Baas. . . For God's sake smile for once in your life!" he growled with an oath, and, snatching up a glass of whiskey and water, threw the contents at the half-caste.

Krool did not stir, and some of the liquid caught him in the face. Slowly he drew out an old yellow handkerchief and wiped his cheeks, his eyes fixed with a kind of impersonal scrutiny on Barry Whalen and the scene before him.

The night was well forward, and an air of recklessness and dissipation pervaded this splendid room in De Lancy Scovel's house. The air was thick with tobacco-smoke, trays were scattered about, laden with stubs of cigars and ashes, and empty and half-filled glasses were everywhere. Some of the party had already gone, their gaming instinct satisfied for the night, their pockets lighter than when they came; and the tables where they had sat were in a state of disorder more suggestive of a "dive" than of the house of one who lived in Grosvenor Square.

No servant came to clear away the things. It was a rule of the establishment that at midnight the household went to bed, and the host and his guests looked after themselves thereafter. The friends of De Lancy Scovel called him "Cupid," because of his cherubic face, but he was more gnome than cherub at heart. Having come into his fortune by being a henchman to abler men than himself, he was almost over-zealous to retain it, knowing that he could never get it again; yet he was hospitable with the income he had to spend. He was the Beau Brummel of that coterie which laid the foundation of prosperity on the Rand; and his house was a marvel of order and crude elegance— save when he had his roulette and poker parties, and then it was the shambles of murdered niceties. Once or twice a week his friends met here; and it was not mendaciously said that small fortunes were lost and won within these walls "between drinks."

The critical nature of things on the Rand did not lessen the gaming or the late hours, the theatrical entertainments and social functions at which Al'mah or another sang at a fabulous fee; or from which a dancer took away a pocketful of gold—partly fee. Only a few of all the group, great and small, kept a quiet pace and cherished their nerves against possible crisis or disaster; and these were consumed by inward anxiety, because all the others looked to them for a lead, for policy, for the wise act and the manoeuvre that would win.

Rudyard Byng was the one person who seemed equally compacted of both elements. He was a powerful figure in the financial inner circle; but he was one of those who frequented De Lancy Scovel's house; and he had, in his own house, a roulette-table and a card-room like a banqueting-hall. Wallstein, Wolff, Barry Whalen, Fleming, Hungerford, Reuter, and the others of the inner circle he laughed at in a good-natured way for coddling themselves, and called them—not without some truth—valetudinarians. Indeed, the hard life of the Rand in the early days, with the bad liqueur and the high veld air, had brought to most of the Partners inner physical troubles of some kind; and their general abstention was not quite voluntary moral purpose.

Of them all, except De Lancy Scovel, Rudyard was most free from any real disease or physical weakness which could call for the care of a doctor. With a powerful constitution, he had kept his general health fairly, though strange fits of depression had consumed him of late, and the old strong spring and resilience seemed going, if not gone, from his mind and body. He was not that powerful virile animal of the day when he caught Al'mah in his arms and carried her off the stage at Covent Garden. He was vaguely conscious of the great change in him, and Barry Whalen, who, with all his faults, would have gone to the gallows for him, was ever vividly conscious of it, and helplessly resented the change. At the time of the Jameson Raid Rudyard Byng had gripped the situation with skill, decision, and immense resource, giving as much help to the government of the day as to his colleagues and all British folk on the Rand.

But another raid was nearing, a raid upon British territory this time. The Rand would be the centre of a great war; and Rudyard Byng was not the man he had been, in spite of his show of valour and vigour at the Glencader Mine. Indeed, that incident had shown a certain physical degeneracy—he had been too slow in recovering from the few bad hours spent in the death-trap. The government at Whitehall still consulted him, still relied upon his knowledge and his natural tact; but secret as his conferences were with the authorities, they were not so secret that criticism was not viciously at work. Women jealous of Jasmine, financiers envious of Rudyard, Imperial politicians resentful of his influence, did their best to present him in the worst light possible. It was more than whispered that he sat too long over his wine, and that his desire for fiery liquid at other than meal-times was not in keeping with the English climate, but belonged to lands of drier weather and more absorptive air.

"What damned waste!" was De Lancy Scovel's attempt at wit as Krool dried his face and put the yellow handkerchief back into his pocket. The others laughed idly and bethought themselves of their own glasses, and the croupier again set the ball spinning and drew their eyes.

"Faites vos jeux!" the croupier called, monotonously, and the jingle of coins followed.

"The Baas—where the Baas?" came again the harsh voice from the doorway.

"Gone—went an hour ago," said De Lancy Scovel, coming forward. "What is it, Krool?"

"The Baas—"

"The Baas!" mocked Barry Whalen, swinging round again. "The Baas is gone to find a rope to tie Oom Paul to a tree, as Oom Paul tied you at Lichtenburg."

Slowly Krool's eyes went round the room, and then settled on Barry Whalen's face with owl-like gravity. "What the Baas does goes good," he said. "When the Baas ties, Alles zal recht kom."

He turned away now with impudent slowness, then suddenly twisted his body round and made a grimace of animal-hatred at Barry Whalen, his teeth showing like those of a wolf.

"The Baas will live long as he want," he added, "but Oom Paul will have your heart—and plenty more," he added, malevolently, and moved into the darkness without, closing the door behind him.

A shudder passed through the circle, for the uncanny face and the weird utterance had the strange reality of fate. A gloom fell on the gamblers suddenly, and they slowly drew into a group, looking half furtively at one another.

The wheel turned on the roulette-table, the ball clattered.

"Rien ne va plus!" called the croupier; but no coins had fallen on the green cloth, and the wheel stopped spinning for the night, as though by common consent.

"Krool will murder you some day, Barry," said Fleming, with irritation. "What's the sense in saying things like that to a servant?"

"How long ago did Rudyard leave?" asked De Lancy Scovel, curiously. "I didn't see him go. He didn't say good-night to me. Did he to you—to any of you?"

"Yes, he said to me he was going," rejoined Barry Whalen.

"And to me," said Melville, the Pole, who in the early days on the Rand had been a caterer. His name then had been Joseph Sobieski, but this not fitting well with the English language, he had searched the directory of London till he found the impeachably English combination of Clifford Melville. He had then cut his hair and put himself into the hands of a tailor in Conduit Street, and they had turned him into— what he was.

"Yes, Byng thed good-night to me—deah old boy," he repeated. "'I'm so damned thleepy, and I have to be up early in the morning,' he thed to me."

"Byng's example's good enough. I'm off," said Fleming, stretching up his arms and yawning.

"Byng ought to get up earlier in the morning—much earlier," interposed De Lancy Scovel, with a meaning note in his voice.

"Why?" growled out Barry Whalen.

"He'd see the Outlander early-bird after the young domestic worm," was the slow reply.

For a moment a curious silence fell upon the group. It was as though some one had heard what had been said—some one who ought not to have heard.

That is exactly what had happened. Rudyard had not gone home. He had started to do so; but, remembering that he had told Krool to come at twelve o'clock if any cables arrived, that he might go himself to the cable-office, if necessary, and reply, he passed from the hallway into a little room off the card-room, where there was a sofa, and threw himself down to rest and think. He knew that the crisis in South Africa must come within a few hours; that Oom Paul would present an ultimatum before the British government was ready to act; and that preparations must be made on the morrow to meet all chances and consequences. Preparations there had been, but conditions altered from day to day, and what had been arranged yesterday morning required modification this evening.

He was not heedless of his responsibilities because he was at the gaming-table; but these were days when he could not bear to be alone.

Yet he could not find pleasure in the dinner-parties arranged by Jasmine, though he liked to be with her—liked so much to be with her, and yet wondered how it was he was not happy when he was beside her. This night, however, he had especially wished to be alone with her, to dine with her a deux, and he had been disappointed to find that she had arranged a little dinner and a theatre-party. With a sigh he had begged her to arrange her party without him, and, in unusual depression, he had joined "the gang," as Jasmine called it, at De Lancy Scovel's house.

Here he moved in a kind of gloom, and had a feeling as though he were walking among pitfalls. A dread seemed to descend upon him and deaden his natural buoyancy. At dinner he was fitful in conversation, yet inclined to be critical of the talk around him. Upon those who talked excitedly of war and its consequences, with perverse spirit he fell like a sledge-hammer, and proved their information or judgment wrong. Then, again, he became amiable and almost sentimental in his attitude toward them all, gripping the hands of two or three with a warmth which more than surprised them. It was as though he was subconsciously aware of some great impending change. It may be there whispered through the clouded space that lies between the dwelling-house of Fate and the place where a man's soul lives the voice of that Other Self, which every man has, warning him of darkness, or red ruin, or a heartbreak coming on.

However that may be, he had played a good deal during the evening, had drunk more than enough brandy and soda, had then grown suddenly heavy-hearted and inert. At last he had said good-night, and had fallen asleep in the little dark room adjoining the card-room.

Was it that Other Self which is allowed to come to us as our trouble or our doom approaches, who called sharply in his ear as De Lancy Scovel said, "Byng ought to get up earlier in the morning—much earlier."

Rudyard wakened upon the words without stirring—just a wide opening of the eyes and a moveless body. He listened with, as it were, a new sense of hearing, so acute, so clear, that it was as though his friends talked loudly in his very ears.

"He'd see the Outlander early-bird after the young domestic worm."

His heart beat so loud that it seemed his friends must hear it, in the moment's silence following these suggestive words.

"Here, there's enough of this," said Barry Whalen, sharply, upon the stillness. "It's nobody's business, anyhow. Let's look after ourselves, and we'll have enough to do, or I don't know any of us."

"But it's no good pretending," said Fleming. "There isn't one of us but 'd put ourselves out a great deal for Byng. It isn't human nature to sit still and do naught, and say naught, when things aren't going right for him in the place where things matter most.

"Can't he see? Doesn't he see—anything?" asked a little wizened lawyer, irritably, one who had never been married, the solicitor of three of their great companies.

"See—of course he doesn't see. If he saw, there'd be hell—at least," replied Barry Whalen, scornfully.

"He's as blind as a bat," sighed Fleming.

"He got into the wrong garden and picked the wrong flower—wrong for him," said another voice. "A passion-flower, not the flower her name is," added De Lancy Scovel, with a reflective cynicism.

"They they there's no doubt about it—she's throwing herself away. Ruddy isn't in it, deah old boy, so they they," interposed Clifford Melville, alias Joseph Sobieski of Posen. "Diplomathy is all very well, but thith kind of diplomathy is not good for the thoul." He laughed as only one of his kidney can laugh.

Upon the laugh there came a hoarse growl of anger. Barry Whalen was standing above Mr. Clifford Melville with rage in every fibre, threat in every muscle.

"Shut up—curse you, Sobieski! It's for us, for any and every one, to cut the throats of anybody that says a word against her. We've all got to stand together. Byng forever, is our cry, and Byng's wife is Byng—before the world. We've got to help him—got to help him, I say."

"Well, you've got to tell him first. He's got to know it first," interposed Fleming; "and it's not a job I'm taking on. When Byng's asleep he takes a lot of waking, and he's asleep in this thing."

"And the world's too wide awake," remarked De Lancy Scovel, acidly. "One way or another Byng's got to be waked. It's only him can put it right."

No one spoke for a moment, for all saw that Barry Whalen was about to say something important, coming forward to the table impulsively for the purpose, when a noise from the darkened room beyond fell upon the silence.

De Lancy Scovel heard, Fleming heard, others heard, and turned towards the little room. Sobieski touched Barry Whalen's arm, and they all stood waiting while a hand slowly opened wide the door of the little room, and, white with a mastered agitation, Byng appeared.

For a moment he looked them all full in the face, yet as though he did not see them; and then, without a word, as they stepped aside to make way for him, he passed down the room to the outer hallway.

At the door he turned and looked at them again. Scorn, anger, pride, impregnated with a sense of horror, were in his face. His white lips opened to speak, but closed again, and, turning, he stepped out of their sight.

No one followed. They knew their man.

"My God, how he hates us!" said Barry Whalen, and sank into a chair at the table, with his head between his hands.

The cheeks of the little wizened lawyer glistened with tears, and De Lancy Scovel threw open a window and leaned out, looking into the night remorsefully.

XVII

Is There No Help for these Things?

Slowly, heavily, like one drugged, Rudyard Byng made his way through the streets, oblivious of all around him. His brain was like some engine pounding at high pressure, while all his body was cold and lethargic. His anger at those he left behind was almost madness, his humiliation was unlike anything he had ever known. In one sense he was not a man of the world. All his thoughts and moods and habits had been essentially primitive, even in the high social and civilized surroundings of his youth; and when he went to South Africa, it was to come into his own—the large, simple, rough, adventurous life. His powerful and determined mind was confined in its scope to the big essential things. It had a rare political adroitness, but it had little intellectual subtlety. It had had no preparation for the situation now upon him, and its accustomed capacity was suddenly paralyzed. Like some huge ship staggered by the sea, it took its punishment with heavy, sullen endurance. Socially he had never, as it were, seen through a ladder; and Jasmine's almost uncanny brilliance of repartee and skill in the delicate contest of the mind had ever been a wonder to him, though less so of late than earlier in their married life. Perhaps this was because his senses were more used to it, more blunted; or was it because something had gone from her—that freshness of mind and body, that resilience of temper and spirit, without which all talk is travail and weariness? He had never thought it out, though he was dimly conscious of some great loss—of the light gone from the evening sky.

Yes, it was always in the evening that he had most longed to see "his girl"; when the day's work was done; when the political and financial stress had subsided; or when he had abstracted himself from it all and turned his face towards home. For the big place in Park Lane had really been home to him, chiefly because, or alone because, Jasmine had made it what it was; because in every room, in every corner, was the product of her taste and design. It had been home because it was associated with her. But of late ever since his five months' visit to South Africa without her the year before—there had come a change, at first almost imperceptible, then broadening and deepening.

At first it had vexed and surprised him; but at length it had become a feeling natural to, and in keeping with, a scheme of life in which they saw little of each other, because they saw so much of other people. His primitive soul had rebelled against it at first, not bitterly, but confusedly; because he knew that he did not know why it was; and he thought that if he had patience he would come to understand it in time. But the understanding did not come, and on that ominous, prophetic day before they went to Glencader, the day when Ian Stafford had dined with Jasmine alone after their meeting in Regent Street, there had been a wild, aching protest against it all. Not against Jasmine—he did not blame her; he only realized that she was different from what he had thought she was; that they were both different from what they had been; and that—the light had gone from the evening sky.

But from first to last he had always trusted her. It had never crossed his mind, when she "made up" to men in her brilliant, provoking, intoxicating way, that there was any lack of loyalty to him. It simply never crossed his mind. She was his wife, his girl, his flower which he had plucked; and there it was, for the universe to see, for the universe to heed as a matter of course. For himself, since he had married her, he had never thought of another woman for an instant, except either to admire or to criticize her; and his criticism was, as Jasmine had said, "infantile." The sum of it was, he was married to the woman of his choice, she was married to the man of her choice; and there it was, there it was, a great, eternal, settled fact. It was not a thing for speculation or doubt or reconsideration.

Always, when he had been troubled of late years, his mind had involuntarily flown to South Africa, as a bird flies to its nest in the distant trees for safety, from the spoiler or from the storm. And now, as he paced the streets with heavy, almost blundering tread,—so did the weight of slander drag him down—his thoughts suddenly saw a picture which had gone deep down into his soul in far-off days. It was after a struggle with Lobengula, when blood had been shed and lives lost, and the backbone of barbarism had been broken south of the Zambesi for ever and ever and ever. He had buried two companions in arms whom he had loved in that way which only those know who face danger on the plain, by the river, in the mountain, or on the open road together. After they had been laid to rest in the valley where the great baboons came down to watch the simple cortege pass, where a stray lion stole across the path leading to the grave, he had gone on alone to a spot in the Matoppos, since made famous and sacred.

Where John Cecil Rhodes sleeps on that high plateau of convex hollow stone, with the great natural pillars standing round like sentinels, and all the rugged unfinished hills tumbling away to an unpeopled silence, he came that time to rest his sorrowing soul. The woods, the wild animal life, had been left behind, and only a peaceful middle world between God and man greeted his stern eyes.

Now, here in London, at that corner where the lonely white statue stands by Londonderry House, as he moved in a dream of pain, with vast weights like giant manacles hampering every footstep, inwardly raging that into his sweet garden of home the vile elements of slander had been thrown, yet with a terrible and vague fear that something had gone terribly wrong with him, that far-off day spent at the Matoppos flashed upon his sight.

Through streets upon streets he had walked, far, far out of his way, subconsciously giving himself time to recover before he reached his home; until the green quiet of Hyde Park, the soft depths of its empty spaces, the companionable and commendable trees, greeted his senses. Then, here, suddenly there swam before his eyes the bright sky over those scarred and jagged hills beyond the Matoppos, purple and grey, and red and amethyst and gold, and his soul's sight went out over the interminable distance of loneliness and desolation which only ended where the world began again, the world of fighting men. He saw once more that tumbled waste of primeval creation, like a crazed sea agitated by some Horror underneath, and suddenly transfixed in its plunging turmoil—a frozen concrete sorrow, with all active pain gone. He heard the loud echo of his feet upon that hollow plateau of rock, with convex skin of stone laid upon convex skin, and then suddenly the solid rock which gave no echo under his tread, where Rhodes lies buried. He saw all at once, in the shining horizon at different points, black, angry, marauding storms arise and roar and burst: while all the time above his head there was nothing but sweet sunshine, into which the mists of the distant storms drifted, and rainbows formed above him. Upon those hollow rocks the bellow of the storms was like the rumbling of the wheels of a million gun-carriages; and yet high overhead there were only the bright sun and faint drops of rain falling like mystic pearls.

And then followed—he could hear it again, so plainly, as his eyes now sought the friendly shades of the beeches and the elms yonder in Hyde Park!—upon the air made denser by the storm, the call of a lonely bird from one side of the valley. The note was deep and strong and clear, like the bell-bird of the Australian salt-bush plains beyond the Darling River, and it rang out across the valley, as though a soul desired its mate; and then was still. A moment, and there came across the valley from the other side, stealing deep sweetness from the hollow rocks, the answer of the bird which had heard her master's call. Answering, she called too, the viens ici of kindred things; and they came nearer and nearer and nearer, until at last their two voices were one.

In that wild space there had been worked out one of the great wonders of creation, and under the dim lamps of Park Lane, in his black, shocked mood, Rudyard recalled it all by no will of his own. Upon his eye and brain the picture had been registered, and in its appointed time, with an automatic suggestion of which he was ignorant and innocent, it came to play its part and to transform him.

The thought of it all was like a cool hand laid upon his burning brow. It gave him a glimpse of the morning of life.

The light was gone from the evening sky: but was it gone forever?

As he entered his house now he saw upon a Spanish table in the big hall a solitary bunch of white roses—a touch of simplicity in an area of fine artifice. Regarding it a moment, black thoughts receded, and choosing a flower from the vase he went slowly up the stairs to Jasmine's room.

He would give her this rose as the symbol of his faith and belief in her, and then tell her frankly what he had heard at De Lancy Scovel's house.

For the moment it did not occur to him that she might not be at home. It gave him a shock when he opened the door and found her room empty. On her bed, like a mesh of white clouds, lay the soft linen and lace and the delicate clothes of the night; and by the bed were her tiny blue slippers to match the blue dressing-gown. Some gracious things for morning wear hung over a chair; an open book with a little cluster of violets and a tiny mirror lay upon a table beside a sofa; a footstool was placed at a considered angle for her well-known seat on the sofa where the soft-blue lamp-shade threw the light upon her book; and a little desk with dresden-china inkstand and penholder had little pockets of ribbon-tied letters and bills—even business had an air of taste where Jasmine was. And there on a table beside her bed was a large silver-framed photograph of himself turned at an angle toward the pillow where she would lay her head.

How tender and delicate and innocent it all was! He looked round the room with new eyes, as though seeing everything for the first time. There was another photograph of himself on her dressing-table. It had no companion there; but on another table near were many photographs; four of women, the rest of men: celebrities, old friends like Ian Stafford—and M. Mennaval.

His face hardened. De Lancy Scovel's black slander swept through his veins like fire again, his heart came up in his throat, his fingers clinched.

Presently, as he stood with clouded face and mist in his eyes, Jasmine's maid entered, and, surprised at seeing him, retreated again, but her eyes fastened for a moment strangely on the white rose he held in his hand. Her glance drew his own attention to it again. Going over to the gracious and luxurious bed, with its blue silk canopy, he laid the white rose on her pillow. Somehow it was more like an offering to the dead than a lover's tribute to the living. His eyes were fogged, his lips were set. But all he was then in mind and body and soul he laid with the rose on her pillow.

As he left the rose there, his eyes wandered slowly over this retreat of rest and sleep: white robe-de-nuit, blue silk canopy, blue slippers, blue dressing-gown—all blue, the colour in which he had first seen her.

Slowly he turned away at last and went to his own room. But the picture followed him. It kept shining in his eyes. Krool's face suddenly darkened it.

"You not ring, Baas," Krool said.

Without a word Rudyard waved him away, a sudden and unaccountable fury in his mind. Why did the sight of Krool vex him so?

"Come back," he said, angrily, before the door of the bedroom closed.

Krool returned.

"Weren't there any cables? Why didn't you come to Mr. Scovel's at midnight, as I told you?"

"Baas, I was there at midnight, but they all say you come home, Baas. There the cable—two." He pointed to the dressing-table.

Byng snatched them, tore them open, read them.

One had the single word, "Tomorrow." The other said, "Prepare." The code had been abandoned. Tragedy needs few words.

They meant that to-morrow Kruger's ultimatum would be delivered and that the worst must be faced.

He glanced at the cables in silence, while Krool watched him narrowly, covertly, with a depth of purpose which made his face uncanny.

"That will do, Krool; wake me at seven," he said, quietly, but with suppressed malice in his tone.

Why was it that at that moment he could, with joy, have taken Krool by the neck and throttled him? All the bitterness, anger and rage that he had felt an hour ago concentrated themselves upon Krool—without reason, without cause. Or was it that his deeper Other Self had whispered something to his mind about Krool—something terrible and malign?

In this new mood he made up his mind that he would not see Jasmine till the morning. How late she was! It was one o'clock, and yet this was not the season. She had not gone to a ball, nor were these the months of late parties.

As he tossed in his bed and his head turned restlessly on his pillow, Krool's face kept coming before him, and it was the last thing he saw, ominous and strange, before he fell into a heavy but troubled sleep.

Perhaps the most troubled moment of the night came an hour after he went to bed.

Then it was that a face bent over him for a minute, a fair face, with little lines contracting the ripe lips, which were redder than usual, with eyes full of a fevered brightness. But how harmonious and sweetly ordered was the golden hair above! Nothing was gone from its lustre, nothing robbed it of its splendour. It lay upon her forehead like a crown. In its richness it seemed a little too heavy for the tired face beneath, almost too imperial for so slight and delicate a figure.

Rudyard stirred in his sleep, murmuring as she leaned over him; and his head fell away from her hand as she stretched out her fingers with a sudden air of pity—of hopelessness, as it might seem from her look. His face restlessly turned to the wall—a vexed, stormy, anxious face and head, scarred by the whip of that overlord more cruel and tyrannous than Time, the Miserable Mind.

She drew back with a little shudder. "Poor Ruddy!" she said, as she had said that evening when Ian Stafford came to her after the estranging and scornful years, and she had watched Rudyard leave her—to her fate and to her folly.

"Poor Ruddy!"

With a sudden frenzied motion of her hands she caught her breath, as though some pain had seized her. Her eyes almost closed with the shame that reached out from her heart, as though to draw the veil of her eyelids over the murdered thing before her—murdered hope, slaughtered peace: the peace of that home they had watched burn slowly before their eyes in the years which the locust had eaten.

Which the locust had eaten—yes, it was that. More than once she had heard Rudyard tell of a day on the veld when the farmer surveyed his abundant fields with joy, with the gay sun flaunting it above; and suddenly there came a white cloud out of the west, which made a weird humming, a sinister sound. It came with shining scales glistening in the light and settled on the land acre upon acre, morgen upon morgen; and when it rose again the fields, ready for the harvest, were like a desert— the fields which the locust had eaten. So had the years been, in which Fortune had poured gold and opportunity and unlimited choice into her lap. She had used them all; but she had forgotten to look for the Single Secret, which, like a key, unlocks all doors in the House of Happiness.

"Poor Ruddy!" she said, but even as she said it for the second time a kind of anger seemed to seize her.

"Oh, you fool—you fool!" she whispered, fiercely. "What did you know of women! Why didn't you make me be good? Why didn't you master me—the steel on the wrist—the steel on the wrist!"

With a little burst of misery and futile rage she went from the room, her footsteps uneven, her head bent. One of the open letters she carried dropped from her hand onto the floor of the hall outside. She did not notice it. But as she passed inside her door a shadowy figure at the end of the hall watched her, saw the letter drop, and moved stealthily forward towards it. It was Krool.

How heavy her head was! Her worshipping maid, near dead with fatigue, watched her furtively, but avoided the eyes in the mirror which had a half-angry look, a look at once disturbed and elated, reckless and pitiful. Lablanche was no reader of souls, but there was something here beyond the usual, and she moved and worked with unusual circumspection and lightness of touch. Presently she began to unloose the coils of golden hair; but Jasmine stopped her with a gesture of weariness.

"No, don't," she said. "I can't stand your touch tonight, Lablanche. I'll do the rest myself. My head aches so. Good-night."

"I will be so light with it, madame," Lablanche said, protestingly.

"No, no. Please go. But the morning, quite early."

"The hour, madame?"

"When the letters come, as soon as the letters come, Lablanche—the first post. Wake me then."

She watched the door close, then turned to the mirror in front of her and looked at herself with eyes in which brooded a hundred thoughts and feelings: thoughts contradictory, feelings opposed, imaginings conflicting, reflections that changed with each moment; and all under the spell of a passion which had become in the last few hours the most powerful influence her life had ever known. Right or wrong, and it was wrong, horribly wrong; wise or unwise, and how could the wrong be wise! she knew she was under a spell more tyrannous than death, demanding more sacrifices than the gods of Hellas.

Self-indulgent she had been, reckless and wilful and terribly modern, taking sweets where she found them. She had tried to squeeze the orange dry, in the vain belief that Wealth and Beauty can take what they want, when they want it, and that happiness will come by purchase; only to find one day that the thing you have bought, like a slave that revolts, stabs you in your sleep, and you wake with wide-eyed agony only to die, or to live—with the light gone from the evening sky.

Suddenly, with the letters in her hand with which she had entered the room, she saw the white rose on her pillow. Slowly she got up from the dressing-table and went over to the bed in a hushed kind of way. With a strange, inquiring, half-shrinking look she regarded the flower. One white rose. It was not there when she left. It had been brought from the hall below, from the great bunch on the Spanish table. Those white roses, this white rose, had come from one who, selfish as he was, knew how to flatter a woman's vanity. From that delicate tribute of flattery and knowledge Rudyard had taken this flowering stem and brought it to her pillow.

It was all too malevolently cynical. Her face contracted in pain and shame. She had a soul to which she had never given its chance. It had never bloomed. Her abnormal wilfulness, her insane love of pleasure, her hereditary impulses, had been exercised at the expense of the great thing in her, the soul so capable of memorable and beautiful deeds.

As she looked at the flower, a sense of the path by which she had come, of what she had left behind, of what was yet to chance, shuddered into her heart.

That a flower given by Adrian Fellowes should be laid upon her pillow by her husband, by Rudyard Byng, was too ghastly or too devilishly humorous for words; and both aspects of the thing came to her. Her face became white, and almost mechanically she put the letters she held on a writing-table near; then coming to the bed again she looked at the rose with a kind of horror. Suddenly, however, she caught it up, and bursting into a laugh which was shrill and bitter she threw it across the room. Still laughing hysterically, with her golden hair streaming about her head, folding her round like a veil which reached almost to her ankles, she came back to the chair at the dressing-table and sat down.

Slowly drawing the wonderful soft web of hair over her shoulders, she began to weave it into one wide strand, which grew and grew in length till it was like a great rope of spun gold. Inch by inch, foot by foot it grew, until at last it lay coiled in her lap like a golden serpent, with a kind of tension which gave it life, such as Medusa's hair must have known as the serpent-life entered into it. There is—or was—in Florence a statue of Medusa, seated, in her fingers a strand of her hair, which is beginning to coil and bend and twist before her horror-stricken eyes; and this statue flashed before Jasmine's eyes as she looked at the loose ends of gold falling beyond the blue ribbon with which she had tied the shining rope.

With the mad laughter of a few moments before still upon her lips, she held the flying threads in her hand, and so strained was her mind that it would not have caused her surprise if they had wound round her fingers or given forth forked tongues. She laughed again—a low and discordant laugh it was now.

"Such imaginings—I think I must be mad," she murmured.

Then she leaned her elbows on the dressing-table and looked at herself in the glass.

"Am I not mad?" she asked herself again. Then there stole across her face a strange, far-away look, bringing a fresh touch of beauty to it, and flooding it for a moment with that imaginative look which had been her charm as a girl, a look of far-seeing and wonder and strange light.

"I wonder—if I had had a mother!" she said, wistfully, her chin in her hand. "If my mother had lived, what would I have been?"

She reached out to a small table near, and took from it a miniature at which she looked with painful longing. "My dear, my very dear, you were so sweet, so good," she said. "Am I your daughter, your own daughter—me? Ah, sweetheart mother, come back to me! For God's sake come—now. Speak to me if you can. Are you so very far away? Whisper—only whisper, and I shall hear.

"Oh, she would, she would, if she could!" her voice wailed, softly. "She would if she could, I know. I was her youngest child, her only little girl. But there is no coming back. And maybe there is no going forth;

only a blackness at the last, when all stops—all stops, for ever and ever and ever, amen! . . . Amen—so be it. Ah, I even can't believe in that! I can't even believe in God and Heaven and the hereafter. I am a pagan, with a pagan's heart and a pagan's ways."

She shuddered again and closed her eyes for a moment. "Ruddy had a glimpse, one glimpse, that day, the day that Ian came back. Ruddy said to me that day, 'If you had lived a thousand years ago you would have had a thousand lovers.' . . . And it is true—by all the gods of all the worlds, it is true. Pleasure, beauty, is all I ever cared for—pleasure, beauty, and the Jasmine-flower. And Ian—and Ian, yes, Ian! I think I had soul enough for one true thing, even if I was not true."

She buried her face in her hands for a moment, as though to hide a great burning.

"But, oh, I wonder if I did ever love Ian, even! I wonder. . . Not then, not then when I deserted him and married Rudyard, but now—now? Do—do I love him even now, as we were to-day with his arms round me, or is it only beauty and pleasure and—me? . . . Are they really happy who believe in God and live like—like her?" She gazed at her mother's portrait again. "Yes, she was happy, but only for a moment, and then she was gone—so soon. And I shall never see her, I who never saw her with eyes that recall. . . And if I could see her, would I? I am a pagan—would I try to be like her, if I could? I never really prayed, because I never truly felt there was a God that was not all space, and that was all soul and understanding. And what is to come of it, or what will become of me? . . . I can't go back, and going on is madness. Yes, yes, it is madness, I know—madness and badness—and dust at the end of it all. Beauty gone, pleasure gone. . . I do not even love pleasure now as I did. It has lost its flavour; and I do not even love beauty as I did. How well I know it! I used to climb hills to see a sunset; I used to walk miles to find the wood anemones and the wild violets; I used to worship a pretty child. . . a pretty child!"

She shrank back in her chair and pondered darkly. "A pretty child. . . Other people's pretty children, and music and art and trees and the sea, and the colours of the hills, and the eyes of wild animals. . . and a pretty child. I wonder, I wonder if—"

But she got no farther with that thought. "I shall hate everything on earth if it goes from me, the beauty of things; and I feel that it is going. The freshness of sense has gone, somehow. I am not stirred as I used to be, not by the same things. If I lose that sense I shall kill myself. Perhaps that would be the easiest way now. Just the overdose of—"

She took a little phial from the drawer of the dressing-table. "Just the tiny overdose and 'good-bye, my lover, good-bye.'" Again that hard little laugh of bitterness broke from her. "Or that needle Mr. Mappin had at Glencader. A thrust of the point, and in an instant gone, and no one to know, no one to discover, no one to add blame to blame, to pile shame upon shame. Just blackness—blackness all at once, and no light or anything any more. The fruit all gone from the trees, the garden all withered, the bower all ruined, the children all dead—the pretty children all dead forever, the pretty children that never were born, that never lived in Jasmine's garden."

As there had come to Rudyard premonition of evil, so to-night, in the hour of triumph, when, beyond peradventure, she had got for Ian Stafford what would make his career great, what through him gave England security in her hour of truth, there came now to her something of the real significance of it all.

She had got what she wanted. Her pride had been appeased, her vanity satisfied, her intellect flattered, her skill approved, and Ian was hers. But the cost?

Words from Swinburne's threnody on Baudelaire came to her mind. How often she had quoted them for their sheer pagan beauty! It was the kind of beauty which most appealed to her, which responded to the element of fatalism in her, the sense of doom always with her since she was a child, in spite of her gaiety, her wit, and her native eloquence. She had never been happy, she had never had a real illusion, never aught save the passion of living, the desire to conquer unrest:

"And now, no sacred staff shall break in blossom,
No choral salutation lure to light
The spirit sick with perfume and sweet night,
And Love's tired eyes and hands and barren bosom.
There is no help for these things, none to mend and none to mar
Not all our songs, oh, friend, can make Death clear or
make Life durable
But still with rose and ivy and wild vine,
And with wild song about this dust of thine,
At least I fill a place where white dreams dwell,
And wreathe an unseen shrine."

"'And Love's tired eyes and hands and barren bosom. . . There is no help for these things, none to mend and none to mar. . .'" A sob rose in her throat. "Oh, the beauty of it, the beauty and the misery and the despair of it!" she murmured.

Slowly she wound and wound the coil of golden hair about her neck, drawing it tighter, fold on fold, tighter and tighter.

"This would be the easiest way—this," she whispered. "By my own hair! Beauty would have its victim then. No one would kiss it any more, because it killed a woman. . . No one would kiss it any more."

She felt the touch of Ian Stafford's lips upon it, she felt his face buried in it. Her own face suffused, then Adrian Fellowes' white rose, which Rudyard had laid upon her pillow, caught her eye where it lay on the floor. With a cry as of a hurt animal she ran to her bed, crawled into it, and huddled down in the darkness, shivering and afraid.

Something had discovered her to herself for the first time. Was it her own soul? Had her Other Self, waking from sleep in the eternal spaces, bethought itself and come to whisper and warn and help? Or was it Penalty, or Nemesis, or that Destiny which will have its toll for all it gives of beauty, or pleasure, or pride, or place, or pageantry?

"Love's tired eyes and hands and barren bosom"—

The words kept ringing in her ears. They soothed her at last into a sleep which brought no peace, no rest or repose.

XVIII

LANDRASSY'S LAST STROKE

Midnight—one o'clock, two o'clock, three o'clock. Big Ben boomed the hours, and from St. James's Palace came the stroke of the quarters, lighter, quicker, almost pensive in tone. From St. James's Street below came no sounds at last. The clatter of the hoofs of horses had ceased, the rumble of drays carrying their night freights, the shouts of the newsboys making sensation out of rumours made in a newspaper office, had died away. Peace came, and a silver moon gave forth a soft light, which embalmed the old thoroughfare, and added a tenderness to its workaday dignity. In only one window was there a light at three o'clock. It was the window of Ian Stafford's sitting-room.

He had not left the Foreign Office till nearly ten o'clock, then had had a light supper at his club, had written letters there, and after a long walk up and down the Mall had, with reluctant feet, gone to his chambers.

The work which for years he had striven to do for England had been accomplished. The Great Understanding was complete. In the words of the secretary of the American Embassy, "Mennaval had delivered the goods," and an arrangement had been arrived at, completed this very night, which would leave England free to face her coming trial in South Africa without fear of trouble on the flank or in the rear.

The key was turned in the lock, and that lock had been the original device and design of Ian Stafford. He had done a great work for civilization and humanity; he had made improbable, if not impossible, a European war. The Kaiser knew it, Franz Joseph knew it, the Czar knew it; the White House knew it, and its master nodded with satisfaction, for John Bull was waking up—"getting a move on." America might have her own family quarrel with John Bull, but when it was John Bull versus the world, not even James G. Blaine would have been prepared to see the old lion too deeply wounded. Even Landrassy, ambassador of Slavonia, had smiled grimly when he met Ian Stafford on the steps of the Moravian Embassy. He was artist enough to appreciate a well-played game, and, in any case, he had had done all that mortal man could in the way of intrigue and tact and device. He had worked the international press as well as it had ever been worked; he had distilled poison here and rosewater there; he had again and again baffled the British Foreign Office, again and again cut the ground from under Ian Stafford's feet; and if he could have staved off the pact, the secret international pact, by one more day, he would have gained the victory for himself, for his country, for the alliance behind him.

One day, but one day, and the world would never have heard of Ian Stafford. England would then have approached her conflict with the cup of trembling at her lips, and there would be a new disposition of power in Europe, a new dominating force in the diplomacy and the relations of the peoples of the world. It was Landrassy's own last battle-field of wit and scheming, of intellect and ambition. If he failed in this, his sun would set soon. He was too old to carry on much longer. He could not afford to wait. He was at the end of his career, and he had meant this victory to be the crown of his long services to Slavonia and the world.

But to him was opposed a man who was at the beginning of his career, who needed this victory to give him such a start as few men get in that field of retarded rewards, diplomacy. It had been a man at the end of the journey, and a man at the beginning, measuring skill, playing as desperate a game as was ever played. If Landrassy won—Europe a red battle-field, England at bay; if Ian Stafford won—Europe at peace, England secure. Ambition and patriotism intermingled, and only He who made human nature knew how much was pure patriotism and how much pure ambition. It was a great stake. On this day of days to Stafford destiny hung shivering, each hour that passed was throbbing with unparalleled anxiety, each minute of it was to be the drum-beat of a funeral march or the note of a Te Deum.

Not more uncertain was the roulette-wheel spinning in De Lancy Scovel's house than the wheel of diplomacy which Ian Stafford had set spinning. Rouge et noire—it was no more, no less. But Ian had won; England had won. Black had been beaten.

Landrassy bowed suavely to Ian as they met outside Mennaval's door in the early evening of this day when the business was accomplished, the former coming out, the latter going in.

"Well, Stafford," Landrassy said in smooth tones and with a jerk of the head backward, "the tables are deserted, the croupier is going home. But perhaps you have not come to play?"

Ian smiled lightly. "I've come to get my winnings—as you say," he retorted.

Landrassy seemed to meditate pensively. "Ah yes, ah yes, but I'm not sure that Mennaval hasn't bolted with the bank and your winnings, too!"

His meaning was clear—and hateful. Before Ian had a chance to reply, Landrassy added in a low, confidential voice, saturated with sardonic suggestion, "To tell you the truth, I had ceased to reckon with women in diplomacy. I thought it was dropped with the Second Empire; but you have started a new dispensation—evidemment, evidemment. Still Mennaval goes home with your winnings. Eh bien, we have to pay for our game! Allons gai!"

Before Ian could reply—and what was there to say to insult couched in such highly diplomatic language?—Landrassy had stepped sedately away, swinging his gold-headed cane and humming to himself.

"Duelling had its merits," Ian said to himself, as soon as he had recovered from the first effect of the soft, savage insolence. "There is no way to deal with our Landrassys except to beat them, as I have done, in the business of life."

He tossed his head with a little pardonable pride, as it were, to soothe his heart, and then went in to Mennaval. There, in the arrangements to be made with Moravia he forgot the galling incident; and for hours afterward it was set aside. When, however, he left his club, his supper over, after scribbling letters which he put in his pocket absent-mindedly, and having completed his work at the Foreign Office, it came back to his mind with sudden and scorching force.

Landrassy's insult to Jasmine rankled as nothing had ever rankled in his mind before, not even that letter which she had written him so long ago announcing her intended marriage to Byng. He was fresh from the first triumph of his life: he ought to be singing with joy, shouting to the four corners of the universe his pride, walking on air, finding the world a good, kind place made especially for him—his oyster to open, his nut which he had cracked; yet here he was fresh from the applause of his chief, with a strange heaviness at his heart, a gloom upon his mind.

Victory in his great fight—and love; he had them both and so he said to himself as he opened the door of his rooms and entered upon their comfort and quiet. He had love, and he had success; and the one had helped to give him the other, helped in a way which was wonderful, and so brilliantly skilful and delicate. As he poured out a glass of water, however, the thought stung him that the nature of the success and its value depended on the nature of the love and its value. As the love was, so was the success, no higher, no different, since the one, in some deep way, begot the other. Yes, it was certain that the thing could not have been done at this time without Jasmine, and if not at this time, then the chances were a thousand to one that it never could be done at any time; for Britain's enemies would be on her back while she would have to fight in South Africa. The result of that would mean a shattered, humiliated land, with a people in pawn to the will of a rising power across the northern sea. That it had been prevented just in the nick of time was due to Jasmine, his fate, the power that must beat in his veins till the end of all things.

Yet what was the end to be? To-day he had buried his face in her wonderful cloud of hair and had kissed her; and with it, almost on the instant, had come the end of his great struggle for England and himself; and for that he was willing to pay any price that time and Nemesis might demand—any price save one.

As he thought of that one price his lips tightened, his brow clouded, his eyes half closed with shame.

Rudyard Byng was his friend, whose bread he had eaten, whom he had known since they were boys at school. He remembered acutely Rudyard's words to him that fateful night when he had dined with Jasmine alone—"You will have much to talk about, to say to each other, such old friends as you are." He recalled how Rudyard had left them, trusting them, happy in the thought that Jasmine would have a pleasant evening with the old friend who had first introduced him to her, and that the old friend would enjoy his eager hospitality. Rudyard had blown his friend's trumpet wherever men would listen to him; had proclaimed Stafford as the coming man: and this was what he had done to Rudyard!

This was what he had done; but what did he propose to do? What of the future? To go on in miserable intrigue, twisting the nature, making demands upon life out of all those usual ways in which walk love and companionship—paths that lead through gardens of poppies, maybe, but finding grey wilderness at the end? Never, never the right to take the loved one by the hand before all world and say: "We two are one, and the reckoning of the world must be made with both." Never to have the right to stand together in pride before the wide-eyed many and say: "See what you choose to see, say what you choose to say, do what you choose to do, we do not care." The open sharing of worldly success; the inner joys which the world may not see—these things could not be for Jasmine and for him.

Yet he loved her. Every fibre in his being thrilled to the thought of her. But as his passion beat like wild music in his veins, a blindness suddenly stole into his sight, and in deep agitation he got up, opened the window, and looked out into the night. For long he stood gazing into the quiet street, and watched a daughter of the night, with dilatory steps and neglected mien, go up towards the more frequented quarter of Piccadilly. Life was grim in so much of it, futile in more, feeble at the best, foolish in the light of a single generation or a single century or a thousand years. It was only reasonable in the vast proportions of eternity. It had only little sips of happiness to give, not long draughts of joy. Who drank deep, long draughts—who of all the men and women he had ever known? Who had had the primrose path without the rain of fire, the cinders beneath the feet, the gins and the nets spread for them?

Yet might it not be that here and there people were permanently happy? And had things been different, might not he and Jasmine have been of the radiant few? He desired her above all things; he was willing to sacrifice all—all for her, if need be; and yet there was that which he could not, would not face. All or nothing—all or nothing. If he must drink of the cup of sorrow and passion mixed, then it would be from the full cup.

With a stifled exclamation he sat down and began to write. Again and again he stopped to think, his face lined and worn and old; then he wrote on and on. Ambition, hope, youth, the Foreign Office, the chancelleries of Europe, the perils of impending war, were all forgotten, or sunk into the dusky streams of subconsciousness. One thought dominated him. He was playing the game that has baffled all men, the game of eluding destiny; and, like all men, he must break his heart in the playing.

"Jasmine," he wrote, "this letter, this first real letter of love which I have ever written you, will tell you how great that love is. It will tell you, too, what it means to me, and what I see before us. To-day I surrendered to you all of me that would be worth your keeping, if it was so that you might take and keep it. When I kissed you, I set the seal upon my eternal offering to you. You have given me success. It is for that I thank you with all my soul, but it is not for that I love you. Love flows from other fountains than gratitude. It rises from the well which has its springs at the beginning of the world, where those beings lived who loved before there were any gods at all, or any faiths, or any truths save the truth of being.

"But it is because what I feel belongs to something in me deeper than I have ever known that, since we parted a few hours ago, I see all in a new light. You have brought to me what perhaps could only have come as it did—through fire and cloud and storm. I did not will it so, indeed, I did not wish it so, as you know; but it came in spite of all. And I shall speak to you of it as to my own soul. I want no illusions, no self-deception, no pretense to be added to my debt to you. With wide-open eyes I want to look at it. I know that this love of mine for you is my fate, the first and the last passion of my soul. And to have known it with all its misery,—for misery there must be; misery, Jasmine, there is—to have known it, to have felt it, the great overwhelming thing, goes far to compensate for all the loss it so terribly exposes. It has brought me, too, the fruit of life's ambition. With the full revelation of all that I feel for you came that which gives me place in the world, confers on me the right to open doors which otherwise were closed to me. You have done this for me, but what have I done for you? One thing at least is forced upon me, which I must do now while I have the sight to see and the mind to understand.

"I cannot go on with things as they are. I cannot face Rudyard and give myself to hourly deception. I think that yesterday, a month ago, I could have done so, but not now. I cannot walk the path which will be paved with things revolting to us both. My love for you, damnable as it would seem in the world's eyes, prevents it. It is not small enough to be sustained or made secure in its furfilment by the devices of intrigue. And I know that if it is so with me, it must be a thousand times so with you. Your beauty would fade and pass under the stress and meanness of it; your heart would reproach me even when you smiled; you would learn to hate me even when you were resting upon my hungry heart. You would learn to loathe the day when you said, Let me help you. Yet, Jasmine, I know that you are mine; that you were mine long ago, even when you did not know, and were captured by opportunity to do what, with me, you felt you could not do. You were captured by it; but it has not proved what it promised. You have not made the best of the power into which you came, and you could not do so, because the spring from which all the enriching waters of married life flow was dry. Poor Jasmine—poor illusion of a wild young heart which reached out for the golden city of the mirage!

"But now. . . Two ways spread out, and only two, and one of these two I must take—for your sake. There is the third way, but I will not take it—for your sake and for my own. I will not walk in it ever. Already my feet are burned by the fiery path, already I am choked by the smoke and the ashes. No. I cannot atone for what has been, but I can try and gather up the chances that are left.

"You must come with me away—away, to start life afresh, somewhere, somehow; or I must go alone on some enterprise from which I shall not return. You cannot bear what is, but, together, having braved the world, we could look into each other's eyes without shrinking, knowing that we had been at least true to each other, true at the last to the thing that binds us, taking what Fate gave without repining, because we had faced all that the world could do against us. It would mean that I should leave diplomacy forever, give up all that so far has possessed me in the business of life; but I should not lament. I have done the one big thing I wanted to do, I have cut a swath in the field. I have made some principalities and powers reckon with me. It may be I have done all I was meant to do in doing that—it may be. In any case, the thing I did would stand as an accomplished work—it would represent one definite and original thing; one piece of work in design all my own, in accomplishment as much yours as mine. . . To go then—together—with only the one big violence to the conventions of the world, and take the law into our own hands? Rudyard, who understands Life's violence, would understand that; what he could never understand would be perpetual artifice, unseemly secretiveness. He himself would have been a great filibuster in the olden days; he would have carried off the wives and daughters of the chiefs and kings he conquered; but he would never have stolen into the secret garden at night and filched with the hand of the sneak-thief—never.

"To go with me—away, and start afresh. There will be always work to do, always suffering humanity to be helped. We should help because we would have suffered, we should try to set right the one great mistake you made in not coming to me and so fulfilling the old promise. To set that error right, even though it be by wronging Rudyard by one great stroke—that is better than hourly wronging him now with no surcease of that wrong. No, no, this cannot go on. You could not have it so. I seem to feel that you are writing to me now, telling me to begone forever, saying that you had given me gifts—success and love; and now to go and leave you in peace.

"Peace, Jasmine, it is that we cry for, pray for, adjure the heavens for in the end. And all this vast, passionate love of mine is the strife of the soul for peace, for fruition.

"That peace we may have in another way: that I should go forever, now, before the terrible bond of habit has done its work, and bound us in chains that never fall, that even remain when love is dead and gone, binding the cold cadre to the living pain. To go now, with something accomplished, and turn my back forever on the world, with one last effort to do the impossible thing for some great cause, and fail and be lost forever—do you not understand? Face it, Jasmine, and try to see it in its true light. . . I have a friend, John Caxton— you know him. He is going to the Antarctic to find the futile thing, but the necessary thing so far as the knowledge of the world is concerned. With him, then, that long quiet and in the far white spaces to find peace—forever.

"You? . . . Ah, Jasmine, habit, the habit of enduring me, is not fixed, and in my exit there would be the agony of the moment, and then the comforting knowledge that I had done my best to set things right. Perhaps it is the one way to set things right; the fairest to you, the kindest, and that which has in it most love. The knowledge of a great love ended—yours and mine—would help you to give what you

can give with fuller soul. And, maybe, to be happy with
Rudyard at the last! Maybe, to be happy with him, without
this wonderful throbbing pulse of being, but with quiet,
and to get a measure of what is due to you in the scheme
of things. Destiny gives us in life so much and no more: to
some a great deal in a little time, to others a little over a great
deal of time, but never the full cup and the shining sky over
long years. One's share small it must be, but one's share!
And it may be, in what has come to-day, in the hour of my
triumph, in the business of life, in the one hour of revealing
love, it may be I have had my share. . . And if that is so, then
peace should be my goal, and peace I can have yonder in the
snows. No one would guess that it was not accident, and I
should feel sure that I had stopped in time to save you from
the worst. But it must be the one or the other.

"The third way I cannot, will not, take, nor would you
take it willingly. It would sear your heart and spirit, it would
spoil all that makes you what you are. Jasmine, once for all I
am your lover and your friend. I give you love and I give you
friendship—whatever comes; always that, always friendship.
Tempus fugit sed amicitia est.

"In my veins is a river of fire, and my heart is wrenched
with pain; but in my soul is that which binds me to you,
together or apart, in life, in death. . . Good-night. . . Good-
morrow.

Your Man,

Ian

"P.S.—I will come for your reply at eleven to-morrow.

Ian

He folded the letter slowly and placed it in an envelope which was
lying loose on the desk with the letters he had written at the Trafalgar
Club, and had forgotten to post. When he had put the letter inside the
envelope and stamped it, he saw that the envelope was one carrying the
mark of the Club. By accident he had brought it with the letters written
there. He hesitated a moment, then refrained from opening the letter
again, and presently went out into the night and posted all his letters.

XIX

To-morrow. . . Prepare!

K rool did not sleep. What he read in a letter he had found in a hallway, what he knew of those dark events in South Africa, now to culminate in a bitter war, and what, with the mysterious psychic instinct of race, he divined darkly and powerfully, all kept his eyes unsleeping and his mind disordered. More than any one, he knew of the inner story of the Baas' vrouw during the past week and years; also he had knowledge of what was soon to empty out upon the groaning earth the entrails of South Africa; but how he knew was not to be discovered. Even Rudyard, who thought he read him like a book, only lived on the outer boundaries of his character. Their alliance was only the durable alliance of those who have seen Death at their door, and together have driven him back.

Barry Whalen had regarded Krool as a spy; all Britishers who came and went in the path to Rudyard's door had their doubts or their dislike of him; and to every servant of the household he was a dark and isolated figure. He never interfered with the acts of his fellow-servants, except in so far as those acts affected his master's comfort; and he paid no attention to their words except where they affected himself.

"When you think it's a ghost, it's only Krool wanderin' w'ere he ain't got no business," was the angry remark of the upper-housemaid, whom his sudden appearance had startled in a dim passage one day.

"Lor'! what a turn you give me, Mr. Krool, spookin' about where there's no call for you to be," she had said to him, and below stairs she had enlarged upon his enormities greatly.

"And Mrs. Byng, she not like him better as we do," was the comment of Lablanche, the lady's maid. "A snake in the grass—that is what Madame think."

Slowly the night passed for Krool. His disturbed brain was like some dark wood through which flew songless birds with wings of night; through which sped the furtive dwellers of the grass and the earth-covert. The real and the imaginative crowded the dark purlieus. He was the victim of his blood, his beginnings off there beyond the Vaal, where the veld was swept by the lightning and the storm, the home of wild dreams, and of a loneliness terrible and strange, to which the man who once had tasted its awful pleasures returned and returned again, until he was, at the last, part of its loneliness, its woeful agitations and its reposeless quiet.

It was not possible for him to think or be like pure white people, to do as they did. He was a child of the kopje, the spruit, and the dun veld, where men dwelt with weird beings which were not men—presences that whispered, telling them of things to come, blowing the warnings of Destiny across the waste, over thousands and thousands of miles. Such as he always became apart and lonely because of this companionship of silence and the unseen. More and more they withdrew themselves, unwittingly and painfully, from the understanding and companionship of the usual matter-of-fact, commonplace, sensible people—the settler, the emigrant, and the British man. Sinister they became, but with the helplessness of those in whom the under-spirit of life has been working, estranging them, even against their will, from the rest of the world.

So Krool, estranged, lonely, even in the heart of friendly, pushing, jostling London, still was haunted by presences which whispered to him, not with the old clearness of bygone days, but with confused utterances and clouded meaning; and yet sufficient in dark suggestion for him to know that ill happenings were at hand, and that he would be in the midst of them, an instrument of Fate. All night strange shapes trooped past his clouded eyes, and more than once, in a half-dream, he called out to his master to help him as he was helped long ago when that master rescued him from death.

Long before the rest of the house was stirring, Krool wandered hither and thither through the luxurious rooms, vainly endeavouring to occupy himself with his master's clothes, boots, and belongings. At last he stole into Byng's room and, stooping, laid something on the floor; then reclaiming the two cables which Rudyard had read, crumpled up, and thrown away, he crept stealthily from the room. His face had a sombre and forbidding pleasure as he read by the early morning light the discarded messages with their thunderous warnings—"To-morrow. . . Prepare!"

He knew their meaning well enough. "To-morrow" was here, and it would bring the challenge from Oom Paul to try the might of England against the iron courage of those to whom the Vierkleur was the symbol of sovereignty from sea to sea and the ruin of the Rooinek.

"Prepare!" He knew vastly more than those responsible men in position or in high office, who should know a thousand times as much more. He knew so much that was useful—to Oom Paul; but what he knew he did not himself convey, though it reached those who welcomed it eagerly and grimly. All that he knew, another also near to the Baas also knew, and knew it before Krool; and reaped the reward of knowing.

Krool did not himself need to betray the Baas direct; and, with the reasoning of the native in him, he found it possible to let another be the means and the messenger of betrayal. So he soothed his conscience.

A little time before they had all gone to Glencader, however, he had discovered something concerning this agent of Paul Kruger in the heart of the Outlander camp, whom he employed, which had roused in him the worst passions of an outcast mind. Since then there had been no trafficking with the traitor—the double traitor, whom he was now plotting to destroy, not because he was a traitor to his country, but because he was a traitor to the Baas. In his evil way, he loved his master as a Caliban might love an Apollo. That his devotion took forms abnormal and savage in their nature was due to his origin and his blood. That he plotted to secure the betrayal of the Baas' country and the Outlander interest, while he would have given his life for the Baas, was but the twisted sense of a perverted soul.

He had one obsession now—to destroy Adrian Fellowes, his agent for Paul Kruger in the secret places of British policy and in the house of the Partners, as it were. But how should it be done? What should be the means? On the very day in which Oom Paul would send his ultimatum, the means came to his hand.

"Prepare!" the cable to the Baas had read. The Baas would be prepared for the thunderbolt to be hurled from Pretoria; but he would have no preparation for the thunderbolt which would fall at his feet this day in this house, where white roses welcomed the visitor at the door-way and the beauty of Titians and Botticellis and Rubens' and Goyas greeted him in the luxuriant chambers. There would be no preparation for that war which rages most violently at a fireside and in the human heart.

XX

THE FURNACE DOOR

It was past nine o'clock when Rudyard wakened. It was nearly ten before he turned to leave his room for breakfast. As he did so he stooped and picked up an open letter lying on the floor near the door.

His brain was dazed and still surging with the terrible thoughts which had agonized him the night before. He was as in a dream, and was only vaguely conscious of the fugitive letter. He was wondering whether he would go at once to Jasmine or wait until he had finished breakfast. Opening the door of his room, he saw the maid entering to Jasmine with a gown over her arm.

No, he would not go to her till she was alone, till she was dressed and alone. Then he would tell her all, and take her in his arms, and talk with her—talk as he had never talked before. Slowly, heavily, he went to his study, where his breakfast was always eaten. As he sat down he opened, with uninterested inquiry, the letter he had picked up inside the door of his room. As he did so he vaguely wondered why Krool had overlooked it as he passed in and out. Perhaps Krool had dropped it. His eyes fell on the opening words. . . His face turned ashen white. A harsh cry broke from him.

At eleven o'clock to the minute Ian Stafford entered Byng's mansion and was being taken to Jasmine's sitting-room, when Rudyard appeared on the staircase, and with a peremptory gesture waved the servant away. Ian was suddenly conscious of a terrible change in Rudyard's appearance. His face was haggard and his warm colour had given place to a strange blackish tinge which seemed to underlie the pallor—the deathly look to be found in the faces of those stricken with a mortal disease. All strength and power seemed to have gone from the face, leaving it tragic with uncontrolled suffering. Panic emotion was uppermost, while desperate and reckless purpose was in his eyes. The balance was gone from the general character and his natural force was like some great gun loose from its fastenings on the deck of a sea-stricken ship. He was no longer the stalwart Outlander who had done such great work in South Africa and had such power in political London and in international finance. The demoralization which had stealthily gone on for a number of years was now suddenly a debacle of will and body. Of the superb physical coolness and intrepid mind with which he had sprung upon the stage of Covent Garden Opera House to rescue Al'mah nothing seemed left; or, if it did remain, it was shocked out of its bearings. His eyes were almost glassy as he looked at Ian Stafford, and animal-like hatred was the dominating note of his face and carriage.

"Come with me, Stafford: I want to speak to you," he said, hoarsely. "You've arrived when I wanted you—at the exact time."

"Yes, I said I would come at eleven," responded Stafford, mechanically. "Jasmine expects me at eleven."

"In here," Byng said, pointing to a little morning-room.

As Stafford entered, he saw Krool's face, malign and sombre, show in a doorway of the hall. Was he mistaken in thinking that Krool flashed a look of secret triumph and yet of obscure warning? Warning? There was trouble, strange and dreadful trouble, here; and the wrenching thought had swept into his brain that he was the cause of it all, that he was to be the spring and centre of dreadful happenings.

He was conscious of something else purely objective as he entered the room—of music, the music of a gay light opera being played in the adjoining room, from which this little morning-room was separated only by Indian bead-curtains. He saw idle sunlight play upon these beads, as he sat down at the table to which Rudyard motioned him. He was also subconsciously aware who it was that played the piano beyond there with such pleasant skill. Many a time thereafter, in the days to come, he would be awakened in the night by the sound of that music, a love-song from the light opera "A Lady of London," which had just caught the ears of the people in the street.

Of one thing he was sure: the end of things had come—the end of all things that life meant to him had come. Rudyard knew! Rudyard, sitting there at the other side of the table and leaning toward him with a face where, in control of all else, were hate and panic emotion—he knew.

The music in the next room was soft, persistent and searching. As Ian waited for Rudyard to speak he was conscious that even the words of the silly, futile love-song:

> *"Not like the roses shall our love be, dear*
> *Never shall its lovely petals fade,*
> *Singing, it will flourish till the world's last year*
> *Happy as the song-birds in the glade."*

Through it all now came Rudyard's voice.

"I have a letter here," the voice said, and he saw Rudyard slowly take it from his pocket. "I want you to read it, and when you have read it, I want you to tell me what you think of the man who wrote it."

He threw a letter down on the table—a square white envelope with the crest of the Trafalgar Club upon it. It lay face downward, waiting for his hand.

So it had come. His letter to Jasmine which told all—Rudyard had read it. And here was the end of everything—the roses faded before they had bloomed an hour. It was not for them to flourish "till the world's last year."

His hand reached out for the letter. With eyes almost blind he raised it, and slowly and mechanically took the document of tragedy from the envelope. Why should Rudyard insist on his reading it? It was a devilish revenge, which he could not resent. But time—he must have time; therefore he would do Rudyard's bidding, and read this thing he had written, look at it with eyes in which Penalty was gathering its mists.

So this was the end of it all—friendship gone with the man before him; shame come to the woman he loved; misery to every one; a home-life shattered; and from the souls of three people peace banished for evermore.

He opened out the pages with a slowness that seemed almost apathy, while the man opposite clinched his hands on the table spasmodically. Still the music from the other room with cheap, flippant sensuousness stole through the burdened air:

"Singing, it will flourish till the world's last year—"

He looked at the writing vaguely, blindly. Why should this be exacted of him, this futile penalty? Then all at once his sight cleared; for this handwriting was not his—this letter was not his; these wild, passionate phrases—this terrible suggestiveness of meaning, these references to the past, this appeal for further hours of love together, this abjectly tender appeal to Jasmine that she would wear one of his white roses when he saw her the next day—would she not see him between eleven and twelve o'clock?—all these words were not his.

They were written by the man who was playing the piano in the next room; by the man who had come and gone in this house like one who had the right to do so; who had, as it were, fed from Rudyard Byng's hand; who lived on what Byng paid him; who had been trusted with the innermost life of the household and the life and the business of the master of it.

The letter was signed, Adrian.

His own face blanched like the face of the man before him. He had braced himself to face the consequences of his own letter to the woman he loved, and he was face to face with the consequences of another man's letter to the same woman, to the woman who had two lovers. He was face to face with Rudyard's tragedy, and with his own. . . She, Jasmine, to whom he had given all, for whom he had been ready to give up all—career, fame, existence—was true to none, unfaithful to all, caring for none, but pretending to care for all three—and for how many others? He choked back a cry.

"Well—well?" came the husband's voice across the table. "There's one thing to do, and I mean to do it." He waved a hand towards the music-room. "He's in the next room there. I mean to kill him—to kill him—now. I wanted you to know why, to know all, you, Stafford, my old friend and hers. And I'm going to do it now. Listen to him there!"

His words came brokenly and scarce above a whisper, but they were ghastly in their determination, in their loathing, their blind fury. He was gone mad, all the animal in him alive, the brain tossing on a sea of disorder.

"Now!" he said, suddenly, and, rising, he pushed back his chair. "Give that to me."

He reached out his hand for the letter, but his confused senses were suddenly arrested by the look in Ian Stafford's face, a look so strange, so poignant, so insistent, that he paused. Words could not have checked his blind haste like that look. In the interval which followed, the music from the other room struck upon the ears of both, with exasperating insistence:

"Not like the roses shall our love be, dear—"

Stafford made no motion to return the letter. He caught and held Rudyard's eyes.

"You ask me to tell you what I think of the man who wrote this letter," he said, thickly and slowly, for he was like one paralyzed, regaining his speech with blanching effort: "Byng, I think what you think—all you think; but I would not do what you want to do."

As he had read the letter the whole horror of the situation burst upon him. Jasmine had deceived her husband when she turned to himself, and that was to be understood—to be understood, if not to be pardoned. A woman might marry, thinking she cared, and all too soon, sometimes before the second day had dawned, learn that shrinking and repugnance which not even habit can modify or obscure. A girl might be mistaken, with her heart and nature undeveloped, and with that closer intimate life with another of another sex still untried. With the transition from maidenhood to wifehood, fateful beyond all transitions, yet unmade, she might be mistaken once; as so many have been in the revelations of first intimacy; but not twice, not the second time. It was not possible to be mistaken in so vital a thing twice. This was merely a wilful, miserable degeneracy. Rudyard had been wronged—terribly wronged—by himself, by Jasmine; but he had loved Jasmine since she was a child, before Rudyard came—in truth, he all but possessed her when Rudyard came; and there was some explanation, if no excuse, for that betrayal; but this other, it was incredible, it was monstrous. It was incredible but yet it was true. Thoughts that overturned all his past, that made a melee of his life, rushed and whirled through his mind as he read the letter with assumed deliberation when he saw what it was. He read slowly that he might make up his mind how to act, what to say and do in this crisis. To do—what? Jasmine had betrayed him long ago when she had thrown him over for Rudyard, and now she had betrayed him again after she had married Rudyard, and betrayed Rudyard, too; and for whom this second betrayal? His heart seemed to shrink to nothingness. This business dated far beyond yesterday. The letter furnished that sure evidence.

What to do? Like lightning his mind was made up. What to do? Ah, but one thing to do—only one thing to do—save her at any cost, somehow save her! Whatever she was, whatever she had done, however she had spoiled his life and destroyed forever his faith, yet he too had betrayed this broken man before him, with the look in his eyes of an animal at bay, ready to do the last irretrievable thing. Even as her shameless treatment of himself smote him; lowered him to that dust which is ground from the heels of merciless humanity—even as it sickened his soul beyond recovery in this world, up from the lowest depths of his being there came the indestructible thing. It was the thing that never dies, the love that defies injury, shame, crime, deceit, and desertion, and lives pityingly on, knowing all, enduring all, desiring no touch, no communion, yet prevailing—the indestructible thing.

He knew now in a flash what he had to do. He must save her. He saw that Rudyard was armed, and that the end might come at any moment.

There was in the wronged husband's eyes the wild, reckless, unseeing thing which disregards consequences, which would rush blindly on the throne of God itself to snatch its vengeance. He spoke again: and just in time.

"I think what you think, Byng, but I would not do what you want to do. I would do something else."

His voice was strangely quiet, but it had a sharp insistence which caused Rudyard to turn back mechanically to the seat he had just left. Stafford saw the instant's advantage which, if he did not pursue, all would be lost. With a great effort he simulated intense anger and indignation.

"Sit down, Byng," he said, with a gesture of authority. He leaned over the table, holding the other's eyes, the letter in one clinched hand. "Kill him—," he said, and pointed to the other room, from which came the maddening iteration of the jingling song—"you would kill him for his hellish insolence, for this infamous attempt to lead your wife astray, but what good will it do to kill him?"

"Not him alone, but her too," came the savage, uncontrolled voice from the uncontrolled savagery of the soul.

Suddenly a great fear shot up in Stafford's heart. His breath came in sharp, breaking gasps. Had he—had he killed Jasmine?

"You have not—not her?"

"No—not yet." The lips of the avenger suddenly ceased twitching, and they shut with ominous certainty.

An iron look came into Stafford's face. He had his chance now. One word, one defense only! It would do all, or all would be lost—sunk in a sea of tragedy. Diplomacy had taught him the gift of control of face and gesture, of meaning in tone and word. He made an effort greater than he had ever put forward in life. He affected an enormous and scornful surprise.

"You think—you dare to think that she—that Jasmine—"

"Think, you say! The letter—that letter—"

"This letter—this letter, Byng—are you a fool? This letter, this preposterous thing from the universal philanderer, the effeminate erotic! It is what it is, and it is no more. Jasmine—you know her. Indiscreet—yes; always indiscreet in her way, in her own way, and always daring. A coquette always. She has coquetted all her life; she cannot help it. She doesn't even know it. She led him on from sheer wilfulness. What did it matter to her that he was of no account! She led him on, to be at her feet like the rest, like bigger and better men—like us all. Was there ever a time when she did not want to master us? She has coquetted since—ah, you do not know as I do, her old friend! She has coquetted since she was a little child. Coquetted, and no more. We have all been her slaves—yes, long before you came—all of us. Look at Mennaval! She—"

With a distracted gesture Byng interrupted. "The world believes the worst. Last night, by accident, I heard at De Lancy Scovel's house that she and Mennaval—and now this—!"

But into the rage, the desperation in the wild eyes, was now creeping an eager look—not of hope, but such a look as might be in eyes that were striving to see through darkness, looking for a glimmer of day in the black hush of morning before the dawn. It was pitiful to see the strong man tossing on the flood of disordered understanding, a willing castaway, yet stretching out a hand to be saved.

"Oh, last night, Mennaval, you say, and to-day—this!" Stafford held up the letter. "This means nothing against her, except indiscretion, and indiscretion which would have been nothing if the man had not been what he is. He is of the slime. He does not matter, except that he has dared—!"

"He has dared, by God—!"

All Byng's rage came back, the lacerated pride, the offended manhood, the self-esteem which had been spattered by the mud of slander, by the cynical defense, or the pitying solicitude of his friends—of De Lancy Scovel, Barry Whalen, Sobieski the Polish Jew, Fleming, Wolff, and the rest. The pity of these for him—for Rudyard Byng, because the flower in his garden, his Jasmine-flower, was swept by the blast of calumny! He sprang from his chair with an ugly oath.

But Stafford stepped in front of him. "Sit down, Byng, or damn yourself forever. If she is innocent—and she is—do you think she would ever live with you again, after you had dragged her name into the dust of the criminal courts and through the reek of the ha'penny press? Do you think Jasmine would ever forgive you for suspecting her? If you want to drive her from you forever, then kill him, and go and tell her that you suspect her. I know her—I have known her all her life, long before you came. I care what becomes of her. She has many who care what becomes of her—her father, her brother, many men, and many women who have seen her grow up without a mother. They understand her, they believe in her, because they have known her over all the years.

They know her better than you. Perhaps they care for her—perhaps any one of them cares for her far more than you do."

Now there came a new look into the big, staring eyes. Byng was as one fascinated; light was breaking in on his rage, his besmirched pride, his vengeance; hope was stealing tremblingly into his face.

"She was more to me than all the world—than twenty worlds. She—"

He hesitated, then his voice broke and his body suddenly shook violently, as tears rose in the far, deep wells of feeling and tried to reach the fevered eyes. He leaned his head in his big, awkward hands.

Stafford saw the way of escape for Jasmine slowly open out, and went on quickly. "You have neglected her "—Rudyard's head came up in angry protest—"not wilfully; but you have neglected her. You have been too easy. You should lead, not follow, where a woman is concerned. All women are indiscreet, all are a little dishonourable on opportunity; but not in the big way, only in the small, contemptible way, according to our code. We men are dishonourable in the big way where they are concerned. You have neglected her, Byng, because you have not said, 'This way, Jasmine. Come with me. I want you; and you must came, and come now.' She wanted your society, wanted you all the time; but while you did not have her on the leash she went playing—playing. That is it, and that is all. And now, if you want to keep her, if you want her to live on with you, I warn you not to tell her you know of the insult this letter contains, nor ever say what would make her think you suspected her. If you do, you will bid good-bye to her forever. She has bold blood in her veins, rash blood. Her grandfather—"

"I know—I know." The tone was credulous, understanding now. Hope stole into the distorted face.

"She would resent your suspicion. She, then, would do the mad thing, not you. She would be as frenzied as you were a moment ago; and she would not listen to reason. If you dared to hint outside in the world, that you believed her guilty, there are some of her old friends who would feel like doing to you what you want to do to that libertine in there, to Al'mah's lover—"

"Good God, Stafford—wait!"

"I don't mean Barry Whalen, Fleming, De Lancy Scovel, and the rest. They are not her old friends, and they weren't yours once—that breed; but the others who are the best, of whom you come, over there in Herefordshire, in Dorset, in Westmorland, where your and her people lived, and mine. You have been too long among the Outlanders, Byng. Come back, and bring Jasmine with you. And as for this letter—"

Byng reached out his hand for it.

"No, it contains an insult to your wife. If you get it into your hands, you will read it again, and then you will do some foolish thing, for you have lost grip of yourself. Here is the only place for such stuff—an outburst of sensuality!"

He threw the letter suddenly into the fire. Rudyard sprang to his feet as though to reclaim it, but stood still bewildered, as he saw Stafford push it farther into the coals.

Silent, they watched shrivel such evidence as brings ruin upon men and women in courts of law.

"Leave the whole thing—leave Fellowes to me," Stafford said, after a slight pause. "I will deal with him. He shall leave the country to-night. I will see to that. He shall go for three years at least. Do not see him. You will not contain yourself, and for your own chance of happiness with the woman you love, you must do nothing, nothing at all now."

"He has keys, papers—"

"I will see to that; I will see to everything. Now go, at once. There is enough for you to do. The war, Oom Paul's war, will be on us to day. Do you hear, Byng—to-day! And you have work to do for this your native country and for South Africa, your adopted country. England and the Transvaal will be at each other's throat before night. You have work to do. Do it. You are needed. Go, and leave this wretched business in my hands. I will deal with Fellowes—adequately."

The rage had faded from Byng's fevered eyes, and now there was a moisture in them, a look of incalculable relief. To believe in Jasmine, that was everything to him. He had not seen her yet, not since he left the white rose on her pillow last night—Adrian Fellowes' tribute; and after he had read the letter, he had had no wish to see her till he had had his will and done away with Fellowes forever. Then he would see her—for the last time: and she should die, too,—with himself. That had been his purpose. Now all was changed. He would not see her now, not till Fellowes was gone forever. Then he would come again, and say no word which would let her think he knew what Fellowes had written. Yes, Stafford was right. She must not know, and they must start again, begin life again together, a new understanding in his heart, new purposes in their existence. In these few minutes Stafford had taught him much, had showed him where he had been wrong, had revealed to him Jasmine's nature as he never really understood it.

At the door, as Stafford helped him on with a light overcoat, he took a revolver from his pocket.

"That's the proof of what I meant to do," he said; "and this is proof of what I mean to do," he added, as he handed over the revolver and Stafford's fingers grasped it with a nervous force which he misinterpreted.

"Ah yes," he exclaimed, sadly, "you don't quite trust me yet—not quite, Stafford; and I don't wonder; but it's all right. . . You've been a good, good friend to us both," he added. "I wish Jasmine might know how good a friend you've been. But never mind. We'll pay the debt sometime, somehow, she and I. When shall I see you again?"

At that moment a clear voice rang out cheerily in the distance. "Rudyard—where are you, Ruddy?" it called.

A light broke over Byng's haggard face. "Not yet?" he asked Stafford.

"No, not yet," was the reply, and Byng was pushed through the open door into the street.

"Ruddy—where are you, Ruddy?" sang the voice like a morning song.

Then there was silence, save for the music in the room beyond the little room where the two men had sat a few moments ago.

The music was still poured forth, but the tune was changed. Now it was "Pagliacci"—that wonderful passage where the injured husband pours out his soul in agony.

Stafford closed the doors of the little room where he and Byng had sat, and stood an instant listening to the music. He shuddered as the passionate notes swept over his senses. In this music was the note of the character of the man who played—sensuous emotion, sensual delight. There are men who by nature are as the daughters of the night, primary prostitutes, with no minds, no moral sense; only a sensuous organization which has a gift of shallow beauty, while the life is never deep enough for tears nor high enough for real joy.

In Stafford's pocket was the revolver which Byng had given him. He took it out, and as he did so, a flush swept over his face, and every nerve of his body tingled.

"That way out?" he thought. "How easy—and how selfish. . . If one's life only concerned oneself. . . But it's only partly one's own from first to last." . . . Then his thoughts turned again to the man who was playing "Pagliacci." "I have a greater right to do it than Byng, and I'd have a greater joy in doing it; but whatever he is, it is not all his fault." Again he shuddered. "No man makes love like that to a woman unless she lets him, . . . until she lets him." Then he looked at the fire where the cruel testimony had shrivelled into smoke. "If it had been read to a jury. . . Ah, my God! How many he must have written her like that. . . How often. . ."

With an effort he pulled himself together. "What does it matter now! All things have come to an end for me. There is only one way. My letter to her showed it. But this must be settled first. Then to see her for the last time, to make her understand. . ."

He went to the beaded curtain, raised it, and stepped into the flood of warm sunlight. The voluptuous, agonizing music came in a wave over him. Tragedy, poignant misery, rang through every note, swelled in a stream which drowned the senses. This man-devil could play, Stafford remarked, cynically, to himself.

"A moment—Fellowes," he said, sharply.

The music frayed into a discord and stopped.

XXI

THE BURNING FIERY FURNACE

There was that in Stafford's tone which made Fellowes turn with a start. It was to this room that Fellowes had begged Jasmine to come this morning, in the letter which Krool had so carefully placed for his master to find, after having read it himself with minute scrutiny. It was in this room they had met so often in those days when Rudyard was in South Africa, and where music had been the medium of an intimacy which had nothing for its warrant save eternal vanity and curiosity, the evil genius of the race of women. Here it was that Krool's antipathy to Jasmine and fierce hatred of Fellowes had been nurtured. Krool had haunted the room, desiring the end of it all; but he had been disarmed by a smiling kindness on Jasmine's part, which shook his purpose again and again.

It had all been a problem which Krool's furtive mind failed to master. If he went to the Baas with his suspicions, the chance was that he would be flayed with a sjambok and turned into the streets; if he warned Jasmine, the same thing might happen, or worse. But fate had at last played into his hands, on the very day that Oom Paul had challenged destiny, when all things were ready for the ruin of the hated English.

Fate had sent him through the hallway between Jasmine's and Rudyard's rooms in the moment when Jasmine had dropped Fellowes' letter; and he had seen it fall. He knew not what it was, but it might be of importance, for he had seen Fellowes' handwriting on an envelope among those waiting for Jasmine's return home. In a far dark corner he had waited till he saw Lablanche enter her mistress' room hurriedly, without observing the letter. Then he caught it up and stole away to the library, where he read it with malevolent eyes.

He had left this fateful letter where Rudyard would see it when he rose in the morning. All had worked out as he had planned, and now, with his ear against the door which led from the music-room, he strained to hear what passed between Stafford and Fellowes.

"Well, what is it?" asked Fellowes, with an attempt to be casual, though there was that in Stafford's face which gave him anxiety, he knew not why. He had expected Jasmine, and, instead, here was

Stafford, who had been so much with her of late; who, with Mennaval, had occupied so much of her time that she had scarcely spoken to him, and, when she did so, it was with a detachment which excluded him from intimate consideration.

His face wore a mechanical smile, as his pale blue eyes met the dark intensity of Stafford's. But slowly the peach-bloom of his cheeks faded and his long, tapering fingers played nervously with the leather-trimming of the piano-stool.

"Anything I can do for you, Stafford?" he added, with attempted nonchalance.

"There is nothing you can do for me," was the meaning reply, "but there is something you can do advantageously for yourself, if you will think it worth while."

"Most of us are ready to do ourselves good turns. What am I to do?"

"You will wish to avoid it, and yet you will do yourself a good turn in not avoiding it."

"Is that the way you talk in diplomatic circles—cryptic, they call it, don't they?"

Stafford's chin hardened, and a look of repulsion and disdain crossed over his face.

"It is more cryptic, I confess, than the letter which will cause you to do yourself a good turn."

Now Fellowes' face turned white. "What letter?" he asked, in a sharp, querulous voice.

"The letter you wrote Mrs. Byng from the Trafalgar Club yesterday."

Fellowes made a feint, an attempt at bravado. "What business is it of yours, anyhow? What rights have you got in Mrs. Byng's letters?"

"Only what I get from a higher authority."

"Are you in sweet spiritual partnership with the Trinity?"

"The higher authority I mean is Mr. Byng. Let us have no tricks with words, you fool."

Fellowes made an ineffective attempt at self-possession.

"What the devil. . . why should I listen to you?" There was a peevish stubbornness in the tone.

"Why should you listen to me? Well, because I have saved your life. That should be sufficient reason for you to listen."

"Damnation—speak out, if you've got anything to say! I don't see what you mean, and you are damned officious. Yes, that's it—damned officious." The peevishness was becoming insolent recklessness.

Slowly Stafford drew from his pocket the revolver Rudyard had given him. As Fellowes caught sight of the glittering steel he fell back against the piano-stool, making a clatter, his face livid.

Stafford's lips curled with contempt. "Don't squirm so, Fellowes. I'm not going to use it. But Mr. Byng had it, and he was going to use it. He was on his way to do it when I appeared. I stopped him. . . I will tell you how. I endeavoured to make him believe that she was absolutely innocent, that you had only been an insufferably insolent, presumptuous, and lecherous cad—which is true. I said that, though you deserved shooting, it would only bring scandal to Rudyard Byng's honourable wife, who had been insulted by the lover of Al'mah and the would-be betrayer of an honest girl—of Jigger's sister. . . Yes, you may well start. I know of what stuff you are, how you had the soul and body of one of the most credulous and wonderful women in the world in your hands, and you went scavenging. From Al'mah to the flower-girl! . . . I think I should like to kill you myself for what you tried to do to Jigger's sister; and if it wasn't here"—he handled the little steel weapon with an eager fondness—"I think I'd do it. You are a pest."

Cowed, shivering, abject, Fellowes nervously fell back. His body crashed upon the keys of the piano, producing a hideous discord. Startled, he sprang aside and with trembling hands made gestures of appeal.

"Don't—don't! Can't you see I'm willing! What is it you want me to do? I'll do it. Put it away. . . Oh, my God—Oh!" His bloodless lips were drawn over his teeth in a grimace of terror.

With an exclamation of contempt Stafford put the weapon back into his pocket again. "Pull yourself together," he said. "Your life is safe for the moment; but I can say no more than that. After I had proved the lady's innocence—you understand, after I had proved the lady's innocence to him—"

"Yes, I understand," came the hoarse reply.

"After that, I said I would deal with you; that he could not be trusted to do so. I said that you would leave England within twenty-four hours, and that you would not return within three years. That was my pledge. You are prepared to fulfil it?"

"To leave England! It is impossible—"

"Perhaps to leave it permanently, and not by the English Channel, either, might be worse," was the cold, savage reply. "Mr. Byng made his terms."

Fellowes shivered. "What am I to do out of England—but, yes, I'll go, I'll go," he added, as he saw the look in Stafford's face and thought of the revolver so near to Stafford's hand.

"Yes, of course you will go," was the stern retort. "You will go, just as I say."

"What shall I do abroad?" wailed the weak voice.

"What you have always done here, I suppose—live on others," was the crushing reply. "The venue will be changed, but you won't change, not you. If I were you, I'd try and not meet Jigger before you go. He doesn't know quite what it is, but he knows enough to make him reckless."

Fellowes moved towards the door in a stumbling kind of way. "I have some things up-stairs," he said.

"They will be sent after you to your chambers. Give me the keys to the desk in the secretary's room."

"I'll go myself, and—"

"You will leave this house at once, and everything will be sent after you—everything. Have no fear. I will send them myself, and your letters and private papers will not be read. . . You feel you can rely on me for that—eh?"

"Yes. . . I'll go now. . . abroad. . . where?"

"Where you please outside the United Kingdom."

Fellowes passed heavily out through the other room, where his letter had been read by Stafford, where his fate had been decided. He put on his overcoat nervously and went to the outer door.

Stafford came up to him again. "You understand, there must be no attempt to communicate here. . . You will observe this?"

Fellowes nodded. "Yes, I will. . . Good-night," he added, absently.

"Good-day," answered Stafford, mechanically.

The outer door shut, and Stafford turned again to the little room where so much had happened which must change so many lives, bring so many tears, divert so many streams of life.

How still the house seemed now! It had lost all its charm and homelikeness. He felt stifled. Yet there was the warm sun streaming through the doorway of the music-room, making the beaded curtains shine like gold.

As he stood in the doorway of the little morning-room, looking in with bitter reflection and dreading beyond words what now must come—his meeting with Jasmine, the story he must tell her, and the exposure of a truth so naked that his nature revolted from it, he heard a footstep behind him. It was Krool.

Stafford looked at the saturnine face and wondered how much he knew; but there was no glimmer of revelation in Krool's impassive look. The eyes were always painful in their deep animal-like glow, and they seemed more than usually intense this morning; that was all.

"Will you present my compliments to Mrs. Byng, and say—"

Krool, with a gesture, stopped him.

"Mrs. Byng is come now," he said, making a gesture towards the staircase. Then he stole away towards the servants' quarters of the house. His work had been well done, of its kind, and he could now await consequences.

Stafford turned to the staircase and saw—in blue, in the old sentimental blue—Jasmine slowly descending, a strange look of apprehension in her face.

Immediately after calling out for Rudyard a little while before, she had discovered the loss of Adrian Fellowes' letter. Hours before this she had read and re-read Ian's letter, that document of pain and purpose, of tragical, inglorious, fatal purpose. She was suddenly conscious of an air of impending catastrophe about her now. Or was it that the catastrophe had come? She had not asked for Adrian Fellowes' letter, for if any servant had found it, and had not returned it, it was useless asking; and if Rudyard had found it—if Rudyard had found it. . . !

Where was Rudyard? Why had he not come to her, Why had he not eaten the breakfast which still lay untouched on the table of his study? Where was Rudyard?

Ian's eyes looked straight into hers as she came down the staircase, and there was that in them which paralyzed her. But she made an effort to ignore the apprehension which filled her soul.

"Good-morning. Am I so very late?" she said, gaily, to him, though there was a hollow note in her voice.

"You are just in time," he answered in an even tone which told nothing.

"Dear me, what a gloomy face! What has happened? What is it? There seems to be a Cassandra atmosphere about the place—and so early in the day, too."

"It is full noon—and past," he said, with acute meaning, as her daintily shod feet met the floor of the hallway and glided towards him. How often he had admired that pretty flitting of her feet!

As he looked at her he was conscious, with a new force, of the wonder of that hair on a little head as queenly as ever was given to the modern world. And her face, albeit pale, and with a strange tremulousness in it now, was like that of some fairy dame painted by Greuze. All last night's agony was gone from the rare blue eyes, whose lashes drooped so ravishingly betimes, though that droop was not there as she looked at Ian now.

She beat a foot nervously on the floor. "What is it—why this Euripidean air in my simple home? There's something wrong, I see. What is it? Come, what is it, Ian?"

Hesitatingly she laid a hand upon his arm, but there was no loving-kindness in his look. The arms which yesterday—only yesterday—had clasped her passionately and hungrily to his breast now hung inert at his side. His eyes were strange and hard.

"Will you come in here," he said, in an arid voice, and held wide the door of the room where he and Rudyard had settled the first chapter of the future and closed the book of the past.

She entered with hesitating step. Then he shut the door with an accentuated softness, and came to the table where he had sat with Rudyard. Mechanically she took the seat which Rudyard had occupied, and looked at him across the table with a dread conviction stealing over her face, robbing it of every vestige of its heavenly colour, giving her eyes a staring and solicitous look.

"Well, what is it? Can't you speak and have it over?" she asked, with desperate impatience.

"Fellowes' letter to you—Rudyard found it," he said, abruptly.

She fell back as though she had been struck, then recovered herself. "You read it?" she gasped.

"Rudyard made me read it. I came in when he was just about to kill Fellowes."

She gave a short, sharp cry, which with a spasm of determination her fingers stopped.

"Kill him—why?" she asked in a weak voice, looking down at her trembling hands which lay clasped on the table before her.

"The letter—Fellowes' letter to you."

"I dropped it last night," she said, in a voice grown strangely impersonal and colourless. "I dropped it in Rudyard's room, I suppose."

She seemed not to have any idea of excluding the terrible facts, but to be speaking as it were to herself and of something not vital, though her whole person was transformed into an agony which congealed the lifeblood.

Her voice sounded tuneless and ragged. "He read it—Rudyard read a letter which was not addressed to him! He read a letter addressed to me—he read my letter. . . It gave me no chance."

"No chance—?"

A bitter indignation was added to the cheerless discord of her tones. "Yes, I had a chance, a last chance—if he had not read the letter. But now, there is no chance. . . You read it, too. You read the letter which was addressed to me. No matter what it was—my letter, you read it."

"Rudyard said to me in his terrible agitation, 'Read that letter, and then tell me what you think of the man who wrote it.' . . . I thought it was the letter I wrote to you, the letter I posted to you last night. I thought it was my letter to you."

Her eyes had a sudden absent look. It was as though she were speaking in a trance. "I answered that letter—your letter. I answered it this morning. Here is the answer. . . here." She laid a letter on the table before him, then drew it back again into her lap. "Now it does not matter. But it gives me no chance. . ."

There was a world of despair and remorse in her voice. Her face was wan and strained. "No chance, no chance," she whispered.

"Rudyard did not kill him?" she asked, slowly and cheerlessly, after a moment, as though repeating a lesson. "Why?"

"I stopped him. I prevented him."

"You prevented him—why?" Her eyes had a look of unutterable confusion and trouble. "Why did you prevent it—you?"

"That would have hurt you—the scandal, the grimy press, the world."

Her voice was tuneless, and yet it had a strange, piteous poignancy. "It would have hurt me—yes. Why did you not want to hurt me?"

He did not answer. His hands had gone into his pockets, as though to steady their wild nervousness, and one had grasped the little weapon of steel which Rudyard had given him. It produced some strange, malignant effect on his mind. Everything seemed to stop in him, and he was suddenly possessed by a spirit which carried him into that same region where Rudyard had been. It was the region of the abnormal. In it one moves in a dream, majestically unresponsive to all outward things, numb, unconcerned, disregarding all except one's own agony, which seems to neutralize the universe and reduce all life's problems to one formula of solution.

"What did you say to him that stopped him?" she asked in a whisper of awed and dreadful interest, as, after an earthquake, a survivor would speak in the stillness of dead and unburied millions.

"I said the one thing to say," he answered after a moment, involuntarily laying the pistol on the table before him—doing it, as it were, without conscious knowledge.

It fascinated Jasmine, the ugly, deadly little vehicle of oblivion. Her eyes fastened on it, and for an instant stared at it transfixed; then she recovered herself and spoke again.

"What was the one thing to say?" she whispered.

"That you were innocent—absolutely, that—"

Suddenly she burst into wild laughter—shrill, acrid, cheerless, hysterical, her face turned upward, her hands clasped under her chin, her body shaking with what was not laughter, but the terrifying agitation of a broken organism.

He waited till she had recovered somewhat, and then he repeated his words.

"I said that you were innocent absolutely; that Fellowes' letter was the insolence and madness of a voluptuary, that you had only been wilful and indiscreet, and that—"

In a low, mechanical tone from which was absent any agitation, he told her all he had said to Rudyard, and what Rudyard had said to him. Every word had been burned into his brain, and nearly every word was now repeated, while she sat silent, looking at her hands clasped on the table before her. When he came to the point where Rudyard went from the house, leaving Stafford to deal with Fellowes, she burst again into laughter, mocking, wilful, painful.

"You were left to set things right, to be the lord high executioner—you, Ian!"

How strange his name sounded on her lips now—foreign, distant, revealing the nature of the situation more vividly than all the words which had been said, than all that had been done.

"Rudyard did not think of killing you, I suppose," she went on, presently, with a bitter motion of the lips, and a sardonic note creeping into the voice.

"No, I thought of that," he answered, quietly, "as you know." His eyes sought the weapon on the table involuntarily. "That would have been easy enough," he added. "I was not thinking of myself, or of Fellowes, but only of you—and Rudyard."

"Only of me—and Rudyard," she repeated with drooping eyes, which suddenly became alive again with feeling and passion and wildness. "Wasn't it rather late for that?"

The words stung him beyond endurance. He rose and leaned across the table towards her.

"At least I recognized what I had done, what you had done, and I tried to face it. I did not disguise it. My letter to you proves that. But nevertheless I was true to you. I did not deceive you—ever. I loved you—ah, I loved you as few women have been loved! . . . But you, you might have made a mistake where Rudyard was concerned, made the mistake once, but if you wronged him, you wronged me infinitely more. I was ready to give up all, throw all my life, my career, to the winds, and prove myself loyal to that which was more than all; or I was willing to eliminate myself from the scene forever. I was willing to pay the price— any price—just to stand by what was the biggest thing in my life. But you were true to nothing—to nothing—to nobody."

"If one is untrue—once, why be true at all ever?" she said with an aching laugh, through which tears ran, though none dropped from her eyes. "If one is untrue to one, why not to a thousand?"

Again a mocking laugh burst from her. "Don't you see? One kiss, a wrong? Why not, then, a thousand kisses! The wrong came in the moment that the one kiss was given. It is the one that kills, not the thousand after."

There came to her mind again—and now with what sardonic force— Rudyard's words that day before they went to Glencader: "If you had lived a thousand years ago you would have had a thousand lovers."

"And so it is all understood between you and Rudyard," she added, mechanically. "That is what you have arranged for me—that I go on living as before with Rudyard, while I am not to know from him anything has happened; but to accept what has been arranged for me, and to be repentant and good and live in sackcloth. It has been arranged, has it, that Rudyard is to believe in me?"

"That has not been arranged."

"It has been arranged that I am to live with him as before, and that he is to pretend to love me as before, and—"

"He does love you as before. He has never changed. He believed in you, was so pitifully eager to believe in you even when the letter—"

"Where is the letter?"

He pointed to the fire.

"Who put it in the fire?" she asked. "You?"

He inclined his head.

"Ah yes, always so clever! A burst of indignation at his daring to suspect me even for an instant, and with a flourish into the fire, the evidence. Here is yours—your letter. Would you like to put it into the fire also?" she asked, and drew his letter from the folds of her dress.

"But, no, no, no—" She suddenly sprang to her feet, and her eyes had a look of agonized agitation. "When I have learned every word by heart, I will burn it myself—for your sake." Her voice grew softer, something less discordant came into it. "You will never understand. You could never understand me, or that letter of Adrian Fellowes to me, and that he could dare to write me such a letter. You could never understand it. But I understand you. I understand your letter. It came while I was—while I was broken. It healed me, Ian. Last night I wanted to kill myself. Never mind why. You would not understand. You are too good to understand. All night I was in torture, and then this letter of yours—it was a revelation. I did not think that a man lived like you, so true, so kind, so mad. And so I wrote you a letter, ah, a letter from my soul! and then came down to this—the end of all. The end of everything—forever."

"No, the beginning if you will have it so. . . Rudyard loves you. . ."

She gave a cry of agony. "For God's sake—oh, for God's sake, hush! . . . You think that now I could. . ."

"Begin again with new purpose."

"Purpose! Oh, you fool! You fool! You fool—you who are so wise sometimes! You want me to begin again with Rudyard: and you do not want me to begin again—with you?"

He was silent, and he looked her in the eyes steadily.

"You do not want me to begin again with you, because you believe me—because you believed the worst from that letter, from Adrian Fellowes' letter. . . You believed, yet you hypnotized Rudyard into not believing. But did you, after all? Was it not that he loves me, and that he wanted to be deceived, wanted to be forced to do what he has done? I know him better than you. But you are right, he would have spoken to me about it if you had not warned him."

"Then begin again—"

"You do not want me any more." The voice had an anguish like the cry of the tragic music in "Elektra." "You do not want what you wanted yesterday—for us together to face it all, Ian. You do not want it? You hate me."

His face was disturbed by emotion, and he did not speak for a moment.

In that moment she became transformed. With a sudden tragic motion she caught the pistol from the table and raised it, but he wrenched it from her hand.

"Do you think that would mend anything?" he asked, with a new pity in his heart for her. "That would only hurt those who have been hurt enough already. Be a little magnanimous. Do not be selfish. Give others a chance."

"You were going to do it as an act of unselfishness," she moaned. "You were going to die in order to mend it all. Did you think of me in that? Did you think I would or could consent to that? You believed in me, of course, when you wrote it. But did you think that was magnanimous— when you had got a woman's love, then to kill yourself in order to cure her? Oh, how little you know! . . . But you do not want me now. You do not believe in me now. You abhor me. Yet if that letter had not fallen into Rudyard's hands we might perhaps have now been on our way to begin life again together. Does that look as though there was some one else that mattered—that mattered?"

He held himself together with all his power and will. "There is one way, and only one way," he said, firmly. "Rudyard loves you. Begin again with him." His voice became lower. "You know the emptiness of your home. There is a way to make some recompense to him. You can pay your debt. Give him what he wants so much. It would be a link. It would bind you. A child. . ."

"Oh, how you loathe me!" she said, shudderingly. "Yesterday—and now. . . No, no, no," she added, "I will not, cannot live with Rudyard. I cannot wrench myself from one world into another like that. I will not live with him any more. . . There—listen."

Outside the newsboys were calling:

"Extra speshul! Extra speshul! All about the war! War declared! Extra speshul!"

"War! That will separate many," she added. "It will separate Rudyard and me. . . No, no, there will be no more scandal. . . But it is the way of escape—the war."

"The way of escape for us all, perhaps," he answered, with a light of determination in his eyes. "Good-bye," he added, after a slight pause. "There is nothing more to say."

He turned to go, but he did not hold out his hand, nor even look at her.

"Tell me," she said, in a strange, cold tone, "tell me, did Adrian Fellowes—did he protect me? Did he stand up for me? Did he defend me?"

"He was concerned only for himself," Ian answered, hesitatingly.

Her face hardened. Pitiful, haggard lines had come into it in the last half-hour, and they deepened still more.

"He did not say one word to put me right?"

Ian shook his head in negation. "What did you expect?" he said.

She sank into a chair, and a strange cruelty came into her eyes, something so hard that it looked grotesque in the beautiful setting of her pain-worn, exquisite face.

So utter was her dejection that he came back from the door and bent over her.

"Jasmine," he said, gently, "we have to start again, you and I—in different paths. They will never meet. But at the end of the road—peace. Peace the best thing of all. Let us try and find it, Jasmine."

"He did not try to protect me. He did not defend me," she kept saying to herself, and was only half conscious of what Ian said to her.

He touched her shoulder. "Nothing can set things right between you and me, Jasmine," he added, unsteadily, "but there's Rudyard—you must help him through. He heard scandal about Mennaval last night at De Lancy Scovel's. He didn't believe it. It rests with you to give it all the lie. . . Good-bye."

In a moment he was gone. As the door closed she sprang to her feet. "Ian—Ian—come back," she cried. "Ian, one word—one word."

But the door did not open again. For a moment she stood like one transfixed, staring at the place whence he had vanished, then, with a moan, she sank in a heap on the floor, and rocked to and fro like one demented.

Once the door opened quietly, and Krool's face showed, sinister and furtive, but she did not see it, and the door closed again softly.

At last the paroxysms passed, and a haggard face looked out into the world of life and being with eyes which were drowned in misery.

"He did not defend me—the coward!" she murmured; then she rose with a sudden effort, swayed, steadied herself, and arranged her hair in the mirror over the mantelpiece. "The low coward!" she said again. "But before he leaves. . . before he leaves England. . ."

As she turned to go from the room, Rudyard's portrait on the wall met her eyes. "I can't go on, Rudyard," she said to it. "I know that now."

Out in the streets, which Ian Stafford travelled with hasty steps, the newsboys were calling:

"War declared! All about the war!"

"That is the way out for me," Stafford said, aloud, as he hastened on. "That opens up the road. . . I'm still an artillery officer."

He directed his swift steps toward Pall Mall and the War Office.

XXII

In Which Fellowes Goes a Journey

Kruger's ultimatum, expected though it was, shook England as nothing had done since the Indian mutiny, but the tremour of national excitement presently gave way to a quiet, deep determination.

An almost Oriental luxury had gone far to weaken the fibre of that strong and opulent middle-class who had been the backbone of England, the entrenched Philistines. The value of birth as a moral asset which had a national duty and a national influence, and the value of money which had a social responsibility and a communal use, were unrealized by the many nouveaux riches who frequented the fashionable purlieus; who gave vast parties where display and extravagance were the principal feature; who ostentatiously offered large sums to public objects. Men who had made their money where copper or gold or oil or wool or silver or cattle or railways made commercial kings, supported schemes for the public welfare brought them by fine ladies, largely because the ladies were fine; and they gave substantial sums—upon occasion—for these fine ladies' fine causes. Rich men, or reputed rich men, whose wives never appeared, who were kept in secluded quarters in Bloomsbury or Maida Vale, gave dinners at the Savoy or the Carlton which the scrapings of the aristocracy attended; but these gave no dinners in return.

To get money to do things, no matter how,—or little matter how; to be in the swim, and that swim all too rapidly washing out the real people—that was the almost universal ambition. But still the real people, however few or many, in the time of trouble came quietly into the necessary and appointed places with the automatic precision of the disciplined friend of the state and of humanity; and behind them were folk of the humbler sort, the lower middle-class, the labouring-man. Of these were the landpoor peer, with his sense of responsibility cultivated by daily life and duty in his county, on the one hand; the professional man of all professions, the little merchant, the sailor, the clerk and artisan, the digger and delver, on the other; and, in between, those people in the shires who had not yet come to be material and gross, who had old-fashioned ideas of the duty of the citizen and the

Christian. In the day of darkness these came and laid what they had at the foot of the altar of sacrifice.

This at least the war did: it served as a sieve to sift the people, and it served as the solvent of many a life-problem.

Ian Stafford was among the first to whom it offered "the way out," who went to it for the solution of their own set problem. Suddenly, as he stood with Jasmine in the little room where so many lives were tossed into the crucible of Fate that morning, the newsboy's voice shouting, "War declared!" had told him the path he must tread.

He had astonished the War Office by his request to be sent to the Front with his old arm, the artillery, and he was himself astonished by the instant assent that was given. And now on this October day he was on his way to do two things—to see whether Adrian Fellowes was keeping his promise, and to visit Jigger and his sister.

There had not been a week since the days at Glencader when he had not gone to the sordid quarters in the Mile End Road to see Jigger, and to hear from him how his sister was doing at the opera, until two days before, when he had learned from Lou herself what she had suffered at the hands of Adrian Fellowes. That problem would now be settled forever; but there remained the question of Jigger, and that must be settled, whatever the other grave problems facing him. Jigger must be cared for, must be placed in a position where he could have his start in life. Somehow Jigger was associated with all the movements of his life now, and was taken as part of the problem. What to do? He thought of it as he went eastward, and it did not seem easy to settle it. Jigger himself, however, cut the Gordian knot.

When he was told that Stafford was going to South Africa, and that it was a question as to what he—Jigger—should now do, in what sphere of life his abnormally "cute" mind must run, he answered, instantly.

"I'm goin' wiv y'r gryce," he said. "That's it—stryght. I'm goin' out there wiv you."

Ian shook his head and smiled sadly. "I'm afraid that's not for you, Jigger. No, think again."

"Ain't there work in Souf Afriker—maybe not in the army itself, y'r gryce? Couldn't I have me chanct out there? Lou's all right now, I bet; an' I could go as easy as can be."

"Yes, Lou will be all right now," remarked Stafford, with a reflective irony.

"I ain't got no stiddy job here, and there's work in Souf Afriker, ain't they? Couldn't I get a job holdin' horses, or carryin' a flag, or cleanin' the guns, or nippin' letters about—couldn't I, y'r gryce? I'm only askin' to go wiv you, to work, same as ever I did before I was run over. Ain't I goin' wiv you, y'r gryce?"

With a sudden resolve Stafford laid a hand on his shoulder. "Yes, you are going 'wiv' me, Jigger. You just are, horse, foot, and artillery. There'll be a job somewhere. I'll get you something to do, or—"

"Or bust, y'r gryce?"

So the problem lessened, and Ian's face cleared a little. If all the difficulties perplexing his life would only clear like that! The babe and the suckling had found the way so simple, so natural; and it was a comforting way, for he had a deep and tender regard for this quaint, clever waif who had drifted across his path.

To-morrow he would come and fetch Jigger: and Jigger's face followed him into the coming dusk, radiant and hopeful and full of life—of life that mattered. Jigger would go out to "Souf Afriker" with all his life before him, but he, Ian Stafford, would go with all his life behind him, all mile-stones passed except one.

So, brooding, he walked till he came to an underground station, and there took a train to Charing Cross. Here he was only a little distance away from the Embankment, where was to be found Adrian Fellowes; and with bent head he made his way among the motley crowd in front of the station, scarcely noticing any one, yet resenting the jostle and the crush. Suddenly in the crowd in front of him he saw Krool stealing along with a wide-awake hat well down over his eyes. Presently the sinister figure was lost in the confusion. It did not occur to him that perhaps Krool might be making for the same destination as himself; but the sight of the man threw his mind into an eddy of torturing thoughts.

The flare of light, white and ghastly, at Charing Cross was shining on a moving mass of people, so many of whom were ghastly also—derelicts of humanity, ruins of womanhood, casuals, adventurers, scavengers of life, prowlers who lived upon chance, upon cards, upon theft, upon women, upon libertines who waited in these precincts for some foolish and innocent woman whom they could entrap. Among them moved also the thousand other good citizens bent upon catching trains or wending their way home from work; but in the garish, cruel light, all, even the good, looked evil in a way, and furtive and unstable. To-night, the crowd were far more restless than usual, far more irritating in their purposeless movements. People sauntered, jerked themselves forward, moved in and out, as it were, intent on going everywhere and nowhere;

and the excitement possessing them, the agitation in the air, made them seem still more exasperating, and bewildering. Newsboys with shrill voices rasped the air with invitations to buy, and everywhere eager, nervous hands held out their half-pennies for the flimsy sensational rags.

Presently a girl jostled Stafford, then apologized with an endearing word which brought a sick sensation to his brain; but he only shook his head gravely at her. After all, she had a hard trade and it led nowhere—nowhere.

"Coming home with me, darling?" she added in response to his meditative look. Anything that was not actual rebuff was invitation to her blunted sense. "Coming home with me—?"

Home! A wave of black cynicism, of sardonic mirth passed through Stafford's brain. Home—where the business of this poor wayfarer's existence was carried on, where the shopkeeper sold her wares in the inner sanctuary! Home. . . He shook the girl's hand from his elbow and hastened on.

Yet why should he be angered with her, he said to himself. It was not moral elevation which had made him rough with her, but only that word Home she used. . . The dire mockery of it burned his mind like a corrosive acid. He had had no home since his father died years ago,—his mother had died when he was very young—and his eldest brother had taken possession of the family mansions, placing them in the control of his foreign wife, who sat in his mother's chair and in her place at table.

He had wished so often in the past for a home of his own, where he could gather round him young faces and lose himself in promoting the interests of those for whom he had become forever responsible. He had longed for the Englishman's castle, for his own little realm of interest where he could be supreme; and now it was never to be.

The idea gained in sacred importance as it receded forever from all possibility. In far-off days it had been associated with a vision in blue, with a face like a dresden-china shepherdess and hair like Aphrodite's. Laughter and wit and raillery had been part of the picture; and long evenings in the winter-time, when they two would read the books they both loved, and maybe talk awhile of world events in which his work had place; in which his gifts were found, shaping, influencing, producing. The garden, the orchard—he loved orchards—the hedges of flowering ivy and lilacs; and the fine grey and chestnut horses driven by his hand or hers through country lanes; the smell of the fallen leaves in the autumn evenings; or the sting of the bracing January wind across the moors or where the woodcock awaited its spoiler. All these had been in the vision. It was all over now. He had seen an image, it had vanished, and he was in the desert alone.

A band was playing "The Banks o' Garry Owen," and the tramp of marching men came to his ears. The crowd surged round him, pushed him, forced him forward, carried him on, till the marching men came near, were alongside of him—a battalion of Volunteers, going to the war to see "Kruger's farmers bite the dust!"—a six months' excursion, as they thought. Then the crowd, as it cheered jostled him against the wall of the shops, and presently he found himself forced down Buckingham Street. It was where he wished to go in order to reach Adrian Fellowes' apartments. He did not notice, as he was practically thrown into the street, that Krool was almost beside him.

The street was not well lighted, and he looked neither to right nor left. He was thinking hard of what he would say to Adrian Fellowes, if, and when, he saw him.

But not far behind him was a figure that stole along in the darker shadows of the houses, keeping at some distance. The same figure followed him furtively till he came into that part of the Embankment where Adrian Fellowes' chambers were; then it fell behind a little, for here the lights were brighter. It hung in the shadow of a door-way and watched him as he approached the door of the big building where Adrian Fellowes lived.

Presently, as he came nearer, Stafford saw a hansom standing before the door. Something made him pause for a moment, and when, in the pause, the figure of a woman emerged from the entrance and hastily got into the hansom, he drew back into the darkness of a doorway, as the man did who was now shadowing him; and he waited till it turned round and rolled swiftly away. Then he moved forward again. When not far from the entrance, however, another cab—a four-wheeler—discharged its occupant at a point nearer to the building than where he waited. It was a woman. She paid the cabman, who touched his hat with quick and grateful emphasis, and, wheeling his old crock round, clattered away. The woman glanced along the empty street swiftly, and then hurried to the doorway which opened to Adrian Fellowes' chambers.

Instantly Stafford recognized her. It was Jasmine, dressed in black and heavily veiled. He could not mistake the figure—there was none other like it; or the turn of her head—there was only one such head in all England. She entered the building quickly.

There was nothing to do but wait until she came out again. No passion stirred in him, no jealousy, no anger. It was all dead. He knew why she had come; or he thought he knew. She would tell the man who had said no word in defense of her, done nothing to protect her, who let the worst be believed, without one protest of her innocence, what she thought of him. She was foolish to go to him, but women do mad things, and they must not be expected to do the obviously sensible thing when the crisis of their lives has come. Stafford understood it all.

One thing he was certain Jasmine did not know—the intimacy between Fellowes and Al'mah. He himself had been tempted to speak of it in their terrible interview that morning; but he had refrained. The ignominy, the shame, the humiliation of that would have been beyond her endurance. He understood; but he shrank at the thought of the nature of the interview which she must have, at the thought of the meeting at all.

He would have some time to wait, no doubt, and he made himself easy in the doorway, where his glance could command the entrance she had used. He mechanically took out a cigar-case, but after looking at the cigars for a moment put them away again with a sigh. Smoking would not soothe him. He had passed beyond the artificial.

His waiting suddenly ended. It seemed hardly three minutes after Jasmine's entrance when she appeared in the doorway again, and, after a hasty glance up and down the street, sped away as swiftly as she could, and, at the corner, turned up sharply towards the Strand. Her movements had been agitated, and, as she hurried on, she thrust her head down into her muff as a woman would who faced a blinding rain.

The interview had been indeed short. Perhaps Fellowes had already gone abroad. He would soon find out.

He mounted the deserted staircase quickly and knocked at Fellowes' door. There was no reply. There was a light, however, and he knocked again. Still there was no answer. He tried the handle of the door. It turned, the door gave, and he entered. There was no sound. He knocked at an inner door. There was no reply, yet a light showed in the room. He turned the handle. Entering the room, he stood still and looked round. It seemed empty, but there were signs of packing, of things gathered together hastily.

Then, with a strange sudden sense of a presence in the room, he looked round again. There in a far corner of the large room was a couch, and on it lay a figure—Adrian Fellowes, straight and still—and sleeping.

Stafford went over. "Fellowes," he said, sharply.

There was no reply. He leaned over and touched a shoulder. "Fellowes!" he exclaimed again, but something in the touch made him look closely at the face half turned to the wall. Then he knew.

Adrian Fellowes was dead.

Horror came upon Stafford, but no cry escaped him. He stooped once more and closely looked at the body, but without touching it. There was no sign of violence, no blood, no disfigurement, no distortion, only a look of sleep—a pale, motionless sleep.

But the body was warm yet. He realized that as his hand had touched the shoulder. The man could only have been dead a little while.

Only a little while: and in that little while Jasmine had left the house with agitated footsteps.

"He did not die by his own hand," Stafford said aloud.

He rang the bell loudly. No one answered. He rang and rang again, and then a lazy porter came.

XXIII

"More was Lost at Mohacksfield"

Eastminster House was ablaze. A large dinner had been fixed for this October evening, and only just before half-past eight Jasmine entered the drawing-room to receive her guests. She had completely forgotten the dinner till very late in the afternoon, when she observed preparations for which she had given instructions the day before. She was about to leave the house upon the mission which had drawn her footsteps in the same direction as those of Ian Stafford, when the butler came to her for information upon some details. These she gave with an instant decision which was part of her equipment, and then, when the butler had gone, she left the house on foot to take a cab at the corner of Piccadilly.

When she returned home, the tables in the dining-room were decorated, the great rooms were already lighted, and the red carpet was being laid down at the door. The footmen looked up with surprise as she came up the steps, and their eyes followed her as she ascended the staircase with marked deliberation.

"Well, that's style for you," said the first footman. "Takin' an airin' on shanks' hosses."

"And a quarter of an hour left to put on the tirara," sniggered the second footman. "The lot is asked for eight-thirty."

"Swells, the bunch, windin' up with the brother of an Emperor—'struth!"

"I'll bet the Emperor's brother ain't above takin' a tip about shares on the Rand, me boy."

"I'll bet none of 'em ain't. That's why they come—not forgetting th' grub and the fizz."

"What price a title for the Byng Baas one of these days! They like tips down there where the old Markis rumbles through his beard—and a lot of hands to be greased. And grease it costs a lot, political grease does. But what price a title—Sir Rudyard Byng, Bart., wot oh!"

"Try another shelf higher up, and it's more like it. Wot a head for a coronet 'ers! W'y—"

But the voice of the butler recalled them from the fields of imagination, and they went with lordly leisure upon the business of the household.

Socially this was to be the day of Jasmine's greatest triumph. One of the British royal family was, with the member of another great reigning family, honouring her table—though the ladies of neither were to be present; and this had been a drop of chagrin in her cup. She had been unaware of the gossip there had been of late,—though it was unlikely the great ladies would have known of it—and she would have been slow to believe what Ian had told her this day, that men had talked lightly of her at De Lancy Scovel's house. Her eyes had been shut; her wilful nature had not been sensitive to the quality of the social air about her. People came—almost "everybody" came—to her house, and would come, of course, until there was some open scandal; until her husband intervened. Yet everybody did not come. The royal princesses had not found it convenient to come; and this may have meant nothing, or very much indeed. To Jasmine, however, as she hastily robed herself for dinner, her mind working with lightning swiftness, it did not matter at all; if all the kings and queens of all the world had promised to come and had not come, it would have meant nothing to her this night of nights.

In her eyes there was the look of one who has seen some horrible thing, though she gave her orders with coherence and decision as usual, and with great deftness she assisted her maid in the hasty toilette. Her face was very pale, save for one or two hectic spots which took the place of the nectarine bloom so seldom absent from her cheeks, and in its place was a new, shining, strange look like a most delicate film—the transfiguring kind of look which great joy or great pain gives.

Coming up the staircase from the street, she had seen Krool enter her husband's room more hastily than usual, and had heard him greeted sharply—something that sounded strange to her ears, for Rudyard was uniformly kind to Krool. Never had Rudyard's voice sounded as it did now. Of course it was her imagination, but it was like a voice which came from some desolate place, distant, arid and alien. That was not the voice in which he had wooed her on the day when they heard of Jameson's Raid. That was not the voice which had spoken to her in broken tones of love on the day Ian first dined with her after her marriage—that fateful, desperate day. This was a voice which had a cheerless, fretful note, a savage something in it. Presently they two would meet, and she knew how it would be—an outward semblance, a superficial amenity and confidence before their guests; the smile of intimacy, when there was no intimacy, and never, never, could be again; only acting, only make-believe, only the artifice of deceit.

Yet when she was dressed—in pure white, with only a string of pearls, the smallest she had, round her neck—she was like that white flower which had been placed on her pillow last night.

Turning to leave the bedroom she caught sight of her face and figure again in the big mirror, and she seemed to herself like some other woman. There was that strange, distant look of agony in her eyes, that transfiguring look in the face; there was the figure somehow gone slimmer in these few hours; and there was a frail appearance which did not belong to her.

As she was about to leave the room to descend the stairs, there came a knock at the door. A bunch of white violets was handed in, with a pencilled note in Rudyard's handwriting.

White violets—white violets!

The note read, "Wear these to-night, Jasmine."

White violets—how strange that he should send them! These they send for the young, the innocent, and the dead. Rudyard had sent them to her—from how far away! He was there just across the hallway, and yet he might have been in Bolivia, so far as their real life was concerned.

She was under no illusion. This day, and perhaps a few, a very few others, must be lived under the same roof, in order that they could separate without scandal; but things could never go on as in the past. She had realized that the night before, when still that chance of which she had spoken to Stafford was hers; when she had wound the coil of her wonderful hair round her throat, and had imagined that self-destruction which has tempted so many of more spiritual make than herself. It was melodramatic, emotional, theatrical, maybe; but the emotional, the theatrical, the egotistic mortal has his or her tragedy, which is just as real as that which comes to those of more spiritual vein, just as real as that which comes to the more classical victim of fate. Jasmine had the deep defects of her qualities. Her suffering was not the less acute because it found its way out with impassioned demonstration.

There was, however, no melodrama in the quiet trembling with which she took the white violets, the symbol of love and death. She was sure that Rudyard was not aware of their significance and meaning, but that did not modify the effect upon her. Her trouble just now was too deep for tears, too bitter for words, too terrible for aught save numb endurance. Nothing seemed to matter in a sense, and yet the little routine of life meant so much in its iron insistence. The habits of convention are so powerful that life's great issues are often obscured by them. Going to her final doom a woman would stop to give the last careful touch to her hair—the mechanical obedience to long habit. It is not vanity, not littleness, but habit; never shown with subtler irony than in the case of Madame de Langrois, who, pacing the path to her execution at Lille, stooped, picked up a pin from the ground, and fastened it in her gown—the tyranny of habit.

Outside her own room Jasmine paused for a moment and looked at the closed door of Rudyard's room. Only a step—and yet she was kept apart from him by a shadow so black, so overwhelming, that she could not penetrate it. It smothered her sight. No, no, that little step could not be taken; there was a gulf between them which could not be bridged.

There was nothing to say to Rudyard except what could be said upon the surface, before all the world, as it were; things which must be said through an atmosphere of artificial sounds, which would give no response to the agonized cries of the sentient soul. She could make believe before the world, but not alone with Rudyard. She shrank within herself at the idea of being alone with him.

As she went down-stairs a scene in a room on the Thames Embankment, from which she had come a half hour ago, passed before her vision. It was as though it had been imprinted on the film of her eye and must stay there forever.

When would the world know that Adrian Fellowes lay dead in the room on the Embankment? And when they knew it, what would they say? They would ask how he died—the world would ask how he died. The Law would ask how he died.

How had he died? Who killed him? Or did he die by his own hand? Had Adrian Fellowes, the rank materialist, the bon viveur, the man-luxury, the courage to kill himself by his own hand? If not, who killed him? She shuddered. They might say that she killed him.

She had seen no one on the staircase as she had gone up, but she had dimly seen another figure outside in the terrace as she came out, and there was the cabman who drove her to the place. That was all.

Now, entering the great drawing-room of her own house she shuddered as though from an icy chill. The scene there on the Embankment—her own bitter anger, her frozen hatred; then the dead man with his face turned to the wall; the stillness, the clock ticking, her own cold voice speaking to him, calling; then the terrified scrutiny, the touch of the wrist, the realization, the moment's awful horror, the silence which grew more profound, the sudden paralysis of body and will. . . And then—music, strange, soft, mysterious music coming from somewhere inside the room, music familiar and yet unnatural, a song she had heard once before, a pathetic folk-song of eastern Europe, "More Was Lost at Mohacksfield." It was a tale of love and loss and tragedy and despair.

Startled and overcome, she had swayed, and would have fallen, but that with an effort of the will she had caught at the table and saved herself. With the music still creeping in unutterable melancholy through the room, she had fled, closing the door behind her very softly as though not to disturb the sleeper. It had followed her down the staircase and into the street, the weird, unnatural music.

It was only when she had entered a cab in the Strand that she realized exactly what the music was. She remembered that Fellowes had bought a music-box which could be timed to play at will—even days ahead, and he had evidently set the box to play at this hour. It did so, a strange, grim commentary on the stark thing lying on the couch, nerveless as though it had been dead a thousand years. It had ceased to play before Stafford entered the room, but, strangely enough, it began again as he said over the dead body, "He did not die by his own hand."

Standing before the fireplace in the drawing-room, awaiting the first guest, Jasmine said to herself: "No, no, he had not the courage to kill himself."

Some one had killed him. Who was it? Who killed him—Rudyard— Ian—who? But how? There was no sign of violence. That much she had seen. He lay like one asleep. Who was it killed him?

"Lady Tynemouth."

Back to the world from purgatory again. The butler's voice broke the spell, and Lady Tynemouth took her friend in her arms and kissed her.

"So handsome you look, my darling—and all in white. White violets, too. Dear, dear, how sweet, and oh, how triste! But I suppose it's chic. Certainly, it is stunning. And so simple. Just the weeny, teeny string of pearls, like a young under-secretary's wife, to show what she might do if she had a fair chance. Oh, you clever, wonderful Jasmine!"

"My dressmaker says I have no real taste in colours, so I compromised," was Jasmine's reply, with a really good imitation of a smile.

As she babbled on, Lady Tynemouth had been eyeing her friend with swift inquiry, for she had never seen Jasmine look as she did to-night, so ethereal, so tragically ethereal, with dark lines under the eyes, the curious transparency of the skin, and the feverish brightness and far-awayness of the look. She was about to say something in comment, but other guests entered, and it was impossible. She watched, however, from a little distance, while talking gaily to other guests; she watched at the dinner-table, as Jasmine, seated between her two royalties, talked with gaiety, with pretty irony, with respectful badinage; and no one could be so daring with such ceremonious respect at the same time as she. Yet through it all Lady Tynemouth saw her glance many times with a strange, strained inquiry at Rudyard, seated far away opposite her; at another big, round table.

"There's something wrong here," Lady Tynemouth said to herself, and wondered why Ian Stafford was not present. Mennaval was there, eagerly seeking glances. These Jasmine gave with a smiling openness and apparent good-fellowship, which were not in the least compromising. Lady Tynemouth saw Mennaval's vain efforts, and laughed to herself, and presently she even laughed with her neighbour about them.

"What an infant it is!" she said to her table companion. "Jasmine Byng doesn't care a snap of her finger about Mennaval."

"Does she care a snap for anybody?" asked the other. Then he added, with a kind of query in the question apart from the question itself: "Where is the great man—where's Stafford to-night?"

"Counting his winnings, I suppose." Lady Tynemouth's face grew soft. "He has done great things for so young a man. What a distance he has gone since he pulled me and my red umbrella back from the Zambesi Falls!"

Then proceeded a gay conversation, in which Lady Tynemouth was quite happy. When she could talk of Ian Stafford she was really enjoying herself. In her eyes he was the perfect man, whom other women tried to spoil, and whom, she flattered herself, she kept sound and unspoiled by her frank platonic affection.

"Our host seems a bit abstracted to-night," said her table companion after a long discussion about what Stafford had done and what he still might do.

"The war—it means so much to him," said Lady Tynemouth. Yet she had seen the note of abstraction too, and it had made her wonder what was happening in this household.

The other demurred.

"But I imagine he has been prepared for the war for some time. He didn't seem excessively worried about it before dinner, yet he seemed upset too, so pale and anxious-looking."

"I'll make her talk, make her tell me what it is, if there is anything," said Lady Tynemouth to herself. "I'll ask myself to stay with her for a couple of days."

Superficial as Lady Tynemouth seemed to many, she had real sincerity, and she was a friend in need to her friends. She loved Jasmine as much as she could love any woman, and she said now, as she looked at Jasmine's face, so alert, so full of raillery, yet with such an undertone of misery:

"She looks as if she needed a friend."

After dinner she contrived to get her arm through that of her hostess, and gave it an endearing pressure. "May I come to you for a few days, Jasmine?" she asked.

"I was going to ask if you would have me," answered Jasmine, with a queer little smile. "Rudyard will be up to his ears for a few days, and that's a chance for you and me to do some shopping, and some other things together, isn't it?"

She was thinking of appearances, of the best way to separate from Rudyard for a little while, till the longer separation could be arranged without scandal. Ian Stafford had said that things could go on in this house as before, that Rudyard would never hint to her what he knew, or rather what the letter had told him or left untold: but that was impossible. Whatever Rudyard was willing to do, there was that which she could not do. Twenty-four hours had accomplished a complete revolution in her attitude towards life and in her sense of things. Just for these immediate days to come, when the tragedy of Fellowes' death would be made a sensation of the hour, there must be temporary expedients; and Lady Tynemouth had suggested one which had its great advantages.

She could not bear to remain in Rudyard's house; and in his heart of hearts Rudyard would wish the same, even if he believed her innocent; but if she must stay for appearance' sake, then it would be good to have Lady Tynemouth with her. Rudyard would be grateful for time to get his balance again. This bunch of violets was the impulse of a big, magnanimous nature; but it would be followed by the inevitable reaction, which would be the real test and trial.

Love and forgiveness—what had she to do with either! She did not wish forgiveness because of Adrian Fellowes. No heart had been involved in that episode. It had in one sense meant nothing to her. She loved another man, and she did not wish forgiveness of him either. No, no, the whole situation was impossible. She could not stay here. For his own sake Rudyard would not, ought not, to wish her to stay. What might the next few days bring forth?

Who had killed Adrian Fellowes? He was not man enough to take his own life—who had killed him? Was it her husband, after all? He had said to Ian Stafford that he would do nothing, but, with the maggot of revenge and jealousy in their brains, men could not be trusted from one moment to another.

The white violets? Even they might be only the impulse of the moment, one of those acts of madness of jealous and revengeful people. Men had kissed their wives and then killed them—fondled them, and then strangled them. Rudyard might have made up his mind since morning to kill Fellowes, and kill herself, also. Fellowes was gone, and now might come her turn. White violets were the flowers of death, and the first flowers he had ever given her were purple violets, the flowers of life and love.

If Rudyard had killed Adrian Fellowes, there would be an end to everything. If he was suspected, and if the law stretched out its hand of steel to clutch him—what an ignominious end to it all; what a mean finish to life, to opportunity, to everything worth doing!

And she would have been the cause of everything.

The thought scorched her soul.

Yet she talked on gaily to her guests until the men returned from their cigars; as though Penalty and Nemesis were outside even the range of her imagination; as though she could not hear the snap of the handcuffs on Rudyard's—or Ian's—wrists.

Before and after dinner only a few words had passed between her and Rudyard, and that was with people round them. It was as though they spoke through some neutralizing medium, in which all real personal relation was lost. Now Rudyard came to her, however, and in a matter-of-fact voice said: "I suppose Al'mah will be here. You haven't heard to the contrary, I hope? These great singers are so whimsical."

There was no time for Jasmine to answer, for through one of the far entrances of the drawing-room Al'mah entered. Her manner was composed—if possible more composed than usual, and she looked around her calmly. At that moment a servant handed Byng a letter. It contained only a few words, and it ran:

Dear Byng,

Fellowes is gone. I found him dead in his rooms. An inquest will be held to-morrow. There are no signs of violence; neither of suicide or anything else. If you want me, I shall be at my rooms after ten o'clock to-night. I have got all his papers.

Yours ever,
Ian Stafford

Jasmine watched Rudyard closely as he read. A strange look passed over his face, but his hand was steady as he put the note in his pocket. She then saw him look searchingly at Al'mah as he went forward to greet her.

On the instant Rudyard had made up his mind what to do. It was clear that Al'mah did not know that Fellowes was dead, or she would not be here; for he knew of their relations, though he had never told Jasmine. Jasmine did not suspect the truth, or Al'mah would not be where she was; and Fellowes would never have written to Jasmine the letter for which he had paid with his life.

Al'mah was gently appreciative of the welcome she received from both Byng and Jasmine, and she prepared to sing.

"Yes, I think I am in good voice," she said to Jasmine, presently. Then Rudyard went, giving his wife's arm a little familiar touch as he passed, and said:

"Remember, we must have some patriotic things tonight. I'm sure Al'mah will feel so, too. Something really patriotic and stirring. We shall need it—yes we shall need cheering very badly before we've done. We're not going to have a walk-over in South Africa. Cheering up is what we want, and we must have it."

Again he cast a queer, inquiring look at Al'mah, to which he got no response, and to himself he said, grimly: "Well, it's better she should not know it—here."

His mind was in a maze. He moved as in a dream. He was pale, but he had an air of determination. Once he staggered with dizziness, then he righted himself and smiled at some one near. That some one winked at his neighbour.

"It's true, then, what we hear about him," the neighbour said, and suggestively raised fingers to his mouth.

GILBERT PARKER

Al'mah sang as perhaps she had seldom sung. There was in her voice an abandon and tragic intensity, a wonderful resonance and power, which captured her hearers as they had never been captured before. First she sang a love-song, then a song of parting. Afterwards came a lyric of country, which stirred her audience deeply. It was a challenge to every patriot to play his part for home and country. It was an appeal to the spirit of sacrifice; it was an inspiration and an invocation. Men's eyes grew moist.

And now another, a final song, a combination of all—of love, and loss and parting and ruin, and war and patriotism and destiny. With the first low notes of it Jasmine rose slowly from her seat, like one in a dream, and stood staring blindly at Al'mah. The great voice swelled out in a passion of agony, then sank away into a note of despair that gripped the heart.

"But more was lost at Mohacksfield—"

Jasmine had stood transfixed while the first words were sung, then, as the last line was reached, staring straight in front of her, as though she saw again the body of Adrian Fellowes in the room by the river, she gave a cry, which sounded half laughter and half torture, and fell heavily on the polished floor.

Rudyard ran forward and lifted her in his arms. Lady Tynemouth was beside him in an instant.

"Yes, that's right—you come," he said to her, and he carried the limp body up-stairs, the white violets in her dress crushed against his breast.

"Poor child—the war, of course; it means so much to them."

Thus, a kindly dowager, as she followed the Royalties down-stairs.

XXIV

ONE WHO CAME SEARCHING

A lady to see you, sir."

"A lady? What should we be doing with ladies here, Gleg?"

"I'm sure I have no use for them, sir," replied Gleg, sourly. He was in no good humour. That very morning he had been told that his master was going to South Africa, and that he would not be needed there, but that he should remain in England, drawing his usual pay. Instead of receiving this statement with gratitude, Gleg had sniffed in a manner which, in any one else, would have been impertinence; and he had not even offered thanks.

"Well, what do you think she wants? She looks respectable?"

"I don't know about that, sir. It's her ladyship, sir."

"It's what 'ladyship,' Gleg?"

"Her ladyship, sir—Lady Tynemouth."

Stafford looked at Gleg meditatively for a minute, and then said quietly:

"Let me see, you have been with me sixteen years, Gleg. You've forgotten me often enough in that time, but you've never forgotten yourself before. Come to me to-morrow at noon. . . I shall allow you a small pension. Show her ladyship in."

Gone waxen in face, Gleg crept out of the room.

"Seven-and-six a week, I suppose," he said to himself as he went down the stairs. "Seven-and-six for a bit of bonhommy."

With great consideration he brought Lady Tynemouth up, and shut the door with that stillness which might be reverence, or something at its antipodes.

Lady Tynemouth smiled cheerily at Ian as she held out her hand.

"Gleg disapproves of me very greatly. He thinks I am no better than I ought to be."

"I am sure you are," answered Stafford, drily.

"Well, if you don't know, Ian, who does? I've put my head in the lion's mouth before, just like this, and the lion hasn't snapped once," she rejoined, settling herself cozily in a great, green leather-chair. "Nobody would believe it; but there it is. The world couldn't think that you could be so careless of your opportunities, or that I would pay for the candle without burning it."

"On the contrary, I think they would believe anything you told them."

She laughed happily. "Wouldn't you like to call me Alice, 'same as ever,' in the days of long ago? It would make me feel at home after Gleg's icy welcome."

He smiled, looked down at her with admiration, and quoted some lines of Swinburne, alive with cynicism:

> *"And the worst and the best of this is,*
> *That neither is most to blame*
> *If she has forgotten my kisses,*
> *And I have forgotten her name."*

Lady Tynemouth made a plaintive gesture. "I should probably be able to endure the bleak present, if there had been any kisses in the sunny past," she rejoined, with mock pathos. "That's the worst of our friendship, Ian. I'm quite sure the world thinks I'm one of your spent flames, and there never was any fire, not so big as the point of a needle, was there? It's that which hurts so now, little Ian Stafford—not so much fire as would burn on the point of a needle."

"'On the point of a needle,'" Ian repeated, half-abstractedly. He went over to his writing-desk, and, opening a blotter, regarded it meditatively for an instant. As he did so she tapped the floor impatiently with her umbrella, and looked at him curiously, but with a little quirk of humour at the corners of her mouth.

"The point of a needle might carry enough fire to burn up a good deal," he said, reflectively. Then he added, slowly: "Do you remember Mr. Mappin and his poisoned needle at Glencader?"

"Yes, of course. That was a day of tragedy, when you and Rudyard Byng won a hundred Royal Humane Society medals, and we all felt like martyrs and heroes. I had the most creepy dreams afterwards. One night it was awful. I was being tortured with Mr. Mappin's needle horribly by—guess whom? By that half-caste Krool, and I waked up with a little scream, to find Tynie busy pinching me. I had been making such a wurra-wurra, as he called it."

"Well, it is a startling idea that there's poison powerful enough to make a needle-point dipped in it deadly."

"I don't believe it a bit, but—"

Pausing, she flicked a speck of fluff from her black dress—she was all in black, with only a stole of pure white about her shoulders. "But tell me," she added, presently—"for it's one of the reasons why I'm here now—what happened at the inquest to-day? The evening papers are not out, and you were there, of course, and gave evidence, I suppose. Was it very trying? I'm sure it was, for I've never seen you look so pale. You are positively haggard, Ian. You don't mind that from an old friend, do you? You look terribly ill, just when you should look so well."

"Why should I look so well?" He gazed at her steadily. Had she any glimmering of the real situation? She was staying now in Byng's house, and two days had gone since the world had gone wrong; since Jasmine had sunk to the floor unconscious as Al'mah sang, "More was lost at Mohacksfield."

"Why should you look so well? Because you are the coming man, they say. It makes me so proud to be your friend—even your neglected, if not quite discarded, friend. Every one says you have done such splendid work for England, and that now you can have anything you want. The ball is at your feet. Dear man, you ought to look like a morning-glory, and not as you do. Tell me, Ian, are you ill, or is it only the reaction after all you've done?"

"No doubt it's the reaction," he replied.

"I know you didn't like Adrian Fellowes much," she remarked, watching him closely. "He behaved shockingly at the Glencader Mine affair—shockingly. Tynie was for pitching him out of the house, and taking the consequences; but, all the same, a sudden death like that all alone must have been dreadful. Please tell me, what was the verdict?"

"Heart failure was the verdict; with regret for a promising life cut short, and sympathy with the relatives."

"I never heard that he had heart trouble," was the meditative response. "But—well, of course, it was heart failure. When the heart stops beating, there's heart failure. What a silly verdict!"

"It sounded rather worse than silly," was Ian's comment.

"Did—did they cut him up, to see if he'd taken morphia, or an overdose of laudanum or veronal or something? I had a friend who died of taking quantities of veronal while you were abroad so long—a South American, she was."

He nodded. "It was all quite in order. There were no signs of poison, they said, but the heart had had a shock of some kind. There had been what they called lesion, and all that kind of thing, and not sufficient strength for recovery."

"I suppose Mr. Mappin wasn't present?" she asked, curiously. "I know it is silly in a way, but don't you remember how interested Mr. Fellowes was in that needle? Was Mr. Mappin there?"

"There was no reason why he should be there."

"What witnesses were called?"

"Myself and the porter of Fellowes' apartments, his banker, his doctor—"

"And Al'mah?" she asked, obliquely.

He did not reply at once, but regarded her inquiringly.

"You needn't be afraid to speak about Al'mah," she continued. "I saw something queer at Glencader. Then I asked Tynie, and he told me that—well, all about her and Adrian Fellowes. Was Al'mah there? Did she give evidence?"

"She was there to be called, if necessary," he responded, "but the coroner was very good about it. After the autopsy the authorities said evidence was unnecessary, and—"

"You arranged that, probably?"

"Yes; it was not difficult. They were so stupid—and so kind."

She smoothed out the folds of her dress reflectively, then got up as if with sudden determination, and came near to him. Her face was pale now, and her eyes were greatly troubled.

"Ian," she said, in a low voice, "I don't believe that Adrian Fellowes died a natural death, and I don't believe that he killed himself. He would not have that kind of courage, even in insanity. He could never go insane. He could never care enough about anything to do so. He—did—not—kill—himself. There, I am sure of it. And he did not die a natural death, either."

"Who killed him?" Ian asked, his face becoming more drawn, but his eyes remaining steady and quiet.

She put her hand to her eyes for a moment. "Oh, it all seems so horrible! I've tried to shake it off, and not to think my thoughts, and I came to you to get fresh confidence; but as soon as I saw your face I knew I couldn't have it. I know you are upset too, perhaps not by the same thoughts, but through the same people."

"Tell me all you think or know. Be quite frank," he said, heavily. "I will tell you why later. It is essential that you should be wholly frank with me."

"As I have always been. I can't be anything else. Anyhow, I owe you so much that you have the right to ask me what you will. . . There it is, the fatal thing," she added.

Her eyes were raised to the red umbrella which had nearly carried her over into the cauldron of the Zambesi Falls.

"No, it is the world that owes me a heavy debt," he responded, gallantly. "I was merely selfish in saving you."

Her eyes filled with tears, which she brushed away with a little laugh.

"Ah, how I wish it was that! I am just mean enough to want you to want me, while I didn't want you. That's the woman, and that's all women, and there's no getting away from it. But still I would rather you had saved me than any one else who wasn't bound, like Tynie, to do so."

"Well, it did seem absurd that you should risk so much to keep a sixpenny umbrella," he rejoined, drily.

"How we play on the surface while there's so much that is wearing our hearts out underneath," she responded, wearily. "Listen, Ian, you know what I mean. Whoever killed Adrian Fellowes, or didn't, I am sure that Jasmine saw him dead. Three nights ago when she fainted and went ill to bed, I stayed with her, slept in the same room, in the bed beside hers. The opiate the doctor gave her was not strong enough, and two or three times she half waked, and—and it was very painful. It made my heart ache, for I knew it wasn't all dreams. I am sure she saw Adrian Fellowes lying dead in his room. . . Ian, it is awful, but for some reason she hated him, and she saw him lying dead. If any one knows the truth, you know. Jasmine cares for you—no, no, don't mind my saying it. She didn't care a fig for Mennaval, or any of the others, but she does care for you—cares for you. She oughtn't to, but she does, and she should have married you long ago before Rudyard Byng came. Please don't think I am interfering, Ian. I am not. You never had a better friend than I am. But there's something ghastly wrong. Rudyard is looking like a giant that's had blood-letting, and he never goes near Jasmine, except when some one is with her. It's a bad sign when two people must have some third person about to insulate their self-consciousness and prevent those fatal moments when they have to be just their own selves, and have it out."

"You think there's been trouble between them?" His voice was quite steady, his manner composed.

"I don't think quite that. But there is trouble in that palace. Rudyard is going to South Africa."

"Well, that is not unnatural. I should expect him to do so. I am going to South Africa also."

For a moment she looked at him without speaking, and her face slowly paled. "You are going to the Front—you?"

"Yes—'Back to the army again, sergeant, back to the army again.' I was a gunner, you know, and not a bad one, either, if I do say it."

"You are going to throw up a great career to go to the Front? When you have got your foot at the top of the ladder, you climb down?" Her voice was choking a little.

He made a little whimsical gesture. "There's another ladder to climb. I'll have a try at it, and do my duty to my country, too. I'll have a double-barrelled claim on her, if possible."

"I know that you are going because you will not stay when Rudyard goes," she rejoined, almost irritably.

"What a quixotic idea! Really you are too impossible and wrong-headed."

He turned an earnest look upon her. "No, I give you my word, I am not going because Rudyard is going. I didn't know he was going till you told me. I got permission to go three hours after Kruger's message came."

"You are only feckless—only feckless, as the Scotch say," she rejoined with testy sadness. "Well, since everybody is going, I am going too. I am going with a hospital-ship."

"Well, that would pay off a lot of old debts to the Almighty," he replied, in kindly taunt.

"I haven't been worse than most women, Ian," she replied. "Women haven't been taught to do things, to pay off their debts. Men run up bills and pay them off, and run them up again and again and pay them off; but we, while we run up bills, our ways of paying them off are so few, and so uninteresting."

Suddenly she took from her pocket a letter. "Here is a letter for you," she said. "It was lying on Jasmine's table the night she was taken ill. I don't know why I did it, but I suppose I took it up so that Rudyard should not see it; and then I didn't say anything to Jasmine about it at once. She said nothing, either; but to-day I told her I'd seen the letter addressed to you, and had posted it. I said it to see how she would take it. She only nodded, and said nothing at first. Then after a while she whispered, 'Thank you, my dear,' but in such a queer tone. Ian, she meant you to have the letter, and here it is."

She put it into his hands. He remembered it. It was the letter which Jasmine had laid on the table before him at that last interview when the world stood still. After a moment's hesitation he put it in his pocket.

"If she wished me to have it—" he said in a low voice.

"If not, why, then, did she write it? Didn't she say she was glad I posted it?"

A moment followed, in which neither spoke. Lady Tynemouth's eyes were turned to the window; Stafford stood looking into the fire.

"Tynie is sure to go to South Africa with his Yeomanry," she continued at last. "He'll be back in England next week. I can be of use out there, too. I suppose you think I'm useless because I've never had to do anything, but you are quite wrong. It's in me. If I'd been driven to work when I was a girl, if I'd been a labourer's daughter, I'd have made hats—or cream-cheeses. I'm not really such a fool as you've always thought me, Ian; at any rate, not in the way you've thought me."

His look was gentle, as he gazed into her eyes. "I've never thought you anything but a very sensible and alluring woman, who is only wilfully foolish at times," he said. "You do dangerous things."

"But you never knew me to do a really wrong thing, and if you haven't, no one has."

Suddenly her face clouded and her lips trembled. "But I am a good friend, and I love my friends. So it all hurts. Ian, I'm most upset. There's something behind Adrian Fellowes' death that I don't understand. I'm sure he didn't kill himself; but I'm also sure that some one did kill him." Her eyes sought his with an effort and with apprehension, but with persistency too. "I don't care what the jury said—I know I'm right."

"But it doesn't matter now," he answered, calmly. "He will be buried to-morrow, and there's an end of it all. It will not even be the usual nine days' wonder. I'd forget it, if I were you."

"I can't easily forget it while you remember it," she rejoined, meaningly. "I don't know why or how it affects you, but it does affect you, and that's why I feel it; that's why it haunts me."

Gleg appeared. "A gentleman to see you, sir," he said, and handed Ian a card.

"Where is he?"

"In the dining-room, sir."

"Very good. I will see him in a moment."

When they were alone again, Lady Tynemouth held out her hand. "When do you start for South Africa?" she asked.

"In three days. I join my battery in Natal."

"You will hear from me when I get to Durban," she said, with a shy, inquiring glance.

"You are really going?"

"I mean to organize a hospital-ship and go."

"Where will you get the money?"

"From some social climber," she replied, cynically. His hand was on the door-knob, and she laid her own on it gently. "You are ill, Ian," she said. "I have never seen you look as you do now."

"I shall be better before long," he answered. "I never saw you look so well."

"That's because I am going to do some work at last," she rejoined. "Work at last. I'll blunder a bit, but I'll try a great deal, and perhaps I'll do some good. . . And I'll be there to nurse you if you get fever or anything," she added, laughing nervously—"you and Tynie."

When she was gone he stood looking at the card in his hand, with his mind seeing something far beyond. Presently he rang for Gleg.

"Show Mr. Mappin in," he said.

XXV

Wherein the Lost is Found

In a moment the great surgeon was seated, looking reflectively round him. Soon, however, he said brusquely, "I hope your friend Jigger is going on all right?"

"Yes, yes, thanks to you."

"No, no, Mr. Stafford, thanks to you and Mrs. Byng chiefly. It was care and nursing that did it. If I could have hospitals like Glencader and hospital nurses like Mrs. Byng and Al'mah and yourself, I'd have few regrets at the end of the year. That was an exciting time at Glencader."

Stafford nodded, but said nothing. Presently, after some reference to the disaster at the mine at Glencader and to Stafford's and Byng's bravery, Mr. Mappin said. "I was shocked to hear of Mr. Fellowes' death. I was out of town when it happened—a bad case at Leeds; but I returned early this morning." He paused, inquiringly but Ian said nothing, and he continued, "I have seen the body."

"You were not at the inquest, I think," Ian remarked, casually.

"No, I was not in time for that, but I got permission to view the body."

"And the verdict—you approve?"

"Heart failure—yes." Mr. Mappin's lip curled. "Of course. But he had no heart trouble. His heart wasn't even weak. His life showed that."

"His life showed—?" Ian's eyebrows went up.

"He was very much in society, and there's nothing more strenuous than that. His heart was all right. Something made it fail, and I have been considering what it was."

"Are you suggesting that his death was not natural?"

"Quite artificial, quite artificial, I should say."

Ian took a cigarette, and lighted it slowly. "According to your theory, he must have committed suicide. But how? Not by an effort of the will, as they do in the East, I suppose?"

Mr. Mappin sat up stiffly in his chair. "Do you remember my showing you all at Glencader a needle which had on its point enough poison to kill a man?"

"And leave no trace—yes."

"Do you remember that you all looked at it with interest, and that Mr. Fellowes examined it more attentively than any one else?"

"I remember."

"Well, I was going to kill a collie with it next day."

"A favourite collie grown old, rheumatic—yes, I remember."

"Well, the experiment failed."

"The collie wasn't killed by the poison?"

"No, not by the poison, Mr. Stafford."

"So your theory didn't work except on paper."

"I think it worked, but not with the collie."

There was a pause, while Stafford looked composedly at his visitor, and then he said: "Why didn't it work with the collie?"

"It never had its chance."

"Some mistake, some hitch?"

"No mistake, no hitch; but the wrong needle."

"The wrong needle! I should not say that carelessness was a habit with you." Stafford's voice was civil and sympathetic.

"Confidence breeds carelessness," was Mr. Mappin's enigmatical retort.

"You were over-confident then?"

"Quite clearly so. I thought that Glencader was beyond reproach."

There was a slight pause, and then Stafford, flicking away some cigarette ashes, continued the catechism. "What particular form of reproach do you apply to Glencader?"

"Thieving."

"That sounds reprehensible—and rude."

"If you were not beyond reproach, it would be rude, Mr. Stafford."

Stafford chafed at the rather superior air of the expert, whose habit of bedside authority was apt to creep into his social conversation; but, while he longed to give him a shrewd thrust, he forbore. It was hard to tell how much he might have to do to prevent the man from making mischief. The compliment had been smug, and smugness irritated Stafford.

"Well, thanks for your testimonial," he said, presently, and then he determined to cut short the tardy revelation, and prick the bubble of mystery which the great man was so slowly blowing.

"I take it that you think some one at Glencader stole your needle, and so saved your collie's life," he said.

"That is what I mean," responded Mr. Mappin, a little discomposed that his elaborate synthesis should be so sharply brought to an end.

There was almost a grisly raillery in Stafford's reply. "Now, the collie—were you sufficiently a fatalist to let him live, or did you prepare another needle, or do it in the humdrum way?"

"I let the collie live."

"Hoping to find the needle again?" asked Stafford, with a smile.

"Perhaps to hear of it again."

"Hello, that is rather startling! And you have done so?"

"I think so. Yes, I may say that."

"Now how do you suppose you lost that needle?"

"It was taken from my pocket-case, and another substituted."

"Returning good for evil. Could you not see the difference in the needles?"

"There is not, necessarily, difference in needles. The substitute was the same size and shape, and I was not suspicious."

"And what form does your suspicion take now?"

The great man became rather portentously solemn—he himself would have said "becomingly grave." "My conviction is that Mr. Fellowes took my needle."

Stafford fixed the other with his gaze. "And killed himself with it?"

Mr. Mappin frowned. "Of that I cannot be sure, of course."

"Could you not tell by examining the body?"

"Not absolutely from a superficial examination."

"You did not think a scientific examination necessary?"

"Yes, perhaps; but the official inquest is over, the expert analysis or examination is finished by the authorities, and the superficial proofs, while convincing enough to me, are not complete and final; and so, there you are."

Stafford got and held his visitor's eyes, and with slow emphasis said: "You think that Fellowes committed suicide with your needle?"

"No, I didn't say that."

"Then I fear my intelligence must be failing rapidly. You said—"

"I said I was not sure that he killed himself. I am sure that he was killed by my needle; but I am not sure that he killed himself. Motive and all that kind of thing would come in there."

"Ah—and all that kind of thing! Why should you discard motive for his killing himself?"

"I did not say I discarded motive, but I think Mr. Fellowes the last man in the world likely to kill himself."

"Why, then, do you think he stole the needle?"

"Not to kill himself."

Stafford turned his head away a little. "Come now; this is too tall. You are going pretty far in suggesting that Fellowes took your needle to kill some one else."

"Perhaps. But motive might not be so far to seek."

"What motive in this case?" Stafford's eyes narrowed a little with the inquiry.

"Well, a woman, perhaps."

"You know of some one, who—"

"No. I am only assuming from Mr. Fellowes' somewhat material nature that there must be a woman or so."

"Or so—why 'or so?'" Stafford pressed him into a corner.

"There comes the motive—one too many, when one may be suspicious, or jealous, or revengeful, or impossible."

"Did you see any mark of the needle on the body?"

"I think so. But that would not do more than suggest further delicate, detailed, and final examination."

"You have no trace of the needle itself?"

"None. But surely that isn't strange. If he had killed himself, the needle would probably have been found. If he did not kill himself, but yet was killed by it, there is nothing strange in its not being recovered."

Stafford took on the gravity of a dry-as-dust judge. "I suppose that to prove the case it would be necessary to produce the needle, as your theory and your invention are rather new."

"For complete proof the needle would be necessary, though not indispensable."

Stafford was silent for an instant, then he said: "You have had a look for the little instrument of passage?"

"I was rather late for that, I fear."

"Still, by chance, the needle might have been picked up. However, it would look foolish to advertise for a needle which had traces of atric acid on it, wouldn't it?"

Mr. Mappin looked at Stafford quite coolly, and then, ignoring the question, said, deliberately: "You discovered the body, I hear. You didn't by any chance find the needle, I suppose?"

Stafford returned his look with a cool stare. "Not by any chance," he said, enigmatically.

He had suddenly decided on a line of action which would turn this astute egoist from his half-indicated purpose. Whatever the means of

Fellowes' death, by whomsoever caused, or by no one, further inquiry could only result in revelations hurtful to some one. As Mr. Mappin had surmised, there was more than one woman,—there may have been a dozen, of course—but chance might just pitch on the one whom investigation would injure most.

If this expert was quieted, and Fellowes was safely bestowed in his grave, the tragic incident would be lost quickly in the general excitement and agitation of the nation. The war-drum would drown any small human cries of suspicion or outraged innocence. Suppose some one did kill Adrian Fellowes? He deserved to die, and justice was satisfied, even if the law was marauded. There were at least four people who might have killed Fellowes without much remorse. There was Rudyard, there was Jasmine, there was Lou the erstwhile flower-girl—and himself. It was necessary that Mappin, however, should be silenced, and sent about his business.

Stafford suddenly came over to the table near to his visitor, and with an assumed air of cold indignation, though with a little natural irritability behind all, said "Mr. Mappin, I assume that you have not gone elsewhere with your suspicions?"

The other shook his head in negation.

"Very well, I should strongly advise you, for your own reputation as an expert and a man of science, not to attempt the rather cliche occupation of trying to rival Sherlock Holmes. Your suspicions may have some distant justification, but only a man of infinite skill, tact, and knowledge, with an almost abnormal gift for tracing elusive clues and, when finding them, making them fit in with fact—only a man like yourself, a genius at the job, could get anything out of it. You are not prepared to give the time, and you could only succeed in causing pain and annoyance beyond calculation. Just imagine a Scotland Yard detective with such a delicate business to do. We have no Hamards here, no French geniuses who can reconstruct crimes by a kind of special sense. Can you not see the average detective blundering about with his ostentatious display of the obvious; his mind, which never traced a motive in its existence, trying to elucidate a clue? Well, it is the business of the Law to detect and punish crime. Let the Law do it in its own way, find its own clues, solve the mysteries given it to solve. Why should you complicate things? The official fellows could never do what you could do, if you were a detective. They haven't the brains or initiative or knowledge. And since you are not a detective, and can't devote yourself to this most delicate problem, if there be any problem at all, I would suggest—I imitate your own rudeness—that you mind your own business."

He smiled, and looked down at his visitor with inscrutable eyes.

At the last words Mr. Mappin flushed and looked consequential; but under the influence of a smile, so winning that many a chancellerie of Europe had lost its irritation over some skilful diplomatic stroke made by its possessor, he emerged from his atmosphere of offended dignity and feebly returned the smile.

"You are at once complimentary and scathing, Mr. Stafford," he said; "but I do recognize the force of what you say. Scotland Yard is beneath contempt. I know of cases—but I will not detain you with them now. They bungle their work terribly at Scotland Yard. A detective should be a man of imagination, of initiative, of deep knowledge of human nature. In the presence of a mystery he should be ready to find motives, to construct them and put them into play, as though they were real—work till a clue was found. Then, if none is found, find another motive and work on that. The French do it. They are marvels. Hamard is a genius, as you say. He imagines, he constructs, he pursues, he squeezes out every drop of juice in the orange. . . You see, I agree with you on the whole, but this tragedy disturbed me, and I thought that I had a real clue. I still believe I have, but cui bono?"

"Cui bono indeed, if it is bungled. If you could do it all yourself, good. But that is impossible. The world wants your skill to save life, not to destroy it. Fellowes is dead—does it matter so infinitely, whether by his own hand or that of another?"

"No, I frankly say I don't think it does matter infinitely. His type is no addition to the happiness of the world."

They looked at each other meaningly, and Mappin responded once again to Stafford's winning smile.

It pleased him prodigiously to feel Stafford lay a firm hand on his arm and say: "Can you, perhaps, dine with me to-night at the Travellers' Club? It makes life worth while to talk to men like you who do really big things."

"I shall be delighted to come for your own reasons," answered the great man, beaming, and adjusting his cuffs carefully.

"Good, good. It is capital to find you free." Again Stafford caught the surgeon's arm with a friendly little grip.

Suddenly, however, Mr. Mappin became aware that Stafford had turned desperately white and worn. He had noticed this spent condition when he first came in, but his eyes now rediscovered it. He regarded Stafford with concern.

"Mr. Stafford," he said, "I am sure you do not realize how much below par you are. . . You have been under great strain—I know, we all know, how hard you have worked lately. Through you, England launches her ship of war without fear of complications; but it has told on you heavily. Nothing is got without paying for it. You need rest, and you need change."

"Quite so—rest and change. I am going to have both now," said Stafford with a smile, which was forced and wan.

"You need a tonic also, and you must allow me to give you one," was the brusque professional response.

With quick movement he went over to Stafford's writing-table, and threw open the cover of the blotter.

In a flash Stafford was beside him, and laid a hand upon the blotter, saying with a smile, of the kind which had so far done its work—

"No, no, my friend, I will not take a tonic. It's only a good sleep I want; and I'll get that to-night. But I give my word, if I'm not all right to-morrow, if I don't sleep, I'll send to you and take your tonic gladly."

"You promise?"

"I promise, my dear Mappin."

The great man beamed again: and he really was solicitous for his new-found friend.

"Very well, very well—Stafford," he replied. "It shall be as you say. Good-bye, or, rather, au revoir!"

"A la bonne heure!" was the hearty response, as the door opened for the great surgeon's exit.

When the door was shut again, and Stafford was alone, he staggered over to the writing-desk. Opening the blotter, he took something up carefully and looked at it with a sardonic smile.

"You did your work quite well," he said, reflectively.

It was such a needle as he had seen at Glencader in Mr. Mappin's hand. He had picked it up in Adrian Fellowes' room.

"I wonder who used you," he said in a hard voice. "I wonder who used you so well. Was it—was it Jasmine?"

With a trembling gesture he sat down, put the needle in a drawer, locked it, and turned round to the fire again.

"Was it Jasmine?" he repeated, and he took from his pocket the letter which Lady Tynemouth had given him. For a moment he looked at it unopened—at the beautiful, smooth handwriting so familiar to his eyes; then he slowly broke the seal, and took out the closely written pages.

XXVI

Jasmine's Letter

"Ian, oh, Ian, what strange and dreadful things you have written to me!" Jasmine's letter ran—the letter which she told him she had written on that morning when all was lost. "Do you realize what you have said, and, saying it, have you thought of all it means to me? You have tried to think of what is best, I know, but have you thought of me? When I read your letter first, a flood of fire seemed to run through my veins; then I became as though I had been dipped in ether, and all the winds of an arctic sea were blowing over me.

"To go with you now, far away from the world in which we live and in which you work, to begin life again, as you say—how sweet and terrible and glad it would be! But I know, oh, I know myself and I know you! I am like one who has lived forever. I am not good, and I am not foolish, I am only mad; and the madness in me urges me to that visionary world where you and I could live and work and wander, and be content with all that would be given us—joy, seeing, understanding, revealing, doing.

"But Ian, it is only a visionary world, that world of which you speak. It does not exist. The overmastering love, the desire for you that is in me, makes for me the picture as it is in your mind; but down beneath all, the woman in me, the everlasting woman, is sure there is no such world.

"Listen, dear child—I call you that, for though I am only twenty-five I seem as aged as the Sphinx, and, like the Sphinx that begets mockery, so my soul, which seems to have looked out over unnumbered centuries, mocks at this world which you would make for you and me. Listen, Ian. It is not a real world, and I should not—and that is the pitiful, miserable part of it—I should not make you happy, if I were in that world with you. To my dire regret I know it. Suddenly you have roused in me what I can honestly say I have never felt before—strange, reckless, hungry feelings. I am like some young dweller of the jungle which, cut off from its kind tries, with a passion that eats and eats and eats away his very flesh to get back to its kind, to his mate, to that other wild child of nature which waits for the one appeasement of primeval desire.

"Ian, I must tell you the whole truth about myself as I understand it. I am a hopeless, painful contradiction; I have always been so. I have always wanted to be good, but something has always driven me where the flowers have a poisonous sweetness, where the heart grows bad. I want to cry to you, Ian, to help me to be good; and yet something drives me on to want to share with you the fruit which turns to dust and ashes in the long end. And behind all that again, some tiny little grain of honour in me says that I must not ask you to help me; says that I ought never to look into your eyes again, never touch your hand, nor see you any more; and from the little grain of honour comes the solemn whisper, 'Do not ruin him; do not spoil his life.'

"Your letter has torn my heart, so that it can never again be as it was before, and because there is some big, noble thing in you, some little, not ignoble thing is born in me. Ian, you could never know the anguished desire I have to be with you always, but, if I keep sane at all, I will not go—no, I will not go with you, unless the madness carries me away. It would kill you. I know, because I have lived so many thousands of years. My spirit and my body might be satisfied, the glory in having you all my own would be so great; but there would be no joy for you. To men like you, work is as the breath of life. You must always be fighting for something, always climbing higher, because you see some big thing to do which is so far above you.

"Yes, men like you get their chance sooner or later, because you work, and are ready to take the gifts of Fate when they appear and before they pass. You will be always for climbing, if some woman does not drag you back. That woman may be a wife, or it may be a loving and living ghost of a wife like me. Ian, I could not bear to see what would come at last—the disappointment in your face the look of hope gone from your eyes; your struggle to climb, and the struggle of no avail. Sisyphus had never such a task as you would have on the hill of life, if I left all behind here and went with you. You would try to hide it; but I would see you growing older hourly before my eyes. You would smile—I wonder if you know what sort of wonderful, alluring thing your smile is, Ian?— and that smile would drive me to kill myself, and so hurt you still more. And so it is always an everlasting circle of penalty and pain when you take the laws of life you get in the mountains in your hands and break them in pieces on the rocks in the valleys, and make new individual laws out of harmony with the general necessity.

"Isn't it strange, Ian, that I who can do wrong so easily still know so well and value so well what is right? It is my mother in me and my grandfather in me, both of them fighting for possession. Let me empty out my heart before you, because I know—I do not know why, but I do know, as I write—that some dark cloud lowers, gathers round us, in which we shall be lost, shall miss the touch of hand and never see each other's face again. I know it, oh so surely! I did not really love you years ago, before I married Rudyard; I did not love you when I married him; I did not love him, I could not really love any one. My heart was broken up in a thousand pieces to give away in little bits to all who came. But I cared for you more than I cared for any one else—so much more; because you were so able and powerful, and were meant to do such big things; and I had just enough intelligence to want to understand you; to feel what you were thinking, to grasp its meaning, however dimly. Yet I have no real intellect. I am only quick and rather clever—sharp, as Jigger would say, and with some cunning, too. I have made so many people believe that I am brilliant. When I think and talk and write, I only give out in a new light what others like you have taught me; give out a loaf where you gave me a crumb; blow a drop of water into a bushel of bubbles. No, I did not love you, in the big way, in those old days, and maybe it is not love I feel for you now; but it is a great and wonderful thing, so different from the feeling I once had. It is very powerful, and it is also very cruel, because it smothers me in one moment, and in the next it makes me want to fly to you, heedless of consequences.

"And what might those consequences be, Ian, and shall I let you face them? The real world, your world, England, Europe, would have no more use for all your skill and knowledge and power, because there would be a woman in the way. People who would want to be your helpers, and to follow you, would turn away when they saw you coming; or else they would say the superficial things which are worse than blows in the face to a man who wants to feel that men look to him to help solve the problems perplexing the world. While it may not be love I feel for you, whatever it is, it makes me a little just and unselfish now. I will not—unless a spring-time madness drives me to it to-day—I will not go with you.

"As for the other solution you offer, deceiving the world as to your purposes, to go far away upon some wild mission, and to die!

"Ah, no, you must not cheat the world so; you must not cheat yourself so! And how cruel it would be to me! Whatever I deserve—and in leaving you to marry Rudyard I deserved heavy punishment—still I do not deserve the torture which would follow me to the last day of my life if, because of me, you sacrificed that which is not yours alone, but which belongs to all the world. I loathe myself when I think of the old wrong that I did you; but no leper woman could look upon herself with such horror as I should upon myself, if, for the new wrong I have done you, you were to take your own life.

"These are so many words, and perhaps they will not read to you as real. That is perhaps because I am only shallow at the best; am only, as you once called me, 'a little burst of eloquence.' But even I can suffer, and I believe that even I can love. You say you cannot go on as things are; that I must go with you or you must die; and yet you do not wish me to go with you. You have said that, too. But do you not wonder what would become of me, if either of these alternatives is followed? A little while ago I could deceive Rudyard, and put myself in pretty clothes with a smile, and enjoy my breakfast with him and look in his face boldly, and enjoy the clothes, and the world and the gay things that are in it, perhaps because I had no real moral sense. Isn't it strange that out of the thing which the world would condemn as most immoral, as the very degradation of the heart and soul and body, there should spring up a new sense that is moral—perhaps the first true glimmering of it? Oh, dear love of my life, comrade of my soul, something has come to me which I never had before, and for that, whatever comes, my lifelong gratitude must be yours! What I now feel could never have come except through fire and tears, as you yourself say, and I know so well that the fire is at my feet, and the tears—I wept them all last night, when I too wanted to die.

"You are coming at eleven to-day, Ian—at eleven. It is now eight. I will try and send this letter to reach you before you leave your rooms. If not, I will give it to you when you come—at eleven. Why did you not say noon—noon—twelve of the clock? The end and the beginning! Why did you not say noon, Ian? The light is at its zenith at noon, at twelve; and the world is dark at twelve—at midnight. Twelve at noon; twelve at night; the light and the dark—which will it be for us, Ian? Night or noon? I wonder, oh, I wonder if, when I see you I shall have the strength to say, 'Yes, go, and come again no more.' Or whether, in spite of everything, I shall wildly say, 'Let us go away together.' Such is the kind of woman that I am. And you—dear lover, tell me truly what kind of man are you?

Your JASMINE

He read the letter slowly, and he stopped again and again as though to steady himself. His face became strained and white, and once he poured brandy and drank it off as though it were water. When he had finished the letter he went heavily over to the fire and dropped it in. He watched it burn, until only the flimsy carbon was left.

"If I had not gone till noon," he said aloud, in a nerveless voice—"if I had not gone till noon. . . Fellowes—did she—or was it Byng?"

He was so occupied with his thoughts that he was not at first conscious that some one was knocking.

"Come in," he called out at last.

The door opened and Rudyard Byng entered.

"I am going to South Africa, Stafford," he said, heavily. "I hear that you are going, too; and I have come to see whether we cannot go out together."

XXVII

Krool

A message from Mr. Byng to say that he may be a little late, but he says will you go on without him? He will come as soon as possible."

The footman, having delivered himself, turned to withdraw, but Barry Whalen called him back, saying, "Is Mr. Krool in the house?"

The footman replied in the affirmative. "Did you wish to see him, sir?" he asked.

"Not at present. A little later perhaps," answered Barry, with a glance round the group, who eyed him curiously.

At a word the footman withdrew. As the door closed, little black, oily Sobieski dit Melville said with an attempt at a joke, "Is 'Mr.' Krool to be called into consultation?"

"Don't be so damned funny, Melville," answered Barry. "I didn't ask the question for nothing."

"These aren't days when anybody guesses much," remarked Fleming. "And I'd like to know from Mr. Kruger, who knows a lot of things, and doesn't gas, whether he means the mines to be safe."

They all looked inquiringly at Wallstein, who in the storms which rocked them all kept his nerve and his countenance with a power almost benign. His large, limpid eye looked little like that belonging to an eagle of finance, as he had been called.

"It looked for a while as though they'd be left alone," said Wallstein, leaning heavily on the table, "but I'm not so sure now." He glanced at Barry Whalen significantly, and the latter surveyed the group enigmatically.

"There's something evidently waiting to be said," remarked Wolff, the silent Partner in more senses than one. "What's the use of waiting?"

Two or three of those present looked at Ian Stafford, who, standing by the window, seemed oblivious of them all. Byng had requested him to be present, with a view to asking his advice concerning some international aspect of the situation, and especially in regard to Holland and Germany. The group had welcomed the suggestion eagerly, for on this side of the question they were not so well equipped as on others.

But when it came to the discussion of inner local policy there seemed hesitation in speaking freely before him. Wallstein, however, gave a reassuring nod and said, meaningly:

"We took up careful strategical positions, but our camp has been overlooked from a kopje higher than ours."

"We have been the victims of treachery for years," burst out Fleming, with anger. "Nearly everything we've done here, nearly everything the Government has done here, has been known to Kruger—ever since the Raid."

"I think it could have been stopped," said the once Sobieski, with an ugly grimace, and an attempt at an accent which would suit his new name. "Byng's to blame. We ought to have put down our feet from the start. We're Byng-ridden."

"Keep a civil tongue, Israel," snarled Barry Whalen. "You know nothing about it, and that is the state in which you most shine—in your natural state of ignorance, like the heathen in his blindness. But before Byng comes I'd better give you all some information I've got."

"Isn't it for Byng to hear?" asked Fleming.

"Very much so; but it's for you all to decide what's to be done. Perhaps Mr. Stafford can help us in the matter, as he has been with Byng very lately." Wallstein looked inquiringly towards Stafford.

The group nodded appreciatively, and Stafford came forward to the table, but without seating himself. "Certainly you may command me," he said. "What is the mystery?"

In short and abrupt sentences Barry Whalen, with an occasional interjection and explanation from Wallstein, told of the years of leakage in regard to their plans, of moves circumvented by information which could only have been got by treacherous means either in South Africa or in London.

"We didn't know for sure which it was," said Barry, "but the proof has come at last. One of Kruger's understrappers from Holland was successfully tapped, and we've got proof that the trouble was here in London, here in this house where we sit—Byng's home."

There was a stark silence, in which more than one nodded significantly, and looked round furtively to see how the others took the news.

"Here is absolute proof. There were two in it here—Adrian Fellowes and Krool."

"Adrian Fellowes!"

It was Ian Stafford's voice, insistent and inquiring.

"Here is the proof, as I say." Barry Whalen leaned forward and pushed a paper over on the table, to which were attached two or three smaller papers and some cablegrams. "Look at them. Take a good look at them and see how we've been done—done brown. The hand that dipped in the same dish, as it were, has handed out misfortune to us by the bucketful. We've been carted in the house of a friend."

The group, all standing, leaned over, as Barry Whalen showed them the papers, one by one, then passed them round for examination.

"It's deadly," said Fleming. "Men have had their throats cut or been hanged for less. I wouldn't mind a hand in it myself."

"We warned Byng years ago," interposed Barry, "but it was no use. And we've paid for it par and premium."

"What can be done to Krool?" asked Fleming.

"Nothing particular—here," said Barry Whalen, ominously.

"Let's have the dog in," urged one of the group.

"Without Byng's permission?" interjected Wallstein.

There was a silence. The last time any of them, except Wallstein, had seen Byng, was on the evening when he had overheard the slanders concerning Jasmine, and none had pleasant anticipation of this meeting with him now. They recalled his departure when Barry Whalen had said, "God, how he hates us." He was not likely to hate them less, when they proved that Fellowes and Krool had betrayed him and them all. They had a wholesome fear of him in more senses than one, because, during the past few years, while Wallstein's health was bad, Byng's position had become more powerful financially, and he could ruin any one of them, if he chose. A man like Byng in "going large" might do the Samson business. Besides, he had grown strangely uncertain in his temper of late, and, as Barry Whalen had said, "It isn't good to trouble a wounded bull in the ring."

They had him on the hip in one way through the exposure of Krool, but they were all more or less dependent on his financial movements. They were all enraged at Byng because he had disregarded all warnings regarding Krool; but what could they do? Instinctively they turned now to Stafford, whose reputation for brains and diplomacy was so great and whose friendship with Byng was so close.

Stafford had come to-day for two reasons: to do what he could to help Byng—for the last time; and to say to Byng that they could not travel together to South Africa. To make the long journey with him was beyond his endurance. He must put the world between Rudyard and himself; he must efface all companionship. With this last act, begotten of the blind confidence Rudyard had in him, their intercourse must cease forever. This would be easy enough in South Africa. Once at the Front, it was as sure as anything on earth that they would never meet again. It was torture to meet him, and the day of the inquest, when Byng had come to his rooms after his interview with Lady Tynemouth and Mr. Mappin, he had been tried beyond endurance.

"Shall we have Krool in without Byng's permission? Is it wise?" asked Wallstein again. He looked at Stafford, and Stafford instantly replied:

"It would be well to see Krool, I think. Your action could then be decided by Krool's attitude and what he says."

Barry Whalen rang the bell, and the footman came. After a brief waiting Krool entered the room with irritating deliberation and closed the door behind him.

He looked at no one, but stood contemplating space with a composure which made Barry Whalen almost jump from his seat in rage.

"Come a little closer," said Wallstein in a soothing voice, but so Wallstein would have spoken to a man he was about to disembowel.

Krool came nearer, and now he looked round at them all slowly and inquiringly. As no one spoke for a moment he shrugged his shoulders.

"If you shrug your shoulders again, damn you, I'll sjambok you here as Kruger did at Vleifontein," said Barry Whalen in a low, angry voice. "You've been too long without the sjambok."

"This is not the Vaal, it is Englan'," answered Krool, huskily. "The Law—here!"

"Zo you stink ze law of England would help you—eh?" asked Sobieski, with a cruel leer, relapsing into his natural vernacular.

"I mean what I say, Krool," interposed Barry Whalen, fiercely, motioning Sobieski to silence. "I will sjambok you till you can't move, here in England, here in this house, if you shrug your shoulders again, or lift an eyebrow, or do one damned impudent thing."

He got up and rang a bell. A footman appeared. "There is a rhinoceros-hide whip, on the wall of Mr. Byng's study. Bring it here," he said, quietly, but with suppressed passion.

"Don't be crazy, Whalen," said Wallstein, but with no great force, for he would richly have enjoyed seeing the spy and traitor under the whip. Stafford regarded the scene with detached, yet deep and melancholy interest.

While they waited, Krool seemed to shrink a little; but as he watched like some animal at bay, Stafford noticed that his face became venomous and paler, and some sinister intention showed in his eyes.

The whip was brought and laid upon the table beside Barry Whalen, and the footman disappeared, looking curiously at the group and at Krool.

Barry Whalen's fingers closed on the whip, and now a look of fear crept over Krool's face. If there was one thing calculated to stir with fear the Hottentot blood in him, it was the sight of the sjambok. He had native tendencies and predispositions out of proportion to the native blood in him—maybe because he had ever been treated more like a native than a white man by his Boer masters in the past.

As Stafford viewed the scene, it suddenly came home to him how strange was this occurrence in Park Lane. It was medieval, it belonged to some land unslaked of barbarism. He realized all at once how little these men around him represented the land in which they were living, and how much they were part of the far-off land which was now in the throes of war.

To these men this was in one sense an alien country. Through the dulled noises of London there came to their ears the click of the wheels of a cape-wagon, the crack of the Kaffir's whip, the creak of the disselboom. They followed the spoor of a company of elephants in the East country, they watched through the November mist the blesbok flying across the veld, a herd of quaggas taking cover with the rheebok, or a cloud of locusts sailing out of the sun to devastate the green lands. Through the smoky smell of London there came to them the scent of the wattle, the stinging odour of ten thousand cattle, the reek of a native kraal, the sharp sweetness of orange groves, the aromatic air of the karoo, laden with the breath of a thousand wild herbs. Through the drizzle of the autumn rain they heard the wild thunderbolt tear the trees from earthly moorings. In their eyes was the livid lightning that searched in spasms of anger for its prey, while there swept over the brown, aching veld the flood which filled the spruits, which made the rivers seas, and ploughed fresh channels through the soil. The luxury of this room, with its shining mahogany tables, its tapestried walls, its rare fireplace and massive overmantel brought from Italy, its exquisite stained-glass windows, was only part of a play they were acting; it was not their real life.

And now there was not one of them that saw anything incongruous in the whip of rhinoceros-hide lying on the table, or clinched in Barry

Whalen's hand. On the contrary, it gave them a sense of supreme naturalness. They had lived in a land where the sjambok was the symbol of progress. It represented the forward movement of civilization in the wilderness. It was the vierkleur of the pioneer, without which the long train of capewagons, with the oxen in longer coils of effort, would never have advanced; without which the Kaffir and the Hottentot would have sacrificed every act of civilization. It prevented crime, it punished crime, it took the place of the bowie-knife and the derringer of that other civilization beyond the Mississippi; it was the lock to the door in the wild places, the open sesame to the territories where native chiefs ruled communal tribes by playing tyrant to the commune. It was the rod of Aaron staying the plague of barbarism. It was the sceptre of the veldt. It drew blood, it ate human flesh, it secured order where there was no law, and it did the work of prison and penitentiary. It was the symbol of authority in the wilderness.

It was race.

Stafford was the only man present who saw anything incongruous in the scene, and yet his travels in the East his year in Persia, Tibet and Afghanistan, had made him understand things not revealed to the wise and prudent of European domains. With Krool before them, who was of the veld and the karoo, whose natural habitat was but a cross between a krall and the stoep of a dopper's home, these men were instantly transported to the land where their hearts were in spite of all, though the flesh-pots of the West End of London had turned them into by-paths for a while. The skin had been scratched by Krool's insolence and the knowledge of his treachery, and the Tartar showed—the sjambok his scimitar.

In spite of himself, Stafford was affected by it all. He understood. This was not London; the scene had shifted to Potchefstroom or Middleburg, and Krool was transformed too. The sjambok had, like a wizard's wand, as it were, lifted him away from England to spaces where he watched from the grey rock of a kopje for the glint of an assegai or the red of a Rooinek's tunic: and he had done both in his day.

"We've got you at last, Krool," said Wallstein. "We have been some time at it, but it's a long lane that has no turning, and we have you—"

"Like that—like that, jackal!" interjected Barry Whalen, opening and shutting his lean fingers with a gesture of savage possession.

"What?" asked Krool, with a malevolent thrust forward of his head. "What?"

"You betrayed us to Kruger," answered Wallstein, holding the papers. "We have here the proof at last."

"You betrayed England and her secrets, and yet you think that the English law would protect you against this," said Barry Whalen, harshly, handling the sjambok.

"What I betray?" Krool asked again. "What I tell?"

With great deliberation Wallstein explained.

"Where proof?" Krool asked, doggedly.

"We have just enough to hang you," said Wallstein, grimly, and lifted and showed the papers Barry Whalen had brought.

An insolent smile crossed Krool's face.

"You find out too late. That Fellowes is dead. So much you get, but the work is done. It not matter now. It is all done—altogether. Oom Paul speaks now, and everything is his—from the Cape to the Zambesi, everything his. It is too late. What can to do?" Suddenly ferocity showed in his face. "It come at last. It is the end of the English both sides the Vaal. They will go down like wild hogs into the sea with Joubert and Botha behind them. It is the day of Oom Paul and Christ. The God of Israel gives to his own the tents of the Rooineks."

In spite of the fierce passion of the man, who had suddenly disclosed a side of his nature hitherto hidden—the savage piety of the copper Boer impregnated with stereotyped missionary phrasing, Ian Stafford almost laughed outright. In the presence of Jews like Sobieski it seemed so droll that this half-caste should talk about the God of Israel, and link Oom Paul's name with that of Christ the great liberator as partners in triumph.

In all the years Krool had been in England he had never been inside a place of worship or given any sign of that fanaticism which, all at once, he made manifest. He had seemed a pagan to all of his class, had acted as a pagan.

Barry Whalen, as well as Ian Stafford, saw the humour of the situation, while they were both confounded by the courageous malice of the traitor. It came to Barry's mind at the moment, as it came to Ian Stafford's, that Krool had some card to play which would, to his mind, serve him well; and, by instinct, both found the right clue. Barry's anger became uneasiness, and Stafford's interest turned to anxiety.

There was an instant's pause after Krool's words, and then Wolff the silent, gone wild, caught the sjambok from the hands of Barry Whalen. He made a movement towards Krool, who again suddenly shrank, as he would not have shrunk from a weapon of steel.

"Wait a minute," cried Fleming, seizing the arm of his friend. "One minute. There's something more." Turning to Wallstein, he said, "If Krool consents to leave England at once for South Africa, let him go. Is it agreed? He must either be dealt with adequately, or get out. Is it agreed?"

"I do what I like," said Krool, with a snarl, in which his teeth showed glassily against his drawn lips. "No one make me do what I not want."

"The Baas—you have forgotten him," said Wallstein.

A look combined of cunning, fear and servility crossed Krool's face, but he said, morosely:

"The Baas—I will do what I like."

There was a singular defiance and meaning in his tone, and the moment seemed critical, for Barry Whalen's face was distorted with fury. Stafford suddenly stooped and whispered a word in Wallstein's ear, and then said:

"Gentlemen, if you will allow me, I should like a few words with Krool before Mr. Byng comes. I think perhaps Krool will see the best course to pursue when we have talked together. In one sense it is none of my business, in another sense it is everybody's business. A few minutes, if you please, gentlemen." There was something almost authoritative in his tone.

"For Byng's sake—his wife—you understand," was all Stafford had said under his breath, but it was an illumination to Wallstein, who whispered to Stafford.

"Yes, that's it. Krool holds some card, and he'll play it now."

By his glance and by his word of assent, Wallstein set the cue for the rest, and they all got up and went slowly into the other room. Barry Whalen was about to take the sjambok, but Stafford laid his hand upon it, and Barry and he exchanged a look of understanding.

"Stafford's a little bit of us in a way," said Barry in a whisper to Wallstein as they left the room. "He knows, too, what a sjambok's worth in Krool's eyes."

When the two were left alone, Stafford slowly seated himself, and his fingers played idly with the sjambok.

"You say you will do what you like, in spite of the Baas?" he asked, in a low, even tone.

"If the Baas hurt me, I will hurt. If anybody hurt me, I will hurt."

"You will hurt the Baas, eh? I thought he saved your life on the Limpopo."

A flush stole across Krool's face, and when it passed again he was paler than before. "I have save the Baas," he answered, sullenly.

"From what?"

"From you."

With a powerful effort, Stafford controlled himself. He dreaded what was now to be said, but he felt inevitably what it was.

"How—from me?"

"If that Fellowes' letter come into his hands first, yours would not matter. She would not go with you."

Stafford had far greater difficulty in staying his hand than had Barry Whalen, for the sjambok seemed the only reply to the dark suggestion. He realized how, like the ostrich, he had thrust his head into the sand, imagining that no one knew what was between himself and Jasmine. Yet here was one who knew, here was one who had, for whatever purpose, precipitated a crisis with Fellowes to prevent a crisis with himself.

Suddenly Stafford thought of an awful possibility. He fastened the gloomy eyes of the man before him, that he might be able to see any stir of emotion, and said: "It did not come out as you expected?"

"Altogether—yes."

"You wished to part Mr. and Mrs. Byng. That did not happen."

"The Baas is going to South Africa."

"And Mr. Fellowes?"

"He went like I expec'."

"He died—heart failure, eh?"

A look of contempt, malevolence, and secret reflection came into Krool's face. "He was kill," he said.

"Who killed him?"

Krool was about to shrug his shoulders, but his glance fell on the sjambok, and he made an ugly gesture with his lean fingers. "There was yourself. He had hurt you—you went to him. . . Good! There was the Baas, he went to him. The dead man had hurt him. . . Good!"

Stafford interrupted him by an exclamation. "What's that you say— the Baas went to Mr. Fellowes?"

"As I tell the vrouw, Mrs. Byng, when she say me go from the house to-day—I say I will go when the Baas send me."

"The Baas went to Mr. Fellowes—when?"

"Two hours before you go, and one hour before the vrouw, she go."

Like some animal looking out of a jungle, so Krool's eyes glowed from beneath his heavy eyebrows, as he drawled out the words.

"The Baas went—you saw him?"

"With my own eyes."

"How long was he there?"

"Ten minutes."

"Mrs. Byng—you saw her go in?"

"And also come out."

"And me—you followed me—you saw me, also?"

"I saw all that come, all that go in to him."

With a swift mind Stafford saw his advantage—the one chance, the one card he could play, the one move he could make in checkmate, if, and when, necessary. "So you saw all that came and went. And you came and went yourself!"

His eyes were hard and bright as he held Krool's, and there was a sinister smile on his lips.

"You know I come and go—you say me that?" said Krool, with a sudden look of vague fear and surprise. He had not foreseen this.

"You accuse yourself. You saw this person and that go out, and you think to hold them in your dirty clutches; but you had more reason than any for killing Mr. Fellowes."

"What?" asked Krool, furtively.

"You hated him because he was a traitor like yourself. You hated him because he had hurt the Baas."

"That is true altogether, but—"

"You need not explain. If any one killed Mr. Fellowes, why not you? You came and went from his rooms, too."

Krool's face was now yellowish pale. "Not me. . . it was not me."

"You would run a worse chance than any one. Your character would damn you—a partner with him in crime. What jury in the world but would convict you on your own evidence? Besides, you knew—"

He paused to deliver a blow on the barest chance. It was an insidious challenge which, if it failed, might do more harm to others, might do great harm, but he plunged. "You knew about the needle."

Krool was cowed and silent. On a venture Stafford had struck straight home.

"You knew that Mr. Fellowes had stolen the needle from Mr. Mappin at Glencader," he added.

"How you know that?" asked Krool, in a husky, ragged voice.

"I saw him steal it—and you?"

"No. He tell me."

"What did he mean to do with it?"

A look came into Krool's eyes, malevolent and barbaric.

"Not to kill himself," he reflected. "There is always some one a man or a woman want kill."

There was a hideous commonplaceness in the tone which struck a chill to Stafford's heart.

"No doubt there is always some one you want to kill. Now listen, Krool. You think you've got a hold over me—over Mrs. Byng. You threaten. Well, I have passed through the fire of the coroner's inquest. I have nothing to fear. You have. I saw you in the street as you watched. You came behind me—"

He remembered now the footsteps that paused when he did, the figure behind his in the dark, as he watched for Jasmine to come out from Fellowes' rooms, and he determined to plunge once more.

"I recognized you, and I saw you in the Strand just before that. I did not speak at the inquest, because I wanted no scandal. If I had spoken, you would have been arrested. Whatever happened your chances were worse than those of any one. You can't frighten me, or my friends in there, or the Baas, or Mrs. Byng. Look after your own skin. You are the vile scum of the earth,"—he determined to take a strong line now, since he had made a powerful impression on the creature before him—"and you will do what the Baas likes, not what you like. He saved your life. Bad as you are, the Baas is your Baas for ever and ever, and what he wants to do with you he will do. When his eyes look into yours, you will think the lightning speaks. You are his slave. If he hates you, you will die; if he curses you, you will wither."

He played upon the superstitious element, the native strain again. It was deeper in Krool than anything else.

"Do you think you can defy them?" Stafford went on, jerking a finger towards the other room. "They are from the veld. They will have you as sure as the crack of a whip. This is England, but they are from the veld. On the veld you know what they would do to you. If you speak against the Baas, it is bad for you; if you speak against the Baas' vrouw it will be ten times worse. Do you hear?"

There was a strange silence, in which Stafford could feel Krool's soul struggling in the dark, as it were—a struggle as of black spirits in the grey dawn.

"I wait the Baas speak," Krool said at last, with a shiver.

There was no time for Stafford to answer. Wallstein entered the room hurriedly. "Byng has come. He has been told about him," he said in French to Stafford, and jerking his head towards Krool.

Stafford rose. "It's all right," he answered in the same language. "I think things will be safe now. He has a wholesome fear of the Baas."

He turned to Krool. "If you say to the Baas what you have said to me about Mr. Fellowes or about the Baas's vrouw, you will have a bad time. You will think that wild hawks are picking out your vitals. If you have sense, you will do what I tell you."

Krool's eyes were on the door through which Wallstein had come. His gaze was fixed and tortured. Stafford had suddenly roused in him some strange superstitious element. He was like a creature of a lower order awaiting the approach of the controlling power. It was, however, the door behind him which opened, and he gave a start of surprise and terror. He knew who it was. He did not turn round, but his head bent forward, as though he would take a blow from behind, and his eyes almost closed. Stafford saw with a curious meticulousness the long eyelashes touch the grey cheek.

"There's no fight in him now," he said to Byng in French. "He was getting nasty, but I've got him in order. He knows too much. Remember that, Byng."

Byng's look was as that of a man who had passed through some chamber of torture, but the flabbiness had gone suddenly from his face, and even from his figure, though heavy lines had gathered round the mouth and scarred the forehead. He looked worn and much thinner, but there was a look in his eyes which Stafford had never seen there—a new look of deeper seeing, of revelation, of realization. With all his ability and force, Byng had been always much of a boy, so little at one with the hidden things—the springs of human conduct, the contradictions of human nature, the worst in the best of us, the forces that emerge without warning in all human beings, to send them on untoward courses and at sharp tangents to all the habits of their existence and their character. In a real sense he had been very primitive, very objective in all he thought and said and did. With imagination, and a sensitive organization out of keeping with his immense physique, it was still only a visualizing sense which he had, only a thing that belongs to races such as those of which Krool had come.

A few days of continuous suffering begotten by a cataclysm, which had rent asunder walls of life enclosing vistas he had never before seen; these had transformed him. Pain had given him dignity of a savage kind, a grim quiet which belonged to conflict and betokened grimmer purpose. In the eyes was the darkness of the well of despair; but at his lips was iron resolution.

In reply to Stafford he said quietly: "All right, I understand. I know how to deal with Krool."

As Stafford withdrew, Byng came slowly down the room till he stood at the end of the table opposite to Krool.

Standing there, he looked at the Boer with hard eyes.

"I know all, Krool," he said. "You sold me and my country—you tried to sell me and my country to Oom Paul. You dog, that I snatched from the tiger death, not once but twice."

"It is no good. I am a Hottentot. I am for the Boer, for Oom Paul. I would have die for you, but—"

"But when the chance came to betray the thing I cared for more than I would twenty lives—my country—you tried to sell me and all who worked with me."

"It would be same to you if the English go from the Vaal," said the half-caste, huskily, not looking into the eyes fixed on him. "But it matter to me that the Boer keep all for himself what he got for himself. I am half Boer. That is why."

"You defend it—tell me, you defend it?"

There was that in the voice, some terrible thing, which drew Krool's eyes in spite of himself, and he met a look of fire and wrath.

"I tell why. If it was bad, it was bad. But I tell why, that is all. If it is not good, it is bad, and hell is for the bad; but I tell why."

"You got money from Oom Paul for the man—Fellowes?" It was hard for him to utter the name.

Krool nodded.

"Every year—much?"

Again Krool nodded.

"And for yourself—how much?"

"Nothing for myself; no money, Baas."

"Only Oom Paul's love!"

Krool nodded again.

"But Oom Paul flayed you at Vleifontein; tied you up and skinned you with a sjambok. . . That didn't matter, eh? And you went on loving him. I never touched you in all the years. I gave you your life twice. I gave you good money. I kept you in luxury—you that fed in the cattle-kraal; you that had mealies to eat and a shred of biltong when you could steal it; you that ate a steinbok raw on the Vaal, you were so wild for meat. . . I took you out of that, and gave you this."

He waved an arm round the room, and went on: "You come in and go out of my room, you sleep in the same cart with me, you eat out of the same dish on trek, and yet you do the Judas trick. Slim—god of gods, how slim! You are the snake that crawls in the slime. It's the native in you, I suppose. . . But see, I mean to do to you as Oom Paul did. It's the only thing you understand. It's the way to make you straight and true, my sweet Krool."

Still keeping his eyes fixed on Krool's eyes, his hand reached out and slowly took the sjambok from the table. He ran the cruel thing through his fingers as does a prison expert the cat-o'-nine-tails before laying on the lashes of penalty. Into Krool's eyes a terror crept which never had been there in the old days on the veld when Oom Paul had flayed him. This was not the veld, and he was no longer the veld-dweller with skin like the rhinoceros, all leather and bone and endurance. And this was not Oom Paul, but one whom he had betrayed, whose wife he had sought to ruin, whose subordinate he had turned into a traitor. Oom Paul had been a mere savage master; but here was a master whose very tongue could excoriate him like Oom Paul's sjambok; whom, at bottom, he loved in his way as he had never loved anything; whom he had betrayed, not realizing the hideous nature of his deed; having argued that it was against England his treachery was directed, and that was a virtue in his eyes; not seeing what direct injury could come to Byng through it. He had not seen, he had not understood, he was still uncivilized; he had only in his veins the morality of the native, and he had tried to ruin his master's wife for his master's sake; and when he had finished with Fellowes as a traitor, he was ready to ruin his confederate—to kill him—perhaps did kill him!

"It's the only way to deal with you, Hottentot dog!"

The look in Krool's eyes only increased Byng's lust of punishment. What else was there to do? Without terrible scandal there was no other way to punish the traitor, but if there had been another way he would still have done this. This Krool understood; behind every command the Baas had ever given him this thing lay—the sjambok, the natural engine of authority.

Suddenly Byng said with a voice of almost guttural anger: "You dropped that letter on my bedroom floor—that letter, you understand? . . . Speak."

"I did it, Baas."

Byng was transformed. Slowly he laid down the sjambok, and as slowly took off his coat, his eyes meanwhile fastening those of the wretched man before him. Then he took up the sjambok again.

"You know what I am going to do with you?"

"Yes, Baas."

It never occurred to Byng that Krool would resist; it did not occur to Krool that he could resist. Byng was the Baas, who at that moment was the Power immeasurable. There was only one thing to do—to obey.

"You were told to leave my house by Mrs. Byng, and you did not go."

"She was not my Baas."

"You would have done her harm, if you could?"

"So, Baas."

With a low cry Byng ran forward, the sjambok swung through the air, and the terrible whip descended on the crouching half-caste.

Krool gave one cry and fell back a little, but he made no attempt to resist.

Suddenly Byng went to a window and threw it open.

"You can jump from there or take the sjambok. Which?" he said with a passion not that of a man wholly sane. "Which?"

Krool's wild, sullen, trembling look sought the window, but he had no heart for that enterprise—thirty feet to the pavement below.

"The sjambok, Baas," he said.

Once again Byng moved forward on him, and once again Krool's cry rang out, but not so loud. It was like that of an animal in torture.

In the next room, Wallstein and Stafford and the others heard it, and understood. Whispering together they listened, and Stafford shrank away to the far side of the room; but more than one face showed pleasure in the sound of the whip and the moaning.

It went on and on.

Barry Whalen, however, was possessed of a kind of fear, and presently his face became troubled. This punishment was terrible. Byng might kill the man, and all would be as bad as could be. Stafford came to him.

"You had better go in," he said. "We ought to intervene. If you don't, I will. Listen. . ."

It was a strange sound to hear in this heart of civilization. It belonged to the barbaric places of the earth, where there was no law, where every pioneer was his own cadi.

With set face Barry Whalen entered the room. Byng paused for an instant and looked at him with burning, glazed eyes that scarcely realized him.

"Open that door," he said, presently, and Barry Whalen opened the door which led into the big hall.

"Open all down to the street," Byng said, and Barry Whalen went forward quickly.

Like some wild beast Krool crouched and stumbled and moaned as he ran down the staircase, through the outer hall, while a servant with scared face saw Byng rain savage blows upon the hated figure.

On the pavement outside the house, Krool staggered, stumbled, and fell down; but he slowly gathered himself up, and turned to the doorway, where Byng stood panting with the sjambok in his hand.

"Baas!—Baas!" Krool said with livid face, and then he crept painfully away along the street wall.

A policeman crossed the road with a questioning frown and the apparent purpose of causing trouble, but Barry Whalen whispered in his ear, and told him to call that evening and he would hear all about it. Meanwhile a five-pound note in a quick palm was a guarantee of good faith.

Presently a half-dozen people began to gather near the door, but the benevolent policeman moved them on.

At the top of the staircase Jasmine met her husband. She shivered as he came up towards her.

"Will you come to me when you have finished your business?" she said, and she took the sjambok gently from his hand.

He scarcely realized her. He was in a dream; but he smiled at her, and nodded, and passed on to where the others awaited him.

XXVIII

"The Battle Cry of Freedom"

Slowly Jasmine returned to her boudoir. Laying the sjambok on the table among the books in delicate bindings and the bowls of flowers, she stood and looked at it with confused senses for a long time. At last a wan smile stole to her lips, but it did not reach her eyes. They remained absorbed and searching, and were made painfully sad by the wide, dark lines under them. Her fair skin was fairer than ever, but it was delicately faded, giving her a look of pensiveness, while yet there was that in her carriage and at her mouth which suggested strength and will and new forces at work in her. She carried her head, weighted by its splendour of golden hair, as an Eastern woman carries a goulah of water. There was something pathetic yet self-reliant in the whole figure. The passion slumbering in the eyes, however, might at any moment burst forth in some wild relinquishment of control and self-restraint.

"He did what I should have liked to do," she said aloud. "We are not so different, after all. He is primitive at bottom, and so am I. He gets carried away by his emotions, and so do I."

She took up the whip, examined it, felt its weight, and drew it with a swift jerk through the air.

"I did not even shrink when Krool came stumbling down the stairs, with this cutting his flesh," she said to herself. "Somehow it all seemed natural and right. What has come to me? Are all my finer senses dead? Am I just one of the crude human things who lived a million years ago, and who lives again as crude as those; with only the outer things changed? Then I wore the skins of wild animals, and now I do the same, just the same; with what we call more taste perhaps, because we have ceased to see the beauty in the natural thing."

She touched the little band of grey fur at the sleeve of her clinging velvet gown. "Just a little distance away—that is all."

Suddenly a light flashed up in her eyes, and her face flushed as though some one had angered her. She seized the whip again. "Yes, I could have seen him whipped to death before my eyes—the coward, the abject coward. He did not speak for me; he did not defend me; he did not deny. He let Ian think—death was too kind to him. How dared he hurt me so! . . . Death is so easy a way out, but he would not have taken it. No, no, no, it was not suicide; some one killed him. He could never have taken his own life—never. He had not the courage. . . No; he died of poison or was strangled. Who did it? Who did it? Was it Rudyard? Was it. . . ? Oh, it wears me out—thinking, thinking, thinking!"

She sat down and buried her face in her hands. "I am doomed—doomed," she moaned. "I was doomed from the start. It must always have been so, whatever I did. I would do it again, whatever I did; I know I would do it again, being what I was. It was in my veins, in my blood from the start, from the very first days of my life."

All at once there flashed through her mind again, as on that night so many centuries ago, when she had slept the last sleep of her life as it was, Swinburne's lines on Baudelaire:

"There is no help for these things, none to mend and none to mar; Not all our songs, oh, friend, can make death clear Or make life durable. . ."

"'There is no help for these things,'" she repeated with a sigh which seemed to tear her heart in twain. "All gone—all. What is there left to do? If death could make it better for any one, how easy! But everything would be known—somehow the world would know, and every one would suffer more. Not now—no, not now. I must live on, but not here. I must go away. I must find a place to go where Rudyard will not come. There is no place so far but it is not far enough. I am twenty-five, and all is over—all is done for me. I have nothing that I want to keep, there is nothing that I want to do except to go—to go and to be alone. Alone, always alone now. It is either that, or be Jezebel, or—"

The door opened, and the servant brought a card to her. "His Excellency, the Moravian ambassador," the footman said.

"Monsieur Mennaval?" she asked, mechanically, as though scarcely realizing what he had said.

"Yes, ma'am, Mr. Mennaval."

"Please say I am indisposed, and am sorry I cannot receive him to-day," she said.

"Very good, ma'am." The footman turned to go, then came back.

"Shall I tell the maid you want her?" he asked, respectfully.

"No, why should you?" she asked.

"I thought you looked a bit queer, ma'am," he responded, hastily. "I beg your pardon, ma'am."

She rewarded him with a smile. "Thank you, James, I think I should like her after all. Ask her to come at once."

When he had gone she leaned back and shut her eyes. For a moment she was perfectly motionless, then she sat up again and looked at the card in her hand.

"M. Mennaval—M. Mennaval," she said, with a note so cynical that it betrayed more than her previous emotion, to such a point of despair her mind had come.

M. Mennaval had played his part, had done his service, had called out from her every resource of coquetry and lure; and with wonderful art she had cajoled him till he had yielded to influence, and Ian had turned the key in the international lock. M. Mennaval had been used with great skill to help the man who was now gone from her forever, whom perhaps she would never see again; and who wanted never to see her again, never in all time or space. M. Mennaval had played his game for his own desire, and he had lost; but what had she gained where M. Mennaval had lost? She had gained that which now Ian despised, which he would willingly, so far as she was concerned, reject with contempt. . . And yet, and yet, while Ian lived he must still be grateful to her that, by whatever means, she had helped him to do what meant so much to England. Yes, he could not wholly dismiss her from his mind; he must still say, "This she did for me—this thing, in itself not commendable, she did for me; and I took it for my country."

Her eyes were open, and her garden had been invaded by those revolutionaries of life and time, Nemesis, Penalty, Remorse. They marauded every sacred and secret corner of her mind and soul. They came with whips to scourge her. Nothing was private to her inner self now. Everything was arrayed against her. All life doubled backwards on her, blocking her path.

M. Mennaval—what did she care for him! Yet here he was at her door asking payment for the merchandise he had sold to her: his judgment, his reputation as a diplomatist, his freedom, the respect of the world— for how could the world respect a man at whom it laughed, a man who had hoped to be given the key to a secret door in a secret garden!

As Jasmine sat looking at the card, the footman entered again with a note.

"His Excellency's compliments," he said, and withdrew.

She opened the letter hesitatingly, held it in her hand for a moment without reading it, then, with an impulsive effort, did so. When she had finished, she gave a cry of anger and struck her tiny clinched hand upon her knee.

The note ran:

"Chere amie, you have so much indisposition in these days. It is all too vexing to your friends. The world will be surprised, if you allow a migraine to come between us. Indeed, it will be shocked. The world understands always so imperfectly, and I have no gift of explanation. Of course, I know the war has upset many, but I thought you could not be upset so easily—no, it cannot be the war; so I must try and think what it is. If I cannot think by tomorrow at five o'clock, I will call again to ask you. Perhaps the migraine will be better. But, if you will that migraine to be far away, it will fly, and then I shall be near. Is it not so? You will tell me to-morrow at five, will you not, belle amie?

A toi, M. M.

THE WORDS SCORCHED HER EYES. They angered her, scourged her. One of life's Revolutionaries was insolently ravaging the secret place where her pride dwelt. Pride—what pride had she now? Where was the room for pride or vanity? . . . And all the time she saw the face of a dead man down by the river—a face now beneath the sod. It flashed before her eyes at moments when she least could bear it, to agitate her soul.

M. Mennaval—how dare he write to her so! "Chere amie" and "A toi"—how strange the words looked now, how repulsive and strange! It did not seem possible that once before he had written such words to her. But never before had these epithets or others been accompanied by such meaning as his other words conveyed.

"I will not see him to-morrow. I will not see him ever again, if I can help it," she said bitterly, and trembling with agitation. "I shall go where I shall not be found. I will go to-night."

The door opened. Her maid entered. "You wanted me, madame?" asked the girl, in some excitement and very pale.

"Yes, what is the matter? Why so agitated?" Jasmine asked.

The maid's eyes were on the sjambok. She pointed to it. "It was that, madame. We are all agitated. It was terrible. One had never seen anything like that before in one's life, madame—never. It was like the days—yes, of slavery. It was like the galleys of Toulon in the old days. It was—"

"There, don't be so eloquent, Lablanche. What do you know of the galleys of Toulon or the days of slavery?"

"Madame, I have heard, I have read, I—"

"Yes, but did you love Krool so?"

The girl straightened herself with dramatic indignation. "Madame, that man, that creature, that toad—!"

"Then why so exercised? Were you so pained at his punishment? Were all the household so pained?"

"Every one hated him, madame," said the girl, with energy.

"Then let me hear no more of this impudent nonsense," Jasmine said, with decision.

"Oh, madame, to speak to me like this!" Tears were ready to do needful service.

"Do you wish to remain with me, Lablanche?"

"Ah, madame, but yes—"

"Then my head aches, and I don't want you to make it worse. . . And, see, Lablanche, there is that grey walking-suit; also the mauve dressing-gown, made by Loison; take them, if you can make them fit you; and be good."

"Madame, how kind—ah, no one is like you, madame—!"

"Well, we shall see about that quite soon. Put out at once every gown of mine for me to see, and have trunks ready to pack immediately; but only three trunks, not more."

"Madame is going away?"

"Do as I say, Lablanche. We go to-night. The grey gown and the mauve dressing-gown that Loison made, you will look well in them. Quick, now, please."

In a flutter Lablanche left the room, her eyes gleaming.

She had had her mind on the grey suit for some time, but the mauve dressing-gown as well—it was too good to be true.

She almost ran into Lady Tynemouth's arms as the door opened. With a swift apology she sped away, after closing the door upon the visitor.

Jasmine rose and embraced her friend, and Lady Tynemouth subsided into a chair with a sigh.

"My dear Jasmine, you look so frail," she said. "A short time ago I feared you were going to blossom into too ripe fruit, now you look almost a little pinched. But it quite becomes you, mignonne—quite. You have dark lines under your eyes, and that transparency of skin—it is quite too fetching. Are you glad to see me?"

"I would have seen no one to-day, no one, except you or Rudyard."

"Love and duty," said Lady Tynemouth, laughing, yet acutely alive to the something so terribly wrong, of which she had spoken to Ian Stafford.

"Why is it my duty to see you, Alice?" asked Jasmine, with the dry glint in her tone which had made her conversation so pleasing to men.

"You clever girl, how you turn the tables on me," her friend replied, and then, seeing the sjambok on the table, took it up. "What is this formidable instrument? Are you flagellating the saints?"

"Not the saints, Alice."

"You don't mean to say you are going to scourge yourself?"

Then they both smiled—and both immediately sighed. Lady Tynemouth's sympathy was deeply roused for Jasmine, and she meant to try and win her confidence and to help her in her trouble, if she could; but she was full of something else at this particular moment, and she was not completely conscious of the agony before her.

"Have you been using this sjambok on Mennaval?" she asked with an attempt at lightness. "I saw him leaving as I came in. He looked rather dejected—or stormy, I don't quite know which."

"Does it matter which? I didn't see Mennaval today."

"Then no wonder he looked dejected and stormy. But what is the history of this instrument of torture?" she asked, holding up the sjambok again.

"Krool."

"Krool! Jasmine, you surely don't mean to say that you—"

"Not I—it was Rudyard. Krool was insolent—a half-caste, you know."

"Krool—why, yes, it was he I saw being helped into a cab by a policeman just down there in Piccadilly. You don't mean that Rudyard—"

She pushed the sjambok away from her.

"Yes—terribly."

"Then I suppose the insolence was terrible enough to justify it."

"Quite, I think." Jasmine's voice was calm.

"But of course it is not usual—in these parts."

"Rudyard is not usual in these parts, or Krool either. It was a touch of the Vaal."

Lady Tynemouth gave a little shudder. "I hope it won't become fashionable. We are altogether too sensational nowadays. But, seriously, Jasmine, you are not well. You must do something. You must have a change."

"I am going to do something—to have a change."

"That's good. Where are you going, dear?"

"South. . . And how are you getting on with your hospital-ship?"

Lady Tynemouth threw up her hands. "Jasmine, I'm in despair. I had set my heart upon it. I thought I could do it easily, and I haven't done it, after trying as hard as can be. Everything has gone wrong, and now Tynie cables I mustn't go to South Africa. Fancy a husband forbidding a wife to come to him."

"Well, perhaps it's better than a husband forbidding his wife to leave him."

"Jasmine, I believe you would joke if you were dying."

"I am dying."

There was that in the tone of Jasmine's voice which gave her friend a start. She eyed her suddenly with a great anxiety.

"And I'm not jesting," Jasmine added, with a forced smile. "But tell me what has gone wrong with all your plans. You don't mind what Tynemouth says. Of course you will do as you like."

"Of course; but still Tynie has never 'issued instructions' before, and if there was any time I ought to humour him it is now. He's so intense about the war! But I can't explain everything on paper to him, so I've written to say I'm going to South Africa to explain, and that I'll come back by the next boat, if my reasons are not convincing."

In other circumstances Jasmine would have laughed. "He will find you convincing," she said, meaningly.

"I said if he found my reasons convincing."

"You will be the only reason to him."

"My dear Jasmine, you are really becoming sentimental. Tynie would blush to discover himself being silly over me. We get on so well because we left our emotions behind us when we married."

"Yours, I know, you left on the Zambesi," said Jasmine, deliberately.

A dull fire came into Lady Tynemouth's eyes, and for an instant there was danger of Jasmine losing a friend she much needed; but Lady Tynemouth had a big heart, and she knew that her friend was in a mood when anything was possible, or everything impossible.

So she only smiled, and said, easily: "Dearest Jasmine, that umbrella episode which made me love Ian Stafford for ever and ever without even amen came after I was married, and so your pin doesn't prick, not a weeny bit. No, it isn't Tynie that makes me sad. It's the Climbers who won't pay."

"The Climbers? You want money for—"

"Yes, the hospital-ship; and I thought they'd jump at it; but they've all been jumping in other directions. I asked the Steuvenfeldts, the

Boulters, the Felix Fowles, the Brutons, the Sheltons, and that fellow Mackerel, who has so much money he doesn't know what to do with it and twenty others; and Mackerel was the only one who would give me anything at all large. He gave me ten thousand pounds. But I want fifty—fifty, my beloved. I'm simply broken-hearted. It would do so much good, and I could manage the thing so well, and I could get other splendid people to help me to manage it—there's Effie Lyndhall and Mary Meacham. The Mackerel wanted to come along, too, but I told him he could come out and fetch us back—that there mustn't be any scandal while the war was on. I laugh, my dear, but I could cry my eyes out. I want something to do—I've always wanted something to do. I've always been sick of an idle life, but I wouldn't do a hundred things I might have done. This thing I can do, however, and, if I did it, some of my debt to the world would be paid. It seems to me that these last fifteen years in England have been awful. We are all restless; we all have been going, going—nowhere; we have all been doing, doing—nothing; we have all been thinking, thinking, thinking—of ourselves. And I've been a playbody like the rest; I've gone with the Climbers because they could do things for me; I've wanted more and more of everything— more gadding, more pleasure, more excitement. It's been like a brass-band playing all the time, my life this past ten years. I'm sick of it. It's only some big thing that can take me out of it. I've got to make some great plunge, or in a few years more I'll be a middle-aged peeress with nothing left but a double chin, a tongue for gossip, and a string of pearls. There must be a bouleversement of things as they are, or good-bye to everything except emptiness. Don't you see, Jasmine, dearest?"

"Yes yes, I see." Jasmine got up, went to her desk, opened a drawer, took out a book, and began to write hastily. "Go on," she said as she wrote; "I can hear what you are saying."

"But are you really interested?"

"Even Tynemouth would find you interesting and convincing. Go on."

"I haven't anything more to say, except that nothing lies between me and flagellation and the sack cloth,"—she toyed with the sjambok— "except the Climbers; and they have failed me. They won't play—or pay."

Jasmine rose from the desk and came forward with a paper in her hand. "No, they have not failed you, Alice," she said, gently. "The Climbers seldom really disappoint you. The thing is, you must know how to talk to them, to say the right thing, the flattering, the tactful, and the nice sentimental thing,—they mostly have middle-class sentimentality—and then you get what you want. As you do now. There. . ."

She placed in her friend's hand a long, narrow slip of paper. Lady Tynemouth looked astonished, gazed hard at the paper, then sprang to her feet, pale and agitated.

"Jasmine—you—this—sixty thousand pounds!" she cried. "A cheque for sixty thousand pounds—Jasmine!"

There was a strange brilliance in Jasmine's eyes, a hectic flush on her cheek.

"It must not be cashed for forty-eight hours; but after that the money will be there."

Lady Tynemouth caught Jasmine's shoulders in her trembling yet strong fingers, and looked into the wild eyes with searching inquiry and solicitude.

"But, Jasmine, it isn't possible. Will Rudyard—can you afford it?"

"That will not be Rudyard's money which you will get. It will be all my own."

"But you yourself are not rich. Sixty thousand pounds—why?"

"It is because it is a sacrifice to me that I give it; because it is my own; because it is two-thirds of what I possess. And if all is needed before we have finished, then all shall go."

Alice Tynemouth still held the shoulders, still gazed into the eyes which burned and shone, which seemed to look beyond this room into some world of the soul or imagination. "Jasmine, you are not crazy, are you?" she asked, excitedly. "You will not repent of this? It is not a sudden impulse?"

"Yes, it is a sudden impulse; it came to me all at once. But when it came I knew it was the right thing, the only thing to do. I will not repent of it. Have no fear. It is final. It is sure. It means that, like you, I have found a rope to drag myself out of this stream which sweeps me on to the rapids."

"Jasmine, do you mean that you will—that you are coming, too?"

"Yes, I am going with you. We will do it together. You shall lead, and I shall help. I have a gift for organization. My grandfather? he—"

"All the world knows that. If you have anything of his gift, we shall not fail. We shall feel that we are doing something for our country— and, oh, so much for ourselves! And we shall be near our men. Tynie and Ruddy Byng will be out there, and we shall be ready for anything if necessary. But Rudyard, will he approve?" She held up the cheque.

Jasmine made a passionate gesture. "There are times when we must do what something in us tells us to do, no matter what the consequences. I am myself. I am not a slave. If I take my own way in the pleasures of life, why should I not take it in the duties and the business of life?"

Her eyes took on a look of abstraction, and her small hand closed on the large, capable hand of her friend. "Isn't work the secret of life? My grandfather used to say it was. Always, always, he used to say to me, 'Do something, Jasmine. Find a work to do, and do it. Make the world look at you, not for what you seem to be, but for what you do. Work cures nearly every illness and nearly every trouble'—that is what he said. And I must work or go mad. I tell you I must work, Alice. We will work together out there where great battles will be fought."

A sob caught her in the throat, and Alice Tynemouth wrapped her round with tender arms. "It will do you good, darling," she said, softly. "It will help you through—through it all, whatever it is."

For an instant Jasmine felt that she must empty out her heart; tell the inner tale of her struggle; but the instant of weakness passed as suddenly as it came, and she only said—repeating Alice Tynemouth's words: "Yes, through it all, through it all, whatever it is." Then she added: "I want to do something big. I can, I can. I want to get out of this into the open world. I want to fight. I want to balance things somehow—inside myself. . ."

All at once she became very quiet. "But we must do business like business people. This money: there must be a small committee of business men, who—"

Alice Tynemouth finished the sentence for her. "Who are not Climbers?"

"Yes. But the whole organization must be done by ourselves—all the practical, unfinancial work. The committee will only be like careful trustees."

There was a new light in Jasmine's eyes. She felt for the moment that life did not end in a cul de sac. She knew that now she had found a way for Rudyard and herself to separate without disgrace, without humiliation to him. She could see a few steps ahead. When she gave Lablanche instructions to put out her clothes a little while before, she did not know what she was going to do; but now she knew. She knew how she could make it easier for Rudyard when the inevitable hour came,—and it was here—which should see the end of their life together. He need not now sacrifice himself so much for her sake.

She wanted to be alone, and, as if divining her thought, Lady Tynemouth embraced her, and a moment later there was no sound in the room save the ticking of the clock and the crackle of the fire.

How silent it was! The world seemed very far away. Peace seemed to have taken possession of the place, and Jasmine's stillness as she sat by the fire staring into the embers was a part of it. So lost was she that she was not conscious of an opening door and of a footstep. She was roused by a low voice.

"Jasmine!"

She did not start. It was as though there had come a call, for which she had waited long, and she appeared to respond slowly to it, as one would to a summons to the scaffold. There was no outward agitation now, there was only a cold stillness which seemed little to belong to the dainty figure which had ever been more like a decoration than a living utility in the scheme of things. The crisis had come which she had dreaded yet invited—that talk which they two must have before they went their different ways. She had never looked Rudyard in the eyes direct since the day when Adrian Fellowes died. They had met, but never quite alone; always with some one present, either the servants or some other. Now they were face to face.

On Rudyard's lips was a faint smile, but it lacked the old bonhomie which was part of his natural equipment; and there were still sharp, haggard traces of the agitation which had accompanied the expulsion of Krool.

For an instant the idea possessed her that she would tell him everything there was to tell, and face the consequences, no matter what they might be. It was not in her nature to do things by halves, and since catastrophe was come, her will was to drink the whole cup to the dregs. She did not want to spare herself. Behind it all lay something of that terrible wilfulness which had controlled her life so far. It was the unlovely soul of a great pride. She did not want to be forgiven for anything. She did not want to be condoned. There was a spirit of defiance which refused to accept favours, preferring punishment to the pity or the pardon which stooped to make it easier for her. It was a dangerous pride, and in the mood of it she might throw away everything, with an abandonment and recklessness only known to such passionate natures.

The mood came on her all at once as she stood and looked at Rudyard. She read, or she thought she read in his eyes, in his smile, the superior spirit condescending to magnanimity, to compassion; and her whole nature was instantly up in arms. She almost longed on the instant to strip herself bare, as it were, and let him see her as she really was, or as, in her despair, she thought she really was. The mood in which she had talked to Lady Tynemouth was gone, and in its place a spirit of revolt was at work. A certain sullenness which Rudyard and no one else had ever seen came into her eyes, and her lips became white with an ominous determination. She forgot him and all that he would suffer if she told him the whole truth; and the whole truth would, in her passion, become far more than the truth: she was again the egoist, the centre of the universe. What happened to her was the only thing which mattered in all the world. So it had ever been; and her beauty and her wit and her youth and the habit of being spoiled had made it all possible, without those rebuffs and that confusion which fate provides sooner or later for the egoist.

"Well," she said, sharply, "say what you wish to say. You have wanted to say it badly. I am ready."

He was stunned by what seemed to him the anger and the repugnance in her tone.

"You remember you asked me to come, Jasmine, when you took the sjambok from me."

He nodded towards the table where it lay, then went forward and picked it up, his face hardening as he did so.

Like a pendulum her mood swung back. By accident he had said the one thing which could have moved her, changed her at the moment. The savage side of him appealed to her. What he lacked in brilliance and the lighter gifts of raillery and eloquence and mental give-and-take, he had balanced by his natural forces—from the power-house, as she had called it long ago. Pity, solicitude, the forced smile, magnanimity, she did not want in this black mood. They would have made her cruelly audacious, and her temper would have known no license; but now, suddenly, she had a vision of him as he stamped down the staircase, his coat off, laying the sjambok on the shoulders of the man who had injured her so, who hated her so, and had done so over all the years. It appealed to her.

In her heart of hearts she was sure he had done it directly or indirectly for her sake; and that was infinitely more to her than that he should stoop from the heights to pick her up. He was what he was because Heaven had made him so; and she was what she was because Heaven had forgotten to make her otherwise; and he could not know or understand how she came to do things that he would not do. But she could know and understand why his hand fell on Krool like that of Cain on Abel. She softened, changed at once.

"Yes, I remember," she said. "I've been upset. Krool was insolent, and I ordered him to go. He would not."

"I've been a fool to keep him all these years. I didn't know what he was—a traitor, the slimmest of the slim, a real Hottentot-Boer. I was pigheaded about him, because he seemed to care so much about me. That counts for much with the most of us."

"Alice Tynemouth saw a policeman help him into a cab in Piccadilly and take him away. Will there be trouble?"

A grim look crossed his face. "I think not," he responded. "There are reasons. He has been stealing information for years, and sending it to Kruger, he and—"

He stopped short, and into his face came a look of sullen reticence.

"Yes, he and—and some one else? Who else?" Her face was white. She had a sudden intuition.

He met her eyes. "Adrian Fellowes—what Fellowes knew, Krool knew, and one way or another, by one means or another, Fellowes knew a great deal."

The knowledge of Adrian Fellowes' treachery and its full significance had hardly come home to him, even when he punished Krool, so shaken was he by the fact that the half-caste had been false to him. Afterwards, however, as the Partners all talked together upstairs, the enormity of the dead man's crime had fastened on him, and his brain had been stunned by the terrible thought that directly or indirectly Jasmine had abetted the crime. Things he had talked over with her, and with no one else, had got to Kruger's knowledge, as the information from South Africa showed. She had at least been indiscreet, had talked to Fellowes with some freedom or he could not have known what he did. But directly, knowingly abetted Fellowes? Of course, she had not done that; but her foolish confidences had abetted treachery, had wronged him, had helped to destroy his plans, had injured England.

He had savagely punished Krool for insolence to her and for his treachery, but a new feeling had grown up in him in the last half-hour. Under the open taunts of his colleagues, a deep resentment had taken possession of him that his work, so hard to do, so important and critical, should have been circumvented by the indiscretions of his wife.

Upon her now this announcement came with crushing force. Adrian Fellowes had gained from her—she knew it all too well now—that which had injured her husband; from which, at any rate, he ought to have been immune. Her face flushed with a resentment far greater than that of Rudyard's, and it was heightened by a humiliation which overwhelmed her. She had been but a tool in every sense, she, Jasmine Byng, one who ruled, had been used like a—she could not form the comparison in her mind—by a dependent, a hanger-on of her husband's bounty; and it was through her, originally, that he had been given a real chance in life by Rudyard.

"I am sorry," she said, calmly, as soon as she could get her voice. "I was the means of your employing him."

"That did not matter," he said, rather nervously. "There was no harm in that, unless you knew his character before he came to me."

"You think I did?"

"I cannot think so. It would have been too ruthless—too wicked."

She saw his suffering, and it touched her. "Of course I did not know that he could do such a thing—so shameless. He was a low coward. He did not deserve decent burial," she added. "He had good fortune to die as he did."

"How did he die?" Rudyard asked her, with a face so unlike what it had always been, so changed by agitation, that it scarcely seemed his. His eyes were fixed on hers.

She met them resolutely. Did he ask her in order to see if she had any suspicion of himself? Had he done it? If he had, there would be some mitigation of her suffering. Or was it Ian Stafford who had done it? One or the other—but which?

"He died without being made to suffer," she said. "Most people who do wrong have to suffer."

"But they live on," he said, bitterly.

"That is no great advantage unless you want to live," she replied. "Do you know how he died?" she added, after a moment, with sharp scrutiny.

He shook his head and returned her scrutiny with added poignancy. "It does not matter. He ceases to do any more harm. He did enough."

"Yes, quite enough," she said, with a withered look, and going over to her writing-table, stood looking at him questioningly. He did not speak again, however.

Presently she said, very quietly, "I am going away."

"I do not understand."

"I am going to work."

"I understand still less."

She took from the writing-table her cheque-book, and handed it to him. He looked at it, and read the counterfoil of the cheque she had given to Alice Tynemouth.

He was bewildered. "What does this mean?" he asked.

"It is for a hospital-ship."

"Sixty thousand pounds! Why, it is nearly all you have."

"It is two-thirds of what I have."

"Why—in God's name, why?"

"To buy my freedom," she answered, bitterly.

"From what?"

"From you."

He staggered back and leaned heavily against a bookcase.

"Freedom from me!" he exclaimed, hoarsely.

He had had terribly bitter and revengeful feelings during the last hour, but all at once his real self emerged, the thing that was deepest in him. "Freedom from me? Has it come to that?"

"Yes, absolutely. Do you remember the day you first said to me that something was wrong with it all,—the day that Ian Stafford dined after his return from abroad? Well, it has been all wrong—cruelly wrong. We haven't made the best of things together, when everything was with us to do so. I have spoiled it all. It hasn't been what you expected."

"Nor what you expected?" he asked, sharply.

"Nor what I expected; but you are not to blame for that."

Suddenly all he had ever felt for her swept through his being, and sullenness fled away. "You have ceased to love me, then. . . See, that is the one thing that matters, Jasmine. All else disappears beside that. Do you love me? Do you love me still? Do you love me, Jasmine? Answer that."

He looked like the ghost of his old dead self, pleading to be recognized.

His misery oppressed her. "What does one know of one's self in the midst of all this—of everything that has nothing to do with love?" she asked.

What she might have said in the dark mood which was coming on her again it is hard to say, but from beneath the window of the room which looked on Park Lane, there came the voice of a street-minstrel, singing to a travelling piano, played by sympathetic fingers, the song:

"She is far from the land where her young hero sleeps, And lovers around her are sighing—"

The simple pathos of the song had nothing to do with her own experience or her own case, but the flood of it swept through her veins like tears. She sank into a chair and listened for a moment with eyes shining, then she sprang up in an agitation which made her tremble and her face go white.

"No, no, no, Rudyard, I do not love you," she said, swiftly. "And because I do not love you, I will not stay. I never loved you, never truly loved you at any time. I never knew myself—that is all that I can say. I never was awake till now. I never was wholly awake till I saw you driving Krool into the street with the sjambok."

She flung up her hands. "For God's sake, let me be truthful at last. I don't want to hurt you—I have hurt you enough, but I do not love you; and I must go. I am going with Alice Tynemouth. We are going together to do something. Maybe I shall learn what will make life possible."

He reached out his arms towards her with a sudden tenderness.

"No, no, no, do not touch me," she cried. "Do not come near me. I must be alone now, and from now on and on. . . You do not understand, but I must be alone. I must work it out alone, whatever it is."

She got up with a quick energy, and went over to the writing-table again. "It may take every penny I have got, but I shall do it, because it is the thing I feel I must do."

"You have millions, Jasmine," he said, in a low, appealing voice.

She looked at him almost fiercely again. "No, I have what is my own, my very own, and no more," she responded, bitterly. "You will do your work, and I will do mine. You will stay here. There will be no scandal, because I shall be going with Alice Tynemouth, and the world will not misunderstand."

"There will be no scandal, because I am going, too," he said, firmly.

"No, no, you cannot, must not, go," she urged.

"I am going to South Africa in two days," he replied. "Stafford was going with me, but he cannot go for a week or so. He will help you, I am sure, with forming your committee and arranging, if you will insist on doing this thing. He is still up-stairs there with the rest of them. I will get him down now, I—"

"Ian Stafford is here—in this house?" she asked, with staring eyes. What inconceivable irony it all was! She could have shrieked with that laughter which is more painful far than tears.

"Yes, he is up-stairs. I made him come and help us—he knows the international game. He will help you, too. He is a good friend—you will know how good some day."

She went white and leaned against the table.

"No, I shall not need him," she said. "We have formed our committee."

"But when I am gone, he can advise you, he can—"

"Oh—oh!" she murmured, and swayed forward, fainting.

He caught her and lowered her gently into a chair.

"You are only mad," he whispered to ears which heard not as he bent over her. "You will be sane some day."

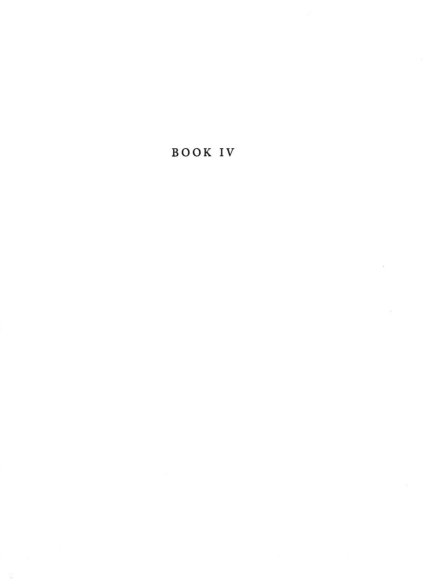

BOOK IV

XXIX

The Menace of the Mountain

Far away, sharply cutting the ether, rise the great sterile peaks and ridges. Here a stark, bare wall like a prison which shuts in a city of men forbidden the blithe world of sun and song and freedom; yonder, a giant of a lost world stretched out in stony ease, sleeping on, while over his grey quiet, generations of men pass. First came savage, warring, brown races alien to each other; then following, white races with faces tanned and burnt by the sun, and smothered in unkempt beard and hair—men restless and coarse and brave, and with ancient sins upon them; but with the Bible in their hands and the language of the prophets on their lips; with iron will, with hatred as deep as their race-love is strong; they with their cattle and their herds, and the clacking wagons carrying homes and fortunes, whose women were housewives and warriors too. Coming after these, men of fairer aspect, adventurous, self-willed, intent to make cities in the wilderness; to win open spaces for their kinsmen, who had no room to swing the hammer in the workshops of their far-off northern island homes; or who, having room, stood helpless before the furnaces where the fires had left only the ashes of past energies.

Up there, these mountains which, like Marathon, look on the sea. But lower the gaze from the austere hills, slowly to the plains below. First the grey of the mountains, turning to brown, then the bare bronze rock giving way to a tumbled wilderness of boulders, where lizards lie in the sun, where the meerkat startles the gazelle. Then the bronze merging into a green so deep and strong that it resembles a blanket spread upon the uplands, but broken by kopjes, shelterless and lonely, rising here and there like watch-towers. After that, below and still below, the flat and staring plain, through which runs an ugly rift turning and twisting like a snake, and moving on and on, till lost in the arc of other hills away to the east and the south: a river in the waste, but still only a muddy current stealing between banks baked and sterile, a sinister stream, giving life to the veld, as some gloomy giver of good gifts would pay a debt of atonement.

On certain Dark Days of 1899-1900, if you had watched these turgid waters flow by, your eyes would have seen tinges of red like blood;

and following the stain of red, gashed lifeless things, which had been torn from the ranks of sentient beings.

Whereupon, lifting your eyes from the river, you would have seen the answer to your question—masses of men mounted and unmounted, who moved, or halted, or stood like an animal with a thousand legs controlled by one mind. Or again you would have observed those myriad masses plunging across the veld, still in cohering masses, which shook and broke and scattered, regathering again, as though drawn by a magnet, but leaving stark remnants in their wake.

Great columns of troops which had crossed the river and pushed on into a zone of fierce fire, turn and struggle back again across the stream; other thousands of men, who had not crossed, succour their wounded, and retreat steadily, bitterly to places of safety, the victims of blunders from which come the bloody punishment of valour.

Beyond the grey mountains were British men and women waiting for succour from forces which poured death in upon them from the malevolent kopjes, for relief from the ravages of disease and hunger. They waited in a straggling town of the open plain circled by threatening hills, where the threat became a blow, and the blow was multiplied a million times. Gaunt, fighting men sought to appease the craving of starvation by the boiled carcasses of old horses; in caves and dug-outs, feeble women, with undying courage, kept alive the flickering fires of life in their children; and they smiled to cheer the tireless, emaciated warriors who went out to meet death, or with a superior yet careful courage stayed to receive or escape it.

When night came, across the hills and far away in the deep blue, white shaking streams of light poured upward, telling the besieged forces over there at Lordkop that rescue would come, that it was moving on to the mountain. How many times had this light in the sky flashed the same grave pledge in the mystic code of the heliograph, "We are gaining ground—we will reach you soon." How many times, however, had the message also been, "Not yet—but soon."

Men died in this great camp from wounds and from fever, and others went mad almost from sheer despair; yet whenever the Master Player called, they sprang to their places with a new-born belief that he who had been so successful in so many long-past battles would be right in the end with his old rightness, though he had been wrong so often on the Dreitval.

Others there were who were sick of the world and wished "to be well out of it"—as they said to themselves. Some had been cruelly injured, and desire of life was dead in them; others had given injury, and remorse had slain peace. Others still there were who, having done evil all their lives, knew that they could not retrace their steps, and yet shrank from a continuance of the old bad things.

Some indeed, in the red futile sacrifice, had found what they came to find; but some still were left whose recklessness did not avail. Comrades fell beside them, but, unscathed, they went on fighting. Injured men were carried in hundreds to the hospitals, but no wounds brought them low. Bullets were sprayed around them, but none did its work for them. Shells burst near, yet no savage shard mutilated their bodies.

Of these was Ian Stafford.

Three times he had been in the fore-front of the fight where Death came sweeping down the veld like rain, but It passed him by. Horses and men fell round his guns, yet he remained uninjured.

He was patient. If Death would not hasten to meet him, he would wait. Meanwhile, he would work while he could, but with no thought beyond the day, no vision of the morrow.

He was one of the machines of war. He was close to his General, he was the beloved of his men, still he was the man with no future; though he studied the campaign with that thoroughness which had marked his last years in diplomacy.

He was much among his own wounded, much with others who were comforted by his solicitude, by the courage of his eye, and the grasp of his firm, friendly hand. It was at what the soldiers called the Stay Awhile Hospital that he came in living touch again with the life he had left behind.

He knew that Rudyard Byng had come to South Africa; but he knew no more. He knew that Jasmine had, with Lady Tynemouth, purchased a ship and turned it into a hospital at a day's notice; but as to whether these two had really come to South Africa, and harboured at the Cape, or Durban, he had no knowledge. He never looked at the English newspapers which arrived at Dreitval River. He was done with that old world in which he once worked; he was concerned only for this narrow field where an Empire's fate was being solved.

Night, the dearest friend of the soldier, had settled on the veld. A thousand fires were burning, and there were no sounds save the murmuring voices of myriads of men, and the stamp of hoofs where the Cavalry and Mounted Infantry horses were picketed. Food and fire, the priceless comfort of a blanket on the ground, and a saddle or kit for a pillow gave men compensation for all the hardships and dangers of the day; and they gave little thought to the morrow.

The soldier lives in the present. His rifle, his horse, his boots, his blanket, the commissariat, a dry bit of ground to sleep on—these are the things which occupy his mind. His heroism is incidental, the commonplace impulse of the moment. He does things because they are there to do, not because some great passion, some exaltation, seizes him. His is the real simple life. So it suddenly seemed to Stafford as he left his tent, after he had himself inspected every man and every horse in his battery that lived through the day of death, and made his way towards the Stay Awhile Hospital.

"This is the true thing," he said to himself as he gazed at the wide camp. He turned his face here and there in the starlight, and saw human life that but now was moving in the crash of great guns, the shrieking of men terribly wounded, the agony of mutilated horses, the bursting of shells, the hissing scream of the pom-pom, and the discordant cries of men fighting an impossible fight.

"There is no pretense here," he reflected. "It is life reduced down to the bare elements. There is no room for the superficial thing. It's all business. It's all stark human nature."

At that moment his eye caught one of those white messages of the sky flashing the old bitter promise, "We shall reach you soon." He forgot himself, and a great spirit welled up in him.

"Soon!" The light in the sky shot its message over the hills.

That was it—the present, not the past. Here was work, the one thing left to do.

"And it has to be done," he said aloud, as he walked on swiftly, a spring to his footstep. Presently he mounted and rode away across the veld. Buried in his thoughts, he was only subconsciously aware of what he saw until, after near an hour's riding, he pulled rein at the door of the Stay Awhile Hospital, which was some miles in the rear of the main force.

As he entered, a woman in a nurse's garb passed him swiftly. He scarcely looked at her; he was only conscious that she was in great haste. Her eyes seemed looking at some inner, hidden thing, and, though they glanced at him, appeared not to see him or to realize more than that some one was passing. But suddenly, to both, after they had passed, there came an arrest of attention. There was a consciousness, which had nothing to do with the sight of the eyes, that a familiar presence had gone by. Each turned quickly, and their eyes came back from regarding the things of the imagination, and saw each other face to face. The nurse gave an exclamation of pleasure and ran forward.

Stafford held out a hand. It seemed to him, as he did it, that it stretched across a great black gulf and found another hand in the darkness beyond.

"Al'mah!" he said, in a voice of protest as of companionship.

Of all those he had left behind, this was the one being whom to meet was not disturbing. He wished to encounter no one of that inner circle of his tragic friendship; but he realized that Al'mah had had her tragedy too, and that her suffering could not be less than his own. The same dark factor had shadowed the lives of both. Adrian Fellowes had injured them both through the same woman, had shaken, if not shattered, the fabric of their lives. However much they two were blameworthy, they had been sincere, they had been honourable in their dishonour, they had been "falsely true." They were derelicts of life, with the comradeship of despair as a link between them.

"Al'mah," he said again, gently. Then, with a bitter humour, he added, "You here—I thought you were a prima donna!"

The flicker of a smile crossed her odd, fine, strong face. "This is grand opera," she said. "It is the Nibelungen Ring of England."

"To end in the Twilight of the Gods?" he rejoined with a hopeless kind of smile.

They turned to the outer door of the hospital and stepped into the night. For a moment they stood looking at the great camp far away to right and left, and to the lone mountains yonder, where the Boer commandoes held the passes and trained their merciless armament upon all approaches. Then he said at last: "Why have you come here? You had your work in England."

"What is my work?" she asked.

"To heal the wounded," he answered.

"I am trying to do that," she replied.

"You are trying to heal bodies, but it is a bigger, greater thing to heal the wounded mind."

"I am trying to do that too. It is harder than the other."

"Whose minds are you trying to heal?" he questioned, gently.

"'Physician heal thyself' was the old command, wasn't it? But that is harder still."

"Must one always be a saint to do a saintly thing?" he asked.

"I am not clever," she replied, "and I can't make phrases. But must one always be a sinner to do a wicked thing? Can't a saint do a wicked thing, and a sinner do a good thing without being called the one or the other?"

"I don't think you need apologize for not being able to make phrases. I suppose you'd say there is neither absolute saintliness nor absolute wickedness, but that life is helplessly composite of both, and that black really may be white. You know the old phrase, 'Killing no murder.'"

She seemed to stiffen, and her lips set tightly for a minute; then, as though by a great effort, she laughed bitterly.

"Murder isn't always killing," she replied. "Don't you remember the protest in Macbeth, 'Time was, when the brains were out the man would die'?" Then, with a little quick gesture towards the camp, she added, "When you think of to-day, doesn't it seem that the brains are out, and yet that the man still lives? I'm not a soldier, and this awful slaughter may be the most wonderful tactics, but it's all beyond my little mind."

"Your littleness is not original enough to attract notice," he replied with kindly irony. "There is almost an epidemic of it. Let us hope we shall have an antidote soon."

There was a sudden cry from inside the hospital. Al'mah shut her eyes for a moment, clinched her fingers, and became very pale; then she recovered herself, and turned her face towards the door, as though waiting for some one to come out.

"What is the matter?" he asked. "Some bad case?"

"Yes—very bad," she replied.

"One you've been attending?"

"Yes."

"What arm—the artillery?" he asked with sudden interest.

"Yes, the artillery."

He turned towards the door of the hospital again. "One of my men? What battery? Do you know?"

"Not yours—Schiller's."

"Schiller's! A Boer?"

She nodded. "A Boer spy, caught by Boer bullets as he was going back."

"When was that?"

"This morning early."

"The little business at Wortmann's Drift?"

She nodded. "Yes, there."

"I don't quite understand. Was he in our lines—a Boer spy?"

"Yes. But he wore British uniform, he spoke English. He was an Englishman once."

Suddenly she came up close to him, and looked into his face steadily. "I will tell you all," she said scarce above a whisper. "He came to spy, but he came also to see his wife. She had written to ask him not to join the Boers, as he said he meant to do; or, if he had, to leave them and join his own people. He came, but not to join his fellow-countrymen. He came to get money from his wife; and he came to spy."

An illuminating thought shot into Stafford's mind. He remembered something that Byng once told him.

"His wife is a nurse?" he asked in a low tone.

"She is a nurse."

"She knew, then, that he was a spy?" he asked.

"Yes, she knew. I suppose she ought to be tried by court-martial. She did not expose him. She gave him a chance to escape. But he was shot as he tried to reach the Boer lines."

"And was brought back here to his wife—to you! Did he let them"— he nodded towards the hospital—"know he was your husband?"

When she spoke again her voice showed strain, but it did not tremble. "Of course. He would not spare me. He never did. It was always like that."

He caught her hand in his. "You have courage enough for a hundred," he said.

"I have suffered enough for a hundred," she responded.

Again that sharp cry rang out, and again she turned anxiously towards the door.

"I came to South Africa on the chance of helping him in some way," she replied. "It came to me that he might need me."

"You paid the price of his life once to Kruger—after the Raid, I've heard," he said.

"Yes, I owed him that, and as much more as was possible," she responded with a dark, pained look.

"His life is in danger—an operation?" he questioned.

"Yes. There is one chance; but they could not give him an anaesthetic, and they would not let me stay with him. They forced me away—out here." She appeared to listen again. "That was his voice—that crying," she added presently.

"Wouldn't it be better he should go? If he recovers there would only be—"

"Oh yes, to be tried as a spy—a renegade Englishman! But he would rather live in spite of that, if it was only for an hour."

"To love life so much as that—a spy!" Stafford reflected.

"Not so much love of life as fear of—" She stopped short.

"To fear—silence and peace!" he remarked darkly, with a shrug of his shoulders. Then he added: "Tell me, if he does not die, and if—if he is pardoned by any chance, do you mean to live with him again?"

A bitter laugh broke from her. "How do I know? What does any woman know what she will do until the situation is before her! She may mean to do one thing and do the complete opposite. She may mean to hate, and will end by loving. She may mean to kiss and will end by killing. She may kiss and kill too all in one moment, and still not be inconsistent. She would have the logic of a woman. How do I know what I would do—what I will do!"

The door of the hospital opened. A surgeon came out, and seeing Al'mah, moved towards the two. Stafford went forward hurriedly, but Al'mah stood like one transfixed. There was a whispered word, and then Stafford came back to her.

"You will not need to do anything," he said.

"He is gone—like that!" she whispered in an awed voice. "Death, death—so many die!" She shuddered.

Stafford passed her arm through his, and drew her towards the door of the hospital.

A half-hour later Stafford emerged again from the hospital, his head bent in thought. He rode slowly back to his battery, unconscious of the stir of life round him, of the shimmering white messages to the besieged town beyond the hills. He was thinking of the tragedy of the woman he had left tearless and composed beside the bedside of the man who had so vilely used her. He was reflecting how her life, and his own, and the lives of at least three others, were so tangled together that what twisted the existence of one disturbed all. In one sense the woman he had just left in the hospital was nothing to him, and yet now she seemed to be the only living person to whom he was drawn.

He remembered the story he had once heard in Vienna of a man and a woman who both had suffered betrayal, who both had no longer a single illusion left, who had no love for each other at all, in whom indeed love was dead—a mangled murdered thing; and yet who went away to Corfu together, and there at length found a pathway out of despair in the depths of the sea. Between these two there had never been even the faint shadow of romance or passion; but in the terrible mystery of pain and humiliation, they had drawn together to help each other, through a breach of all social law, in pity of each other. He apprehended the real meaning of the story when Vienna was alive with it, but he understood far, far better now.

A pity as deep as any feeling he had ever known had come to him as he stood with Al'mah beside the bed of her dead renegade man; and it seemed to him that they two also might well bury themselves in the desert together, and minister to each other's despair. It was only the swift thought of a moment, which faded even as it saw the light; but it had its origin in that last flickering sense of human companionship which dies in the atmosphere of despair. "Every man must live his dark hours alone," a broken-down actor once said to Stafford as he tried to cheer him when the last thing he cared for had been taken from him— his old, faded, misshapen wife; when no faces sent warm glances to him across the garish lights. "It is no use," this Roscius had said, "every man must live his dark hours alone."

That very evening, after the battle of the Dreitval, Jigger, Stafford's trumpeter, had said a thing to him which had struck a chord that rang in empty chambers of his being. He had found Jigger sitting disconsolate beside a gun, which was yet grimy and piteous with the blood of men who had served it, and he asked the lad what his trouble was.

In reply Jigger had said, "When it 'it 'm 'e curled up like a bit o' shaving. An' when I done what I could 'e says, 'It's a speshul for one now, an' it's lonely goin',' 'e says. When I give 'im a drink 'e says, 'It 'd do me more good later, little 'un'; an' 'e never said no more except, 'One at a time is the order—only one.'"

Not even his supper had lifted the cloud from Jigger's face, and Stafford had left the lad trying to compose a letter to the mother of the dead man, who had been an especial favourite with the trumpeter from the slums.

Stafford was roused from his reflections by the grinding, rumbling sound of a train. He turned his face towards the railway line.

"A troop-train—more food for the dragons," he said to himself. He could not see the train itself, but he could see the head-light of the locomotive, and he could hear its travail as it climbed slowly the last incline to the camp.

"Who comes there!" he said aloud, and in his mind there swept a premonition that the old life was finding him out, that its invisible forces were converging upon him. But did it matter? He knew in his soul that he was now doing the right thing, that he had come out in the open where all the archers of penalty had a fair target for their arrows. He wished to be "Free among the dead that are wounded and that lie in the grave and are out of remembrance;" but he would do no more to make it so than tens of thousands of other men were doing on these battle-fields.

"Who comes there!" he said again, his eyes upon the white, round light in the distance, and he stood still to try and make out the black, winding, groaning thing.

Presently he heard quick footsteps.

A small, alert figure stopped short, a small, abrupt hand saluted. "The General Commanding 'as sent for you, sir."

It was trumpeter Jigger of the Artillery.

"Are you the General's orderly, then?" asked Stafford quizzically.

"The orderly's gone w'ere 'e thought 'e'd find you, and I've come w'ere I know'd you'd be, sir."

"Where did he think he'd find me?"

"Wiv the 'osses, sir."

A look of gratification crossed Stafford's face. He was well known in the army as one who looked after his horses and his men. "And what made you think I was at the hospital, Jigger?"

"Becos you'd been to the 'osses, sir."

"Did you tell the General's orderly that?"

"No, your gryce—no, sir," he added quickly, and a flush of self-reproach came to his face, for he prided himself on being a real disciplinarian, a disciple of the correct thing. "I thought I'd like 'im to see our 'osses, an' 'ow you done 'em, an' I'd find you as quick as 'e could, wiv a bit to the good p'r'aps."

Stafford smiled. "Off you go, then. Find that orderly. Say, Colonel Stafford's compliments to the General Commanding and he will report himself at once. See that you get it straight, trumpeter."

Jigger would rather die than not get it straight, and his salute made that quite plain.

"It's made a man of him, anyhow," Stafford said to himself, as he watched the swiftly disappearing figure. "He's as straight as a nail, body and mind—poor little devil. . . How far away it all seems!"

A quarter of an hour later he was standing beside the troop-train which he had seen labouring to its goal. It was carrying the old regiment of the General Officer Commanding, who had sent Stafford to its Colonel with an important message. As the two officers stood together watching the troops detrain and make order out of the chaos of baggage and equipment, Stafford's attention was drawn to a woman some little distance away, giving directions about her impedimenta.

"Who is the lady?" he asked, while in his mind was a sensible stir of recognition.

"Ah, there's something like the real thing!" his companion replied. "She is doing a capital bit of work. She and Lady Tynemouth have got a hospital-ship down at Durban. She's come to link it up better with the camp. It's Rudyard Byng's wife. They're both at it out here."

"Who comes there!" Stafford had exclaimed a moment before with a sense of premonition.

Jasmine had come.

He drew back in the shadow as she turned round towards them.

"To the Stay Awhile—right!" he heard a private say in response to her directions.

He saw her face, but not clearly. He had glimpse of a Jasmine not so daintily pretty as of old, not so much of a dresden-china shepherdess; but with the face of a woman who, watching the world with understanding eyes, and living with an understanding heart, had taken on something of the mysterious depths of the Life behind life. It was only a glimpse he had, but it was enough. It was more than enough.

"Where is Byng?" he asked his fellow-officer.

"He's been up there with Tain's Brigade for a fortnight. He was in Kimberley, but got out before the investment, went to Cape Town, and came round here—to be near his wife, I suppose."

"He is soldiering, then?"

"He was a Colonel in the Rand Rifles once. He's with the South African Horse now in command of the regiment attached to Tain. Tain's out of your beat—away on the right flank there."

Presently Stafford saw Jasmine look in their direction; then, on seeing Stafford's companion, came forward hastily. The Colonel left Stafford and went to meet her.

A moment afterwards, she turned and looked at Stafford. Her face was now deadly pale, but it showed no agitation. She was in the light of an electric lamp, and he was in the shadow. For one second only she gazed at him, then she turned and moved away to the cape-cart awaiting her. The Colonel saw her in, then returned to Stafford.

"Why didn't you come and be introduced?" the Colonel asked. "I told her who you were."

"Hospital-ships are not in my line," Stafford answered casually. "Women and war don't go together."

"She's a nurse, she's not a woman," was the paradoxical reply.

"She knows Byng is here?"

"I suppose so. It looks like a clever bit of strategy—junction of forces. There's a lot of women at home would like the chance she has—at a little less cost."

"What is the cost?"

"Well, that ship didn't cost less than a hundred thousand pounds."

"Is that all?"

The Colonel looked at Stafford in surprise: but Stafford was not thinking of the coin.

XXX

"And Never the Twain Shall Meet!"

As the cape-cart conveying Jasmine to the hospital moved away from the station, she settled down into the seat beside the driver with the helplessness of one who had received a numbing blow. Her body swayed as though she would faint, and her eyes closed, and stayed closed for so long a time, that Corporal Shorter, who drove the rough little pair of Argentines, said to her sympathetically:

"It's all right, ma'am. We'll be there in a jiffy. Don't give way."

This friendly solicitude had immediate effect. Jasmine sat up, and thereafter held herself as though she was in her yellow salon yonder in London.

"Thank you," she replied serenely to Corporal Shorter. "It was a long, tiring journey, and I let myself go for a moment."

"A good night's rest'll do you a lot of good, ma'am," he ventured. Then he added, "Beggin' pardon, ain't you Mrs. Colonel Rudyard Byng?"

She turned and looked at the man inquiringly. "Yes, I am Mrs. Byng."

"Thank you, ma'am. Now how did I know? Why," he chuckled, "I saw a big B on your hand-bag, and I knew you was from the hospital-ship—they told me that at the Stay Awhile; and the rest was easy, ma'am. I had a mate along o' your barge. He was one of them the Boers got at Talana Hill. They chipped his head-piece nicely—just like the 4.7's flay the kopjes up there. My mate's been writing to me about you. We're a long way from home, Joey and me, and a bit o' kindness is a bit of all right to us."

"Where is your home?" Jasmine asked, her fatigue and oppression lifting.

He chuckled as though it were a joke, while he answered: "Australia onct and first. My mate, Joey Clynes, him that's on your ship, we was both born up beyond Bendigo. When we cut loose from the paternal leash, so to speak, we had a bit of boundary-riding, rabbit-killing, shearing and sun-downing—all no good, year by year. Then we had a bit o' luck and found a mob of warrigals—horses run wild, you know. We stalked 'em for days in the droughttime to a water-course, and got 'em, and coaxed 'em along till the floods come; then we sold 'em, and with the hard tin shipped for to see the world. So it was as of old. And by and by we found ourselves down here, same as all the rest, puttin' in a bit o' time for the Flag."

Jasmine turned on him one of those smiles which had made her so many friends in the past—a smile none the less alluring because it had lost that erstime flavour of artifice and lure which, however hidden, had been part of its power. Now it was accompanied by no slight drooping of the eyelids. It brightened a look which was direct and natural.

"It's a good thing to have lived in the wide distant spaces of the world," she responded. "A man couldn't easily be mean or small where life is so simple and so large."

His face flushed with pleasure. She was so easy to get on with, he said to himself; and she certainly had a wonderfully kind smile. But he felt too that she needed greater wisdom, and he was ready to give it—a friendly characteristic of the big open spaces "where life is so simple and so large."

"Well, that might be so 'long o' some continents," he remarked, "but it wasn't so where Joey Clynes and me was nourished, so to speak. I tripped up on a good many mean things from Bendigo to Thargomindah and back around. The back-blocks has its tricks as well as the towns, as you would see if you come across a stock-rider with a cheque to be broke in his hand. I've seen six months' wages go bung in a day with a stock-rider on the gentle jupe. But again, peradventure, I've seen a man that had lost ten thousand sheep tramp fifty miles in a blazing sun with a basket of lambs on his back, savin' them two switherin' little papillions worth nothin' at all, at the risk of his own life—just as mates have done here on this salamanderin' veld; same as Colonel Byng did to-day along o' Wortmann's Drift."

Jasmine had been trying to ask a question concerning her husband ever since the man had mentioned his name, and had not been able to do so. She had never spoken of him directly to any one since she had left England; had never heard from him; had written him no word; was, so far as the outer acts of life were concerned, as distant from him as Corporal Shorter was from his native Bendigo. She had been busy as she had never before been in her life, in a big, comprehensive, useful way. It had seemed to her in England, as she carried through the negotiations for the Valoria, fitted it out for the service it was to render, directed its administration over the heads of the committee appointed, for form's sake, to assist Lady Tynemouth and herself, that the spirit of her grandfather was over her, watching her, inspiring her. This had become almost an obsession with her. Her grandfather had had belief in her, delight in her; and now the innumerable talks she had had with him, as to the way he had done things, gave her confidence and a key to what she had to do. It was the first real work; for what she did for Ian Stafford in diplomacy was only playing upon the weakness of human nature with a skilled intelligence, with an instinctive knowledge of men and a capacity for managing them. The first real pride she had ever felt soothed her angry soul.

Her grandfather had been more in her mind than any one else—than either Rudyard or Ian Stafford. Towards both of these her mind had slowly and almost unconsciously changed, and she wished to think about neither. There had been a revolution in her nature, and all her tragic experience, her emotions, and her faculties, had been shaken into a crucible where the fire of pain and revolt burned on and on and on. From the crucible there had come as yet no precipitation of life's elements, and she scarcely knew what was in her heart. She tried to smother every thought concerning the past. She did not seek to find her bearings, or to realize in what country of the senses and the emotions she was travelling.

One thing was present, however, at times, and when it rushed over her in its fulness, it shook her as the wind shakes the leaf on a tree—a sense of indignation, of anger, or resentment. Against whom? Against all. Against Rudyard, against Ian Stafford; but most of all, a thousand times most against a dead man, who had been swept out of life, leaving behind a memory which could sting murderously.

Now, when she heard of Rudyard's bravery at Wortmann's Drift, a curious thrill of excitement ran through her veins, or it would be truer to say that a sensation new and strange vibrated in her blood. She had heard many tales of valour in this war, and more than one hero of the Victoria Cross had been in her charge at Durban; but as a child's heart might beat faster at the first words of a wonderful story, so she felt a faint suffocation in the throat and her brooding eyes took on a brighter, a more objective look, as she heard the tale of Wortmann's Drift.

"Tell me about it," she said, yet turned her head away from her eager historian.

Corporal Shorter's words were addressed to the smallest pink ear he had ever seen except on a baby, but he was only dimly conscious of that. He was full of a man's pride in a man's deed.

"Well, it was like this," he recited. "Gunter's horse bolted—Dick Gunter's in the South African Horse same as Colonel Byng—his lot. Old Gunter's horse gits away with him into the wide open. I s'pose there'd been a hunderd Boers firing at the runaway for three minutes, and at last off comes Gunter. He don't stir for a minute or more, then we see him pick himself up a bit quick, but settle back again. And while we was lookin' and tossin' pennies like as to his chances out there, a grey New Zealand mare nips out across the veld stretchin' every string. We knowed her all right, that grey mare—a regular Mrs. Mephisto, w'ich belongs to Colonel Byng. Do the Boojers fire at him? Don't they! We could see the spots of dust where the bullets struck, spittin', spittin', spittin', and Lord knows how many hunderd more there was that didn't hit the ground. An' the grey mare gets there. As cool as a granadillar, down drops Colonel Byng beside old Gunter; down goes the grey mare—Colonel Byng had taught her that trick, like the Roosian Cossack hosses. Then up on her rolls old Gunter, an' up goes Colonel Byng, and the grey mare switchin' her bobtail, as if she was havin' a bit of mealies in the middle o' the day. But when they was both on, then the band begun to play. Men was fightin' of course, but it looked as if the whole smash stopped to see what the end would be. It was a real pretty race, an' the grey mare takin' it as free as if she was carryin' a little bit of a pipkin like me instead of twenty-six stone. She's a flower, that grey mare! Once she stumbled, an' we knowed it wasn't an ant-bear's hole she'd found in the veld, and that she'd been hurt. But they know, them hosses, that they must do as their Baases do; and they fight right on. She come home with the two all right. She switched round a corner and over a nose of land where that crossfire couldn't hit the lot; an' there was the three of 'em at 'ome for a cup o' tea. Why, ma'am, that done the army as much good to-day, that little go-to-the-devil, you mud-suckers! as though we'd got Schuster's Hill. 'Twas what we needed—an' we got it. It took our eyes off the nasty little fact that half of a regiment was down, an' the other half with their job not done as it was ordered. It made the S.A.'s and the Lynchesters and the Gessex lot laugh. Old Gunter's all right. He's in the Stay Awhile now. You'll be sure to see him. And Colonel Byng's all right, too, except a little bit o' splinter—"

"A bit of splinter—" Her voice was almost peremptory.

"A chip off his wrist like, but he wasn't thinkin' of that when he got back. He was thinkin' of the grey mare; and she was hit in three places, but not to mention. One bullet cut through her ear and through

Colonel Byng's hat as he stooped over her neck; but the luck was with them. They was born to do a longer trek together. A little bit of the same thing in both of 'em, so to speak. The grey mare has a temper like a hunderd wildcats, and Colonel Byng can let himself go too, as you perhaps know, ma'am. We've seen him let loose sometimes when there was shirkers about, but he's all right inside his vest. And he's a good feeder. His men get their tucker all right. He knows when to shut his eyes. He's got a way to make his bunch—and they're the hardest-bit bunch in the army—do anything he wants 'em to. He's as hard himself as ever is, but he's all right underneath the epidermotis."

All at once there flashed before Jasmine's eyes the picture of Rudyard driving Krool out of the house in Park Lane with a sjambok. She heard again the thud of the rhinoceros-whip on the cringing back of the Boer; she heard the moan of the victim as he stumbled across the threshold into the street; and again she felt that sense of suffocation, that excitement which the child feels on the brink of a wonderful romance, the once-upon-a-time moment.

They were nearing the hospital. The driver silently pointed to it. He saw that he had made an impression, and he was content with it. He smiled to himself.

"Is Colonel Byng in the camp?" she asked.

"He's over—'way over, miles and miles, on the left wing with Kearey's brigade now. But old Gunter's here, and you're sure to see Colonel Byng soon—well, I should think."

She had no wish to see Colonel Byng soon. Three days would suffice to do what she wished here, and then she would return to Durban to her work there—to Alice Tynemouth, whose friendship and wonderful tactfulness had helped her in indefinable ways, as a more obvious sympathy never could have done. She would have resented one word which would have suggested that a tragedy was slowly crushing out her life.

Never a woman in the world was more alone. She worked and smiled with eyes growing sadder, yet with a force hardening in her which gave her face a character it never had before. Work had come at the right moment to save her from the wild consequences of a nature maddened by a series of misfortunes and penalties, for which there had been no warning and no preparation.

She was not ready for a renewal of the past. Only a few minutes before she had been brought face to face with Ian Stafford, had seen him look at her out of the shadow there at the station, as though she was an infinite distance away from him; and she had realized with overwhelming force how changed her world was. Ian Stafford, who but a few short months ago had held her in his arms and whispered unforgettable things, now looked at her as one looks at the image of a forgotten thing. She recalled his last words to her that awful day when Rudyard had read the fatal letter, and the world had fallen:

"Nothing can set things right between you and me, Jasmine," he had said. "But there is Rudyard. You must help him through. He heard scandal about Mennaval last night at De Lancy Scovel's. He didn't believe it. It rests with you to give it all the lie. Good-bye."

That had been the end—the black, bitter end. Since then Ian had never spoken a word to her, nor she to him; but he had stood there in the shadow at the station like a ghost, reproachful, unresponsive, indifferent. She recalled now the day when, after three years' parting, she had left him cool, indifferent, and self-contained in the doorway of the sweet-shop in Regent Street; how she had entered her carriage, had clinched her hands, and cried with wilful passion: "He shall not treat me so. He shall show some feeling. He shall! He shall!"

Here was indifference again, but of another land. Hers was not a woman's vanity, in fury at being despised. Vanity, maybe, was still there, but so slight that it made no contrast to the proud turmoil of a nature which had been humiliated beyond endurance; which, for its mistakes, had received accruing penalties as precise as though they had been catalogued; which had waked to find that a whole lifetime had been an error; and that it had no anchor in any set of principles or impelling habits.

And over all there hung the shadow of a man's death, with its black suspicion. When Ian Stafford looked at her from the shadow of the railway-station, the question had flashed into his mind, Did she kill him? Around Adrian Fellowes' death there hung a cloud of mystery which threw a sinister shadow on the path of three people. In the middle of the night, Jasmine started from her sleep with the mystery of the man's death torturing her, and with the shuddering question, Which? on her fevered lips. Was it her husband—was it Ian Stafford? As he galloped over the veld, or sat with his pipe beside the camp-fire, Rudyard Byng was also drawn into the frigid gloom of the ugly thought, and his mind asked the question, Did she kill him? It was as though each who had suffered from the man in life was destined to be menaced by his shade, till it should be exorcised by that person who had taken the useless life, saying, "It was I; I did it!"

As Jasmine entered the hospital, it seemed to her excited imagination as though she was entering a House of Judgment: as though here in a court of everlasting equity she would meet those who had played their vital parts in her life.

What if Rudyard was here! What if in these few days while she was to be here he was to cross her path! What would she say? What would she do? What could be said or done? Bitterness and resentment and dark suspicion were in her mind—and in his. Her pride was less wilful and tempestuous than on the day when she drove him from her; when he said things which flayed her soul, and left her body as though it had been beaten with rods. Her bitterness, her resentment had its origin in the fact that he did not understand—and yet in his crude big way he had really understood better than Ian Stafford. She felt that Rudyard despised her now a thousand times more than ever he had hinted at in that last stifling scene in Park Lane; and her spirit rebelled against it. She would rather that he had believed everything against her, and had made an open scandal, because then she could have paid any debt due to him by the penalty most cruel a woman can bear. But pity, concession, the condescension of a superior morality, were impossible to her proud mind.

As for Ian Stafford, he had left her stripped bare of one single garment of self-respect. His very kindness, his chivalry in defending her; his inflexible determination that all should be over between them forever, that she should be prevailed upon to be to Rudyard more than she had ever been—it all drove her into a deeper isolation. This isolation would have been her destruction but that something bigger than herself, a passion to do things, lifted to idealism a mind which in the past had grown materialistic, which, in gaining wit and mental skill, had missed the meaning of things, the elemental sense.

Corporal Shorter's tale of Rudyard's heroism had stirred her; but she could not have said quite what her feeling was with regard to it. She only knew vaguely that she was glad of it in a more personal than impersonal way. When she shook hands with the cheerful non-com. at the door of the hospital, she gave him a piece of gold which he was loth to accept till she said: "But take it as a souvenir of Colonel Byng's little ride with 'Old Gunter.'"

With a laugh, he took it then, and replied, "I'll not smoke it, I'll not eat it, and I'll not drink it. I'll wear it for luck and God-bless-you!"

XXXI

The Grey Horse and its Rider

It was almost midnight. The camp was sleeping. The forces of destruction lay torpid in the starry shadow of the night. There was no moon, but the stars gave a light that relieved the gloom. They were so near to the eye that it might seem a lancer could pick them from their nests of blue. The Southern Cross hung like a sign of hope to guide men to a new Messiah.

In vain Jasmine had tried to sleep. The day had been too much for her. All that happened in the past four years went rushing past, and she saw herself in scenes which were so tormenting in their reality that once she cried out as in a nightmare. As she did so, she was answered by a choking cry of pain like her own, and, waking, she started up from her couch with poignant apprehension; but presently she realized that it was the cry of some wounded patient in the ward not far from the room where she lay.

It roused her, however, from the half wakefulness which had been excoriated by burning memories, and, hurriedly rising, she opened wide the window and looked out into the night. The air was sharp, but it soothed her hot face and brow, and the wild pulses in her wrists presently beat less vehemently. She put a firm hand on herself, as she was wont to do in these days, when there was no time for brooding on her own troubles, and when, with the duties she had taken upon herself, it would be criminal to indulge in self-pity.

Looking out of the window now into the quiet night, the watch-fires dotting the plain had a fascination for her greater than the wonder of the southern sky and its plaque of indigo sprinkled with silver dust and diamonds. Those fires were the bulletins of the night, telling that around each of them men were sleeping, or thinking of other scenes, or wondering whether the fight to-morrow would be their last fight, and if so, what then? They were to the army like the candle in the home of the cottager. Those little groups of men sleeping around their fires were like a family, where men grow to serve each other as brother serves brother, knowing each other's foibles, but preserving each other's honour for the family's pride, risking life to save each other.

As Jasmine gazed into the gloom, spattered with a delicate radiance which did not pierce the shadows, but only made lively the darkness, she was suddenly conscious of the dull regular thud of horses' hoofs upon the veld. Troops of Mounted Infantry were evidently moving to take up a new position at the bidding of the Master Player. The sound was like the rub-a-dub of muffled hammers. The thought forced itself on her mind that here were men secretly hastening to take part in the grim lottery of life and death, from which some, and maybe many, would draw the black ticket of doom, and so pass from the game before the game was won.

The rumbling roll of hoofs grew distinct. Now they seemed to be almost upon her, and presently they emerged into view from the right, where their progress had been hidden by the hospital-building. When they reached the hospital there came a soft command and, as the troop passed, every face was turned towards the building. It was men full of life and the interest of the great game paying passing homage to their helpless comrades in this place of healing.

As they rode past, a few of the troopers had a glimpse of the figure dimly outlined at the window. Some made kindly jests, cheffing each other—"Your fancy, old sly-boots? Arranged it all, eh? Watch me, Lizzie, as I pass, and wave your lily-white hand!"

But others pressed their lips tightly, for visions of a woman somewhere waiting and watching flashed before their eyes; while others still had only the quiet consciousness of the natural man, that a woman looks at them; and where women are few and most of them are angels,—the battle-field has no shelter for any other—such looks have deep significance.

The troop went by steadily, softly and slowly. After they had all gone past, two horsemen detached from the troop came after. Presently one of them separated from his companion and rode on. The other came towards the hospital at a quick trot, drew bridle very near Jasmine's window, slid to the ground, said a soft word to his charger, patted its neck, and, turning, made for the door of the hospital. For a moment Jasmine stood looking out, greatly moved, she scarcely knew why, by this little incident of the night, and then suddenly the starlight seemed to draw round the patient animal standing at attention, as it were.

Then she saw it was a grey horse.

Its owner, as Corporal Shorter predicted, had come to see "Old Gunter," ere he went upon another expedition of duty. Its owner was Rudyard Byng.

That was why so strange a coldness, as of apprehension or anxiety, had passed through Jasmine when the rider had come towards her out of the night. Her husband was here. If she called, he would come. If she stretched out her hand, she could touch him. If she opened a door, she would be in his presence. If he opened the door behind her, he could—

She stepped back hastily into the room, and drew her night-robe closely about her with sudden flushing of the face. If he should enter her room—she felt in the darkness for her dressing-gown. It was not on the chair beside her bed. She moved hastily, and blundered against a table. She felt for the foot of the bed. The dressing-gown was not there. Her brain was on fire. Where was her dressing-gown? She tried to button the night-dress over her palpitating breast, but abandoned it to throw back her head and gather her golden hair away from her shoulders and breast. All this in the dark, in the safe dusk of her own room. . . Where was her dressing-gown? Where was her maid? Why should she be at such a disadvantage! She reached for the table again and found a match-box. She would strike a light, and find her dressing-gown. Then she abruptly remembered that she had no dressing-gown with her; that she had travelled with one single bag—little more than a hand-bag—and it contained only the emergency equipment of a nurse. She had brought no dressing-gown; only the light outer rain-proof coat which should serve a double purpose. She had forgotten for a moment that she was not in her own house, that she was an army-woman, living a soldier's life. She felt her way to the wall, found the rain-proof coat, and, with trembling fingers, put it on. As she did so a wave of weakness passed over her, and she swayed as though she would fall; but she put a hand on herself and fought her growing agitation.

She turned towards the bed, but stopped abruptly, because she heard footsteps in the hall outside—footsteps she knew, footsteps which for years had travelled towards her, day and night, with eagerness; the quick, urgent footsteps of a man of decision, of impulse, of determination. It was Rudyard's footsteps outside her door, Rudyard's voice speaking to some one; then Rudyard's footsteps pausing; and afterwards a dead silence. She felt his presence; she imagined his hand upon her door. With a little smothered gasp, she made a move forward as though to lock the door; then she remembered that it had no lock. With strained and startled eyes, she kept her gaze turned on the door, expecting to see it open before her. Her heart beat so hard she could hear it pounding against her breast, and her temples were throbbing.

The silence was horrible to her. Her agitation culminated. She could bear it no longer. Blindly she ran to another door which led into the sitting-room of the matron, used for many purposes—the hold-all of the odds and ends of the hospital life; where surgeons consulted, officers waited, and army authorities congregated for the business of the hospital. She found the door, opened it and entered hastily. One light was burning—a lamp with a green shade. She shut the door behind her quickly and leaned against it, closing her eyes with a sense of relief. Presently some movement in the room startled her. She opened her eyes. A figure stood between the green lamp and the farther door.

It was her husband.

Her senses had deceived her. His footsteps had not stopped before her bedroom-door. She had not heard the handle of the door of her bedroom turn, but the handle of the door of this room. The silence which had frightened her had followed his entrance here.

She hastily drew the coat about her. The white linen of her night-dress showed. She thrust it back, and instinctively drew behind the table, as though to hide her bare ankles.

He had started back at seeing her, but had instantly recovered himself. "Well, Jasmine," he said quietly, "we've met in a queer place."

All at once her hot agitation left her, and she became cold and still. She was in a maelstrom of feeling a minute before, though she could not have said what the feeling meant; now she was dominated by a haunting sense of injury, roused by resentment, not against him, but against everything and everybody, himself included. All the work of the last few months seemed suddenly undone—to go for nothing. Just as a drunkard in his pledge made reformation, which has done its work for a period, feels a sudden maddening desire to indulge his passion for drink, and plunges into a debauch,—the last maddening degradation before his final triumph,—so Jasmine felt now the restrictions and self-control of the past few months fall away from her. She emerged from it all the same woman who had flung her married life, her man, and her old world to the winds on the day that Krool had been driven into the street. Like Krool, she too had gone out into the unknown—into a strange land where "the Baas" had no habitation.

Rudyard's words seemed to madden her, and there was a look of scrutiny and inquiry in his eyes which she saw—and saw nothing else there. There was the inquisition in his look which had been there in their last interview when he had said as plainly as man could say, "What did it mean—that letter from Adrian Fellowes?"

It was all there in his eyes now—that hateful inquiry, the piercing scrutiny of a judge in the Judgment House, and there came also into her eyes, as though in consequence, a look of scrutiny too.

"Did you kill Adrian Fellowes? Was it you?" her disordered mind asked.

She had mistaken the look in his eyes. It was the same look as the look in hers, and in spite of all the months that had gone, both asked the same question as in the hour when they last parted. The dead man stood between them, as he had never stood in life—of infinitely more importance than he had ever been in life. He had never come between Rudyard and herself in the old life in any vital sense, not in any sense that finally mattered. He had only been an incident; not part of real life, but part of a general wastage of character; not a disintegrating factor in itself. Ah, no, not Adrian Fellowes, not him! It enraged her that Rudyard should think the dead man had had any sway over her. It was a needless degradation, against which she revolted now.

"Why have you come here—to this room?" she asked coldly.

As a boy flushes when he has been asked a disconcerting question which angers him or challenges his innocence, so Rudyard's face suffused; but the flush faded as quickly as it came. His eyes then looked at her steadily, the whites of them so white because of his bronzed face and forehead, the glance firmer by far than in his old days in London. There was none of that unmanageable emotion in his features, the panic excitement, the savage disorder which were there on the day when Adrian Fellowes' letter brought the crisis to their lives; none of the barbaric storm which drove Krool down the staircase under the sjambok. Here was force and iron strength, though the man seemed older, his thick hair streaked with grey, while there was a deep fissure between the eyebrows. The months had hardened him physically, had freed him from all superfluous flesh; and the flabbiness had wholly gone from his cheeks and chin. There was no sign of a luxurious life about him. He was merely the business-like soldier with work to do. His khaki fitted him as only uniform can fit a man with a physique without defect. He carried in his hand a short whip of rhinoceros-hide, and as he placed his hands upon his hips and looked at Jasmine meditatively, before he answered her question, she recalled the scene with Krool. Her eyes were fascinated by the whip in his hand. It seemed to her, all at once, as though she was to be the victim of his wrath, and that the whip would presently fall upon her shoulders, as he drove her out into the veld. But his eyes drew hers to his own presently, and even while he spoke to her now, the illusion of the sjambok remained, and she imagined his voice to be intermingling with the dull thud of the whip on her shoulders.

"I came to see one of my troop who was wounded at Wortmann's Drift," he answered her.

"Old Gunter," she said mechanically.

"Old Gunter, if you like," he returned, surprised. "How did you know?"

"The world gossips still," she rejoined bitterly.

"Well, I came to see Gunter."

"On the grey mare," she said again like one in a dream.

"On the grey mare. I did not know that you were here, and—"

"If you had known I was here, you would not have come?" she asked with a querulous ring to her voice.

"No, I should not have come if I had known, unless people in the camp were aware that I knew. Then I should have felt it necessary to come."

"Why?" She knew; but she wanted him to say.

"That the army should not talk and wonder. If you were here, it is obvious that I should visit you."

"The army might as well wonder first as last," she rejoined. "That must come."

"I don't know anything that must come in this world," he replied. "We don't control ourselves, and must lies in the inner Mystery where we cannot enter. I had only to deal with the present. I could not come to the General and go again, knowing that you were here, without seeing you. We ought to do our work here without unnecessary cross-firing from our friends. There's enough of that from our foes."

"What right had you to enter my room?" she rejoined stubbornly.

"I am not in your room. Something—call it anything you like—made us meet on this neutral ground."

"You might have waited till morning," she replied perversely.

"In the morning I shall be far from here. Before daybreak I shall be fighting. War waits for no one—not even for you," he added, with more sarcasm than he intended.

Her feelings were becoming chaos again. He was going into battle. Bygone memories wakened, and the first days of their lives together came rushing upon her; but her old wild spirit was up in arms too against the irony of his last words, "Not even for you." Added to this was the rushing remembrance that South Africa had been the medium of all her trouble. If Rudyard had not gone to South Africa, that one five months a year and more ago, when she was left alone, restless, craving for amusement and excitement and—she was going to say romance, but there was no romance in those sordid hours of pleasure-making, when she plucked the fruit as it lay to her hand—ah, if only Rudyard had not gone to South Africa then! That five months held no romance. She had never known but one romance, and it was over and done. The floods had washed it away.

"You are right. War does not wait even for me," she exclaimed. "It came to meet me, to destroy me, when I was not armed. It came in the night as you have come, and found me helpless as I am now."

Suddenly she clasped her hands and wrung them, then threw them above her head in a gesture of despair. "Why didn't God or Destiny, or whatever it is, stop you from coming here! There is nothing between us worth keeping, and there can never be. There is a black sea between us. I never want to see you any more."

In her agitation the coat had fallen away from her white night-dress, and her breast showed behind the parted folds of the linen. Involuntarily his eyes saw. What memories passed through him were too vague to record; but a heavy sigh escaped him, followed, however, by a cloud which gathered on his brow. The shadow of a man's death thrust itself between them. This war might have never been, had it not been for the treachery of the man who had been false to everything and every being that had come his way. Indirectly this vast struggle in which thousands of lives were being lost had come through his wife's disloyalty, however unintentional, or in whatever degree. Whenever he thought of it, his pulses beat faster with indignation, and a deep resentment possessed him.

It was a resentment whose origin was not a mere personal wrong to him, but the betrayal of all that invaded his honour and the honour of his country. The map was dead—so much. He had paid a price—too small.

And Jasmine, as she looked at her husband now, was, oppressed by the same shadow—the inescapable thing. That was what she meant when she said, "There is a black sea between us."

What came to her mind when she saw his glance fall on her breast, she could not have told. But a sudden flame of anger consumed her. The passion of the body was dead in her—atrophied. She was as one through whose veins had passed an icy fluid which stilled all the senses of desire, but never had her mind been so passionate, so alive. In the months lately gone, there had been times when her mind was in a paroxysm of rebellion and resentment and remorse; but in this red corner of the universe, from which the usual world was shut out, from which all domestic existence, all social organization, habit or the amenities of social intercourse were excluded, she had been able to restore her equilibrium. Yet now here, all at once, there was an invasion of this world of rigid, narrow organization, where there was no play; where all men's acts were part of a deadly mortal issue; where the human being was only part of a scheme which allowed nothing of the flexible adaptations of the life of peace, the life of cities, of houses: here was the sudden interposition of a purely personal life, of domestic being—of sex. She was conscious of no reasoning, of no mental protest which could be put into words: she was only conscious of emotions which now shook her with their power, now left her starkly cold, her brain muffled, or again aflame with a suffering as intense as that of Procrustes on his bed of iron.

This it was that seized her now. The glance of his eyes at her bared breast roused her. She knew not why, except that there was an indefinable craving for a self respect which had been violated by herself and others; except that she longed for the thing which she felt he would not give her. The look in his eye offered her nothing of that.

That she mistook what really was in his eyes was not material, though he was thinking of days when he believed he had discovered the secret of life—a woman whose life was beautiful; diffusing beauty, contentment, inspiration and peace. She did not know that his look was the wistful look backward, with no look forward; and that alone. She was living a life where new faculties of her nature were being exercised or brought into active being; she was absorbed by it all; it was part of her scheme for restoring herself, for getting surcease of anguish; but here, all at once, every entrenchment was overrun, the rigidity of the unit was made chaos, and she was tossed by the Spirit of Confusion upon a stormy sea of feeling.

"Will you not go?" she asked in a voice of suppressed passion. "Have you no consideration? It is past midnight."

His anger flamed, but he forced back the words upon his lips, and said with a bitter smile: "Day and night are the same to me always now. What else should be in war? I am going." He looked at the watch at his wrist. "It is half-past one o'clock. At five our work begins—not an eight-hour day. We have twenty-four-hour days here sometimes. This one may be shorter. You never can tell. It may be a one-hour day—or less."

Suddenly he came towards her with hands outstretched. "Dear wife—Jasmine—" he exclaimed.

Pity, memory, a great magnanimity carried him off his feet for a moment, and all that had happened seemed as nothing beside this fact that they might never see each other again; and peace appeared to him the one thing needful after all. The hatred and conflict of the world seemed of small significance beside the hovering presence of an enemy stronger than Time.

She was still in a passion of rebellion against the inevitable—that old impatience and unrealized vanity which had helped to destroy her past. She shrank back in blind misunderstanding from him, for she scarcely heard his words. She mistook what he meant. She was bewildered, distraught.

"No, no—coward!" she cried.

He stopped short as though he had been shot. His face turned white. Then, with an oath, he went swiftly to the window which opened to the floor and passed through it into the night.

An instant later he was on his horse.

A moment of dumb confusion succeeded, then she realized her madness, and the thing as it really was. Running to the window, she leaned out.

She called, but only the grey mare's galloping came back to her awe-struck ears.

With a cry like that of an animal in pain, she sank on her knees on the floor, her face turned towards the stars.

"Oh, my God, help me!" she moaned.

At least here was no longer the cry of doom.

XXXII

The World's Foundling

At last day came. Jasmine was crossing the hallway of the hospital on her way to the dining-room when there came from the doorway of a ward a figure in a nurse's dress. It startled her by some familiar motion. Presently the face turned in her direction, but without seeing her. Jasmine recognized her then. She went forward quickly and touched the nurse's arm.

"Al'mah—it is Al'mah?" she said.

Al'mah's face turned paler, and she swayed slightly, then she recovered herself. "Oh, it is you, Mrs. Byng!" she said, almost dazedly.

After an instant's hesitation she held out a hand. "It's a queer place for it to happen," she added.

Jasmine noticed the hesitation and wondered at the words. She searched the other's face. What did Al'mah's look mean? It seemed composite of paralyzing surprise, of anxiety, of apprehension. Was there not also a look of aversion?

"Everything seems to come all at once," Al'mah continued, as though in explanation.

Jasmine had no inkling as to what the meaning of the words was; and, with something of her old desire to conquer those who were alien to her, she smiled winningly.

"Yes, things concentrate in life," she rejoined.

"I've noticed that," was the reply. "Fate seems to scatter, and then to gather in all at once, as though we were all feather-toys on strings."

After a moment, as Al'mah regarded her with vague wonder, though now she smiled too, and the anxiety, apprehension, and pain went from her face, Jasmine said: "Why did you come here? You had a world to work for in England."

"I had a world to forget in England," Al'mah replied. Then she added suddenly, "I could not sing any longer."

"Your voice—what happened to it?" Jasmine asked.

"One doesn't sing with one's voice only. The music is far behind the voice."

They had been standing in the middle of the hallway. Suddenly Al'mah caught at Jasmine's sleeve. "Will you come with me?" she said.

She led the way into a room which was almost gay with veld everlastings, pictures from illustrated papers, small flags of the navy and the colonies, the Boer Vierkleur and the Union Jack.

"I like to have things cheerful here," Al'mah said almost gaily. "Sometimes I have four or five convalescents in here, and they like a little gaiety. I sing them things from comic operas—Offenbach, Sullivan, and the rest; and if they are very sentimentally inclined I sing them good old-fashioned love-songs full of the musician's tricks. How people adore illusions! I've had here an old Natal sergeant, over sixty, and he was as cracked as could be about songs belonging to the time when we don't know that it's all illusion, and that there's no such thing as Love, nor ever was; but only a kind of mirage of the mind, a sort of phantasy that seizes us, in which we do crazy things, and sometimes, if the phantasy is strong enough, we do awful things. But still the illusions remain in spite of everything, as they did with the old sergeant. I've heard the most painful stories here from men before they died, of women that were false, and injuries done, many, many years ago; and they couldn't see that it wasn't real at all, but just phantasy."

"All the world's mad," responded Jasmine wearily, as Al'mah paused.

Al'mah nodded. "So I laugh a good deal, and try to be cheerful, and it does more good than being too sympathetic. Sympathy gets to be mere snivelling very often. I've smiled and laughed a great deal out here; and they say it's useful. The surgeons say it, and the men say it too sometimes."

"Are you known as Nurse Grattan?" Jasmine asked with sudden remembrance.

"Yes, Grattan was my mother's name. I am Nurse Grattan here."

"So many have whispered good things of you. A Scottish Rifleman said to me a week ago, 'Ech, she's aye see cheery!' What a wonderful thing it is to make a whole army laugh. Coming up here three officers spoke of you, and told of humorous things you had said. It's all quite honest, too. It's a reputation made out of new cloth. No one knows who you are?"

Al'mah flushed. "I don't know quite who I am myself. I think sometimes I'm the world's foundling."

Suddenly a cloud passed over her face again, and her strong whimsical features became drawn.

"I seem almost to lose my identity at times; and then it is I try most to laugh and be cheerful. If I didn't perhaps I should lose my identity altogether. Do you ever feel that?"

"No; I often wish I could."

Al'mah regarded her steadfastly. "Why did you come here?" she asked. "You had the world at your feet; and there was plenty to do in London. Was it for the same reason that brought me here? Was it something you wanted to forget there, some one you wanted to help here?"

Jasmine saw the hovering passion in the eyes fixed on her, and wondered what this woman had to say which could be of any import to herself; yet she felt there was something drawing nearer which would make her shrink.

"No," Jasmine answered, "I did not come to forget, but to try and remember that one belongs to the world, to the work of the world, to the whole people, and not to one of the people; not to one man, or to one family, or to one's self. That's all."

Al'mah's face was now very haggard, but her eyes were burning. "I do not believe you," she said straightly. "You are one of those that have had a phantasy. I had one first fifteen years ago, and it passed, yet it pursued me till yesterday—till yesterday evening. Now it's gone; that phantasy is gone forever. Come and see what it was."

She pointed to the door of another room.

There was something strangely compelling in her tone, in her movements. Jasmine followed her, fascinated by the situation, by the look in the woman's face. The door opened upon darkness, but Jasmine stepped inside, with Almah's fingers clutching her sleeve. For a moment nothing was visible; then, Jasmine saw, dimly, a coffin on two chairs.

"That was the first man I ever loved—my husband," Al'mah said quietly, pointing at the coffin. "There was another, but you took him from me—you and others."

Jasmine gave a little cry which she smothered with her hand; and she drew back involuntarily towards the light of the hallway. The smell of disinfectants almost suffocated her. A cloud of mystery and indefinable horror seemed to envelop her; then a light flooded through her brain. It was like a stream of fire. But with a voice strangely calm, she said, "You mean Adrian Fellowes?"

Al'mah's face was in the shadow, but her voice was full of storm. "You took him from me, but you were only one," she said sharply and painfully. "I found it out at last. I suspected first at Glencader. Then at last I knew. It was an angry, contemptuous letter from you. I had opened it. I understood. When everything was clear, when there was no doubt, when I knew he had tried to hurt little Jigger's sister, when he had made up his mind to go abroad, then, I killed him. Then—I killed him."

Jasmine's cheek was white as Al'mah's apron; but she did not shrink. She came a step nearer, and peered into Al'mah's face, as though to read her inmost mind, as though to see if what she said was really true. She saw not a quiver of agitation, not the faintest horror of memory; only the reflective look of accomplished purpose.

"You—are you insane?" Jasmine exclaimed in a whisper. "Do you know what you have said?"

Al'mah smoothed her apron softly. "Perfectly. I do not think I am insane. I seem not to be. One cannot do insane things here. This is the place of the iron rule. Here we cure madness—the madness of war and other madnesses."

"You had loved him, yet you killed him!"

"You would have killed him though you did not love him. Yes, of course—I know that. Your love was better placed; but it was like a little bird caught by the hawk in the upper air—its flight was only a little one before the hawk found it. Yes, you would have killed Adrian, as I did if you had had the courage. You wanted to do it, but I did it. Do you remember when I sang for you on the evening of that day he died? I sang, 'More Was Lost at Mohacksfield.' As soon as I saw your face that evening I felt you knew all. You had been to his rooms and found him dead. I was sure of that. You remember how La Tosca killed Scarpia? You remember how she felt? I felt so—just like that. I never hesitated. I knew what I wanted to do, and I did it."

"How did you kill him?" Jasmine asked in that matter-of-fact way which comes at those times when the senses are numbed by tragedy.

"You remember the needle—Mr. Mappin's needle? I knew Adrian had it. He showed it to me. He could not keep the secret. He was too weak. The needle was in his pocket-book—to kill me with some day perhaps. He certainly had not the courage to kill himself. . . I went to see him. He was dressing. The pocket-book lay on the table. As I said, he had showed it to me. While he was busy I abstracted the needle. He talked of his journey abroad. He lied—nothing but lies, about himself, about everything. When he had said enough,—lying was easier to him than anything else—I told him the truth. Then he went wild. He caught hold of me as if to strangle me. . . He did not realize the needlepoint when it caught him. If he did, it must have seemed to him only the prick of a pin. . . But in a few minutes it was all over. He died quite peacefully. But it was not very easy getting him on the sofa. He looked sleeping as he lay there. You saw. He would never lie any more to women, to you or to me or any other. It is a good thing to stop a plague, and the simplest way is the best. He was handsome, and his music was very deceiving. It was almost good of its kind, and it was part of him. When I look back I find only misery. Two wicked men hurt me. They spoiled my life, first one and then another; and I went from bad to worse. At least he"— she pointed to the other room—"he had some courage at the very last. He fought, he braved death. The other—you remember the Glencader Mine. Your husband and Ian Stafford went down, and Lord Tynemouth was ready to go, but Adrian would not go. Then it was I began to hate him. That was the beginning. What happened had to be. I was to kill him; and I did. It avenged me, and it avenged your husband. I was glad of that, for Rudyard Byng had done so much for me: not alone that he saved me at the opera, you remember, but other good things. I did his work for him with Adrian."

"Have you no fear—of me?" Jasmine asked.

"Fear of—you? Why?"

"I might hate you—I might tell."

Al'mah made a swift gesture of protest. "Do not say foolish things. You would rather die than tell. You should be grateful to me. Some one had to kill him. There was Rudyard Byng, Ian Stafford, or yourself. It fell to me. I did your work. You will not tell; but it would not matter if you did. Nothing would happen—nothing at all. Think it out, and you will see why."

Jasmine shuddered violently. Her body was as cold as ice.

"Yes, I know. What are you going to do after the war?"

"Back to Covent Garden perhaps; or perhaps there will be no 'after the war.' It may all end here. Who knows—who cares!"

Jasmine came close to her. For an instant a flood of revulsion had overpowered her; but now it was all gone.

"We pay for all the wrong we do. We pay for all the good we get"— once Ian Stafford had said that, and it rang in her ears now. Al'mah would pay, and would pay here—here in this world. Meanwhile, Al'mah was a woman who, like herself, had suffered.

"Let me be your friend; let me help you," Jasmine said, and she took both of Almah's hands in her own.

Somehow Jasmine's own heart had grown larger, fuller, and kinder all at once. Until lately she had never ached to help the world or any human being in all her life; there had never been any of the divine pity which finds its employ in sacrifice. She had been kind, she had been generous, she had in the past few months given service unstinted; but it was more as her own cure for her own ills than yearning compassion for all those who were distressed "in mind, body, or estate."

But since last evening, in the glimmer of the stars, when Rudyard went from her with bitter anger on his lips, and a contempt which threw her far behind him,—since that hour, when, in her helplessness, she had sunk to the ground with an appeal to Something outside herself, her heart had greatly softened. Once before she had appealed to the Invisible—that night before her catastrophe, when she wound her wonderful hair round her throat and drew it tighter and tighter, and had cried out to the beloved mother she had never known. But her inborn, her cultivated, her almost invincible egoism, had not even then been scattered by the bitter helplessness of her life.

That cry last night was a cry to the Something behind all. Only in the last few hours—why, she knew not—her heart had found a new sense. She felt her soul's eyes looking beyond herself. The Something that made her raise her eyes to the stars, which seemed a pervading power, a brooding tenderness and solicitude, had drawn her mind away into the mind of humanity. Her own misery now at last enabled her to see, however dimly, the woes of others; and it did not matter whether the woes were penalties or undeserved chastisement; the new-born pity of her soul made no choice and sought no difference.

As the singing-woman's hands lay in hers, a flush slowly spread over Al'mah's face, and behind the direct power of her eyes there came a light which made them aglow with understanding.

"I always thought you selfish—almost meanly selfish," Al'mah said presently. "I thought you didn't know any real life, any real suffering—only the surface, only disappointment at not having your own happiness; but now I see that was all a mask. You understand why I did what I did?"

"I understand."

"I suppose there would be thousands who would gladly see me in prison and on the scaffold—if they knew—"

Pain travelled across Jasmine's face. She looked Al'mah in the eyes with a look of reproof and command. "Never, never again speak of that to me or to any living soul," she said. "I will try to forget it; you must put it behind you." . . . Suddenly she pointed to the other room where Al'mah's husband lay dead. "When is he to be buried?" she asked.

"In an hour." A change came over Al'mah's face again, and she stood looking dazedly at the door of the room, behind which the dead man lay. "I cannot realize it. It does not seem real," she said. "It was all so many centuries ago, when I was young and glad."

Jasmine admonished her gently and drew her away.

A few moments later an officer approached them from one of the wards. At that moment the footsteps of the three were arrested by the booming of artillery. It seemed as though all the guns of both armies were at work.

The officer's eyes blazed, and he turned to the two women with an impassioned gesture.

"Byng and the S.A.'s have done their trick," he said. "If they hadn't, that wouldn't be going on. It was to follow—a general assault—if Byng pulled it off. Old Blunderbuss has done it this time. His combination's working all right—thanks to Byng's lot."

As he hurried on he was too excited to see Jasmine's agitation.

"Wait!" Jasmine exclaimed, as he went quickly down the hallway. But her voice was scarcely above a whisper, and he did not hear.

She wanted to ask him if Rudyard was safe. She did not realize that he could not know.

But the thunder of artillery told her that Rudyard had had his fighting at daybreak, as he had said.

XXXIII

"Alamachtig!"

When Rudyard flung himself on the grey mare outside Jasmine's window at the Stay Awhile Hospital, and touched her flank with his heel, his heart was heavy with passion, his face hard with humiliation and defeat. He had held out the hand of reconciliation, and she had met it with scorn. He had smothered his resentment, and let the light of peace in upon their troubles, and she had ruthlessly drawn a black curtain between them. He was going upon as dangerous a task as could be set a soldier, from which he might never return, and she had not even said a God-be-with-you—she who had lain in his bosom, been so near, so dear, so cherished:

> *"For Time and Change estrange, estrange—*
> *And, now they have looked and seen us,*
> *Oh, we that were dear, we are all too near,*
> *With the thick of the world between us!"*

How odd it seemed that two beings who had been all in all to each other, who in the prime of their love would have died of protesting shame, if they had been told that they would change towards each other, should come to a day when they would be less to each other than strangers, less and colder and farther off! It is because some cannot bear this desecration of ideals, this intolerable loss of life's assets, that they cling on and on, long after respect and love have gone, after hope is dead.

There had been times in the past few months when such thoughts as these vaguely possessed Rudyard's mind; but he could never, would never, feel that all was over, that the book of Jasmine's life was closed to him; not even when his whole nature was up in arms against the injury she had done him.

But now, as the grey mare reached out to achieve the ground his troopers had covered before him, his brain was in a storm of feeling. After all, what harm had he done her, that he should be treated so? Was he the sinner? Why should he make the eternal concession? Why should he be made to seem the one needing forgiveness? He did not know why. But at the bottom of everything lay a something—a yearning—which would not be overwhelmed. In spite of wrong and injury, it would live on and on; and neither Time nor crime, nor anything mortal could obliterate it from his heart's oracles.

The hoofs of the grey mare fell like the soft thud of a hammer in the sand, regular and precise. Presently the sound and the motion lulled his senses. The rage and humiliation grew less, his face cooled. His head, which had been bent, lifted and his face turned upwards to the stars. The influence of an African night was on him. None that has not felt it can understand it so cold, so sweet, so full of sleep, so stirring with an underlife. Many have known the breath of the pampas beyond the Amazon; the soft pungency of the wattle blown across the salt-bush plains of Australia; the friendly exhilaration of the prairie or the chaparral; the living, loving loneliness of the desert; but yonder on the veld is a life of the night which possesses all the others have, and something of its own besides; something which gets into the bones and makes for forgetfulness of the world. It lifts a man away from the fret of life, and sets his feet on the heights where lies repose.

The peace of the stars crept softly into Rudyard's heart as he galloped gently on to overtake his men. His pulses beat slowly once again, his mind regained its poise. He regretted the oath he uttered, as he left Jasmine; he asked himself if, after all, everything was over and done.

How good the night suddenly seemed! No, it was not all over—unless, unless, indeed, in this fight coming on with the daybreak, Fate should settle it all by doing with him as it had done with so many thousands of others in this war. But even then, would it be all over? He was a primitive man, and he raised his face once more to the heavens. He was no longer the ample millionaire, sitting among the flesh-pots; he was a lean, simple soldier eating his biscuit as though it were the product of the chef of the Cafe Voisin; he was the fighter sleeping in a blanket in the open; he was a patriot after his kind; he was the friend of his race and the lover of one woman.

Now he drew rein. His regiment was just ahead. Daybreak was not far off, and they were near the enemy's position. In a little while, if they were not surprised, they would complete a movement, take a hill, turn the flank of the foe, and, if designed supports came up, have the Boers at a deadly disadvantage. Not far off to the left of him and his mounted infantry there were coming on for this purpose two batteries of artillery and three thousand infantry—Leary's brigade, which had not been in the action the day before at Wortmann's Drift.

But all depended on what he was able to do, what he and his hard-bitten South Africans could accomplish. Well, he had no doubt. War was part chance, part common sense, part the pluck and luck of the devil. He had ever been a gambler in the way of taking chances; he had always possessed ballast even when the London life had enervated, had depressed him; and to men of his stamp pluck is a commonplace: it belongs as eyes and hands and feet belong.

Dawn was not far away, and before daybreak he must have the hill which was the key to the whole position, which commanded the left flank of the foe. An hour or so after he got it, if the artillery and infantry did their portion, a great day's work would be done for England; and the way to the relief of the garrison beyond the mountains would be open. The chance to do this thing was the reward he received for his gallant and very useful fight at Wortmann's Drift twenty-four hours before. It would not do to fail in justifying the choice of the Master Player, who had had enough bad luck in the campaign so far.

The first of his force to salute him in the darkness was his next in command, Barry Whalen. They had been together in the old Rand Rifles, and had, in the words of the Kaffir, been as near as the flea to the blanket, since the day when Rudyard discovered that Barry Whalen was on the same ship bound for the seat of war. They were not youngsters, either of them; but they had the spring of youth in them, and a deep basis of strength and force; and they knew the veld and the veld people. There was no trick of the veldschoen copper for which they were not ready; and for any device of Kruger's lambs they were prepared to go one better. As Barry Whalen had said, "They'll have to get up early in the morning if they want to catch us."

This morning the Boers would not get up early enough; for Rudyard's command had already reached the position from which they could do their work with good chances in their favour; and there had been no sign of life from the Boer trenches in the dusk—naught of what chanced at Magersfontein. Not a shot had been fired, and there would certainly have been firing if the Boer had known; for he could not allow the Rooinek to get to the point where his own position would be threatened or commanded. When Kruger's men did discover the truth, there would be fighting as stiff as had been seen in this struggle for half a continent.

"Is it all right?" whispered Rudyard, as Barry Whalen drew up by him.

"Not a sound from them—not a sign."

"Their trenches should not be more than a few hundred yards on, eh?"

"Their nearest trenches are about that. We are just on the left of Hetmeyer's Kopje."

"Good. Let Glossop occupy the kopje with his squadrons, while we take the trenches. If we can force them back on their second line of trenches, and keep them there till our supports come up, we shall be all right."

"When shall we begin, sir?" asked Barry.

"Give orders to dismount now. Get the horses in the lee of the kopje, and we'll see what Brother Boer thinks of us after breakfast."

Rudyard took out a repeating-watch, and held it in his closed palm. As it struck, he noted the time.

His words were abrupt but composed. "Ten minutes more and we shall have the first streak of dawn. Then move. We shall be on them before they know it."

Barry Whalen made to leave, then turned back. Rudyard understood. They clasped hands. It was the grip of men who knew each other—knew each other's faults and weaknesses, yet trusted with a trust which neither disaster nor death could destroy.

"My girl—if anything happens to me," Barry said.

"You may be sure—as if she were my own," was Rudyard's reply. "If I go down, find my wife at the Stay Awhile Hospital. Tell her that the day I married her was the happiest day of my life, and that what I said then I thought at the last. Everything else is straightened out—and I'll not forget your girl, Barry. She shall be as my own if things should happen that way."

"God bless you, old man," whispered Barry. "Goodbye." Then he recovered himself and saluted. "Is that all, sir?"

"Au revoir, Barry," came the answer; then a formal return of the salute. "That is all," he added brusquely.

They moved forward to the regiment, and the word to dismount was given softly. When the forces crept forward again, it was as infantrymen, moving five paces apart, and feeling their way up to the Boer trenches.

Dawn. The faintest light on the horizon, as it were a soft, grey glimmer showing through a dark curtain. It rises and spreads slowly, till the curtain of night becomes the veil of morning, white and kind.

Then the living world begins to move. Presently the face of the sun shines through the veil, and men's bodies grow warm with active being, and the world stirs with busy life. On the veld, with the first delicate glow, the head of a meerkat, or a springbok, is raised above the gray-brown grass; herds of cattle move uneasily. Then a bird takes flight across the whitening air, another, and then another; the meerkat sits up and begs breakfast of the sun; lizards creep out upon the stones; a snake slides along obscenely foraging. Presently man and beast and all wild things are afoot or a-wing, as though the world was new-created; as though there had never been any mornings before, and this was not the monotonous repetition of a million mornings, when all things living begin the world afresh.

But nowhere seems the world so young and fresh and glad as on the sun-warmed veld. Nowhere do the wild roses seem so pure, or are the aloes so jaunty and so gay. The smell of the karoo bush is sweeter than attar, and the bog-myrtle and mimosa, where they shelter a house or fringe a river, have a look of Arcady. It is a world where any mysterious thing may happen—a world of five thousand years ago—the air so light, so sweetly searching and vibrating, that Ariel would seem of the picture, and gleaming hosts of mailed men, or vast colonies of green-clad archers moving to virgin woods might belong. Something frightens the timid spirit of a springbok, and his flight through the grass is like a phrase of music on a wilful adventure; a bird hears the sighing of the breeze in the mimosa leaves or the swaying shrubs, and in disdain of such slight performance flings out a song which makes the air drunken with sweetness.

A world of light, of commendable trees, of grey grass flecked with flowers, of life having the supreme sense of a freedom which has known no check. It is a life which cities have not spoiled, and where man is still in touch with the primeval friends of man; where the wildest beast and the newest babe of a woman have something in common.

Drink your fill of the sweet intoxicating air with eyes shut till the lungs are full and the heart beats with new fulness; then open them upon the wide sunrise and scan the veld so full of gracious odour. Is it not good and glad? And now face the hills rising nobly away there to the left, the memorable and friendly hills. Is it not—

Upon the morning has crept suddenly a black cloud, although the sun is shining brilliantly. A moment before the dawn all was at peace on the veld and among the kopjes, and only the contented sighing of men and beasts broke the silence, or so it seemed; but with the glimmer of light along the horizon came a change so violent that all the circle of vision was in a quiver of trouble. Affrighted birds, in fluttering bewilderment, swept and circled aimlessly through the air with strange, half-human cries; the jackal and the meerkat, the springbok and the rheebok, trembled where they stood, with heads uplifted, vaguely trying to realize the Thing which was breaking the peace of their world; useless horses which had been turned out of the armies of Boers and British galloped and stumbled and plunged into space in alarm; for they knew what was darkening the morning. They had suffered the madness of battle, and they realized it at its native first value.

There was a battle forward on the left flank of the Boer Army. Behind Hetmeyer's Kopje were the horses of the men whom Rudyard Byng had brought to take a position and hold it till support came and this flank of the Farmer's Army was turned; but the men themselves were at work on the kopjes—the grim work of dislodging the voortrekker people from the places where they burrowed like conies among the rocks.

Just before dawn broke Byng's men were rushing the outer trenches. These they cleared with the wild cries of warriors whose blood was in a tempest. Bayonets dripped red, rifles were fired at hand-to-hand range, men clubbed their guns and fought as men fought in the days when the only fighting was man to man, or one man to many men. Here every "Boojer" and Rooinek was a champion. The Boer fell back because he was forced back by men who were men of the veld like himself; and the Briton pressed forward because he would not be denied; because he was sick of reverses; of going forward and falling back; of taking a position with staggering loss and then abandoning it; of gaining a victory and then not following it up; of having the foe in the hollow of the hand and hesitating to close it with a death-grip; of promising relief to besieged men, and marking time when you had gained a foothold, instead of gaining a foothold farther on.

Byng's men were mostly South-Africans born, who had lived and worked below the Zambesi all their lives; or else those whose blood was in a fever at the thought that a colony over which the British flag flew should be trod by the feet of an invader, who had had his own liberty and independence secured by that flag, but who refused to white men the status given to "niggers" in civilized states. These fighters under Byng had had their fill of tactics and strategy which led nowhere forward;

and at Wortmann's Drift the day before they had done a big thing for the army with a handful of men. They could ride like Cossacks, they could shoot like William Tell, and they had a mind to be the swivel by which the army of Queen Victoria should swing from almost perpetual disaster, in large and small degree, to victory.

From the first trenches on and on to the second trenches higher up! But here the Boer in his burrow with his mauser rifle roaring, and his heart fierce with hatred and anger at the surprise, laid down to the bloody work with an ugly determination to punish remorselessly his fellow-citizens of the veld and the others. It was a fire which only bullet-proof men could stand, and these were but breasts of flesh and muscle, though the will was iron.

Up, up, and up, struggled these men of the indomitable will. Step by step, while man after man fell wounded or dead, they pushed forward, taking what cover was possible; firing as steadily as at Aldershot; never wasting shots, keeping the eye vigilant for the black slouch hat above the rocks, which told that a Boer's head was beneath it, and might be caught by a lightning shot.

Step by step, man by man, troop by troop, they came nearer to the hedges of stone behind which an inveterate foe with grim joy saw a soldier fall to his soft-nosed bullet; while far down behind these men of a forlorn hope there was hurrying up artillery which would presently throw its lyddite and its shrapnel on the top of the hill up where hundreds of Boers held, as they thought, an impregnable position. At last with rushes which cost them almost as dearly in proportion as the rush at Balaclava cost the Light Brigade, Byng's men reached the top, mad with the passion of battle, vengeful in spirit because of the comrades they had lost; and the trenches emptied before them. As they were forsaken, men fought hand to hand and as savagely as ever men fought in the days of Rustum.

In one corner, the hottest that the day saw, Rudyard and Barry Whalen and a scattered handful of men threw themselves upon a greatly larger number of the enemy. For a moment a man here and there fought for his life against two or three of the foe. Of these were Rudyard and Barry Whalen. The khaki of the former was shot through in several places, he had been slashed in the cheek by a bullet, and a bullet had also passed through the muscle of his left forearm; but he was scarcely conscious of it. It seemed as though Fate would let no harm befall him; but, in the very moment, when on another part of the ridge his men were waving their hats in victory, three Boers sprang up before him, ragged and grim and old, but with the fire of fanaticism and race-hatred in their eyes. One of them he accounted for, another he wounded, but the wounded voortrekker—a giant of near seven feet clubbed his rifle, and drove at him. Rudyard shot at close quarters again, but his pistol missed fire.

Just as the rifle of his giant foe swung above him, Byng realized that the third Boer was levelling a rifle directly at his breast. His eyes involuntarily closed as though to draw the curtain of life itself, but, as he did so, he heard a cry—the wild, hoarse cry of a voice he knew so well.

"Baas! Baas!" it called.

Then two shots came simultaneously, and the clubbed rifle brought him to the ground.

"Baas! Baas!"

The voice followed him, as he passed into unconsciousness.

Barry Whalen had seen Rudyard's danger, but had been unable to do anything. His hands were more than full, his life in danger; but in the instant that he had secured his own safety, he heard the cry of "Baas! Baas!" Then he saw the levelled rifle fall from the hands of the Boer who had aimed at Byng, and its owner collapse in a heap. As Rudyard fell beneath the clubbed rifle he heard the cry, "Baas! Baas!" again, and saw an unkempt figure darting among the rocks. His own pistol brought down the old Boer who had felled Byng, and then he realized who it was had cried out, "Baas!"

The last time he had heard that voice was in Park Lane, when Byng, with sjambok, drove a half-caste valet into the street.

It was the voice of Krool. And Krool was now bending over Rudyard's body, raising his head and still murmuring, "Baas—Baas!"

Krool's rifle had saved Rudyard from death by killing one of his own fellow-fighters. Much as Barry Whalen loathed the man, this act showed that Krool's love for the master who had sjamboked him was stronger than death.

Barry, himself bleeding from slight wounds, stooped over his unconscious friend with a great anxiety.

"No, it is nothing," Krool said, with his hand on Rudyard's breast. "The left arm, it is hurt, the head not get all the blow. Alamachtig, it is good! The Baas—it is right with the Baas."

Barry Whalen sighed with relief. He set about to restore Rudyard, as Krool prepared a bandage for the broken head.

Down in the valley the artillery was at work. Lyddite and shrapnel and machine-guns were playing upon the top of the ridge above them, and the infantry—Humphrey's and Blagdon's men—were hurrying up the slope which Byng's pioneers had cleared, and now held. From this position the enemy could be driven from their main position on the summit, because they could be swept now by artillery fire from a point as high as their own.

"A good day's work, old man," said Barry Whalen to the still unconscious figure. "You've done the trick for the Lady at Windsor this time. It's a great sight better business than playing baccarat at DeLancy Scovel's."

Cheering came from everywhere, cries of victory filled the air. As he looked down the valley Barry could see the horses they had left behind being brought, under cover of the artillery and infantry fire, to the hill they had taken. The grey mare would be among them. But Rudyard would not want the grey mare yet awhile. An ambulance-cart was the thing for him.

Barry would have given much for a flask of brandy. A tablespoonful would bring Rudyard back. A surgeon was not needed, however. Krool's hands had knowledge. Barry remembered the day when Wallstein was taken ill in Rudyard's house, and how Krool acted with the skill of a Westminster sawbones.

Suddenly a bugle-call sounded, loud and clear and very near them. Byng had heard that bugle call again and again in this engagement, and once he had seen the trumpeter above the trenches, sounding the advance before more than a half-dozen men had reached the defences of the Boers. The same trumpeter was now running towards them. He had been known in London as Jigger. In South Africa he was familiarly called Little Jingo.

His face was white as he leaned over Barry Whalen to look at Rudyard, but suddenly the blood came back to his cheek.

"He wants brandy," Jigger said.

"Well, go and get it," said Barry sharply.

"I've got it here," was the reply; and he produced a flask.

"Well, I'm damned!" said Barry. "You'll have a gun next, and fire it too!"

"A 4.7," returned Jigger impudently.

As the flask was at Rudyard's lips, Barry Whalen said to Krool, "What do you stay here as—deserter or prisoner? It's got to be one or the other."

"Prisoner," answered Krool. Then he added, "See—the Baas."

Rudyard's eyes were open.

"Prisoner—who is a prisoner?" he asked feebly.

"Me, Baas," whispered Krool, leaning over him.

"He saved your life, Colonel," interposed Barry Whalen.

"I thought it was the brandy," said Jigger with a grin.

XXXIV

"The Alpine Fellow"

To all who fought in the war a change of some sort had come. Those who emerged from it to return to England or her far Dominions, or to stay in the land of the veld, of the kranz and the kloof and the spruit, were never the same again. Something came which, to a degree, transformed them, as the salts of the water and the air permeate the skin and give the blood new life. None escaped the salt of the air of conflict.

The smooth-faced young subaltern who but now had all his life before him, realized the change when he was swept by the leaden spray of death on Spion Kop, and received in his face of summer warmth, or in his young exultant heart, the quietus to all his hopes, impulses and desires. The young find no solace or recompense in the philosophy of those who regard life as a thing greatly over-estimated.

Many a private grown hard of flesh and tense of muscle, with his scant rations and meagre covering in the cold nights, with his long marches and fruitless risks and futile fightings, when he is shot down, has little consolation, save in the fact that the thing he and his comrades and the regiment and the army set out to do is done. If he has to do so, he gives his life with a stony sense of loss which has none of the composure of those who have solace in thinking that what they leave behind has a constantly decreasing value. And here and there some simple soul, more gifted than his comrades, may touch off the meaning of it all, as it appears to those who hold their lives in their hands for a nation's sake, by a stroke of mordant comment.

So it was with that chess-playing private from New Zealand of whom Barry Whalen told Ian Stafford. He told it a few days after Rudyard Byng had won that fight at Hetmeyer's Kopje, which had enabled the Master Player to turn the flank of the Boers, though there was yet grim frontal work to do against machines of Death, carefully hidden and masked on the long hillsides, which would take staggering toll of Britain's manhood.

"From behind Otago there in New Zealand, he came," began Barry, "as fine a fella of thirty-three as ever you saw. Just come, because he heard old Britain callin'. Down he drops the stock-whip, away he shoves the plough, up he takes his little balance from the bank, sticks his chess-box in his pocket, says 'so-long' to his girl, and treks across the world, just to do his whack for the land that gave him and all his that went before him the key to civilization, and how to be happy though alive. . . He was the real thing, the ne plus ultra, the I-stand-alone. The other fellas thought him the best of the best. He was what my father used to call 'a wide man.' He was in and out of a fight with a quirk at the corner of his mouth, as much as to say, 'I've got the hang of this, and it's different from what I thought; but that doesn't mean it hasn't got to be done, and done in style. It's the has-to-be.' And when they got him where he breathes, he fished out the little ivory pawn and put it on a stone at his head, to let it tell his fellow-countrymen how he looked at it—that he was just a pawn in the great game. The game had to be played, and won, and the winner had to sacrifice his pawns. He was one of the sacrifices. Well, I'd like a tombstone the same as that fella from New Zealand, if I could win it as fair, and see as far."

Stafford raised his head with a smile of admiration. "Like the ancients, like the Oriental Emperors to-day, he left his message. An Alexander, with not one world conquered."

"I'm none so sure of that," was Barry's response. "A man that could put such a hand on himself as he did has conquered a world. He didn't want to go, but he went as so many have gone hereabouts. He wanted to stay, but he went against his will, and—and I wish that the grub-hunters, and tuft-hunters, and the blind greedy majority in England could get hold of what he got hold of. Then life 'd be a different thing in Thamesfontein and the little green islands."

"You were meant for a Savonarola or a St. Francis, my bold grenadier," said Stafford with a friendly nod.

"I was meant for anything that comes my way, and to do everything that was hard enough."

Stafford waved a hand. "Isn't this hard enough—a handful of guns and fifteen hundred men lost in a day, and nothing done that you can put in an envelope and send 'to the old folks at 'ome?'"

"Well, that's all over, Colonel. Byng has turned the tide by turning the Boer flank. I'm glad he's got that much out of his big shindy. It'll do him more good than his millions. He was oozing away like a fat old pine-tree in London town. He's got all his balsam in his bones now. I bet he'll get more out of this thing than anybody, more that's worth having. He doesn't want honours or promotion; he wants what'd make his wife sorry to be a widow; and he's getting it."

"Let us hope that his wife won't be put to the test," responded Stafford evenly.

Barry looked at him a little obliquely. "She came pretty near it when we took Hetmeyer's Kopje."

"Is he all right again?" Stafford asked; then added quickly, "I've had so much to do since the Hetmeyer business that I have not seen Byng."

Barry spoke very carefully and slowly. "He's over at Brinkwort's Farm for a while. He didn't want to go to the hospital, and the house at the Farm is good enough for anybody. Anyhow, you get away from the smell of disinfectants and the business of the hospital. It's a snigger little place is Brinkwort's Farm. There's an orchard of peaches and oranges, and there are pomegranate hedges, and plenty of nice flowers in the garden, and a stoep made for candidates for Stellenbosch—as comfortable as the room of a Rand director."

"Mrs. Byng is with him?" asked Stafford, his eyes turned towards Brinkwort's Farm miles away. He could see the trees, the kameel-thorn, the blue-gums, the orange and peach trees surrounding it, a clump or cloud of green in the veld.

"No, Mrs. Byng's not with him," was the reply.

Stafford stirred uneasily, a frown gathered, his eyes took on a look of sombre melancholy. "Ah," he said at length, "she has returned to Durban, then?"

"No. She got a chill the night of the Hetmeyer coup, and she's in bed at the hospital."

Stafford controlled himself. "Is it a bad chill?" he asked heavily. "Is she dangerously ill?" His voice seemed to thicken.

"She was; but she's not so bad that a little attention from a friend would make her worse. She never much liked me; but I went just the same, and took her some veld-roses."

"You saw her?" Stafford's voice was very low.

"Yes, for a minute. She's as thin as she once wasn't," Barry answered, "but twice as beautiful. Her eyes are as big as stars, and she can smile still, but it's a new one—a war-smile, I expect. Everything gets a turn of its own at the Front."

"She was upset and anxious about Byng, I suppose?" Stafford asked, with his head turned away from this faithfulest of friends, who would have died for the man now sitting on the stoep of Brinkwort's house, looking into the bloom of the garden.

"Naturally," was the reply. Barry Whalen thought carefully of what he should say, because the instinct of the friend who loved his friend had told him that, since the night at De Lancy Scovel's house when the name of Mennaval had been linked so hatefully with that of Byng's wife, there had been a cloud over Rudyard's life; and that Rudyard and Jasmine were not the same as of yore.

"Naturally she was upset," he repeated. "She made Al'mah go and nurse Byng."

"Al'mah," repeated Stafford mechanically. "Al'mah!" His mind rushed back to that night at the opera, when Rudyard had sprung from the box to the stage and had rescued Al'mah from the flames. The world had widened since then.

Al'mah and Jasmine had been under the same roof but now; and Al'mah was nursing Jasmine's husband—surely life was merely farce and tragedy.

At this moment an orderly delivered a message to Barry Whalen. He rose to go, but turned back to Stafford again.

"She'd be glad to see you, I'm certain," he said. "You never can tell what a turn sickness will take in camp, and she's looking pretty frail. We all ought to stand by Byng and whatever belongs to Byng. No need to say that to you; but you've got a lot of work and responsibility, and in the rush you mightn't realize that she's more ill than the chill makes her. I hope you won't mind my saying so in my stupid way."

Stafford rose and grasped his hand, and a light of wonderful friendliness and comradeship shone in his eyes.

"Beau chevalier! Beau chevalier!" was all he said, and impulsive Barry Whalen went away blinking; for hard as iron as he was physically, and a fighter of courage, his temperament got into his eyes or at his lips very easily.

Stafford looked after him admiringly. "Lucky the man who has such a friend," he said aloud—"Sans peur et sans reproche! He could not betray a "—the waving of wings above him caught his eye—"he could not betray an aasvogel." His look followed the bird of prey, the servitor of carrion death, as it flew down the wind.

He had absorbed the salt of tears and valour. He had been enveloped in the Will that makes all wills as one, the will of a common purpose;

and it had changed his attitude towards his troubles, towards his past, towards his future.

What Barry had said to him, and especially the tale of the New Zealander, had revealed the change which had taken place. The War had purged his mind, cleared his vision. When he left England he was immersed in egoism, submerged by his own miseries. He had isolated himself in a lazaretto of self-reproach and resentment. The universe was tottering because a woman had played him false. Because of this obsession of self, he was eager to be done with it all, to pay a price which he might have paid, had it been possible to meet Rudyard pistol or sword in hand, and die as many such a man has done, without trying to save his own life or to take the life of another. That he could not do. Rudyard did not know the truth, had not the faintest knowledge that Jasmine had been more to himself than an old and dear friend. To pay the price in any other way than by eliminating himself from the equation was to smirch her name, be the ruin of a home, and destroy all hope for the future.

It had seemed to him that there was no other way than to disappear honourably through one of the hundred gates which the war would open to him—to go where Death ambushed the reckless or the brave, and take the stroke meant for him, on a field of honour all too kind to himself and soothing to those good friends who would mourn his going, those who hoped for him the now unattainable things.

In a spirit of stoic despair he had come to the seat of war. He had invited Destiny to sweep him up in her reaping, by placing himself in the ambit of her scythe; but the sharp reaping-hook had passed him by.

The innumerable exits were there in the wall of life and none had opened to him; but since the evening when he saw Jasmine at the railway station, there had been an opening of doors in his soul hitherto hidden. Beyond these doors he saw glimpses of a new world—not like the one he had lived in, not so green, so various, or tumultuous, but it had the lure of that peace, not sterile or somnolent, which summons the burdened life, or the soul with a vocation, to the hood of a monk—a busy self-forgetfulness.

Looking after Barry Whalen's retreating figure he saw this new, grave world opening out before him; and as the vision floated before his eyes, Barry's appeal that he should visit Jasmine at the hospital came to him.

Jasmine suffered. He recalled Barry's words: "She's as thin as she once wasn't, but twice as beautiful. Her eyes are as big as stars, and she can smile still, but it's a new one—a war-smile, I expect. Everything gets a turn of its own at the Front."

Jasmine suffered in body. He knew that she suffered in mind also. To go to her? Was that his duty? Was it his desire? Did his heart cry out for it either in pity—or in love?

In love? Slowly a warm flood of feeling passed through him. It was dimly borne in on him, as he gazed at the hospital in the distance, that this thing called Love, which seizes upon our innermost selves, which takes up residence in the inner sanctuary, may not be dislodged. It stays on when the darkness comes, reigning in the gloom. Even betrayal, injury, tyranny, do not drive it forth. It continues. No longer is the curtain drawn aside for tribute, for appeal, or for adoration, but It remains until the last footfall dies in the temple, and the portals ate closed forever.

For Stafford the curtain was drawn before the shrine; but love was behind the curtain still.

He would not go to her as Barry had asked. There in Brinkwort's house in the covert of peaches and pomegranates was the man and the only man who should, who must, bring new bloom to her cheek. Her suffering would carry her to Rudyard at the last, unless it might be that one or the other of them had taken Adrian Fellowes' life. If either had done that, there could be no reunion.

He did not know what Al'mah had told Jasmine, the thing which had cleared Jasmine's vision, and made possible a path which should lead from the hospital to the house among the orchard-trees at Brinkwort's Farm.

No, he would not, could not go to Jasmine—unless, it might be, she was dying. A sudden, sharp anxiety possessed him. If, as Barry Whalen suggested, one of those ugly turns should come, which illnesses take in camp, and she should die without a friend near her, without Rudyard by her side! He mounted his horse, and rode towards the hospital.

His inquiries at the hospital relieved his mind. "If there is no turn for the worse, no complications, she will go on all right, and will be convalescent in a few days," the medicine-man had said.

He gave instructions for a message to be sent to him if there was any change for the worse. His first impulse, to tell them not to let her know he had inquired, he set aside. There must not be subterfuge or secrecy any longer. Let Destiny take her course.

As he left the hospital, he heard a wounded Boer prisoner say to a Tommy who had fought with him on opposite sides in the same engagement, "Alles zal recht kom!" All will come right, was the English of it.

Out of the agony of conflict would all come right—for Boer, for Briton, for Rudyard, for Jasmine, for himself, for Al'mah?

As he entered his tent again, he was handed his mail, which had just arrived. The first letter he touched had the postmark of Durban. The address on the envelope was in the handwriting of Lady Tynemouth.

He almost shrank from opening it, because of the tragedy which had come to the husband of the woman who had been his faithful friend over so many years. At an engagement a month before, Tynemouth had been blinded by shrapnel, and had been sent to Durban. To the two letters he had written there had come no answer until now; and he felt that this reply would be a plaint against Fate, a rebellion against the future restraint and trial and responsibility which would be put upon the wife, who was so much of the irresponsible world.

After a moment, however, he muttered a reproach against his own darkness of spirit and his lack of faith in her womanliness, and opened the envelope.

It was not the letter he had imagined and feared. It began by thanking him for his own letter, and then it plunged into the heart of her trouble:

> ". . . Tynie is blind. He will never see again. But his face seems
> to me quite beautiful. It shines, Ian: beauty comes from
> within. Poor old Tynie, who would have thought that the
> world he loved couldn't make that light in his face! I never
> saw it there—did you? It is just giving up one's self to the
> Inevitable. I suppose we mostly are giving up ourselves to
> Ourselves, thinking always of our own pleasure and profit
> and pride, never being content, pushing on and on. . . Ian,
> I'm not going to push on any more. I've done with the
> Climbers. There's too much of the Climbers in us all—not
> social climbing, I mean, but wanting to get somewhere that
> has something for us, out in the big material world. When
> I look at Tynie—he's lying there so peaceful—you might
> think it is a prison he is in. It isn't. He's set free into a world
> where he had never been. He's set free in a world of light
> that never blinds us. If he'd lived to be a hundred with the
> sight of his eyes, he'd never have known that there's a world

that belongs to Allah,—I love that word, it sounds so great and yet so friendly, so gentler than the name by which we call the First One in our language and our religion—and that world is inside ourselves. . . Tynie is always thinking of other people now, wondering what they are doing and how they are doing it. He was talking about you a little while ago, and so admiringly. It brought the tears to my eyes. Oh, I am so glad, Ian, that our friendship has always been so much on the surface, so 'void of offence'—is that the phrase? I can look at it without wincing; and I am glad. It never was a thing of importance to you, for I am not important, and there was no weight of life in it or in me. But even the butterfly has its uses, and maybe I was meant to play a little part in your big life. I like to think it was so. Sometimes a bright day gets a little more interest from the drone of the locust or the glow of a butterfly's wings. I'm not sure that the locust's droning and the bright flutter of the butterfly's wings are not the way Nature has of fastening the soul to the meaning of it all. I wonder if you ever heard the lines—foolish they read, but they are not:

> *"All summer long there was one little butterfly,*
> *Flying ahead of me,*
> *Wings red and yellow, a pretty little fellow,*
> *Flying ahead of me.*
> *One little butterfly, one little butterfly,*
> *What can his message be?—*
> *All summer long, there was one little butterfly*
> *Flying ahead of me.'*

"It may be so that the poet meant the butterfly to mean the joy of things, the hope of things, the love of things flying ahead to draw us on and on into the sunlight and up the steeps, and over the higher hills.

"Ian, I would like to be such a butterfly in your eyes at this moment; perhaps the insignificant means of making you see the near thing to do, and by doing it get a step on towards the Far Thing. You used always to think of the Far Thing. Ah, what ambition you had when I first knew you on the Zambesi, when the old red umbrella, but for you, would have carried me over into the mist and the thunder! Well, you have lost that ambition. I know why you came out here. No one ever told me. The thing behind the words in your letter tells me plainer than words. The last time I saw you in London—do you remember when it was? It was the day that Rudyard Byng drove Krool into Park Lane with the sjambok. Well, that last time, when I met you in the hall as we were both leaving a house of trouble, I felt the truth. Do you remember the day I went to see you when Mr. Mappin came? I felt the truth then more. I often wondered how I could ever help you in the old days. That was an ambition of mine. But I had no brains—no brains like Jasmine's and many another woman; and I was never able to do anything. But now I feel as I never felt anything before in my life. I feel that my time and my chance have come. I feel like a prophetess, like Miriam,—or was it Deborah?—and that I must wind the horn of warning as you walk on the edge of the precipice.

"Ian, it's only little souls who do the work that should be left to Allah, and I don't believe that you can take the reins out of Allah's hands,—He lets you do it, of course, if you insist, for a wilful child must be taught his lesson—without getting smashed up at a sharp corner that you haven't learnt to turn. Ian, there's work for you to do. Even Tynie thinks that he can do some work still. He sees he can, as he never did before; and he talks of you as a man who can do anything if you will. He says that if England wanted a strong man before the war she will want a stronger man afterwards to pick up the pieces, and put them all together again. He says that after we win, reconstruction in South Africa will be a work as big as was ever given to a man, because, if it should fail, 'down will go the whole Imperial show'—that's Tynie's phrase. And he says, why shouldn't you do it here, or why shouldn't you be the man who will guide it all in England? You found the key to England's isolation, to her foreign problem,—I'm quoting Tynie—which meant that the other nations keep hands off in this fight; well, why shouldn't you find another key, that to the future of this Empire? You got European peace for England, and now the problem is how to make this Empire a real thing. Tynie says this, not me. His command of English is better than mine, but neither of us would make a good private secretary, if we had to write letters with words of over two syllables. I've told you what Tynie says, but he doesn't know at all what I know; he doesn't see the danger I see, doesn't realize the mad thing in your brain, the sad thing weighing down your heart—and hers.

"Ian, I feel it on my own heart, and I want it lifted away. Your letter has only one word in it really. That word is Finis. I say, it must not, shall not, be Finis. Look at the escapes you have had in this war. Is not that enough to prove that you have a long way to go yet, and that you have to 'make good' the veld as you trek. To outspan now would be a crime. It would spoil a great life, it would darken memory—even mine, Ian. I must speak the truth. I want you, we all want you, to be the big man you are at heart. Do not be a Lassalle. It is too small. If one must be a slave, then let it be to something greater than one's self, higher—toweringly unattainably higher. Believe me, neither the girl you love nor any woman on earth is entitled to hold in slavery the energies and the mind and hopes of a man who can do big things—or any man at all.

"Ian, Tynie and I have our trials, but we are going to live them down. At first Tynie wanted to die, but he soon said he would see it through—blind at forty. You have had your trials, you have them still; but every gift of man is yours, and every opportunity. Will you not live it all out to the end? Allah knows the exit He wants for us, and He must resent our breaking a way out of the prison of our own making.

"You've no idea how this life of work with Jasmine has brought things home to me—and to Jasmine too. When I see the multitude of broken and maimed victims of war, well, I feel like Jeremiah; but I feel sad too that these poor fellows and those they love must suffer in order to teach us our lesson—us and England. Dear old friend, great man, I am going to quote a verse Tynie read to me last night—oh, how strange that seems! Yet it was so in a sense, he did read to me. Tynie made me say the words from the book, but he read into them all that they were, he that never drew a literary breath. It was a poem Jasmine quoted to him a fortnight ago— Browning's 'Grammarian,' and he stopped me at these words:

> *"'Thither our path lies; wind we up the heights:*
> *Wait ye the warning?*
> *Our low life was the level's and the night's;*
> *He's for the morning.'*

"Tynie stopped me there, and said, 'That's Stafford. He's the Alpine fellow!' . . ."

A few sentences more and then the letter ended on a note of courage, solicitude and friendship. And at the very last she said:

> "It isn't always easy to find the key to things, but you will find it, not because you are so clever, but because at heart you are so good. . . We both send our love, and don't forget that England hasn't had a tenth of her share of Ian Stafford. . ."

Then there followed a postscript which ran:

> "I always used to say, 'When my ship comes home,' I'd have this or that. Well, here is the ship—mine and Jasmine's, and it has come Home for me, and for Jasmine, too, I hope."

Stafford looked out over the veld. He saw the light of the sun, the joy of summer, the flowers, the buoyant hills, where all the guns were silent now; he saw a blesbok in the distance leaping to join its fellows of a herd which had strayed across the fields of war; he felt that stir of vibrant life in the air which only the new lands know; and he raised his head with the light of resolve growing in his eyes.

"Don't forget that England hasn't had a tenth of her share of Ian Stafford," Alice Tynemouth had said.

Looking round, he saw men whose sufferings were no doubt as great as his own or greater; but they were living on for others' sakes. Despair retreated before a woman's insight.

"The Alpine fellow" wanted to live now.

XXXV

AT BRINKWORT'S FARM

"What are you doing here, Krool?" The face of the half-caste had grown more furtive than it was in the London days, and as he looked at Stafford now, it had a malignant expression which showed through the mask of his outward self-control.

"I am prisoner," Krool answered thickly.

"When—where?" Stafford inquired, his eye holding the other's.

"At Hetmeyer's Kopje."

"But what are you—a prisoner—doing here at Brinkwort's Farm?"

"I was hurt. They take me hospital, but the Baas, he send for me."

"They let you come without a guard?"

"No—not. They are outside"—Krool jerked a finger towards the rear of the house—"with the biltong and the dop."

"You are a liar, Krool. There may be biltong, but there is no dop."

"What matters!" Krool's face had a leer. He looked impudently at Stafford, and Stafford read the meaning behind the unveiled insolence: Krool knew what no one else but Jasmine and himself knew with absolute certainty. Krool was in his own country, more than half a savage, with the lust of war in his blood, with memories of a day in Park Lane when the sjambok had done its ugly work, and Ian Stafford had, as Krool believed, placed it in the hands of the Baas.

It might be that this dark spirit, this Nibelung of the tragedy of the House of Byng, would even yet, when the way was open to a reconstructed life for Jasmine and Rudyard, bring catastrophe.

The thought sickened him, and then black anger took possession of him. The look he cast on the bent figure before him in the threadbare frock-coat which had been taken from the back of some dead Boer, with the corded breeches stuck in boots too large for him, and the khaki hat which some vanished Tommy would never wear again, was resolute and vengeful.

Krool must not stay at Brinkwort's Farm. He must be removed. If the Caliban told Rudyard what he knew, there could be but one end to it all; and Jasmine's life, if not ruined, must ever be, even at the best, lived under the cover of magnanimity and compassion. That would break her spirit, would take from her the radiance of temperament which alone could make life tolerable to her or to others who might live with her under the same roof. Anxiety possessed him, and he swiftly devised means to be rid of Krool before harm could be done. He was certain harm was meant—there was a look of semi-insanity in Krool's eyes. Krool must be put out of the way before he could speak with the Baas. . . But how?

With a great effort Stafford controlled himself. Krool must be got rid of at once, must be sent back to the prisoners' quarters and kept there. He must not see Byng now. In a few more hours the army would move on, leaving the prisoners behind, and Rudyard would presently move on with the army. This was Byng's last day at Brinkwort's Farm, to which he himself had come to-day lest Rudyard should take note of his neglect, and their fellow-officers should remark that the old friendship had grown cold, and perhaps begin to guess at the reason why.

"You say the Baas sent for you?" he asked presently.

"Yes."

"To sjambok you again?"

Krool made a gesture of contempt. "I save the Baas at Hetmeyer's Kopje. I kill Piet Graaf to do it."

There was a look of assurance in the eyes of the mongrel, which sent a wave of coldness through Stafford's veins and gave him fresh anxiety.

He was in despair. He knew Byng's great, generous nature, and he dreaded the inconsistency which such men show—forgiving and forgetting when the iron penalty should continue and the chains of punishment remain.

He determined to know the worst. "Traitor all round!" he said presently with contempt. "You saved the Baas by killing Piet Graaf— have you told the Baas that? Has any one told the Baas that? The sjambok is the Baas' cure for the traitor, and sometimes it kills to cure. Do you think that the Baas would want his life through the killing of Piet Graaf by his friend Krool, the slim one from the slime?"

As a sudden tempest twists and bends a tree, contorts it, bows its branches to the dust, transforms it from a thing of beauty to a hag of Walpurgis, so Stafford's words transformed Krool. A passion of rage possessed him. He looked like one of the creatures that waited on Wotan in the nether places. He essayed to speak, but at first could not. His body bent forward, and his fingers spread out in a spasm of hatred, then clinched with the stroke of a hammer on his knees, and again opened and shut in a gesture of loathsome cruelty.

At length he spoke, and Stafford listened intently, for now Caliban was off his guard, and he knew the worst that was meant.

"Ah, you speak of traitor—you! The sjambok for the traitor, eh? The sjambok—fifty strokes, a hunderd strokes—a t'ousand! Krool—Krool is a traitor, and the sjambok for him. What did he do? What did Krool do? He help Oom Paul against the Rooinek—against the Philistine. He help the chosen against the children of Hell.

"What did Krool do? He tell Oom Paul how the thieves would to come in the night to sold him like sheep to a butcher, how the t'ousand wolves would swarm upon the sheepfold, and there would be no homes for the voortrekker and his vrouw, how the Outlander would sit on our stoeps and pick the peaches from our gardens. And he tell him other things good for him to hear."

Stafford was conscious of the smell of orchard blossoms blown through the open window, of the odour of the pomegranate in the hedge; but his eyes were fascinated by the crouching passion of the figure before him and the dissonance of the low, unhuman voice. There was no pause in the broken, turgid torrent, which was like a muddy flood pouring over the boulders of a rapid.

"Who the traitor is? Is it the man that tries to save his homeland from the wolf and the worm? I kill Piet Graaf to save the Baas. The Baas an' I, we understand—on the Limpopo we make the unie. He is the Baas, and I am his slave. All else nothing is. I kill all the people of the Baas' country, but I die for the Baas. The Baas kill me if he will it. So it was set down in the bond on the Limpopo. If the Baas strike, he strike; if he kill, he kill. It is in the bond, it is set down. All else go. Piet Graaf, he go. Oom Paul, he go. Joubert, Cronje, Botha, they all go, if the Baas speak. It is written so. On the Limpopo it is written. All must go, if the Baas speak—one, two, three, a t'ousand. Else the bond is water, and the spirits come in the night, and take you to the million years of torment. It is nothing to die—pain! But only the Baas is kill me. It is written so. Only the Baas can hurt me. Not you, nor all the verdomde Rooineks out there"—he pointed to the vast camp out on the veld—"nor the Baas' vrouw. Do I not know all about the Baas' vrouw! She cannot hurt me. . ." He spat on the ground. "Who is the traitor? Is it Krool? Did Krool steal from the Baas? Krool is the Baas' slave; it is only the friend of the Baas that steal from him—only him is traitor. I kill Piet Graaf to save the Baas. No one kills you to save the Baas! I saw you with your arms round the Baas' vrouw. So I go tell the Baas all. If he kill me—it is the Baas. It is written."

He spat on the ground again, and his eyes grown red with his passion glowered on Stafford like those of some animal of the jungle.

Stafford's face was white, and every nerve in his body seemed suddenly to be wrenched by the hand of torture. What right had he to resent this abominable tirade, this loathsome charge by such a beast? Yet he would have shot where he stood the fellow who had spoken so of "the Baas' vrouw," if it had not come to him with sudden conviction that the end was not to be this way. Ever since he had read Alice Tynemouth's letter a new spirit had been working in him. He must do nothing rash. There was enough stain on his hands now without the added stain of blood. But he must act; he must prevent Krool from telling the Baas. Yonder at the hospital was Jasmine, and she and her man must come together here in this peaceful covert before Rudyard went forward with the army. It must be so.

Two sentries were beyond the doorway. He stepped quickly to the stoep and summoned them. They came. Krool watched with eyes that, at first, did not understand.

Stafford gave an order. "Take the prisoner to the guard. They will at once march him back to the prisoners' camp."

Now Krool understood, and he made as if to spring on Stafford, but a pistol suddenly faced him, and he knew well that what Stafford would not do in cold blood, he would do in the exercise of his duty and as a soldier before these Rooinek privates. He stood still; he made no resistance.

But suddenly his voice rang out in a guttural cry—"Baas!"

In an instant a hand was clapped on his mouth, and his own dirty neckcloth provided a gag.

The storm was over. The native blood in him acknowledged the logic of superior force, and he walked out quietly between the sentries. Stafford's move was regular from a military point of view. He was justified in disposing of a dangerous and recalcitrant prisoner. He could find a sufficient explanation if he was challenged.

As he turned round from the doorway through which Krool had disappeared, he saw Al'mah, who had entered from another room during the incident.

A light came to Stafford's face. They two derelicts of life had much in common—the communion of sinners who had been so much sinned against.

"I heard his last words about you and—her," she said in a low voice.

"Where is Byng?" he asked anxiously.

"In the kloof near by. He will be back presently."

"Thank God!"

Al'mah's face was anxious. "I don't know what you are going to say to him, or why you have come," she said, "but—"

"I have come to congratulate him on his recovery."

"I understand. I want to say some things to you. You should know them before you see him. There is the matter of Adrian Fellowes."

"What about Adrian Fellowes?" Stafford asked evenly, yet he felt his heart give a bound and his brain throb.

"Does it matter to you now? At the inquest you were—concerned."

"I am more concerned now," he rejoined huskily.

He suddenly held out a hand to her with a smile of rare friendliness. There came over him again the feeling he had at the hospital when they talked together last, that whatever might come of all the tragedy and sorrow around them they two must face irretrievable loss.

She hesitated a moment, and then as she took his outstretched hand she said, "Yes, I will take it while I can."

Her eyes went slowly round the room as though looking for something—some point where they might rest and gather courage maybe, then they steadied to his firmly.

"You knew Adrian Fellowes did not die a natural death—I saw that at the inquest."

"Yes, I knew."

"It was a poisoned needle."

"I know. I found the needle."

"Ah! I threw it down afterwards. I forgot about it."

Slowly the colour left Stafford's face, as the light of revelation broke in upon his brain. Why had he never suspected her? His brain was buzzing with sounds which came from inner voices—voices of old thoughts and imaginings, like little beings in a dark forest hovering on the march of the discoverer. She was speaking, but her voice seemed to come through a clouded medium from a great distance to him.

"He had hurt me more than any other—than my husband or her. I did it. I would do it again. . . I had been good to him. . . I had suffered, I wanted something for all I had lost, and he was. . ."

Her voice trailed away into nothing, then rose again presently. "I am not sorry. Perhaps you wonder at that. But no, I do not hate myself for it—only for all that went before it. I will pay, if I have to pay, in my own way. . . Thousands of women die who are killed by hands that carry no weapon. They die of misery and shame and regret. . . This one man died because. . ."

He did not hear, or if he heard he did not realize what she was saying now. One thought was ringing through his mind like bells pealing. The gulf of horrible suspicion between Rudyard and Jasmine was closed. So long as it yawned, so long as there was between them the accounting for Adrian Fellowes' death, they might have come together, but there would always have been a black shadow between—the shadow that hangs over the scaffold.

"They should know the truth," he said almost peremptorily.

"They both know," she rejoined calmly. "I told him this evening. On the day I saw you at the hospital, I told her."

There was silence for a moment, and then he said: "She must come here before he joins his regiment."

"I saw her last night at the hospital," Al'mah answered. "She was better. She was preparing to go to Durban. I did not ask her if she was coming, but I was sure she was not. So, just now, before you came, I sent a message to her. It will bring her. . . It does not matter what a woman like me does."

"What did you say to her?"

"I wrote, 'If you wish to see him before the end, come quickly.' She will think he is dying."

"If she resents the subterfuge?"

"Risks must be taken. If he goes without their meeting—who can tell! Now is the time—now. I want to see it. It must be."

He reached out both hands and took hers, while she grew pale. Her eyes had a strange childishly frightened look.

"You are a good woman, Al'mah," he said.

A quivering, ironical laugh burst from her lips. Then, suddenly, her eyes were suffused.

"The world would call it the New Goodness then," she replied in a voice which told how deep was the well of misery in her being.

"It is as old as Allah," he replied.

"Or as old as Cain?" she responded, then added quickly, "Hush! He is coming."

An instant afterwards she was outside among the peach trees, and Rudyard and Stafford faced each other in the room she had just left.

As Al'mah stood looking into the quivering light upon the veld, her fingers thrust among the blossoms of a tree which bent over her, she heard horses' hoofs, and presently there came round the corner of the house two mounted soldiers who had brought Krool to Brinkwort's Farm. Their prisoner was secured to a stirrup-leather, and the neckcloth was still binding his mouth.

As they passed, Krool turned towards the house, eyes showing like flames under the khaki trooper's hat, which added fresh incongruity to the frock-coat and the huge top-boots.

The guard were now returning to their post at the door-way.

"What has happened?" she asked, with a gesture towards the departing Krool.

"A bit o' lip to Colonel Stafford, ma'am," answered one of the guard. "He's got a tongue like a tanner's vat, that goozer. Wants a lump o' lead in 'is baskit 'e does."

"'E done a good turn at Hetmeyer's Kopje," added the Second. "If it hadn't been for 'im the S.A.'s would have had a new Colonel"—he jerked his head towards the house, from which came the murmur of men's voices talking earnestly.

"Whatever 'e done it for, it was slim, you can stake a tidy lot on that, ma'am," interjected the First. "He's the bottom o' the sink, this half-caste Boojer is."

The Second continued: "If I 'ad my way 'e'd be put in front at the next push-up, just where the mausers of his pals would get 'im. 'E's done a lot o' bitin' in 'is time—let 'im bite the dust now, I sez. I'm fair sick of treatin' that lot as if they was square fighters. Why, 'e'd fire on a nurse or an ambulanche, that tyke would."

"There's lots like him in yonder," urged the First, as a hand was jerked forward towards the hills, "and we're goin' to get 'em this time—goin' to get 'em on the shovel. Their schanses and their kranzes and their ant-bear dugouts ain't goin' to help them this mop-up. We're goin' to get the tongue in the hole o' the buckle this time. It's over the hills and far away, and the Come-in-Elizas won't stop us. When the howitzers with their nice little balls of lyddite physic get opening their bouquets to-morrow—"

"Who says to-morrow?" demanded the Second.

"I says to-morrow. I know. I got ears, and 'im that 'as ears to 'ear let 'im 'ear—that's what the Scripture saith. I was brought up on the off side of a vicarage."

He laughed eagerly at his own joke, chuckling till his comrade followed up with a sharp challenge.

"I bet you never heard nothin' but your own bleatin's—not about wot the next move is, and w'en it is."

The First made quick retort. "Then you lose your bet, for I 'eard Colonel Byng get 'is orders larst night—w'en you was sleepin' at your post, Willy. By to-morrow this time you'll see the whole outfit at it. You'll see the little billows of white rolling over the hills—that's shrapnel. You'll hear the rippin', zippin', zimmin' thing in the air wot makes you sick; for you don't know who it's goin' to 'it. That's shells. You'll hear a thousand blankets being shook—that's mausers and others. You'll see regiments marching out o' step, an' every man on his own, which is not how we started this war, not much. And where there's a bit o' rock, you say, 'Ere's a friend, and you get behind it like a man. And w'en there's nothing to get behind, you get in front, and take your chances, and you get there—right there, over the trenches, over the bloomin' Amalakites, over the hills and far away, where they want the relief they're goin' to get, or I'm a pansy blossom."

"Well, to-morrow can't come quick enough for me," answered the Second. He straightened out his shoulders and eyed the hills in front of him with a calculating air, as though he were planning the tactics of the fight to come.

"We'll all be in it—even you, ma'am," insinuated the First to Al'mah with a friendly nod. "But I'd ruther 'ave my job nor yours. I've done a bit o' nursin'—there was Bob Critchett that got a splinter o' shell in 'is 'ead, and there was Sergeant Hoyle and others. But it gits me where I squeak that kind o' thing do."

Suddenly they brought their rifles to the salute, as a footstep sounded smartly on the stoep. It was Stafford coming from the house.

He acknowledged the salute mechanically. His eyes were fastened on the distance. They had a rapt, shining look, and he walked like one in a pleasant dream. A moment afterwards he mounted his horse with the lightness of a boy, and galloped away.

He had not seen Al'mah as he passed.

In her fingers was crushed a bunch of orange blossoms. A heavy sigh broke from her lips. She turned to go within, and, as she did so, saw

Rudyard Byng looking from the doorway towards the hospital where Jasmine was.

"Will she come?" Al'mah asked herself, and mechanically she wiped the stain of the blossoms from her fingers.

XXXVI

Springs of Healing

Dusk had almost come, yet Jasmine had not arrived at Brinkwort's Farm, the urgency of Al'mah's message notwithstanding. As things stood, it was a matter of life and death; and to Al'mah's mind humanity alone should have sent Jasmine at once to her husband's side. Something of her old prejudice against Jasmine rose up again. Perhaps behind it all was involuntary envy of an invitation to happiness so freely laid at Jasmine's feet, but withheld from herself by Fate. Never had the chance to be happy or the obvious inducement to be good ever been hers. She herself had nothing, and Jasmine still had a chance for all to which she had no right. Her heart beat harder at the thought of it. She was of those who get their happiness first in making others happy—as she would have done with Blantyre, if she had had a chance; as even she tried to do with the man whom she had sent to his account with the firmness and fury of an ancient Greek. The maternal, the protective sense was big in her, and indirectly it had governed her life. It had sent her to South Africa—to protect the wretch who had done his best to destroy her; it had made her content at times as she did her nurse's work in what dreadful circumstances! It was the source of her revolt at Jasmine's conduct and character.

But was it also that, far beneath her criticism of Jasmine, which was, after all, so little in comparison with the new-found affection she really had for her, there lay a kinship, a sympathy, a soul's rapprochement with Rudyard, which might, in happier circumstances, have become a mating such as the world knew in its youth? Was that also in part the cause of her anxiety for Rudyard, and of her sharp disapproval of Jasmine? Did she want to see Rudyard happy, no matter at what cost to Jasmine? Was it the everlasting feminine in her which would make a woman sacrifice herself for a man, if need be, in order that he might be happy? Was it the ancient tyrannical soul in her which would make a thousand women sacrifice themselves for the man she herself set above all others?

But she was of those who do not know what they are, or what they think and feel, till some explosion forces open the doors of their souls and they look upon a new life over a heap of ruins.

She sat in the gathering dusk, waiting, while hope slowly waned. Rudyard also, on the veranda, paced weakly, almost stumblingly, up and down, his face also turning towards the Stay Awhile Hospital. At length, with a heavy sigh, he entered the house and sat down in a great arm-chair, from which old Brinkwort the Boer had laid down the law for his people.

Where was Jasmine? Why did she not hasten to Brinkwort's Farm?

A Staff Officer from the General Commanding had called to congratulate Jasmine on her recovery, and to give fresh instructions which would link her work at Durban effectively with the army as it now moved on to the relief of the town beyond the hills. Al'mah's note had arrived while the officer was with Jasmine, and it was held back until he left. It was then forgotten by the attendant on duty, and it lay for three hours undelivered. Then when it was given to her, no mention was made of the delay.

When the Staff Officer left her, he had said to himself that hers was one of the most alluring and fascinating faces he had ever seen; and he, like Stafford, though in another sphere—that of the Secret Intelligence Department—had travelled far and wide in the world. Perfectly beautiful he did not call her, though her face was as near that rarity as any he had known. He would only have called a woman beautiful who was tall, and she was almost petite; but that was because he himself was over-tall, and her smallness seemed to be properly classed with those who were pretty, not the handsome or the beautiful. But there was something in her face that haunted him—a wistful, appealing delicacy, which yet was associated with an instant readiness of intellect, with a perspicuous judgment and a gift of organization. And she had eyes of blue which were "meant to drown those who hadn't life-belts," as he said.

In one way or another he put all this to his fellow officers, and said that the existence of two such patriots as Byng and Jasmine in one family was unusual.

"Pretty fairly self-possessed, I should say," said Rigby, the youngest officer present at mess. "Her husband under repair at Brinkwort's Farm, in the care of the blue-ribbon nurse of the army, who makes a fellow well if he looks at her, and she studying organization at the Stay Awhile with a staff-officer."

The reply of the Staff Officer was quick and cutting enough for any officers' mess.

"I see by the latest papers from England, that Balfour says we'll muddle through this war somehow," he said. "He must have known you, Rigby. With the courage of the damned you carry a fearsome lot of impedimenta, and you muddle quite adequately. The lady you have traduced has herself been seriously ill, and that is why she is not at Brinkwort's Farm. What a malicious mind you've got! Byng would think so."

"If Rigby had been in your place to-day," interposed a gruff major, "the lady would surely have had a relapse. Convalescence is no time for teaching the rudiments of human intercourse."

Pale and angry, Rigby, who was half Scotch and correspondingly self-satisfied, rejoined stubbornly: "I know what I know. They haven't met since she came up from Durban. Sandlip told me that—"

The Staff Officer broke the sentence. "What Sandlip told you is what Nancy would tell Polly and Polly would tell the cook—and then Rigby would know. But statement number one is an Ananiasism, for Byng saw his wife at the hospital the night before Hetmeyer's Kopje. I can't tell what they said, though, nor what was the colour of the lady's pegnoir, for I am neither Nancy nor Polly nor the cook—nor Rigby."

With a maddened gesture Rigby got to his feet, but a man at his side pulled him down. "Sit still, Baby Bunting, or you'll not get over the hills to-morrow," he said, and he offered Rigby a cigar from Rigby's own cigar-case, cutting off the end, handing it to him and lighting a match.

"Gun out of action: record the error of the day," piped the thin precise voice of the Colonel from the head of the table.

A chorus of quiet laughter met the Colonel's joke, founded on the technical fact that the variation in the firing of a gun, due to any number of causes, though apparently firing under the same conditions, is carted officially "the error of the day" in Admiralty reports.

"Here the incident closed," as the newspapers say, but Rigby the tactless and the petty had shown that there was rumour concerning the relations of Byng and his wife, which Jasmine, at least, imagined did not exist.

When Jasmine read the note Al'mah had sent her, a flush stole slowly over her face, and then faded, leaving a whiteness, behind which was the emanation, not of fear, but of agitation and of shock.

It meant that Rudyard was dying, and that she must go to him. That she must go to him? Was that the thought in her mind—that she must go to him?

If she wished to see him again before he went! That midnight, when he was on his way to Hetmeyer's Kopje, he had flung from her room into the night, and ridden away angrily on his grey horse, not hearing her voice faintly calling after him. Now, did she want to see him—the last time before he rode away again forever, on that white horse called Death? A shudder passed through her.

"Ruddy! Poor Ruddy!" she said, and she did not remember that those were the pitying, fateful words she used on the day when Ian Stafford dined with her alone after Rudyard made his bitter protest against the life they lived. "We have everything—everything," he had said, "and yet—"

Now, however, there was an anguished sob in her voice. With the thought of seeing him, her fingers tremblingly sought the fine-spun strands of hair which ever lay a little loose from the wonder of its great coiled abundance, and then felt her throat, as though to adjust the simple linen collar she wore, making exquisite contrast to the soft simplicity of her dark-blue gown.

She found the attendant who had given her the letter, and asked if the messenger was waiting, and was only then informed that he had been gone three hours or more.

Three hours or more! It might be that Rudyard was gone forever without hearing what she had to say, or knowing whether she desired reconciliation and peace.

She at once gave orders for a cape-cart to take her over to Brinkwort's Farm. The attendant respectfully said that he must have orders. She hastened to the officer in charge of the hospital, and explained. His sympathy translated itself into instant action. Fortunately there was a cart at the door. In a moment she was ready, and the cart sped away into the night across the veld.

She had noticed nothing as she mounted the cart—neither the driver nor the horses; but, as they hurried on, she was roused by a familiar voice saying, "'E done it all right at Hetmeyer's Kopje—done it brown. First Wortmann's Drift, and then Hetmeyer's Kopje, and he'll be over the hills and through the Boers and into Lordkop with the rest of the hold-me-backs."

She recognized him—the first person who had spoken to her of her husband on her arrival, the cheerful Corporal Shorter, who had told her of Wortmann's Drift and the saving of "Old Gunter."

She touched his arm gently. "I am glad it is you," she said in a low tone.

"Not so glad as I am," he answered. "It's a purple shame that you should ha' been took sick when he was mowed down, and that some one else should be healin' 'is gapin' wounds besides 'is lawful wife, and 'er a rifle-shot away! It's a fair shame, that's wot it is. But all's well as ends well, and you're together at the finish."

She shrank from his last words. Her heart seemed to contract; it hurt her as though it was being crushed in a vise. She was used to that pain now. She had felt it—ah, how many times since the night she found Adrian Fellowes' white rose on her pillow, laid there by the man she had sworn at the altar to love, honor, and obey! Her head drooped. "At the finish"—how strange and new and terrible it was! The world stood still for her.

"You'll go together to Lordkop, I expeck," she heard her companion's voice say, and at first she did not realize its meaning; then slowly it came to her. "At the finish" in his words meant the raising of the siege of Lordkop, it meant rescue, victory, restoration. He had not said that Rudyard was dead, that the Book of Rudyard and Jasmine was closed forever. Her mind was in chaos, her senses in confusion. She seemed like one in a vague shifting, agonizing dream.

She was unconscious of what her friendly Corporal was saying. She only answered him mechanically now and then; and he, seeing that she was distraught, talked on in a comforting kind of way, telling her anecdotes of Rudyard, as they were told in that part of the army to which he belonged.

What was she going to do when she arrived? What could she do if Rudyard was dead? If Rudyard was still alive, she would make him understand that she was not the Jasmine of the days "before the flood"—before that storm came which uprooted all that ever was in her life except the old, often anguished, longing to be good, and the power which swept her into bye and forbidden paths. If he was gone, deaf to her voice and to any mortal sound, then—there rushed into her vision the figure of Ian Stafford, but she put that from her with a trembling determination. That was done forever. She was as sure of it as she was sure of anything in the world. Ian had not forgiven her, would never forgive her. He despised her, rejected her, abhorred her. Ian had saved her from the result of Rudyard's rash retaliation and fury, and had then repulsed her, bidden her stand off from him with a magnanimity and a chivalry which had humiliated her. He had protected her from the shame of an open tragedy, and then had shut the door in her face.

Rudyard, with the same evidence as Ian held,—the same letter as proof—he, whatever he believed or thought, he had forgiven her. Only a few nights ago, that night before the fight at Hetmeyer's Kopje, he had opened his arms to her and called her his wife. In Rudyard was some great good thing, something which could not die, which must live on. She sat up straight in the seat of the cart, her hands clinched.

No, no, no, Rudyard was not dead, and he should not die. It mattered not what Al'mah had written, she must have her chance to prove herself; his big soul must have its chance to run a long course, must not be cut off at the moment when so much had been done; when there was so much to do. Ian should see that she was not "just a little burst of eloquence," as he had called her, not just a strumpet, as he thought her; but a woman now, beyond eloquence, far distant from the poppy-fields of pleasure. She was young enough for it to be a virtue in her to avoid the poppy-fields. She was not twenty-six years of age, and to have learned the truth at twenty-six, and still not to have been wholly destroyed by the lies of life, was something which might be turned to good account.

She was sharply roused, almost shocked out of her distraction. Bright lights appeared suddenly in front of her, and she heard the voice of her Corporal saying: "We're here, ma'am, where old Brinkwort built a hospital for one, and that one's yours, Mrs. Byng."

He clucked to his horses and they slackened. All at once the lights seemed to grow larger, and from the garden of Brinkwort's house came the sharp voice of a soldier saying:

"Halt! Who goes there?"

"A friend," was the Corporal's reply.

"Advance, friend, and give the countersign," was brusquely returned.

A moment afterwards Jasmine was in the sweet-smelling garden, and the lights of the house were flaring out upon her.

She heard at the same time the voices of the sentry and of Corporal Shorter in low tones of badinage, and she frowned. It was cruel that at the door of the dead or the dying there should be such levity.

All at once a figure came between her and the light. Instinctively she knew it was Al'mah.

"Al'mah! Al'mah!" she said painfully, and in a voice scarce above a whisper.

The figure of the singing-woman bent over her protectingly, as it might almost seem, and her hands were caught in a warm clasp.

"Am I in time?" Jasmine asked, and the words came from her in gasps.

Al'mah had no repentance for her deception. She saw an agitation which seemed to her deeper and more real than any emotion ever shown by Jasmine, not excepting the tragical night at the Glencader Mine and the morning of the first meeting at the Stay Awhile Hospital. The butterfly had become a thrush that sang with a heart in its throat.

She gathered Jasmine's eyes to her own. It seemed as though she never would answer. To herself she even said, why should she hurry, since all was well, since she had brought the two together living, who had been dead to each other these months past, and, more than all, had been of the angry dead? A little more pain and regret could do no harm, but only good. Besides, now that she was face to face with the result of her own deception, she had a sudden fear that it might go wrong. She had no remorse for the act, but only a faint apprehension of the possible consequences. Suppose that in the shock of discovery Jasmine should throw everything to the winds, and lose herself in arrant egotism once more! Suppose—no, she would suppose nothing. She must believe that all she had done was for the best.

She felt how cold were the small delicate hands in her own strong warm fingers, she saw the frightened appeal of the exquisite haunting eyes, and all at once realized the cause of that agitation—the fear that death had come without understanding, that the door had been forever shut against the answering voices.

"You are in time," she said gently, encouragingly, and she tightened the grasp of her hands.

As the volts of an electric shock quivering through a body are suddenly withdrawn, and the rigidity becomes a ghastly inertness, so Jasmine's hands, and all her body, seemed released. She felt as though she must fall, but she reasserted her strength, and slowly regained her balance, withdrawing her hands from those of Al'mah.

"He is alive—he is alive—he is alive," she kept repeating to herself like one in a dream. Then she added hastily, with an effort to bear herself with courage: "Where is he? Take me."

Al'mah motioned, and in a moment they were inside the house. A sense of something good and comforting came over Jasmine. Here was an old, old room furnished in heavy and simple Dutch style, just as old Elias Brinkwort had left it. It had the grave and heavy hospitableness of a picture of Teniers or Jan Steen. It had the sense of home, the welcome of the cradle and the patriarch's chair. These were both here as they were when Elias Brinkwort and his people went out to join the Boer army in the hills, knowing that the verdomde Rooinek would not loot his house or ravage his belongings.

To Jasmine's eyes, it brought a new strange sense, as though all at once doors had been opened up to new sensations of life. Almost mechanically, yet with a curious vividness and permanency of vision, her eyes drifted from the patriarch's chair to the cradle in the corner; and that picture would remain with her till she could see no more at all. Unbidden and unconscious there came upon her lips a faint smile, and then a door in front of her was opened, and she was inside another room—not a bedroom as she had expected, but a room where the Dutch simplicity and homely sincerity had been invaded by something English and military. This she felt before her eyes fell on a man standing beside a table, fully dressed. Though shaken and worn, it was a figure which had no affinity with death.

As she started back Al'mah closed the door behind her, and she found herself facing Rudyard, looking into his eyes.

Al'mah had miscalculated. She did not realize Jasmine as she really was—like one in a darkened room who leans out to the light and sun. The old life, the old impetuous egoism, the long years of self were not yet gone from a character composite of impulse, vanity and intensity. This had been too daring an experiment with one of her nature, which had within the last few months become as strangely, insistently, even fanatically honest, as it had been elusive in the past. In spite of a tremulous effort to govern herself and see the situation as it really was—an effort of one who desired her good to bring her and Rudyard together, the ruse itself became magnified to monstrous proportions, and her spirit suddenly revolted. She felt that she had been inveigled; that what should have been her own voluntary act of expiation and submission, had been forced upon her, and pride, ever her most secret enemy, took possession of her.

"I have been tricked," she said, with eyes aflame and her body trembling. "You have trapped me here!" There was scorn and indignation in her voice.

He did not move, but his eyes were intent upon hers and persistently held them. He had been near to death, and his vision had been more fully cleared than hers. He knew that this was the end of all or the beginning of all things for them both; and though anger suddenly leaped at the bottom of his heart, he kept it in restraint, the primitive thing of which he had had enough.

"I did not trick you, Jasmine," he answered, in a low voice. "The letter was sent without my knowledge or permission. Al'mah thought she was doing us both a good turn. I never deceived you—never. I should not have sent for you in any case. I heard you were ill and I tried to get up and go to you; but it was not possible. Besides, they would not let me. I wanted to go to you again, because, somehow, I felt that midnight meeting in the hospital was a mistake; that it ended as you would not really wish it to end."

Again, with wonderful intuition for a man who knew so little of women, as he thought, he had said the one thing which could have cooled the anger that drowned the overwhelming gratitude she felt at his being alive—overwhelming, in spite of the fact that her old mad temperament had flooded it for the moment.

He would have gone to her—that was what he had said. In spite of her conduct that midnight, when he was on his way to Hetmeyer's Kopje, he would have come again to her! How, indeed, he must have loved her; or how magnanimous, how impossibly magnanimous, he was!

How thin and worn he was, and how large the eyes were in the face grown hollow with suffering! There were liberal streaks of grey also at his temples, and she noted there was one strand all white just in the centre of his thick hair. A swift revulsion of feeling in her making for peace was, however, sharply arrested by the look in his eyes. It had all the sombreness of reproach—of immitigable reproach. Could she face that look now and through the years to come? It were easier to live alone to the end with her own remorse, drinking the cup that would not empty, on and on, than to live with that look in his eyes.

She turned her head away from him. Her glance suddenly caught a sjambok lying along two nails on the wall. His eyes followed hers, and in the minds of both was the scene when Rudyard drove Krool into the street under just such a whip of rhinoceros-hide.

Something of the old spirit worked in her in spite of all. Idiosyncrasy may not be cauterized, temperament must assert itself, or the personality dies. Was he to be her master—was that the end of it all? She had placed herself so completely in his power by her wilful waywardness and errors. Free from blame, she would have been ruler over him; now she must be his slave!

"Why did you not use it on me?" she asked, in a voice almost like a cry, though it had a ring of bitter irony. "Why don't you use it now? Don't you want to?"

"You were always so small and beautiful," he answered, slowly. "A twenty-stamp mill to crush a bee!"

Again resentment rose in her, despite the far-off sense of joy she had in hearing him play with words. She could forgive almost anything for that—and yet she was real and had not merely the dilettante soul. But why should he talk as though she was a fly and he an eagle? Yet there was admiration in his eyes and in his words. She was angry with herself—and with him. She was in chaos again.

"You treat me like a child, you condescend—"

"Oh, for God's sake—for God's sake!" he interrupted, with a sudden storm in his face; but suddenly, as though by a great mastery of the will, he conquered himself, and his face cleared.

"You must sit down, Jasmine," he said, hurriedly. "You look tired. You haven't got over your illness yet."

He hastily stepped aside to get her a chair, but, as he took hold of it, he stumbled and swayed in weakness, born of an excitement far greater than her own; for he was thinking of the happiness of two people, not of the happiness of one; and he realized how critical was this hour. He had a grasp of the bigger things, and his talk with Stafford of a few hours ago was in his mind—a talk which, in its brevity, still had had the limitlessness of revelation. He had made a promise to one of the best friends that man—or woman—ever had, as he thought; and he would keep it. So he said to himself. Stafford understood Jasmine, and Stafford had insisted that he be not deceived by some revolt on the part of Jasmine, which would be the outcome of her own humiliation, of her own anger with herself for all the trouble she had caused. So he said to himself.

As he staggered with the chair she impulsively ran to aid him.

"Rudyard," she exclaimed, with concern, "you must not do that. You have not the strength. It is silly of you to be up at all. I wonder at Al'mah and the doctor!"

She pushed him to a big arm-chair beside the table and gently pressed him down into the seat. He was very weak, and his hand trembled on the chair-arm. She reached out, as if to take it; but, as though the act was too forward, her fingers slipped to his wrist instead, and she felt his pulse with the gravity of a doctor.

Despite his weakness a look of laughter crept into his eyes and stayed there. He had read the little incident truly. Presently, seeing the whiteness of his face but not the look in his eyes, she turned to the table, and pouring out a glass of water from a pitcher there, held it to his lips.

"Here, Rudyard," she said, soothingly, "drink this. You are faint. You shouldn't have got up simply because I was coming."

As he leaned back to drink from the glass she caught the gentle humour of his look, begotten of the incident of a moment before.

There was no reproach in the strong, clear eyes of blue which even wounds and illness had not faced—only humour, only a hovering joy, only a good-fellowship, and the look of home. She suddenly thought of the room from which she had just come, and it seemed, not fantastically to her, that the look in his eyes belonged to the other room where were the patriarch's chair and the baby's cradle. There was no offending magnanimity, no lofty compassion in his blameless eyes, but a human something which took no account of the years that the locust had eaten, the old mad, bad years, the wrong and the shame of them. There was only the look she had seen the day he first visited her in her own home, when he had played with words she had used in the way she adored, and would adore till she died; when he had said, in reply to her remark that he would turn her head, that it wouldn't make any difference to his point of view if she did turn her head! Suddenly it was all as if that day had come back, although his then giant physical strength had gone; although he had been mangled in the power-house of which they had spoken that day. Come to think of it, she too had been working in the "power-house" and had been mangled also; for she was but a thread of what she was then, but a wisp of golden straw to the sheaf of the then young golden wheat.

All at once, in answer to the humour in his eyes, to the playful bright look, the tragedy and the passion which had flown out from her old self like the flame that flares out of an opened furnace-door, sank back again, the door closed, and all her senses were cooled as by a gentle wind.

Her eyes met his, and the invitation in them was like the call of the thirsty harvester in the sunburnt field. With an abandon, as startling as it was real and true to her nature, she sank down to the floor and buried her face in her hands at his feet. She sobbed deeply, softly.

With an exclamation of gladness and welcome he bent over her and drew her close to him, and his hands soothed her trembling shoulders.

"Peace is the best thing of all, Jasmine," he whispered. "Peace."

They were the last words that Ian had addressed to her. It did not make her shrink now that both had said to her the same thing, for both knew her, each in his own way, better than she had ever known herself; and each had taught her in his own way, but by what different means!

All at once, with a start, she caught Rudyard's arm with a little spasmodic grasp.

"I did not kill Adrian Fellowes," she said, like a child eager to be absolved from a false imputation. She looked up at him simply, bravely.

"Neither did I," he answered gravely, and the look in his eyes did not change. She noted that.

"I know. It was—"

She paused. What right had she to tell!

"Yes, we both know who did it," he added. "Al'mah told me."

She hid her head in her hands again, while he hung over her wisely waiting and watching.

Presently she raised her head, but her swimming eyes did not seek his. They did not get so high. After one swift glance towards his own, they dropped to where his heart might be, and her voice trembled as she said:

"Long ago Alice Tynemouth said I ought to marry a man who would master me. She said I needed a heavy hand over me—and the shackles on my wrists."

She had forgotten that these phrases were her own; that she had used them concerning herself the night before the tragedy.

"I think she was right," she added. "I had never been mastered, and I was all childish wilfulness and vanity. I was never worth while. You took me too seriously, and vanity did the rest."

"You always had genius," he urged, gently, "and you were so beautiful."

She shook her head mournfully. "I was only an imitation always— only a dresden-china imitation of the real thing I might have been, if I had been taken right in time. I got wrong so early. Everything I said or did was mostly imitation. It was made up of other people's acts and words. I could never forget anything I'd ever heard; it drowned any real thing in me. I never emerged—never was myself."

"You were a genius," he repeated again. "That's what genius does. It takes all that ever was and makes it new."

She made a quick spasmodic protest of her hand. She could not bear to have him praise her. She wanted to tell him all that had ever been, all that she ought to be sorry for, was sorry for now almost beyond endurance. She wanted to strip her soul bare before him; but she caught the look of home in his eyes, she was at his knees at peace, and what he thought of her meant so much just now—in this one hour, for this one hour. She had had such hard travelling, and here was a rest-place on the road.

He saw that her soul was up in battle again, but he took her arms, and held them gently, controlling her agitation. Presently, with a great sigh, her forehead drooped upon his hands. They were in a vast theatre of war, and they were part of it; but for the moment sheer waste of spirit and weariness of soul made peace in a turbulent heart.

"It's her real self—at last," he kept saying to himself, "She had to have her chance, and she has got it."

Outside in a dark corner of the veranda, Al'mah was in reverie. She knew from the silence within that all was well. The deep peace of the night, the thing that was happening in the house, gave her a moment's surcease from her own problem, her own arid loneliness. Her mind went back to the night when she had first sung "Manassa" at Covent Garden. The music shimmered in her brain. She essayed to hum some phrases of the opera which she had always loved, but her voice had no resonance or vibration. It trailed away into a whisper.

"I can't sing any more. What shall I do when the war ends? Or is it that I am to end here with the war?" she whispered to herself. . . Again reverie deepened. Her mind delivered itself up to an obsession. "No, I am not sorry I killed him," she said firmly after a long time, "If a price must be paid, I will pay it."

Buried in her thoughts, she was scarcely conscious of voices near by. At last they became insistent to her ears, They were the voices of sentries off duty—the two who had talked to her earlier in the evening, after Ian Stafford had left.

"This ain't half bad, this night ain't," said one. "There's a lot o' space in a night out here."

"I'd like to be 'longside o' some one I know out by 'Ampstead 'Eath," rejoined the other.

"I got a girl in Camden Town," said the First victoriously.

"I got kids—somewheres, I expect," rejoined the Second with a flourish of pride and self-assertion.

"Oh, a donah's enough for me!" returned the First.

"You'll come to the other when you don't look for it neither," declared his friend in a voice of fatality.

"You ain't the only fool in the world, mate, of course. But 'struth, I like this business better. You've got a good taste in your mouth in the morning 'ere."

"Well, I'll meet you on 'Ampstead 'Eath when the war is over, son," challenged the Second.

"I ain't 'opin' and I ain't prophesyin' none this heat," was the quiet reply. "We've got a bit o' hell in front of us yet. I'll talk to you when we're in Lordkop."

"I'll talk to your girl in Camden Town, if you 'appen to don't," was the railing reply.

"She couldn't stand it not but the once," was the retort; and then they struck each other with their fists in rough play, and laughed, and said good-night in the vernacular.

XXXVII

Under the Gun

They had left him for dead in a dreadful circle of mangled gunners who had fallen back to cover in a donga, from a fire so stark that it seemed the hillside itself was discharging myriad bolts of death, as a waterwheel throws off its spray. No enemy had been visible, but far away in front—that front which must be taken—there hung over the ridge of the hills veils of smoke like lace. Hideous sounds tortured the air—crackling, snapping, spitting sounds like the laughter of animals with steel throats. Never was ill work better done than when, on that radiant veld, the sky one vast turquoise vault, beneath which quivered a shimmer of quicksilver light, the pom-poms, the maulers, and the shrapnel of Kruger's men mowed down Stafford and his battery, showered them, drowned them in a storm of lead.

"Alamachtig," said a Rustenburg dopper who, at the end of the day, fell into the hands of the English, "it was like cutting alfalfa with a sickle! Down they tumbled, horses and men, mashed like mealies in the millstones. A damn lot of good horses was killed this time. The lead-grinders can't pick the men and leave the horses. It was a verdomde waste of good horses. The Rooinek eats from a bloody basin this day."

Alamachtig!

At the moment Ian Stafford fell the battle was well launched. The air was shrieking with the misery of mutilated men and horses and the ghoulish laughter of pom-poms. When he went down it seemed to him that human anger had reached its fullest expression. Officers and men alike were in a fury of determination and vengeance. He had seen no fear, no apprehension anywhere, only a defiant anger which acted swiftly, coolly. An officer stepped over the lacerated, shattered body of a comrade of his mess with the abstracted impassiveness of one who finds his way over a puddle in the road; and here were puddles too—puddles of blood. A gunner lifted away the corpse of his nearest friend from the trail and strained and wrenched at his gun with the intense concentration of one who kneads dough in a trough. The sobbing agony of those whom Stafford had led rose up from the ground around him, and voices cried to be put out of pain and torture. These begrimed men around him, with jackets torn by bullets, with bandaged head stained with blood or dragging leg which left a track of blood behind, were not the men who last night were chatting round the camp-fires and making bets as to where the attack would begin to-day.

Stafford was cool enough, however. It was as though an icy liquid had been poured into his veins. He thought more clearly than he had ever done, even in those critical moments of his past when cool thinking was indispensable. He saw the mistake that had been made in giving his battery work which might have been avoided, and with the same result to the battle; but he also saw the way out of it, and he gave orders accordingly. When the horses were lashed to a gallop to take up the new position, which, if they reached, would give them shelter against this fiendish rain of lead, and also enable them to enfilade the foe at advantage, something suddenly brought confusion to his senses, and the clear thinking stopped. His being seemed to expand suddenly to an enormity of chaos and then as suddenly to shrink, dwindle, and fall back into a smother—as though, in falling, blankets were drawn roughly over his head and a thousand others were shaken in the air around him. And both were real in their own way. The thousand blankets flapping in the air were the machine guns of the foe following his battery into a zone of less dreadful fire, and the blankets that smothered him were wrappings of unconsciousness which save us from the direst agonies of body and mind.

The last thing he saw, as his eyes, with a final effort of power, sought to escape from this sudden confusion, was a herd of springboks flinging themselves about in the circle of fire, caught in the struggle of the two armies, and, like wild birds in a hurricane, plunging here and there in flight and futile motion. As unconsciousness enwrapped him the vision of these distraught denizens of the veld was before his eyes. Somehow, in a lightning transformation, he became one with them and was mingled with them.

Time passed.

When his eyes opened again, slowly, heavily, the same vision was before him—the negative left on the film of his sight by his last conscious glance at the world.

He raised himself on his elbow and looked out over the veld. The springboks were still distractedly tossing here and there, but the army to which he belonged had moved on. It was now on its way up the hill lying between them and the Besieged City. He was dimly conscious of this, for the fight round him had ceased, the storm had gone forward. There was noise, great noise, but he was outside of it, in a kind of valley of awful inactivity. All round him was the debris of a world in which he had once lived and moved and worked. How many years—or centuries—was it since he had been in that harvest of death? There was no anomaly. It was not that time had passed; it was that his soul had made so far a journey.

In his sleep among the guns and the piteous, mutilated dead, he had gone a pilgrimage to a Distant Place and had been told the secret of the world. Yet when he first waked, it was not in his mind—only that confusion out of which he had passed to nothingness with the vision of the distracted springboks. Suddenly a torturing thirst came, and it waked him fully to the reality of it all. He was lying in his own blood, in the swath which the battle had cut.

His work was done. This came to him slowly, as the sun clears away the mists of morning. Something—Some One—had reached out and touched him on the shoulder, had summoned him.

When he left Brinkwort's Farm yesterday, it was with the desire to live, to do large things. He and Rudyard had clasped hands, and Rudyard had made a promise to him, which gave him hope that the broken roof-tree would be mended, the shattered walls of home restored. It had seemed to him then that his own mistake was not irreparable, and that the way was open to peace, if not to happiness.

When he first came to this war he had said, "I will do this," and, "I will do that," and he had thought it possible to do it in his own time and because he willed it. He had put himself deliberately in the way of the Scythe, and had thrown himself into its arc of death.

To have his own way by tricking Destiny into giving him release and absolution without penalty—that had been his course. In the hour when he had ceased to desire exit by breaking through the wall and not by the predestined door, the reply of Destiny to him had been: "It is not for you to choose." He had wished to drink the cup of release, had reached out to take it, but presently had ceased to wish to drink it. Then Destiny had said: "Here is the dish—drink it."

He closed his eyes to shut out the staring light, and he wished in a vague way that he might shut out the sounds of the battle—the everlasting boom and clatter, the tearing reverberations. But he smiled too, for he realized that his being where he was alone meant that the army had moved on over that last hill; and that there would soon be the Relief for which England prayed.

There was that to the good; and he had taken part in it all. His battery, a fragment of what it had been when it galloped out to do its work in the early morning, had had its glorious share in the great day's work.

He had had the most critical and dangerous task of this memorable day. He had been on the left flank of the main body, and his battery had suddenly faced a terrific fire from concealed riflemen who had not hitherto shown life at this point. His promptness alone had saved the battery from annihilation. His swift orders secured the gallant withdrawal of the battery into a zone of comparative safety and renewed activity, while he was left with this one abandoned gun and his slain men and fellow-officers.

But somehow it all suddenly became small and distant and insignificant to his senses. He did not despise the work, for it had to be done. It was big to those who lived, but in the long movement of time it was small, distant, and subordinate.

If only the thirst did not torture him, if only the sounds of the battle were less loud in his ears! It was so long since he waked from that long sleep, and the world was so full of noises, the air so arid, and the light of the sun so fierce. Darkness would be peace. He longed for darkness.

He thought of the spring that came from the rocks in the glen behind the house, where he was born in Derbyshire. He saw himself stooping down, kneeling to drink, his face, his eyes buried in the water, as he gulped down the good stream. Then all at once it was no longer the spring from the rock in which he laved his face and freshened his parched throat; a cool cheek touched his own, lips of tender freshness swept his brow, silken hair with a faint perfume of flowers brushed his temples, his head rested on a breast softer than any pillow he had ever known.

"Jasmine!" he whispered, with parched lips and closed eyes. "Jasmine—water," he pleaded, and sank away again into that dream from which he had but just wakened.

It had not been all a vision. Water was here at his tongue, his head was pillowed on a woman's breast, lips touched his forehead.

But it was not Jasmine's breast; it was not Jasmine's hand which held the nozzle of the water-bag to his parched lips.

Through the zone of fire a woman and a young surgeon had made their way from the attending ambulance that hovered on the edge of battle to this corner of death in the great battle-field. It mattered not to the enemy, who still remained in the segment of the circle where they first fought, whether it was man or woman who crossed this zone of fire. No heed could be given now to Red Cross work, to ambulance, nurse, or surgeon. There would come a time for that, but not yet. Here were two races in a life-and-death grip; and there could be no give and take for the wounded or the dead until the issue of the day was closed.

The woman who had come through the zone of fire was Al'mah. She had no right to be where she was. As a nurse her place was not the battle-field; but she had had a premonition of Stafford's tragedy, and in the night had concealed herself in the blankets of an ambulance and had been carried across the veld to that outer circle of battle where wait those who gather up the wreckage, who provide the salvage of war. When she was discovered there was no other course but to allow her to remain; and so it was that as the battle moved on she made her way to where the wounded and dead lay.

A sorely wounded officer, able with the help of a slightly injured gunner to get out of the furnace of fire, had brought word of Stafford's death but with the instinct of those to whom there come whisperings, visions of things, Al'mah felt she must go and find the man with whose fate, in a way, her own had been linked; who, like herself, had been a derelict upon the sea of life; the grip of whose hand, the look of whose eyes the last time she saw him, told her that as a brother loves so he loved her.

Hundreds saw the two make their way across the veld, across the lead-swept plain; but such things in the hour of battle are commonplaces; they are taken as part of the awful game. Neither mauser nor shrapnel nor maxim brought them down as they made their way to the abandoned gun beside which Stafford lay. Yet only one reached Stafford's side, where he was stretched among his dead comrades. The surgeon stayed his course at three-quarters of the distance to care for a gunner whose mutilations were robbed of half their horror by a courage and a humour which brought quick tears to Al'mah's eyes. With both legs gone the stricken fellow asked first for a match to light his cutty pipe and then remarked: "The saint's own luck that there it was with the stem unbroke to give me aise whin I wanted it!

"Shure, I thought I was dead," he added as the surgeon stooped over him, "till I waked up and give meself the lie, and got a grip o' me pipe, glory be!"

With great difficulty Al'mah dragged Stafford under the horseless gun, left behind when the battery moved on. Both forces had thought that nothing could live in that gray-brown veld, and no effort at first was made to rescue or take it. By every law of probability Al'mah and the young surgeon ought to be lying dead with the others who had died, some with as many as twenty bullet wounds in their bodies, while the gunner, who had served this gun to the last and then, alone, had stood at attention till the lead swept him down, had thirty wounds to his credit for England's sake. Under the gun there was some shade, for she threw over it a piece of tarpaulin and some ragged, blood-stained jackets lying near—jackets of men whose wounds their comrades had tried hastily to help when the scythe of war cut them down.

There was shade now, but there was not safety, for the ground was spurting dust where bullets struck, and even bodies of dead men were dishonoured by the insult of new wounds and mutilations.

Al'mah thought nothing of safety, but only of this life which was ebbing away beside her. She saw that a surgeon could do nothing, that the hurt was internal and mortal; but she wished him not to die until she had spoken with him once again and told him all there was to tell—all that had happened after he left Brinkwort's Farm yesterday.

She looked at the drawn and blanched face and asked herself if that look of pain and mortal trouble was the precursor of happiness and peace. As she bathed the forehead of the wounded man, it suddenly came to her that here was the only tragedy connected with Stafford's going: his work was cut short, his usefulness ended, his hand was fallen from the lever that lifted things.

She looked away from the blanched face to the field of battle, towards the sky above it. Circling above were the vile aasvogels, the loathsome birds which followed the track of war, watching, waiting till they could swoop upon the flesh blistering in the sun. Instinctively she drew nearer to the body of the dying man, as though to protect it from the evil flying things. She forced between his lips a little more water.

"God make it easy!" she said.

A bullet struck a wheel beside her, and with a ricochet passed through the flesh of her forearm. A strange look came into her eyes, suffusing them. Was her work done also? Was she here to find the solution of all her own problems—like Stafford—like Stafford? Stooping, she reverently kissed the bloodless cheek. A kind of exaltation possessed her. There was no fear at all. She had a feeling that he would need her on the journey he was about to take, and there was no one else who could help him now. Who else was there beside herself—and Jigger?

Where was Jigger? What had become of Jigger? He would surely have been with Stafford if he had not been hurt or killed. It was not like Jigger to be absent when Stafford needed him.

She looked out from under the gun, as though expecting to find him coming—to see him somewhere on this stricken plain. As she did so she saw the young surgeon, who had stayed to help the wounded gunner, stumbling and lurching towards the gun, hands clasping his side, and head thrust forward in an attitude of tense expectation, as though there was a goal which must be reached.

An instant later she was outside hastening towards him. A bullet spat at her feet, another cut the skirt of her dress, but all she saw was the shambling figure of the man who, but a few minutes before, was so flexible and alert with life, eager to relieve the wounds of those who had fallen. Now he also was in dire need.

She had almost reached him when, with a stiff jerk sideways and an angular assertion of the figure, he came to the ground like a log, ungainly and rigid.

"They got me! I'm hit—twice," he said, with grey lips; with eyes that stared at her and through her to something beyond; but he spoke in an abrupt, professional, commonplace tone. "Shrapnel and mauler," he added, his hands protecting the place where the shrapnel had found him. His staring blue eyes took on a dull cloud, and his whole figure seemed to sink and shrink away. As though realizing and resisting, if not resenting this dissolution of his forces, his voice rang out querulously, and his head made dogmatic emphasis.

"They oughtn't to have done it," the petulant voice insisted. "I wasn't fighting." Suddenly the voice trailed away, and all emphasis, accent, and articulation passed from the sentient figure. Yet his lips moved once again. "Ninety-nine Adelphi Terrace—first floor," he said mechanically, and said no more.

As mechanically as he had spoken, Al'mah repeated the last words. "Ninety-nine Adelphi Terrace, first floor," she said slowly.

They were chambers next to those where Adrian Fellowes had lived and died. She shuddered.

"So he was not married," she said reflectively, as she left the lifeless body and went back to the gun where Stafford lay.

Her arm through which the bullet had passed was painful, but she took no heed of it. Why should she? Hundreds, maybe thousands, were being killed off there in the hills. She saw nothing except the debris of Ian Stafford's life drifting out to the shoreless sea.

He lived still, but remained unconscious, and she did not relax her vigil. As she watched and waited the words of the young surgeon kept ringing in her ears, a monotonous discord, "Ninety-nine Adelphi Terrace—first floor!" Behind it all was the music of the song she had sung at Rudyard Byng's house the evening of the day Adrian Fellowes had died—"More was lost at Mohacksfield."

The stupefaction that comes with tragedy crept over her. As the victim of an earthquake sits down amid vast ruins, where the dead lie unnumbered, speechless, and heedless, so she sat and watched the face of the man beside her, and was not conscious that the fire of the armies was slackening, that bullets no longer spattered the veld or struck the gun where she sat; that the battle had been carried over the hills.

In time help would come, so she must wait. At least she had kept Stafford alive. So far her journey through Hades had been justified. He would have died had it not been for the water and brandy she had forced between his lips, for the shade in which he lay beneath the gun. In the end they would come and gather the dead and wounded. When the battle was over they would come, or, maybe, before it was over.

But through how many hours had there been the sickening monotony of artillery and rifle-fire, the bruit of angry metal, in which the roar of angrier men was no more than a discord in the guttural harmony. Her senses became almost deadened under the strain. Her cheeks grew thinner, her eyes took on a fixed look. She seemed like one in a dream. She was only conscious in an isolated kind of way. Louder than all the noises of the clanging day was the beating of her heart. Her very body seemed to throb, the pulses in her temples were like hammers hurting her brain.

At last she was roused by the sound of horses' hoofs.

So the service-corps were coming at last to take up the wounded and bury the dead. There were so many dead, so few wounded!

The galloping came nearer and nearer. It was now as loud as thunder almost. It stopped short. She gave a sigh of relief. Her vigil was ended. Stafford was still alive. There was yet a chance for him to know that friends were with him at the last, and also what had happened at Brinkwort's Farm after he had left yesterday.

She leaned out to see her rescuers. A cry broke from her. Here was one man frantically hitching a pair of artillery-horses to the gun and swearing fiercely in the Taal as he did so.

The last time she had seen that khaki hat, long, threadbare frock-coat, huge Hessian boots and red neckcloth was at Brinkwort's Farm. The last time she had seen that malevolent face was when its owner was marched away from Brinkwort's Farm yesterday.

It was Krool.

An instant later she had dragged Stafford out from beneath the gun, for it was clear that the madman intended to ride off with it.

When Krool saw her first he was fastening the last hook of the traces with swift, trained fingers. He stood dumfounded for a moment. The superstitious, half-mystical thing in him came trembling to his eyes; then he saw Stafford's body, and he realized the situation. A look of savage hatred came into his face, and he made a step forward with sudden impulse, as though he would spring upon Stafford. His hand was upon a knife at his belt. But the horses plunged and strained, and he saw in the near distance a troop of cavalry.

With an obscene malediction at the body, he sprang upon a horse. A sjambok swung, and with a snort, which was half a groan, the trained horses sprang forward.

"The Rooinek's gun for Oom Paul!" he shouted back over his shoulder.

Most prisoners would have been content to escape and save their skins, but a more primitive spirit lived in Krool. Escape was not enough for him. Since he had been foiled at Brinkwort's Farm and could not reach Rudyard Byng; since he would be shot the instant he was caught after his escape—if he was caught—he would do something to gall the pride of the verdomde English. The gun which the Boers had not dared to issue forth and take, which the British could not rescue without heavy loss while the battle was at its height—he would ride it over the hills into the Boers' camp.

There was something so grotesque in the figure of the half-caste, with his copper-coat flying behind him as the horses galloped away, that a wan smile came to Al'mah's lips. With Stafford at her feet in the staring sun she yet could not take her eyes from the man, the horses, and the gun. And not Al'mah alone shaded and strained eyes to follow the tumbling, bouncing gun. Rifles, maxims, and pom-poms opened fire upon it. It sank into a hollow and was partially lost to sight; it rose again and jerked forward, the dust rising behind it like surf. It swayed and swung, as the horses wildly took the incline of the hills, Krool's sjambok swinging above them; it struggled with the forces that dragged it higher and higher up, as though it were human and understood that it was a British gun being carried into the Boer lines.

At first a battery of the Boers, fighting a rear-guard action, had also fired on it, but the gunners saw quickly that a single British gun was not likely to take up an advance position and attack alone, and their fire died away. Thinking only that some daring Boer was doing the thing with a thousand odds against him, they roared approval as the gun came nearer and nearer.

Though the British poured a terrific fire after the flying battery of one gun, there was something so splendid in the episode; the horses were behaving so gallantly,—horses of one of their own batteries daringly taken by Krool under the noses of the force—that there was scarcely a man who was not glad when, at last, the gun made a sudden turn at a kopje, and was lost to sight within the Boer lines, leaving behind it a little cloud of dust.

Tommy Atkins had his uproarious joke about it, but there was one man who breathed a sigh of relief when he heard of it. That was Barry Whalen. He had every reason to be glad that Krool was out of the way, and that Rudyard Byng would see him no more. Sitting beside the still unconscious Ian Stafford on the veld, Al'mah's reflections were much the same as those of Barry Whalen.

With the flight of Krool and the gun came the end of Al'mah's vigil. The troop of cavalry which galloped out to her was followed by the Red Cross wagons.

XXXVIII

"PHEIDIPPIDES"

At dawn, when the veld breathes odours of a kind pungency and fragrance, which only those know who have made it their bed and friend, the end came to the man who had lain under the gun.

"Pheidippides!" the dying Stafford said, with a grim touch of the humour which had ever been his. He was thinking of the Greek runner who brought the news of victory to Athens and fell dead as he told it.

It almost seemed from the look on Stafford's face that, in very truth, he was laying aside the impedimenta of the long march and the battle, to carry the news to that army of the brave in Walhalla who had died for England before they knew that victory was hers.

"Pheidippides," he repeated, and Rudyard Byng, whose eyes were so much upon the door, watching and waiting for some one to come, pressed his hand and said: "You know the best, Stafford. So many didn't. They had to go before they knew."

"I have my luck," Stafford replied, but yet there was a wistful look in his face.

His eyes slowly closed, and he lay so motionless that Al'mah and Rudyard thought he had gone. He scarcely seemed to notice when Al'mah took the hand that Rudyard had held, and the latter, with quick, noiseless steps, left the room.

What Rudyard had been watching and waiting for was come.

Jasmine was at the door. His message had brought her in time.

"Is it dangerous?" she asked, with a face where tragedy had written self-control.

"As bad as can be," he answered. "Go in and speak to him, Jasmine. It will help him."

He opened the door softly. As Jasmine entered, Al'mah with a glance of pity and friendship at the face upon the bed, passed into another room.

There was a cry in Jasmine's heart, but it did not reach her lips.

She stole to the bed and laid her fingers upon the hand lying white and still upon the coverlet.

At once the eyes of the dying man opened. This was a touch that would reach to the farthest borders of his being—would bring him back from the Immortal Gates. Through the mist of his senses he saw her. He half raised himself. She pillowed his head on her breast. He smiled. A light transfigured his face.

"All's well," he said, with a long sigh, and his body sank slowly down.

"Ian! Ian!" she cried, but she knew that he could not hear.

XXXIX

"The Road is Clear"

The Army had moved on over the hills, into the valley of death and glory, across the parched veld to the town of Lordkop, where an emaciated, ragged garrison had kept faith with all the heroes from Caractacus to Nelson. Courageous legions had found their way to the petty dorp, with its corrugated iron roofs, its dug-outs, its improvised forts, its fever hospitals, its Treasure House of Britain, where she guarded the jewels of her honour.

The menace of the hills had passed, heroes had welcomed heroes and drunk the cup of triumph; but far back in the valleys beyond the hills from which the army had come, there were those who must drink the cup of trembling, the wine of loss.

As the trumpets of victory attended the steps of those remnants of brigades which met the remnants of a glorious garrison in the streets of Lordkop, drums of mourning conducted the steps of those who came to bury the dust of one who had called himself Pheidippides as he left the Day Path and took the Night Road.

Gun-carriage and reversed arms and bay charger, faithful comrades with bent heads, the voice of victory over the grave—"I am the resurrection and the life"—the volleys of honour, the proud salut of the brave to the vanished brave, the quivering farewells of the few who turn away from the fresh-piled earth with their hearts dragging behind—all had been; and all had gone. Evening descended upon the veld with a golden radiance which soothed like prayer.

By the open window at the foot of a bed in the Stay Awhile Hospital a woman gazed into the saffron splendour with an intentness which seemed to make all her body listen. Both melancholy and purpose marked the attitude of the figure.

A voice from the bed at the foot of which she stood drew her gaze away from the sunset sky to meet the bright, troubled eyes.

"What is it, Jigger?" the woman asked gently, and she looked to see that the framework which kept the bedclothes from a shattered leg was properly in its place.

"'E done a lot for me," was the reply. "A lot 'e done, and I dunno how I'll git along now."

There was great hopelessness in the tone.

"He told me you would always have enough to help you get on, Jigger. He thought of all that."

"'Ere, oh, 'ere it ain't that," the lad said in a sudden passion of protest, the tears standing in his eyes. "It ain't that! Wot's money, when your friend wot give it ain't 'ere! I never done nothing for 'im—that's wot I feel. Nothing at all for 'im."

"You are wrong," was the soft reply. "He told me only a few days ago that you were like a loaf of bread in the cupboard—good for all the time."

The tears left the wide blue eyes. "Did 'e say that—did 'e?" he asked, and when she nodded and smiled, he added, "'E's 'appy now, ain't 'e?" His look questioned her eagerly.

For an instant she turned and gazed at the sunset, and her eyes took on a strange mystical glow. A colour came to her face, as though from strong flush of feeling, then she turned to him again, and answered steadily:

"Yes, he is happy now."

"How do you know?" the lad asked with awe in his face, for he believed in her utterly. Then, without waiting for her to answer, he added: "Is it, you hear him say so, as I hear you singin' in my sleep sometimes—singin', singin', as you did at Glencader, that first time I ever 'eerd you? Is it the same as me in my sleep?"

"Yes, it is like that—just like that," she answered, taking his hand, and holding it with a motherly tenderness.

"Ain't you never goin' to sing again?" he added.

She was silent, looking at him almost abstractedly.

"This war'll be over pretty soon now," he continued, "and we'll all have to go back to work."

"Isn't this work?" Al'mah asked with a smile, which had in it something of her old whimsical self.

"It ain't play, and it ain't work," he answered with a sage frown of intellectual effort. "It's a cut above 'em both—that's my fancy."

"It would seem like that," was the response. "What are you going to do when you get back to England?" she inquired.

"I thought I'd ask you that," he replied anxiously. "Couldn't I be a scene-shifter or somefink at the opery w'ere you sing?"

"I'm going to sing again, am I?" she asked.

"You'd have to be busy," he protested admiringly.

"Yes, I'll have to be busy," she replied, her voice ringing a little, "and we'll have to find a way of being busy together."

"His gryce'd like that," he responded.

She turned her face slowly to the evening sky, where grey clouds became silver and piled up to a summit of light. She was silent for a long time.

"If work won't cure, nothing will," she said in a voice scarce above a whisper. Her body trembled a little, and her eyes closed, as though to shut out something that pained her sight.

"I wish you'd sing somethin'—same as you did that night at Glencader, about the green hill far away," whispered the little trumpeter from the bed.

She looked at him for a moment meditatively, then shook her head, and turned again to the light in the evening sky.

"P'raps she's makin' up a new song," Jigger said to himself.

On a kopje overlooking the place where Ian Stafford had been laid to sleep to the call of the trumpets, two people sat watching the sun go down. Never in the years that had gone had there been such silence between them as they sat together. Words had been the clouds in which the lightning of their thoughts had been lost; they had been the disguises in which the truth of things masqueraded. They had not dared to be silent, lest the truth should stalk naked before them. Silence would have revealed their unhappiness; they would not have dared to look closely and deeply into each other's face, lest revelation should force them to say, "It has been a mistake; let us end it." So they had talked and talked and acted, and yet had done nothing and been nothing.

Now they were silent, because they had tossed into the abyss of Time the cup of trembling, and had drunk of the chalice of peace. Over the grave into which, this day, they had thrown the rock-roses and sprigs of the karoo bush, they had, in silence, made pledges to each other, that life's disguises should be no more for them; that the door should be wide open between the chambers where their souls dwelt, each in its own pension of being, with its own individual sense, but with the same light, warmth, and nutriment, and with the free confidence which exempts life from its confessions. There should be no hidden things any more.

There was a smile on the man's face as he looked out over the valley. With this day had come triumph for the flag he loved, for the land where he was born, and also the beginning of peace for the land where he had worked, where he had won his great fortune. He had helped to make this land what it was, and in battle he had helped to save it from disaster.

But there had come another victory—the victory of Home. The coincidence of all the vital values had come in one day, almost in one hour.

Smiling, he laid his hand upon the delicate fingers of the woman beside him, as they rested on her knee. She turned and looked at him with an understanding which is the beginning of all happiness; and a colour came to her cheeks such as he had not seen there for more days than he could count. Her smile answered his own, but her eyes had a sadness which would never wholly leave them. When he had first seen those eyes he had thought them the most honest he had ever known. Looking at them now, with confidence restored, he thought again as he did that night at the opera the year of the Raid.

"It's all before us still, Jasmine," he said with a ring of purpose and a great gentleness in his tone.

Her hand trembled, the shadows deepened in her eyes, but determination gathered at her lips.

Some deep-cherished, deferred resolve reasserted itself.

"But I cannot—I cannot go on until you know all, Rudyard, and then you may not wish to go on," she said. Her voice shook, and the colour went from her lips. "I must be honest now—at last, about everything. I want to tell you—"

He got to his feet. Stooping, he raised her, and looked her squarely in the eyes.

"Tell me nothing, Jasmine," he said. Then he added in a voice of finality, "There is nothing to tell." Holding both her hands tight in one of his own, he put his fingers on her lips.

"A fresh start for a long race—the road is clear," he said firmly.

Looking into his eyes, she knew that he read her life and soul, that in his deep primitive way he understood her as she had been and as she was, and yet was content to go on. Her head drooped upon his breast.

A trumpet-call rang out piercingly sweet across the valley. It echoed and echoed away among the hills.

He raised his head to listen. Pride, vision and power were in his eyes. "It's all before us still, Jasmine," he said again.

Her fingers tightened on his.

THE END

A Note About the Author

Gilbert Parker (1862–1932), also credited as Sir Horatio Gilbert George Parker, 1st Baronet, was a Canadian novelist and British politician. His initial career was in education, working in various schools as a teacher and lecturer. He then traveled abroad to Australia where he became an editor at the *Sydney Morning Herald*. He expanded his writing to include long-form works such as romance fiction. Some of his most notable titles include *Pierre and his People* (1892), *The Seats of the Mighty* and *The Battle of the Strong*.

A Note from the Publisher

Spanning many genres, from non-fiction essays to literature classics to children's books and lyric poetry, Mint Edition books showcase the master works of our time in a modern new package. The text is freshly typeset, is clean and easy to read, and features a new note about the author in each volume. Many books also include exclusive new introductory material. Every book boasts a striking new cover, which makes it as appropriate for collecting as it is for gift giving. Mint Edition books are only printed when a reader orders them, so natural resources are not wasted. We're proud that our books are never manufactured in excess and exist only in the exact quantity they need to be read and enjoyed.

bookfinity™

Discover more of your favorite classics with Bookfinity™.

- Track your reading with custom book lists.
- Get great book recommendations for your personalized Reader Type.
- Add reviews for your favorite books.
- AND MUCH MORE!

Visit **bookfinity.com** and take the fun Reader Type quiz to get started.

Enjoy our classic and modern companion pairings!